A CASE OF YOU

RICK BLECHTA

Cover, title page and author photos by Andre Leduc

LE CONSEIL DES ARTS DU CANADA DEPUIS 1957 | THE CANADA COUNCIL FOR THE ARTS SINCE 1957

We acknowledge the support of the Canada Council for the Arts for our publishing program.

We acknowledge the financial support of the Government of Canada through the Book Publishing Industry Development Program (BPIDP) for our publishing activities.

RendezVous Crime
an imprint of Napoleon & Company
Toronto, Ontario, Canada
www.napoleonandcompany.com

Printed in Canada
Printed on Enviro100 paper from 100% post-consumer fibre

12 11 10 09 08   5 4 3 2 1

Library and Archives Canada Cataloguing in Publication

Blechta, Rick
     A case of you / Rick Blechta.

ISBN 978-1-894917-68-1

          I. Title.

PS8553.L3969C38 2008   C813'.54   C2008-900031-5

This novel is dedicated to my long-time good buddy,
cover art collaborator (on every book I've written),
photographer extraordinaire and partner-in-crime,
Andre Leduc. Thanks for the photos, the advice –
and most of all, your friendship.

Also by Rick Blechta

Knock on Wood
The Lark Ascending
Shooting Straight in the Dark
Cemetery of the Nameless
When Hell Freezes Over

As co-editor:
Dishes to Die For
Dishes to Die For...Again

She had a voice like an angel, smooth and complex as a twenty-year-old single malt, rich as thick cream. Everyone who heard Olivia sing felt as if she could see right into the depths of their souls, that her songs were meant for them alone. This was the magic her artistry conjured. In earlier times, she would have been put to death as a witch.

The real kicker was that Olivia had no idea how the magic worked. She'd just open her mouth and the song was *there*, no deep thought about the meaning of lyrics, no analyzing of how she wanted to shape a phrase, bending, stretching, adding notes until everything fit the way she wanted it to. Her pitch was dead on, and her innate sense of rhythm impeccable. Stunningly artless was the only way to describe her performances.

Her voice could produce with equal ease a mental image of a smoky bar at the end of a long night of drinking to forget a lost love, to high-stepping down the sunny side of the street with a bluebird on her shoulder.

With no apparent effort, she made you believe she knew intimately everything about which she sang.

Such was the talent of Olivia Saint.

CHAPTER 1

Things might have turned out very differently if the slimeball hadn't punched me in the eye.

The knee in the gut that followed hadn't helped. No one appreciates getting dropped by a sucker punch.

"That really wasn't necessary," said the smaller of the two, the one seemingly in charge, as I knelt on the wet sidewalk, gasping for air.

The big one shrugged. "The guy was annoying me." He leaned down until his face was about a foot above mine. "Sorry, bud. No hard feelings, huh?"

He didn't extend a hand to help me up, though. Barely able to breathe, I could only watch helplessly as they pushed Olivia into the back seat of their car, and the smaller one climbed in next to her.

Olivia looked at me once before the door swung shut. Her eyes seemed vacant, her expression devoid of anything that spoke of the spark I knew was there. Since they'd begun talking to her in the club, she hadn't spoken once, had given no indication that she even knew who I was when I'd followed them outside.

"Wait," I finally managed to force out. "Wait!"

The big brute stopped as he was getting in the driver's side and smiled over the roof of the car. "No can do, bud. Got a plane to catch."

As I struggled to my feet, the car did a quick U-turn and drove off down King Street. As they neared the corner of Bathurst, it stopped, and the back door on the driver's side opened.

The smaller man leaned out, holding the lambskin coat I'd bought for Olivia. "Hey, mac!" he shouted. "She says this is for you."

He dropped it to the pavement, and the car screeched around the corner into the night.

I walked as quickly as I could to where the coat lay and bent to pick it up. A greasy smear now marked the back, where it had lain on the streetcar track.

Shaking my head, I went back to the club, cold, wet, sore and very confused about what had just happened.

About a month earlier, Olivia had been spinning around delightedly in front of a store's full-length mirror, telling me how much she absolutely loved my gift, how she'd always wanted a coat like this.

Just now, had she been trying to send me a signal?

By the time I stumbled back into the Sal, my eye had begun to swell shut. Slipping into a chair next to Dom, who was carefully nursing his between-set beer, I signalled for Loraine, the waitress. I needed scotch, certainly a double.

Dom raised an eyebrow. "What the hell did *you* run into?"

"Olivia's gone," I said distractedly.

My comment, though, instantly galvanized Ronald, who sat across the table from me. "You mean gone, as in she's not doing the next set?"

"I mean gone, as in I don't think she's ever going to be doing *anything* with us again."

Loraine came over and took my order with a raised eyebrow. I refused to elucidate until she returned and I'd downed half the scotch in one gulp. With the excitement over, the adrenaline had loosened its grip, leaving me feeling cold and decidedly shaky.

"You look like shit, Andy," Dom observed with an expression pretty well devoid of sympathy.

"Tell me what happened," Ronald ordered.

I took another gulp and felt the booze drop warmly into my belly, then looked across at our problematic pianist. "You didn't see those two guys talking to Olivia right after the set ended?"

Dom answered, "I did."

Ronald's response was typical. "I had some people I needed to talk to."

I held up my glass, signalling Loraine to bring another scotch. At that point, I didn't care if I got a bit tight. In my increasingly wobbly state, I was more worried about staying on my drum stool.

"Tell us what happened!" both my band-mates demanded in unison, causing me at least to smile.

"I was talking to Olivia about trying out those new songs we've been rehearsing, when two guys appeared from nowhere. They butted right in and told me to get lost."

The change that had come over Olivia had been quite startling. One moment she was all bubbly, obviously very happy and excited about how the first set of the night had gone. The next it was as if someone had removed her batteries. She just went dead.

When I didn't move off, the bigger of the two guys pushed between Olivia and me. "Like my friend said, bud, we need to talk to the lady—alone."

I peered around his bulk at Olivia, but she just stared back with that blank expression. Against my better judgement, I moved off, but I did stay close to make sure they weren't hassling her.

They took Olivia to a back corner of the club, conversed quietly with her for a few minutes – the men actually doing all the talking – then accompanied her to the closet-sized space that serves as the Green Salamander's dressing room.

Reappearing immediately, with Olivia wearing her new coat, the party of three headed for the door. Naturally, I followed.

They had their car waiting out by the curb, and when I asked what the hell was going on, I got bopped in the eye and kneed in the gut.

Dom whistled after I finished my story, but Ronald looked angry.

"You mean she's just left us high and dry? Walked out? Well, that's a bullshit thing to do after all we've done for her!"

In no mood for his crap, I shot back, "What we've done for her? Do you think the club would be this full tonight if Olivia hadn't been singing? We couldn't attract flies on a cold, wet night like this before she came along, and you know it!"

"Andy's right, Ron," Dom added, using the shortened form of our pianist's name, fully aware how much it irritated him.

"So what are we supposed to do now?" the pianist asked stupidly.

Getting to my feet, I swallowed my second drink in one gulp. "We get up on the stage, say that Miss Olivia is indisposed and get on with it. Whether she's here or not, we still have to play three sets, unless everyone leaves, which is more than likely once they find out she isn't singing."

I was right about the audience making a beeline for the exit. The early spring weather outside promised to become pretty beastly, with wet snow forecast for later in the night. By the time our second set finished, there were about a dozen customers left, most of them pretty drunk.

"This is just swell," Dom said glumly as he took a miniscule sip of his next beer. "This puts us right back where we started."

Ronald looked at our bassist with disgust. "What are you moaning about? There are other chick singers out there – *if* we decide to go that route again. They're all more trouble than they're worth, if you ask me."

"Come off it!" I said angrily. "None of us has ever worked with someone of Olivia's calibre. Talent like hers doesn't wander in here every night."

"What makes you think she isn't coming back?" Dom asked, guiding the discussion into less contentious waters.

It was a fair question. Neither Olivia nor the two guys who carted her off had given any indication what was going on, but it was her behaviour that had really spooked me. My swollen eye throbbed a reminder as I frowned.

"I should go to the cops," I said.

"For the roughing up you got? Good luck if you didn't have any witnesses." Dom took a bigger swig of his beer. "As for Olivia, did she say she didn't want to go with them? Did she struggle?"

"Well, no."

"Then the cops won't be interested. She's not a child."

"She acts like a child often enough," Ronald grumbled.

"So what can I do?" I asked, ignoring him.

Dom looked up. "You actually serious?"

"Sure. Olivia may be in some kind of trouble. The way those two guys behaved didn't exactly fill me with confidence, even if she didn't protest at all."

Dom nodded. "Remember when I got divorced a few years back? Well, I didn't feel like saying much at the time, but I caught my wife cheating. Actually, I hired a private investigator to find that out for me. He was loud and a little bit cocky, but seemed pretty competent. I could put you in touch with him if you *are* serious."

Suddenly, I realized I was. "Can you give me his phone number?"

"I don't think I have it any more, but I can tell you how to find him."

I took out the small black gig book I carry. "Okay, shoot."

"Know that instrument rental outfit north of the city off Woodbine Avenue?"

"Quinn? Sure."

"This investigator's got an office at the opposite end of the same building. That's how I found him. I was renting some equipment for an out of town gig and stopped in to see him on the spur of the moment. I'd had some suspicions about my wife for a few months. It didn't take this guy long to come up with everything I needed: names, videos, the whole sordid shooting match."

Dom had steadfastly refused to talk about his failed marriage for the past two years, and now I couldn't shut him up long enough to get the information I needed. "Dom! The guy's name?"

"O'Brien. Rob O'Brien. Good guy. I think the company is called O'Brien Investigates."

For the first time in many months, Dom ordered a second beer before we went on for our last set. Old wounds, when reopened before they've completely healed, often need painkillers of one kind or another.

At least that's been my experience.

ᐅᑉᕈᐤ·ᐅᑊᕈᐤ·

Sleet arrived sometime in the middle of the night, lashing the windows of Shannon O'Brien's room in the old farmhouse with enough noise to wake her.

After a half hour of fruitless effort, she decided that sleep would not be returning and switched on the light above her side of the bed. Disgustedly grabbing the pillows, she propped them up behind herself and leaned back to check the alignment. Once comfortable, she picked up the book she was currently reading.

Five minutes later, she hadn't read a single word.

Later that morning, Shannon had to make a decision about taking on a new operative. That normally wasn't a difficult decision, but this time the mix was different. The loss of one of her longtime employees had thrown a monkey wrench the size of Winnipeg into the normally smooth-running machinery of O'Brien Investigates.

Several things in the submitted documentation and subsequent follow-up on the prospective employee had raised red flags, tiny ones, true, but it was the little things in her line of work that bit you in the ass. Normally, she'd just wait for the next resumé, but at the moment the firm *really* needed another person.

The dismissed employee had also been a big blow to Shannon's pride. Warren Duke, experienced and likeable, had been with her since the beginning. He had probably been padding his expenses that long, too, as she'd discovered the previous week. What hurt even more was that she'd only discovered his duplicity by accident.

Shannon did not like failing, but she detested being made a fool of, and Warren had done that in spades.

"I'm getting to old for this shit," she told herself as she dropped the book to the floor, rearranged the pillows and snapped off the light.

Lying on her side, her left arm flopped out to where Michael should be. If he were here now, she'd pull herself against his warmth, and they'd hunker down together against the storm outside. She always felt so safe with him.

As four turned to five, Shannon eventually dozed off, but her dreams were troubled and uneasy.

ᐃᖠᑉᐧᐨᑊᐳ·

After a long night of gigging, I found myself travelling up Highway 404 that miserable Wednesday in driving rain. It was far too early to be up.

April can be a pretty grey month in Southern Ontario, but Toronto always looks extra grimy at the end of a long winter, especially when the highway spray kicks up a four-month accumulation of dirt and salt onto your windshield.

The day reflected my mood perfectly as the traffic crawled along south of Finch Avenue.

As I exited at Steeles, everything halted because of a collision in the intersection. By the time the traffic got moving, I seriously considered turning around and going back home. But my swollen eye was still throbbing, and that hardened my resolve to find out what the hell was going on – and possibly pay back the guy who'd popped me one.

As expected, I hadn't heard a thing from Olivia. I'd toyed with trying to get in touch with her friend Maggie to find out if she knew anything, but considering the bad blood between us, I wasn't sure what good it would do. She'd just blame me for what had happened.

With all these thoughts running through my head, I pulled into the small industrial mall where this O'Brien character had his office. It felt odd to be looking for a private investigator. Other than Dom – and that had certainly been news to me – the only people I knew who consulted private eyes were on TV or lived between the pages of books.

The previous evening's events had so unnerved me, I had just driven up without calling first. Pretty stupid thing to do, if you think about it. What if they'd moved or gone out of business? What if they weren't open regular hours? What *were* regular hours for a PI?

But the gods were with me that day, because O'Brien Investigates was stencilled right on the glass door, and lights were on inside the office.

Getting out of the car, I didn't bother locking it. A thirteen-year-old vehicle doesn't hold much interest to a thief – not when the only things holding it together are paint and rust.

Sticking my head in the door, I was greeted by a middle-aged bottle redhead with long fingernails to match. How she managed to type, especially so fast, with claws like that, I couldn't imagine.

"New client?" she asked without looking up.

"Ah, yes."

The woman stopped long enough to reach behind her for a clipboard with forms on it. Holding it out to me without looking up, she added, "Got a pen or pencil?"

"Yes."

"Good. Please fill this out. We'll be with you in a minute."

I did as I was told, sitting on a cheap plastic chair, the kind you see in high school cafeterias. The whole place looked a little careworn: old filing cabinets, yellowing paint, a carpet that had seen better days and a rather shabby desk – although the computer on it looked new. If it hadn't been for Dom's first-rate recommendation, I probably would have left. Maybe their slogan was "Investigations on a Shoestring Budget".

The form was filled with the usual questions, although they asked for my driver's license number and quite a lot of credit info as well. That caused me to wonder how much I'd be willing to pay to find Olivia. The redhead finished her typing before I reached the bottom and sat staring at me as she tapped a pencil on her desk. At least her tempo was steady.

When I handed her the clipboard, she immediately went through a door to the right of her desk into what I supposed was the boss's office.

Appearing in the doorway shortly after, she said, "Step this way, please."

The smaller room I entered had recently been painted, and the desk was large and new. In one corner was a low circular table with four chairs, although judging by the jumble of papers and file folders on it, it probably didn't see much use. Even more filing cabinets lined the opposite wall, and next to me was an aquarium of slowly waving plants and brightly coloured fish.

Standing just in front of the desk was not the heavyset, middle-aged man with a slouch hat that I'd been imagining. My eyes rested on a slender, honey-blonde with intelligent-looking eyes and a welcoming smile. I guessed her height to be close to five-eight and her age to be somewhere around forty. Dressed casually in jeans, a blouse and a tan jacket, she was quite pretty.

She extended a hand. "I'm Shannon O'Brien." Picking up on the fact that I'd stopped partway into the room, not because of what I saw, but what I'd expected to see, she added, "I'm the proprietor of O'Brien Investigates."

"Um, yeah." When I didn't move, she raised an eyebrow, so I added, "I was expecting someone else."

"This business used to be jointly owned by my ex-husband and me. Obviously, he's no longer here."

Her blunt words were said in a kind way but made it perfectly clear that further illumination would not be forthcoming.

"Won't you sit down?" she asked, indicating a comfortable chair in front of the desk. She looked down at the form I'd filled out. "I see we were recommended by a friend. I don't recognize the name, so it must have been a job Rob worked on."

"Yes, it was. A divorce case."

Something flickered across her face, but it was too fast for me to read, other than that she looked sad. "Is your job also a divorce case?"

"No. It concerns a missing person. At least, I *think* she's missing. Actually, I'm not really sure what's going on."

Ms O'Brien smiled again. "Sounds intriguing. Now, gather your thoughts and just tell me your story from the beginning. I find that's the best way to start any investigation."

CHAPTER 2

I had to cast my mind back four months to our steady gig at The Green Salamander Jazz Nightclub to give its somewhat ponderous full name. The Sal (as it's better known) has been a mainstay on the Toronto jazz scene for over four decades. Located in a basement space on Toronto's King Street West near Portland, it is neither plush nor very spacious. Because of this, it has seldom hosted the really big names, unless it caught them on the way up – or down.

As I set up my drums that frigid Tuesday evening in the first week of December, I could see the end of the line approaching fast, an end to the steady gig we'd had for the past two years. Ronald Xavier Felton, our trio's pianist, refused to acknowledge anything of the kind, but then he was like that. His reality was different from a normal person's. Dom Milano, our bass player, always went with the flow – and the best payday. As long as the Sal paid, he'd play. When it didn't, he'd move on – with or without us. He wasn't mean-spirited, just practical. Jobbing musicians have to be like that.

I cursed under my breath. There were just about no other steady gigs in T.O. these days. Jazz was going through one of its dry periods. Two clubs had closed in the past year. Except for a few annual festivals, a handful of clubs that didn't offer more than three-night gigs and the odd Sunday Jazz Brunch at a few restaurants, my hometown seemed to have firmly turned its back once again on the music I love.

It wasn't as if we hadn't had a good run at the Sal. You couldn't sneeze at knowing where you were going to be every Tuesday through Thursday for two years. With weekend run-outs, weddings, trade shows, corporate receptions and the like, my finances had never looked rosier.

I'd been able to keep Sandra out of my hair about child support *and* had gotten to see a good deal of my daughter Kate. That had certainly made the aftershocks of the breakdown of my marriage much less severe on everyone involved than they might have been if I'd been on the road all the time.

Harry, the club's owner, had begun dropping hints that if business didn't pick up in a big way, he was going to be forced to shut the doors. Considering he was in his late seventies, that made sense, but he'd also been quoted as saying that the only way he'd ever give up his club was to be taken out feet first.

Weekends were still reasonably good, since he could book touring soloists to be backed up by all-star local pick-up groups, but it was our weekday nights that were killing him, and that meant the Ronald Felton Trio wasn't pulling its weight.

What had been our Ronald's brilliant solution? An open mike night. He also wanted to bring in promising local student soloists from programs like the one at Humber College, where he taught two days a week. He'd gleefully told Dom and me that we wouldn't have to pay them, *and* they'd fill the place with all their friends.

Dom, his string bass swathed in its padded soft case, the fabric reminding me of a green quilted diaper, stepped onto the low bandstand and gently laid his baby down.

"Think this is going to work, Andy?" he asked.

"An open mike night for vocalists?" I yanked the strap on my trap case, pulling it tight, and shoved it behind the curtain at the back. "It's only a step above karaoke, for Christ's sake."

"Should be good for a laugh, though."

"The laugh is that Ronald is convinced this will work."

Dom looked up with a grin splitting his face. "We both know he's delusional."

And so it began. That first night didn't have too many disasters, mainly because our "delusional" pianist had salted the audience with a few capable friends, along with some of his Humber students who also sang.

The weeks went on, and as winter slowly began inching its way to spring, word spread – helped along nicely by a piece in the *Toronto Star*. More hopefuls than I would have imagined stepped onto the bandstand to strut their stuff. And surprisingly, more regular patrons began coming, too. I figured it was to witness the frequent train wrecks. Disasters always seem to draw a crowd.

The youthful soloists idea also worked pretty well, so I kept my mouth firmly shut. Harry began talking about wanting to be stuffed and laid out behind the bar when he eventually cashed in his chips.

Then Olivia walked in.

Outside, a February storm was blowing, hopefully one of the last gasps of a miserable three-month stretch of extreme cold and snow, but the Sal was still gratifyingly half filled.

Stepping through the door of the club, she looked like a street person. While I prefer to play with my eyes closed most of the time, floating with the groove I'm laying down, for some reason my eyes were immediately drawn to her.

Her brown hair was long, but badly cut, and her baggy clothes, toque and duffel coat looked as if they were straight out of a Salvation Army bin – which turned out to be the literal truth. The only spot of colour was a bright red scarf.

She wasn't much over five feet, and soaking wet she would have weighed in at not much over a hundred pounds, but there was something about her. She was pretty in a conventional sense – nice lips, cute nose, sort of a heart-shaped face – but her dark eyes gazed right into my soul for a brief moment before she looked away.

I watched her find a perch on one of the tall stools lining the wall in a back corner, places set out for those who wander in alone to catch a set or two. She spent the evening nursing two soft drinks that she paid for from a fistful of small change.

Loraine, the waitress, gave Olivia dirty looks as the level of her drinks got very slowly lower. Tuesdays were generally not good nights for tips, and a couple of colas over the course of an entire evening would hardly pay the rent.

I don't think anyone but me noticed the waif-like woman as she listened to us accompany hopefuls and drunks with equal equanimity, and even I didn't catch Olivia as she slipped off her stool and out the door at the end of the evening.

That would never happen again.

I next came across her in a totally unexpected place on a Saturday afternoon a week or so later.

My elderly car was again in the shop, this time for a new transmission. Since I had missed visiting my daughter Kate the previous weekend because of an out-of-town gig, I'd decided to catch the train out to Oakville, where my ex-wife Sandra was living with her new guy in his three-thousand-plus-square-foot house.

Knowing that yet again that bastard Jeremy would look down his long nose at me, my mind was on other things, so I nearly knocked Olivia down as she panhandled for change in between the subway exit and the lower level entrance to Union Station. The Tim Hortons coffee cup in her hand went flying, the coins tinkling as they bounced all over the concrete. Immediately, two other street people appeared from nowhere, stooped and began snatching them up.

"Oh, damn! I'm sorry!" I said.

The poor girl looked as if she might start crying. It took me a moment to realize who she was. She just stared at me, then stooped to pick up her cup and two nickels and a dime that had fallen nearby.

Turning around, I saw the two interlopers scurrying off with their booty. No honour among thieves.

I pulled a handful of coins out of my pocket and dumped them in her cup. "It's the least I can do."

Big eyes looked at me, and a shy smile lit up her face. "Thanks."

Feeling embarrassed, I hurried off with a muttered, "Well, take care," and went in search of my train.

The whole way out to Oakville, I couldn't get her out of my mind.

She puzzled me. Had the girl wandered into the Sal simply to get warm? It had been a frighteningly cold night, but you didn't often see street people in a jazz club – unless they were on the stage playing…

My daughter kept me busy all afternoon, first at a movie then at one of those indoor putting places. The cab fare to and from the big complex out on Winston Churchill Drive where both were located, along with the cost of lunch, movie and putting set me back more than what I made in one night at the Sal, but it was worth it. I'd missed Kate dreadfully since Sandra had taken up with Jeremy, and we'd had a great afternoon.

Eleven-year-old Kate had begun to remind me of my own mother, all dark, curly hair and a broad, pleasant face. She'd never be a beauty like own mom, but her sense of humour and fierce creativity would stand her in good stead. I'd gotten her interested in music, and she showed some talent on the piano. Sandra pushed her hard in school because Kate was very bright. I had no idea how she'd turn out, but I knew she'd be very good at everything she took up.

Whenever I saw Kate, I tried to show her the best time possible. I'm sure a lot of divorced dads do the same. You have to. Jeremy probably made more in three months than I made in a whole year and could give her just about anything.

There was no question that Kate should live with Sandra. With the hours I kept, it couldn't be any other way – certainly not at her age. Perhaps later that might change, but for now, we had to be satisfied with what felt like stolen moments. Unless I went out of town for a gig, I tried my level best to see her every weekend. We'd share email during the week and talk on the phone. Kate was also after me to get a game system like the one Jeremy had given her so we could both play online. I'd reluctantly promised that I'd get one, not because I wanted to, but because I wasn't about to let the interloper have one more thing that my daughter could share with him and not with me.

So that Sunday it was a bad movie (we agreed on that), pizza and a game of mini-putt, where we both cheated as much as possible. We also laughed a lot, and I forgot for minutes at a time how hollow the whole thing felt. Kate was just as aware as I how we had to fit a whole week of being together into a few short hours.

On the cab ride back to Jeremy's, she cuddled up to me and whispered in my ear how she thought he was a "dork". I squeezed her tight and didn't say a word, mainly because her words hit me so hard. That was the first time she'd said anything on the subject.

"I love you, honey," I managed to say as we pulled up in front of her new home.

"And I love you too, Daddy. You take care of yourself this week. You're beginning to look pretty skinny!"

She kissed my cheek, and I kissed her forehead. Then she ran for the house without another word. Sandra was at the door to let Kate in, and her expression, as she closed it, was as devoid of emotion as ever.

On the train ride back into the city, I worked on my electronic agenda, lining up all the gigs the trio had over the next three months.

Just before the axe had fallen on our marriage, Sandra, Kate and I had discussed going to Disney World. That afternoon, I decided that if I could talk Sandra into allowing it, I'd take Kate there for a week in April. The plane tickets would cost a fortune, let alone rooms, food and Disney World admission, but gigs had been plentiful in the six months since Sandra had split, and I could just afford the trip.

I'd be damned if I was going to let Jeremy get there first with my daughter.

Back at Union Station, the mysterious girl I'd seen at the Sal was still standing outside the subway entrance with her pathetic coffee cup. Snow had begun falling, and that short stretch between the two stations was alive with flakes, dancing as they descended out of the darkness into the light. Even though completely fed up with winter at this point, the sight caught my attention.

It had apparently caught the girl's, too, because she was standing there, head upturned, watching the big flakes descend. From the amazed expression on her face, you'd think she'd never seen snow before.

Noticing that her attention was elsewhere, a punk made a snatch for her cup.

Reaching out, I grabbed his wrist. Although I'm not the bulkiest guy around, drumming has made my forearms pretty strong, and he couldn't shake me off.

"Hey, man! Leggo! What do you think you're doing?"

I leaned forward and said quietly, "Why don't you just hand the girl back her cup?"

"Man, you're some kind of psycho!" the little rat said, rubbing his wrist after he'd done what I'd asked.

"Get lost!"

He did, and when I turned to look at her, the girl was staring back with those deep eyes. "You're the man who was here this afternoon."

"Yes, I was."

"That's twice you've done something nice for me. Thank you."

"My name's Andy. What's yours?"

"Ummm...Olivia."

"Are you always out here, Olivia?"

"Most days. People in Toronto aren't as generous as they like to make out they are."

I laughed. "Don't I know it."

She laughed, too, a nice sound, then her expression changed. "I have to go now."

Without another word, she turned and hurried away.

What had I done to spook her?

The episodes with Olivia at Union Station fell out of my mind over the next week. The car wound up costing a lot more than I'd been led to believe, and when I began seriously looking into taking Kate to Disney World, the cost of *that* little excursion was absolutely staggering.

I knew what Sandra would have told me. "Sell the damn house. You know you need the money."

Fortunately for me, it *was* my house – completely. When my parents had both died within a year of each other, it had been left to me as the only child, and by a stroke of good fortune, I had inherited their estate three weeks before my marriage to Sandra.

But she was right; I could get a good price for it in Toronto's superheated real estate market. Houses like mine in Riverdale often went for upwards of a million bucks, a stunning figure, considering what my dad had paid for it nearly forty years earlier. With that money (pure profit), I could buy a condo and put the rest in a retirement plan. I'd be set for my golden years, right?

But I just couldn't bear the thought of giving it up. It had a soundproof basement studio where I gave lessons to a few students and where I could also rehearse a pretty decent-sized band if I wanted, but it was more than those obvious needs. The place had become part of my psyche, and in my present circumstances, that was a very important thing. Except for a few months at various times over the years, I'd never lived anywhere else.

With a ton of things weighing on my mind, I headed off to the Sal that fateful Tuesday evening, not even really thinking about the gig, let alone a girl I'd only seen three times and had barely spoken to.

Of course, it was raining. It's always raining or snowing or doing something miserable when I have to move my drums. With a steady gig, I could leave them in place for a few nights, but once we finished on

Thursday night, I had to horse them out again. That's the lot of a gigging musician, something you put up with, but it can be a drag – especially if you're a drummer. There are a number of parts to a drum set.

Pulling to the curb in a no-parking zone, I put the blinkers on and opened up the hatchback on my old Honda. Take out the trap case, lay the bass drum on top of it, close the trunk and head for the door to the club. Once inside, take the bass drum off the trap case and take each down the steep stairs. By the time I went back to the car to retrieve the two tom-toms, the rain was really coming down.

Normally I would have parked my heap at the lot down the street and carried the two toms back with me, but I decided to take them in first so I could run from the lot to the club more easily.

I had just stuck my key into the hatchback's lock when a cab swerved to avoid God knows what. It went right down the centre of a puddle next to the car, totally drenching the left leg of my pants.

Cursing, I stared laser beams at the rapidly disappearing cab. A flash of red in a doorway across King Street caught my eye.

It was her – the girl I'd seen at the Sal and Union Station. A streetlight thirty feet away illuminated her face and that red scarf only for a moment before she stepped back, disappearing into the shadows.

If she was here again to listen to the music, why was she waiting outside on such a miserable night?

I thought about going across to say something, but looking down at the sodden condition of my pant leg, I decided against it.

Reaching into the car, I grabbed the two tom cases and took my second load into the club. When I came out again, the doorway opposite was empty.

Ronald was in fine form that night, mainly because a couple of local pianists were in the house. He felt that interlopers (as he referred to them) were always after his gigs. So we defended our turf with a couple of fast opening numbers courtesy of Duke Ellington's fertile imagination. That got the evening's festivities off to a good start.

The way the open mike thing had evolved was that interested singers would speak with Ronald before each set. When he found out what they wanted to perform, he'd arrange the song choices in such a way that we didn't wind up with five ballads in a row, or two people singing the same tune back to back.

The first sets each week were generally the best for two reasons: the people who had come specifically to sing most often wanted to sing early. The third set featured more of the sort of performances that relied on "Dutch courage", the half-drunken person saying, "I can sing better than that clown!" followed by his or her equally drunk acquaintances goading the poor soul on. Those were our "train wrecks" – frightening, pathetic and comical all at the same time.

The girl must have slid in sometime during the first set while my attention was occupied elsewhere. In the second-to-last tune, an older gentleman who'd sung a few times in recent weeks was in the middle of a competent rendition of "Chattanooga Choo-Choo" when I looked over at that dark corner of the club, and there she was. She had on the same worn blue duffel coat and the black toque jammed down on her head. Her face had a small frown of concentration as she mouthed the lyrics with the singer.

I again thought of going over to speak with her but got corralled into a conversation with two of the club regulars. By the time that broke up, we had to start the second set.

As the evening progressed, we had some surprisingly good performances and only a few disasters, none of them too excruciating. Dom, Ronald and I were playing well, and in a few tunes we stretched things out a bit, which left the poor vocalists standing around with nothing to do, but hell, we were feeling good. I forgot about the waif at the back of the club.

We were getting ready to finish off the final set with a couple of non-vocal numbers when the girl appeared next to Ronald's grand piano, staring at us with huge, frightened eyes.

"What is it?" he asked testily. "Do you have a request?"

The girl shook her head. "I want to sing," she said in a tiny voice.

"The open mike night is over. If you want to sing, you'll have to come back next week."

She didn't move. Even with the duffel coat on, it was easy to see she was absolutely quaking in her boots. Coming up to the bandstand had taken a lot of courage on her part.

"I want to sing," she said softly but defiantly.

Dom, perhaps sensing that this might be a good bit of sport, said, "Aw, let her, Ronny," then turned to the girl. "What song, darling?"

She mumbled something indistinguishable.

Ronald decided to remain obnoxious – not much of a stretch for him. "If that's how loud you sing, you're not going to make much of an impression on the audience."

As he stretched out his hand to indicate the sixty or so people still in the club, the poor girl's eyes got wider, and I felt certain she'd bolt. I suddenly remembered she'd told me her name.

"Olivia," I said loudly to attract her attention, "tell us the song you'd like to sing."

She looked at me gratefully. "'Skylark'. Do you know 'Skylark'?"

Ronald rolled his eyes, since a woman had already sung it in the previous set.

"What key do you sing in?" Ronald asked impatiently.

Olivia looked confused. "I don't know."

"Then how can we play it?"

Her eyes pleaded with me for help.

"Can you sing it in the same key that we played it in earlier?" I asked.

"I guess so."

Dom nodded. "B flat then, Ronald. The lady wants to sing."

With her coat, hat and that scarf still on, she stepped onto the bandstand with a look of resolution. It took her a moment to figure out how to drop the mike stand to her height, but finally she looked over at Ronald, and with tight lips, nodded.

One of the two visiting pianists was still in the house, half-potted, having an earnest conversation with one of the better female vocalists of the evening, so Ronald made up a totally different intro to the song than the one he'd used earlier, and it really was quite brilliant. Olivia, totally at sea, turned to me with a frightened look, so I smiled and nodded reassuringly, indicating I'd help her come in.

Ronald finished with an arpeggiated chord roll to the upper end of the piano, and I mouthed "two, three, four" to bring her in.

She turned to the audience, shut her eyes and started to sing. "Skylark, have you anything to say to me..."

I had my brushes out, planning to join in for the second verse, and damn near forgot to come in.

The performance of this very odd girl was, to put it mildly, stunning.

There are always people who insist on talking through every song, regardless of the fact that it's rude, irritating and distracting to those people who want to listen, but especially so to the musicians. By the time Olivia was halfway through the first verse, every eye in the house had turned to the stage. Even the bigmouth at the bar stopped gassing.

It wasn't so much her voice – although no one could possibly have any complaints in that department. What had every person in that club riveted was Olivia's delivery. The girl could flat out *sell* a song like nobody I'd ever heard.

"Skylark" is not a song you can belt out. It must be subtle, wistful, delicate, ingenuous. It's about a young girl asking where her first love might be found. The performance earlier in the evening, which had been quite good, paled to black and white in comparison to the way Olivia was singing.

We always set up with me facing Ronald and Dom in the middle, since he's the glue that holds us together musically, so I had a good view of her. Her eyes were shut tight, and she gripped the mike stand with both hands as if it were saving her from drowning, but her body remained supple, swaying gently with the music. Her awkward-looking outerwear suddenly didn't seem important as the subtle nuance of her melodic shadings washed over us. You could visualize her having run in off the street to tell everyone about her search for love. I felt as if I were hearing this song for the very first time.

The trio rose to the occasion, giving this girl the very best we could – even Ronald. He'll occasionally get overly busy, especially if he's bored or put out. His playing in this song was easily the best he'd done in some months, matching Olivia's understated performance with one of his own. He only took a two-chorus solo before he led her in for the last verse with a gentle nod, and smiled broadly as he ended the song with a gentle whisper of melody high up the keyboard.

For a moment there was silence before everyone remembered to breathe. Then the place just went nuts.

Olivia stood there for a moment with an increasingly fearful expression on her face, then turned, and with everyone cheering, she ran right out of the club as if the devil were at her heels.

"Interesting way to end a performance," Dom observed as he leaned on his bass. "Damn good vocalist, though."

Olivia's singing haunted me the rest of the week. I wished someone had taped it.

The following week, she didn't show up on Tuesday, and I was sure the girl had either got it all out of her system, or had completely freaked herself out. More than one regular asked if "that interesting singer" was coming back. Even Harry inquired if we were going to hire her.

Wednesday noon found me downtown to get my passport renewed, so I took a walk over to Union Station, to see if she was there. Street people are creatures of habit, staking their turf and guarding it jealously.

No sign of her, so I grabbed lunch in one of the fast food joints in the underground city, that maze of interconnected office buildings stretching from the train station all the way up to Dundas Street.

Back at Union for a last try, I got no glory, but some old guy was hawking one of those street newspapers homeless people sell. I'd seen him there the previous time I'd encountered Olivia.

"I'm looking for a girl—"

"Isn't everyone?" he interrupted with a broken-toothed grin.

If he was looking to sell a paper, bad comedy wasn't going to get him there.

"This is a particular girl," I said patiently, "*maybe* five-foot-two, pretty, big eyes, long dark hair, wears a navy duffel coat and a black toque. Not your average street person. Know who I'm talking about?"

The guy looked purposefully down at the sheaf of papers under his arm. I got the message and forked over a tooney, twice what the paper was worth.

"She's here most days. The cops did a sweep of the area, and she skedaddled like all the other panhandlers. Odd one, though. She spooks kind of easy."

"When is she usually around?"

"You ain't a cop, are you?"

"Do I look like a cop?"

He cocked an eyebrow at my stupid question.

"No," I sighed, "I'm not a cop. She's just someone I met."

His grin told me he'd imagined a meeting far different from the reality.

"If she shows, it might be around three, maybe three thirty. The evening rush is usually pretty good."

After that, I felt I'd committed myself to sticking around.

From up above at street level, you can see the open area where Olivia had her spot. In order not to spook her again, I hung out up there, occasionally checking to see if she'd arrived. Luckily, the February weather was a little more moderate that day than it had been, because I had to wait until nearly four o'clock before the black cap and red scarf were directly below me. Her outstretched Tim Hortons cup with two quarters in it jingled loudly when she shook it.

Okay, I'll admit it. I snuck up on her. It wasn't hard, since most of the traffic at that time is headed into the station. I forced my way upstream and came at Olivia from her blind side. When I gently touched her shoulder, she flinched as if I'd struck her.

"Hello, Olivia," I said, smiling to look friendly and harmless.

"What are you doing here?"

"I just wanted to say how much I enjoyed your singing last week. We were all hoping you'd show up last night and sing some more."

"That was a stupid thing for me to do!"

"Why? You were really good."

"That's not what I meant. Now leave me alone." When I didn't immediately disappear, she demanded again, "Leave!"

I smiled. "Let me buy you a cup of coffee. You're shivering."

"No. I'm busy."

"How about a coffee and a ten dollar bill, then? In the time it takes to have a coffee, you won't make that standing here."

The dirty white running shoes she had on looked pretty soaked. I think cold feet swung the deal.

"Okay," she finally said. "Where?"

"How about just inside the station? That way you won't have far to go when we're finished."

I bought her a large double-double and a toasted bagel. We went over to the seats where you wait for the local trains.

Olivia wolfed down the bagel. While she chewed and sipped her coffee, I waited patiently, trying to figure her out.

Toronto has a lot of street people. It's part of our city's shame. But something about this girl didn't seem quite right.

I put her age at well over twenty, far too old to be a runaway. She also didn't have that spaced out look of the alcoholic or druggie. With her torn jeans and ratty coat, her appearance wasn't the best, that was for sure, but her hair wasn't dirty, and she didn't smell. She knew I was studying her but kept her eyes averted.

As the last bit of bagel disappeared, she licked a dab of cream cheese off her finger, and I spoke. "You sing really well, you know."

Her head stayed steadfastly down. "I do?"

"Couldn't you tell by the way the audience reacted?"

She shook her head and gave me a sidelong glance. "I shouldn't have done it."

"Why?"

"Can't tell you."

I took another tack. "If you ever came back again, what song would you want to sing?"

She took a long time to answer. The flow of people around us had increased as the downtown office towers emptied for the day. If she'd wanted to bolt, there would have been little I could have done to stop her, and she had to know that.

"Cole Porter. I like Cole Porter."

"What song?"

"'Just One of Those Things.'"

"You like that one?"

She nodded. "I used to sing it for my daddy."

"You know, if you wanted, you could come down to the club, tonight even, and sing with us. We might be able to offer you a job. You wouldn't have to hang out here any more."

She took that in. "I don't think so."

"Don't worry about being frightened to sing in public. You'd soon get used to that."

"I shouldn't do it."

"Why not? A steady paycheque has to be better than panhandling. Safer, too."

Her eyes suddenly got big again, but she said nothing.

Patting her shoulder, I said, "Come down tonight and sing a couple of Cole Porter tunes with us. Okay?"

I knew I should leave or risk having her run away again, and I also knew next time I wouldn't find her so easily.

As I walked towards the subway, she remained behind, but I could feel her eyes on my back.

Since it was the second night of our three-day gig, I didn't have to set up my drums, but I arrived early to check out the doorways in the area of the Sal. No sign of Olivia.

By the time the first set had ended, I'd convinced myself she wouldn't show. I couldn't have told anyone why it was so important, but I just knew that it was. After all, the girl had only sung one ballad with us.

She had good rhythm and listened to what was going on around her, that was clear. Even Ronald couldn't fault her pitch. I felt confident that whatever makes a great vocalist, she had it in spades.

As we sat down at our usual table, I casually mentioned to Dom and Ronald that I'd seen Olivia and invited her to sit in again. The bass player greeted that news enthusiastically, the pianist phlegmatically. I wondered what his problem was.

She slid in between the second and third sets, and I immediately saw her standing uncertainly by the door. Getting to my feet, I motioned her over to our table. This time, though, she wasn't alone. A woman, definitely older and with less of an air of indecision, followed in her wake.

"I'm glad you made it," I said as I helped her off with her coat.

She had on a reasonably nice black dress. From the way it fit her, it had probably been borrowed or picked up at the Salvation Army Thrift Store or some such place. Still, it looked reasonable, if a bit old-fashioned. Around her neck was another scarf, this time a white silk one that complemented the dress nicely.

Dom slid over two seats to make room for the newcomers. Olivia just about fell into her chair, and I could see she was even more nervous than the week before.

The friend said nothing, and Olivia didn't make an effort to introduce her. She looked to be at least fifteen years older than Olivia and definitely more careworn. Her face had a wary expression, and I got the feeling she'd been dragged down to the Sal against her will, or that Olivia had come against her wishes. She said her name was Maggie, but something told me it also might not be.

Dom leaned over towards the frightened girl and said in his usual friendly manner, "Andy told us you'd like to sit in."

She kept her head down. "He asked me to come."

"So what will you be singing?"

"'Just One of Those Things,'" I answered for her. "Maybe another Cole Porter tune or two."

"Like what?" Ronald asked sharply.

"I know 'I've Got You Under My Skin'," she answered.

"And I suppose you don't know what key you want to sing them in."

I was about to tell Ronald to back off, but Dom saved me the trouble. "Just sing them, honey, and I'll tell you what key they're in. Okay?"

In a very soft voice, Olivia started 'Just One of Those Things' and Dom immediately said, "That's in A."

Her other chosen tune was in G. We were ready to go.

As the other two got ready, I pulled the vocal mike and stand to the centre of the bandstand and turned it on, checking its level.

Ronald insisted on opening the set with a rather Bill Evans-like rendition of the Porter tune "Night and Day", and it went on far too long. I kept my eye on Olivia, but my attention wandered when I did a brief solo at the end of the song. When I opened my eyes, I noticed that both women were missing.

Cursing Ronald under my breath for not starting the set with Olivia's songs, I was about to let him have it when they appeared from the corridor leading to the washrooms. Maggie looked even less happy than before, but Olivia had a very determined glint in her eye as she led the way.

Ronald switched on his mike, announcing to the club that we had a special guest who'd dropped by to sing a few songs. Olivia, having sat down again at our table, popped up immediately and stood there. Dom motioned her towards the bandstand, and she came much more readily than she had the previous time.

"Will somebody help me come in?" she asked shyly.

"Sure thing, sugar," Dom said.

Olivia seemed a bit more relaxed (as evidenced by her actually letting go of the mike stand a few times), and her performance was that much better because of it. Often she'd sink so far into the songs that she actually seemed to become the person described by the lyrics. The effect was quite astonishing and had the patrons of the club mesmerized – not to mention her backup band. The girl could swing, she could shout, she could be tender. I could only imagine what Olivia would be like with a little rehearsing under her belt.

She wound up doing the rest of the set with us. We would suggest songs until we came up with one she thought she could do, she'd sing a few bars so Dom and Ronald could get the key, and we'd be off.

By the end of the set, she had everyone in the palm of her ingenuous hand. That performance was the stuff legends are made of, and I've heard at least three times the number of people who were actually present that night say they were there.

The only person who looked unhappy was Olivia's friend.

As we came off the stand, Dom put his arm around Olivia. "Would you like to sing with us steadily, sugar?"

I thought for a moment that Ronald would object, but he finally nodded in agreement.

I watched her carefully until she said, "I don't know..."

"Why don't you come back tomorrow night and sing some more? You don't have to make up your mind on the spot. Right, gentlemen?" he said, looking more at Ronald than me.

She smiled happily at that, although her friend looked (if possible) even more put out.

"So you'll come back?"

"Maybe," was all she answered as she hurriedly put on her coat.

People tried to talk to Olivia as she made her way to the door, but her friend urged her on. They disappeared into the night as quickly as they'd arrived.

It was the first of many nights for the four of us at the Sal.

CHAPTER 3

Shannon O'Brien had tipped her chair back, the small notebook she was busily scribbling in resting on her crossed legs.

The man sitting on the other side of her desk, Andrew Curran, was of Irish descent, like her. Sizing him up, she guessed his height at six feet, age around thirty-five and thought he looked sturdy enough, though slender. He had a strong face, a shock of nearly black hair and a light complexion, like many whose ancestry was Irish. She decided he should lose the mustache and goatee. The left side of his face was swollen, and he had one hell of a shiner. No wonder the guy was so angry at the joker who'd slugged him.

The story he'd told of his mysterious girl singer had Shannon's antennae twitching. After the ordeal she and her family had undergone at the hands of another "mysterious girl", Shannon had little desire to travel down that path again, but the situation he described had piqued her interest.

She surmised there was a lot Curran hadn't told her, but that could wait. She had the bare bones of his story but needed to ask a few questions before hustling him out the door. She had another appointment breathing down her back.

"Do you think the men who took your friend away might have been bounty hunters?"

Curran looked confused. "I don't understand what you mean."

"You told me they said they had a plane to catch."

"Yeah..."

"Think back to what they said to you. Hear it in your head. Now, do you think they were American?"

He concentrated for a moment, then nodded. "Yes, now that you mention it. They didn't have one of those really recognizable accents, but the big guy used the word 'huh'. A Canadian would have used 'eh'."

Shannon smiled. "Now how about Olivia? Did she use 'huh'?"

"Not that I remember. Her accent is very neutral. She never talked a lot and never about herself." He shook his head. "Actually, I know almost nothing about her."

"But could she be from the States?"

"Maybe. There were certainly things about living in Canada that she didn't seem familiar with."

Shannon nodded but decided to keep her questions about the girl for another time.

"Why do you think those men might be bounty hunters?" Curran asked.

"Do you know anything about this particular brand of slimeball?"

"Not really."

"Well then, for a few reasons." She ticked them off on her fingers. "One, bounty hunters are typically American. They have a system down there that allows this sort of thing. Two, you think the girl might also be from the States. Three, one of them said they had to catch a plane. That's typical, too. If the value of the target warrants it, a private plane is always preferable to leaving the country by car or some sort of public transport. Last of all, there's the way they behaved." She raised one eyebrow to punctuate her point.

"Surely they can't just walk out of Canada with her?"

"Of course they can. The Americans will be the ones to check their ID at the airport, and they certainly aren't going to complain. Bounty hunting is legal in most places down there. As long as they had ID for her, they're golden."

Curran slumped. "Do you think you can find her?"

Shannon put her notebook on the desk and leaned forward. "Are you sure you *want* to find her? Bounty hunters only come after people who are on the run – and usually from bad things."

"But you could be wrong. Maybe they aren't bounty hunters. Maybe she hasn't done anything illegal. Maybe they were kidnapping her."

"You said she went with them willingly."

"They could have threatened Olivia when they were talking to her in the club."

"We're only dealing with suppositions at this point, but your story gives ample reason to believe your girl was on the run, don't you think?"

Curran sighed and nodded. "When she was out in public, she could be pretty jumpy, always looking behind her. Stuff like that."

"Do you want me to see if I can find her? You may not like what I come up with."

"I have to know. Even if Olivia was on the run from something or somebody, she may need my help."

"Okay, then. I need to tell you from the outset that this could get very expensive. We may get lucky, and finding her might come easily, but that's not usually the case. The United States is a very big country. Now you've only referred to this woman as Olivia. I assume she has a last name."

He looked awkward. "She said she didn't want to tell us. Ronald eventually pushed her on that, and she told him it was Saint. None of us thought it was actually her real name, though."

Shannon closed her notebook with a sigh. "Do you have a photo of her?"

Curran picked up a manila envelope he'd had in his lap and took a large photo out, sliding it across the desk. "This is a promo shot we had taken."

She studied it for quite some time. The make-up, lighting and soft focus helped to make a very striking photo of a very striking young woman. Her long brown hair glistened, framing a pale face which held an expression at once shy but also alluring. But there was something about her eyes that made Shannon fight down a shudder. "I'll need to keep this."

Curran nodded. "How much will your services cost?"

She shrugged. "I couldn't begin to say. We'll start with the simple and inexpensive ways to search, of course."

"And that might bring results?

"It often does, now that we have the Internet."

"If we have to go farther, I could always mortgage my house, I suppose."

"I sincerely hope it won't come to that, Mr. Curran. Shall we say a retainer of a thousand dollars? That should be more than sufficient to get this started."

Shannon ran her new client through all the fine print. They then signed an agreement with her secretary as witness.

After showing her new client out the door with a reassuring, "I'll be in touch immediately if we find out anything," she went into her office.

Leaning back in her chair, Shannon wondered what Curran's reaction would have been if she'd asked if he and the girl were romantically entangled.

She spent the remaining time before the next appointment staring at the haunting photo of the girl. The eyes kept drawing her in. There was something dark there, well-hidden and possibly dangerous. Had Curran seen that?

The woman slouched in the same chair Curran had just vacated seemed outwardly to be perfectly calm and relaxed, but Shannon could have easily ticked off five telltale signs broadcasting how incredibly anxious she was.

She didn't look at all as Shannon had expected from the initial phone call. The person on the phone had been all business, very mature sounding. What had entered her office looked more like a street urchin, the type you'd see on Queen Street West or one of those huge joints in the club district – the kind who often got into a lot of trouble.

Height 5'7", solidly built, she obviously worked hard to keep in shape. Her face wouldn't turn too many male heads, but it wasn't unpleasant, a good thing when you didn't want to be too noticeable. What caused more than a few alarm bells to go off was the short purple hair that looked as if it had been hacked at with a dull knife. She had on new jeans, and under an unbuttoned flannel shirt was a T-shirt emblazoned with "You got a problem with that?", not the sort of thing most would choose to wear to a job interview, even a business as casually run as O'Brien Investigates.

Taking her time going over all the documentation and the background check she'd done, Shannon let the prospective employee stew in her own juices. If she couldn't control her nerves in a job interview, what good would she be out on the street?

After five minutes, she looked across the desk, nailing the woman right in the eyes. "When we did our background check, we ran across your name in regards to a death several years ago. Tell me about it."

Now she looked really uneasy. "It involved the murder of a friend. The cops thought the murderer was some escaped wacko, and my friends and I thought it was someone else. We set out to find that person. I got involved more than the others and stirred up some sh – stuff. The real murderer came after me. There was a fight. I got lucky, and he wound up dead."

"I was told you stabbed him in the throat."

Her expression was pained. "I was trying to stab him *anywhere*. He'd already nailed me pretty good."

"Where?"

"Here," she answered, as she pulled her shirt and T-shirt off one shoulder. The ugly scar was very plain. "It went right through the joint into the wall behind me. There was another one in my leg." Her expression changed. "Do you want to see that, too?"

Shannon kept a straight face at the woman's impudence. "My sources tell me he was ex-military. How did you get so good at knife fighting?"

"It's called trying to survive any way you can. Like I said, I got lucky."

The PI nodded. "Okay. Well, everything seems to be in order as far as the documentation goes, Ms Goode. With your qualifications, though, it seems to me you'd be happier with a police service or maybe the Mounties. Why do you want to be a private investigator?"

Goode frowned and straightened up. "I don't think I'd fit in with any police force."

"That's pretty forthright. Why?"

"I've never been able to fit in." She tried a grin, but it didn't quite make the grade. "I tend to be a bit of a loner."

Shannon nodded. Despite the misanthropic characters populating detective novels, good cops had to be team players. If you couldn't manage that, you generally didn't stay a cop for long. The girl had enough sense to realize it.

"You're going to be thirty-three next month. Do you think that might be a little late to start down this road?"

Jackie Goode managed a real smile this time. "How old are you?"

"I'm not just starting out."

"Fair enough. Let's just say it took me a while to find my focus. I think

I can handle whatever is thrown at me – physically and mentally. You can see from the transcripts that the instructors thought I have what it takes."

"How are you at dealing with boredom?"

"You're going to tell me how boring this job is most of the time?"

"Yes."

"Well, the way I look at it, there's boredom and there's boredom."

"Explain."

Goode slouched back in her chair again. "I can handle boredom if it's just the calm before the storm. I don't get discouraged easily. Real boredom is when there's no purpose to what you're doing."

Shannon nodded. It was a good answer. At first, she was not going to hire this woman. Reading between the lines on the transcripts and the background check, it was easy to see that the people who'd trained her thought she was a pain in the butt. They praised only her skills and determination, not her personality. There was little about attitude and interpersonal skills. Those omissions were significant.

The more they talked, though, the more Shannon felt swayed. For one, Goode looked at her levelly at all times, her eyes never shifted away. She meant what she said, and there wasn't any evasiveness in her answers. If she didn't know something, she said so, with refreshing bluntness.

But Shannon also knew without a shadow of a doubt that Jackie Goode might be more trouble than she was worth.

Business had been good lately, too good. Shannon needed one or two more operatives, and she needed them fast. Having to let Warren go last week had been a huge blow. Good help was hard to find these days, and everyone she'd interviewed had knocked themselves out of the running pretty early, usually because they'd been cops who hadn't been able to make the grade. It took only a little digging to come up with the straight goods, if it didn't come out in the interview itself. Doing the background information on the job she'd just accepted might be a good place to start this woman off. Let her do the legwork by way of an extended audition.

Shannon leaned back in an imitation of the woman across from her.

It wasn't lost on Goode, who grinned back at her, tension draining from her body. "Do I have the job?"

"Maybe. I'd like to try you out on something. See how you do. Then we'll talk."

After an extensive briefing about the Curran case, the woman was on her way to the door when Shannon called out, "And lose that hair, Goode. *Way* too noticeable. But I'm sure you knew that."

♪♯ρ·♪♭ρ·

Jackie Goode packed it in for the night around two a.m. She felt completely done in, but it was a good tiredness. On the streetcar ride back to her one-room apartment in Parkdale, she thought back on her eventful day.

The interview that morning had gone way better than the previous ones, perhaps because there'd been a woman behind the desk.

Considering what a straight arrow her (hopefully) new employer seemed to be, she'd shown no outward surprise at the way Jackie looked and acted – except for the crack about her hair as she'd left the office.

When Jackie had called about the job, she'd pictured the person at the other end of the phone as some tough old broad. What she'd found when she got ushered into the office looked more like a "soccer mom".

It was easy to imagine Shannon O'Brien going home at night to a husband, two-and-a-half kids, dog and nice suburban house. But Jackie had done her own digging and knew that this woman had been through a messy divorce, an even messier murder investigation and was currently the girlfriend of a genuine rock and roll legend.

During the lengthy interview, O'Brien had been very undemonstrative, although it was easy to see that her interest had grown as Jackie spoke. In past ones, the shutters behind the eyes of prospective employers had come down pretty quickly and never once cracked open again.

Jackie was well aware that her frank – no, be honest – abrasive way of communicating often put people off, especially men, but she wasn't going to change her stripes just to get a goddamn job. She'd always done things her way, and they should know that right from the beginning.

Today, she'd finally been given all she'd ever asked for: a chance.

What had she accomplished in the twelve hours since being given the assignment? No big breakthroughs, certainly, but she had a much better idea where she wanted to go next with this.

Her best friend, Kit Mason, a well-known guitarist and singer, had been the starting point once Jackie had finally got hold of her in Los Angeles.

"Jackie! How the hell are you?"

"I got a job, Kit, a real live PI job."

"Wow! I always knew you'd make it eventually. I'm so proud of you."

"Well, maybe I'm jumping the gun a bit. I don't really *have* the job yet, but I'm on an extended tryout, shall we say."

"It's still good news. Thanks for letting me know."

"Actually, I called for another reason. I need some info for this job."

"Fire away."

Turned out Kit not only knew who Andrew Curran was, she'd sat in with his band back when she'd been knocking around the bar scene.

"They kicked butt, a really high octane funk band with a great horn section. After all this time, I don't quite remember what he looks like, but I do remember he was pretty damn hot. All the girls went after him. He's also a terrific drummer. What's he up to now?"

"He plays jazz."

"You're kidding! He was always Mr. Funky Drummer."

"He has a steady gig with an outfit called The Ronald Felton Trio at a club near Bathurst and King."

"The Sal?"

"I guess someone hip might call it that," Jackie replied sarcastically.

"I'm not going to rise to your bait, Jackie," Kit laughed. "So why do you want to know about Andy Curran?"

Very concisely, Jackie relayed what she'd been told about Curran's problems. "I want a gut reaction from you on this, Kit," Jackie said at the end. "Is Curran a bad guy or a good guy?"

Her friend didn't hesitate. "Unless something has radically changed, Andy's a good guy with a big white hat. He had that reputation around town – both on and off the bandstand. What do you think?"

"I haven't made his acquaintance yet, but I'm going down to the club tonight to hang."

"Tell him I said hi."

"He's not going to know I'm there. I plan on casing out the client thoroughly. This company's giving me a chance, and I don't aim to screw things up like I usually do."

Jackie's next stop was the public library, where she did an extensive Internet search on anything concerning Curran. There was a surprising amount, much of it going back to his days as a rocker. She even found a photo of his band jamming with a very young Kit Mason, who looked to be around twenty.

For the past eight years, as Curran concentrated more on his jazz career, the hits on the search engines dropped dramatically – no surprise there.

Jackie's pulse quickened when she found references to Curran and this Olivia person. The first were ads and listings stating that Miss Olivia Saint had joined the Felton Trio and would be appearing Tuesdays through Thursdays at the Green Salamander.

Now, following the Olivia trail through the Internet, things began to pick up again. Buzz was slow on her at first, but built quickly as the buzz got around through word of mouth and blogs. She couldn't find any interviews with the girl, no bio information to speak of, so the references usually included the word "mysterious" when describing this rapidly ascending star. The only quote Jackie found that came directly from the girl was, "I only want to sing, and only at the Salamander. My private life is just that, private." The members of Curran's trio were equally protective of their amazing vocalist.

Photos were as hard to come by as information, and most seemed to be shots by members of the club's audience, which they'd then posted on their blogs.

In short, as far as Jackie was concerned, the whole set-up stank. Curran certainly knew more than he had told, and she aimed to get that out of him.

She spent several more hours at the library, carefully collating her extensive notes and references into a binder she'd bought.

The first thing I'll do if I get this job, she thought as she shook the cramps from her writing hand, *is spring for a good laptop.*

After grabbing a slice of pizza at a place on Queen near Bathurst, Jackie wandered down to King and hung a left for the short walk to Portland. Spring seemed to be back again, and the evening still held a hint of the day's warmth. She left her jean jacket stowed in the backpack slung over her shoulder. Time to get her bike out of storage.

Hanging around the entrance for a few minutes, she heard several people grumbling as they left to find other entertainment because this Olivia girl wasn't going to be singing that night. No wonder Curran wanted to find his little vocalist.

It didn't take much skill in making small talk to get one of the waitresses blabbing. Obviously pissed that business had fallen off so sharply the past two nights, the woman was quick to admit the club's owner was thinking of booking another steady act. She had only nice things to say about Olivia, obviously as smitten as everyone else by her vocal skills.

"That kid could sing the leaves off the trees. I'm not ashamed to say I had to wipe tears from my eyes more than once when she sang 'Angel Eyes'. God, she made me love that song!"

"Yeah, but what was she like, you know, personally?" Jackie asked. "I find that talented people most often are creeps."

"Listen, honey," the waitress bristled, "don't you start bad mouthing my girl. She was the sweetest thing you'd ever want to meet. Never said boo to nobody. It used to make my blood boil to hear the way Mr High-and-Mighty Felton used to talk to her."

"He didn't like her?"

"It wasn't that. It's just that Olivia is more like a child than an adult. Everyone knows that, but only Felton took advantage of it. I thought Andy was going to clobber him a couple of times. Felton mouthing off to her even got Dom going once – and that takes a *lot* of doing."

Careful not to make herself obvious, Jackie moved over to the bar for a beer. During the course of the next set, she spoke to the bartender and two regulars, alcoholics who'd made the Salamander their home away from home. All three came across as having the hots to some degree for the missing singer. All three were old enough to be her father, if not her grandfather. More importantly, all three had been at the club the night before when Olivia had been whisked away by the two men who'd roughed up Curran.

"The big guy looked like trouble the moment he walked in," a drunk named Charlie offered.

"If I'd known what they were up to," the bartender growled, "I would have had something to say about it."

He was big enough to be able to back that up, assuming he knew how to handle himself.

Marvin, the other drunk, looked up at Jackie with eyes that seemed to be having trouble focussing. "I really miss our little girl. I wish she'd come back and sing for us again."

He looked as if he might start crying. The bartender suggested to Marvin that he should think about getting home and offered him some coffee, which was refused.

Watching Marvin weave towards the door, Jackie casually asked, "So these two guys and Olivia, what did you see?"

The bartender's eyes narrowed. "Why you so interested?"

She shrugged. "Everybody in here is talking about her, that's all. I came down to hear her sing tonight, and she ain't around. Got me curious, I guess."

"They stopped Olivia as she came offstage after the first set. They talked awhile then went into the dressing room, I guess. Right after, they walked through the club and out. Curran, he's the band's drummer, followed them. He returned after another five minutes I'd say, and it was clear somebody had smacked him around. Ordered a couple of shots of scotch, and that isn't usual for him."

"How would you say the girl looked when she left?"

The bartender thought as he mixed two martinis. "Hard to say. Maybe scared. No, that isn't right. She looked like someone who'd just got the bad news she'd been expecting." As he pulled another pint of draft for Jackie, he looked closely at her. "Sure you ain't a cop? You sure ask questions like one."

Jackie held up her hands. "See? No notebook. Cops always write things down."

"Maybe you got a good memory."

Stories went like that the rest of the night. Everybody who'd heard the girl sing said the same thing: how great she was. Several commented that they expected she'd disappeared because she'd gotten a recording contract and was moving on. All were very protective of her. Olivia was everybody's "little girl", men and women alike.

As for Curran, reviews for him were positive. Those who knew him, liked him. Even Jackie, who knew little about jazz, could tell that he was a terrific drummer. Apparently he kept to himself, although he was friendly. Someone said they'd overheard Curran talking to the bass player about his wife, who'd apparently walked out on him not that long ago.

One woman, alone and obviously on the prowl, mentioned that she'd seen Curran and Olivia leave the club together every night. Maybe she had the hots for the good-looking drummer and felt the girl was queering the deal. That was confirmed when Jackie was leaving. The woman, talking to Curran, was standing a lot closer to him than she needed to.

Later, as she got off the streetcar at Queen and Dowling, Jackie's mind drifted back to her last bit of conversation with the waitress.

"So you think Felton might have something to do with Olivia not being here tonight?"

"Let's just say it wouldn't surprise me, honey. I don't think he could stand the competition."

CHAPTER 4

Shannon looked at the pages of a very neat and well-organized handwritten report. "Textbook style!" her dear old dad would have proclaimed. She was further impressed by the fact that Goode had been waiting in the reception area when she'd arrived at the office. It had taken a long time to put this material together. The woman must have been up half the night.

"This is fine work, Goode," she said, nodding. "You've done well."

"Thanks."

Shannon tipped her chair back. The woman *had* done a good job. Not often did she receive such a detailed report from one of her operatives – and within twenty-four hours. She still had her doubts about Goode's overall suitability, but she had to admit she was impressed. To get to the office from downtown and to be there before the boss had arrived, Jackie would have had to leave well before seven a.m.

"What do you think our next steps should be?"

Goode had obviously thought about that, too, because her answer was quick.

"I need to talk to the client personally. He's obviously keeping information from us."

Shannon nodded. "I got the same impression when I met with him."

She didn't elaborate about her suspicion that Curran and Olivia might have been "an item". Let Goode suss out that bit of information for herself.

"I don't think it would be good if I just showed up at his door, though. Could you set up an interview for me?"

"Not a problem. From your report and what you're saying, it's obvious you don't seem completely sure of him."

Goode looked at her levelly. "I'm sure of no one."

"Have you considered how to approach looking for the girl and the two men who led her off?"

Goode considered for a moment. "Curran told you they said they had a plane to catch."

"Pearson Airport?"

"Wouldn't we have to check all of them?"

"And there's the rub. That's a lot of footwork for possibly no results. Our client has intimated he doesn't have much money available."

"It would have to be a private plane, quite possibly a jet."

Shannon nodded. "I don't have much on today. I'll handle the airports, and you interview our Mr. Curran."

Shannon had been this route at airports quite a few times in her career. Usually it was tracing the movements of executives who had the use of corporate jets, so she already had some connections who might be of help.

Since it was close by, she first tried Buttonville, one of the Toronto area's two small plane airports, but that had led to a quick dead end, so it was on to Pearson on the west side of the city. Toronto Island Airport was a long shot, so it was third on the list.

The area servicing private planes lay on the less trafficked north side of Pearson, the international airport serving Toronto. Surrounded by an industrial wasteland of warehouses, factories, strip clubs, and some small businesses, it was not the prettiest of places. Combined with the airport's wide tracts of open land, it always filled her with an odd sense of loneliness.

In the old days, things were run a lot more loosely. Planes came and went, and unless they were carrying something special, everything was pretty casual. Since 2001, though, security and the less regimented business of private aviation had tightened up considerably. A big cargo plane could be flown into an office building just as easily as a commercial airliner, and no one forgot that.

The day was turning positively warm, but the blustery west wind caught Shannon off guard as she stepped from her SUV. She stood for a moment watching a plane land on the runway nearby and wondered how pilots could keep the damn things so steady with that kind of wind buffeting them.

Having called ahead, she entered a low office building, where a
receptionist waved her through. Her contact, an airport official, was
waiting in the doorway of his office as she walked down the hall.
Actually, he was big enough to stand in as a door.

"Shannon O'Brien, how good to see you," he said as they shook hands.

"Likewise, Fred."

Getting his bulk comfortable behind his desk, he asked, "So you're
looking for information on a plane that left Tuesday evening or early
yesterday morning?"

Fred, who ran the refueling concession for this side of the airport,
had helped O'Brien Investigates on numerous occasions. Shannon
knew his assistance was predicated on the fact that he enjoyed looking
at her.

"There probably would have been three passengers, two men and a
woman." She slid a copy she'd made of Olivia's photo across the desk.
"This is who I'm looking for."

"And the two men accompanying her?"

"Bounty hunters, I believe."

"I hate those guys. Do you have a description of them?"

Shannon had typed up something based on Curran's story. It wasn't
very detailed.

As Fred alternately skimmed the page and stared at the girl's photo,
she said, "I also don't want to draw unnecessary attention to what I'm
looking for."

"Was the girl going willingly?"

"On the surface, from what I've been told."

"Any idea of the destination?"

"There's only sketchy material to work with at this point. We're pretty
sure the men are from the States and quite possibly the girl. I don't know
if she ran away from a legal problem, or if it's something else."

"Sounds a bit like a needle in a haystack to me."

Shannon shrugged. "I've done more with less. Think you can help?"

Fred looked down at the photo again. "Jimmy's here today, and he
was around on Tuesday night. Let's talk to him."

Jimmy turned out to be a wiry guy with grey hair who looked as
tough as an old goat. Fred gave him the photo of Olivia. He stared at it
for a good ten seconds before handing it back.

"I seen her. Tuesday night, some time after eleven."

Shannon asked, "Anyone with her?"

"Two guys."

"Can you describe them?"

Jimmy looked at Fred. "She a cop?"

Fred shook his head. "No, a friend. She's looking for the girl."

The airport employee grunted. "I figured out that much. Look lady, I really didn't pay attention. A cute thing like her I certainly glance at, but I don't have time for guys, know what I mean? And besides, they were in a real big hurry. Wanted their plane refuelled like yesterday."

"So they took off right away?"

"Not really. Their pilot wasn't ready, and it took a while to get through all the formalities. They weren't happy. The shorter of the two guys took the girl onto the plane while they waited."

"And the other person?"

"He drove off in the car almost right away. Can't say if he didn't just return it to the rental place and take a cab back, though."

Shannon filed that bit of information away. Now for the million dollar question. "Any idea where they were flying to?"

"The plane was from the States, if that's what you mean. I believe they flew in from California. Can't really say if they were going back there, though. I was pretty busy that night. Hardly had time to think."

He did have time to ogle a pretty girl, though, and that had been a good thing.

Fred spoke up. "I can get you that information."

Shannon wondered how much it might cost her. A year ago, he'd fleeced her for three hundred dollars for the same sort of info. This time she'd stipulate that he share some of it with Jimmy. The sharp-eyed gas jockey had saved her a lot of time.

As she drove along Highway 401 on the way back to her office, Shannon considered her next move.

According to the flight plan that had been filed, the plane had a final destination of San Diego. That didn't necessarily mean that it couldn't have stopped somewhere first to drop off passengers. Pilots amended their flight plans all the time. She'd have to follow that up. Perhaps the pilot or the owners of the plane would be willing to talk. That would require the proper leverage, since they generally protected their clientele, especially if they were bounty hunters.

The news that the bozo who'd poked her client in the eye might still be around was something that required careful consideration, too. Was there a reason for that? If so, what?

Swinging north onto the 404, Shannon's thoughts were back on Jackie Goode. After their meeting that morning, she had the feeling she might have caught lightning in a bottle. Then again, there was the comment by one of Goode's instructors in a Seneca College Police Foundations course: "The kid's got street smarts and savvy, but she's also got a big mouth and is pigheaded to boot. I'd watch my step with her."

Shannon would keep her on a short lead.

♪♯♩·♪♭♩·

At two o'clock sharp, Jackie walked up the steps of Andrew Curran's house. On one of the tree-lined streets running east off Broadview south of Danforth Avenue, he had an enviable location in one of Toronto's hottest neighbourhoods, speaking in real estate terms.

The house itself looked a tad run down, but the windows were new. The broad porch was in need of fresh paint, the bushes in front of it were overgrown and the cement walk was crumbling. Playing drums must keep him busy – or else he didn't care about protecting his investment.

Curran had been watching for her, because he was waiting behind the storm door as she mounted the steps.

"I'm Jackie Goode," she said, offering her hand.

"Is this going to take long? I thought I answered all the questions yesterday."

He seemed distracted as he led her into the living room.

As she sat down on a small sofa and looked around (not much furniture and most of it new), Jackie pulled a notebook out of her backpack before setting it on the floor. Only one small painting adorned the walls, but she could see marks where several others had once hung. The mantel above the fireplace at the far end was also bare. Frankly, the place looked as if he'd just moved in. The only thing of any consequence was an impressive sound system, a large bookcase crammed with CDs on one wall and another with double layers of books on the opposite side. Mr. Curran obviously liked to listen to music and read.

He made no move to turn on a lamp, and the porch outside cast further darkness into the room. Parking himself on one of those curved IKEA chairs, he didn't lounge back the way the seat was designed to encourage. The man was clearly uneasy.

Jackie made a show of looking for her pen as she considered how to proceed in light of this. "To answer your question," she said, opening her notebook, "I'm hoping this won't take long at all. Do you have someplace you need to be?"

"Just my gig tonight, but there are some other things that need doing before I leave."

She smiled. "Okay, I'll be as speedy as I can."

If it was up to her, she'd take the bold frontal approach and come right out and ask it: "What exactly was your relationship with this woman you've hired us to find?" But that would definitely be a bad idea, considering how stiff her potential employer seemed to be. Still, the idea had its charm...

Curran was staring at her. "When Ms O'Brien called this morning, I thought she had news for me. Have you found out anything?"

Jackie shook her head. "It's pretty early, and you didn't give us much to start with. One thing we're doing is checking all the airports to see if that gives us any fresh leads on where they took your girl."

The client squirmed and coloured a bit at her deliberate choice of words. "I saw you at the club last night," was his deflecting response.

"Seems you're not the only one hung up on this girl. I think half the people I spoke to last night have a crush on her."

This time Curran visibly cringed. Jackie felt a bit sorry for him, but she also didn't like people who lied – or at least played around with the truth.

Making a show of flipping pages in her notebook, she asked, "You worked with Olivia how long?"

"A little under two months."

"You told my employer that she lived on the street. Surely that can't be true."

"Olivia kept to herself. I don't know much more about her than I told Ms O'Brien yesterday."

She pounced, but gently. "How did you get in touch with her then? Go down to the train station whenever you wanted to tell her something?"

Curran flopped back into the chair and looked out the window over

Jackie's shoulder, his eyes far away. She waited silently for a good half-minute.

"I asked Olivia to move in here shortly after we asked her to sing with the trio. Before that, she was sharing a room somewhere in the west end."

"Why didn't you tell us this yesterday?"

"I don't know." He shook his head slowly. "I didn't want you to get the wrong idea. I just want to find out if she's okay. You see, I feel responsible."

"Why?"

"That's sort of hard to explain. Maggie, the friend Olivia shared a room with before she came here, was dead set against her performing. She tried really hard to talk Olivia out of it, really hard. I was pushing on the other side. She is an amazing talent."

"We'll talk about this Maggie a little later. So you asked Olivia to, ah, move in?"

He took a deep breath. "I have a lot of room. You see, my wife and I separated recently, and well, there are three bedrooms not being used. The trio also rehearses here, so Olivia only had to go down to the basement. It just seemed like a good idea."

Now Jackie waited a moment, but it was all for effect. "Did she sleep in her own room?"

Curran coloured deeply. "She had her own room."

His response neatly dodged the question. Jackie decided to move past and circle back later.

"Could I see her bedroom? There might be something there that would give us a clue as to why those men showed up or why she went so willingly."

"I don't believe she did go with them willingly. To me it seemed as if she had no choice."

"That's splitting hairs. What I meant was that she didn't put up a fuss. If someone came after you, would you go so docilely?"

He got up. "I'll show you the room."

Upstairs, the house was even more devoid of furniture. The absent wife had obviously taken nearly everything. The room at the top of the stairs had nothing in it but dust and empty shelves and a laptop computer on a small table. The next (obviously Curran's room) had just the bare bones: a double bed, dresser and small square of carpet.

The daughter's room at least had a couple of stuffed toys and pictures on the walls, mostly her artwork. But the bed and dresser were brand new.

Olivia's room was at the end of the hall next to the bathroom. Curran swung the door back and Jackie pushed past, but stopped, barely through the door.

What was in front of her was like nothing she'd ever seen, unless it was under the influence of drugs. Every surface but the floor and the wall to her left had been painted by a hand that was childlike but at the same time masterful. "Standing in a clearing in the forest," Jackie said out loud.

On the wall opposite the window in the unpainted wall, the forest disappeared into darkness. On the wall in front of her, a clearing extended to a spot where a waterfall gushed over a high cliff. Overhead on the ceiling, a night sky glowed with stars and a crescent moon. Stepping farther into the room, she saw on the wall behind her more forest with the shadowy bulk of mountains rising in the distance. It would take hours of study to appreciate every detail that had been painstakingly painted. The whole effect was quite charming – until you noticed what was under the bushes and behind the trees. Everywhere eyes stared out, big eyes, small ones, and all of them filled with menace. Jackie found the effect profoundly disturbing.

"Olivia did this?"

"My daughter helped a bit when she visited, but this is almost all Olivia's work."

"Did she ever sleep?"

Andrew Curran actually laughed. "Very little. She was especially prone to staying up all night after gigs when she was really wired, but unless she was singing or listening to music, she was up here working. Sometimes she'd do all three at once."

The rest of the room was spartan: a mattress on the floor and a lamp on a low table nearby. Jackie went to the closet, where she found five dresses hanging from a rod and shelving stacked with neatly folded underwear, socks, jeans and a few blouses and sweaters.

"Do you mind?" Jackie asked before starting to go through the clothing to see if anything had been hidden among it.

"There's nothing there," Curran told her as she searched. "I was the one who kept all her clothes in order, otherwise they'd just be scattered around the room."

She continued anyway, then asked, "How about under the mattress?"

"I already looked there. I've searched the entire house."

"When Olivia arrived here, what did she have with her?"

"One clean set of clothes besides what she had on, her duffel coat, a toothbrush, and that's about it."

"And all that's still here?"

"In the closet, except for the duffel coat. I threw that out because it was pretty ratty. Tuesday night she had on a dress, boots and a sheepskin coat I bought her about a month ago. The coat was thrown from the car as they drove off. I believe it might have been a signal."

"What kind of signal?"

"That she wants me to come and find her."

CHAPTER 5

The one big sticking point in my relationship with Olivia was her friend Maggie. For some reason, she seemed to hate me from the moment she walked into the Sal.

A tough woman, you knew immediately that she'd been around the block a few times and trusted nothing and no one. She had blonde hair from a bottle done in a sort of mullet cut, and though around five-five in height, she *might* have weighed a hundred and ten pounds. Life can knock people around, and she gave every impression of having been knocked around a lot. She would have been considered pretty by some, but that edge was draining away quickly as the years passed. I never saw her in anything but tight jeans, high-heeled boots and a fringed leather jacket.

Maggie tagged along to the first rehearsal, held in my basement studio. She plopped herself in a corner, sitting there with her arms folded and a scowl plastered on her face. Occasionally she let out a huge sigh and shook her head, until Ronald had enough and told her to wait upstairs. The stomping footsteps overhead as she paced proved even more annoying.

During a break, Olivia went upstairs, and we could hear raised voices – mostly Maggie's. Olivia soon came back down looking troubled, and for the rest of the afternoon her work could most kindly be described as distracted.

When we packed it in (Ronald in deep disgust), my two bandmates split pretty quickly, but I kept Olivia back. "Is everything okay?"

Her lip trembled as she shook her head. "Maggie is very, very angry with me."

"Why?"

"She just is," was the evasive answer.

"You mean she'd rather see you out panhandling for chump change?"

"I only do that because it's better than hanging around our room while she's..."

"What?"

"Never mind. I shouldn't be saying anything."

Maggie yelled from the top of the stairs, "O, are we going to get out of here sometime before midnight?"

"I'll be right along!" Olivia shouted back, then turned to me. "Look, I've gotta go."

"Will you come back tomorrow?"

"Ronald said we're not rehearsing until Sunday afternoon."

"I thought we could do some extra work. I play a bit of piano and have a huge CD collection. We can go through it and see if there are any songs that tickle your fancy. That way you'll be better prepared for our next rehearsal."

She looked troubled. "I don't know if I should. Maggie will be even more upset."

"Hell with Maggie! You need a lot more rehearsing if you're going to be ready for Tuesday night."

"I don't know..."

"Call me in the morning."

"I don't have a phone."

"Does Maggie?"

"A cell. She knows I'd have no good reason to ask for it."

"Will you come tomorrow?" I pressed.

"I'll try. I could tell Maggie I'm going down to Union Station to work."

Next morning, when I staggered downstairs around eight to brew a pot of coffee, I found Olivia shivering on my front steps. Thanking my lucky stars that I'd bothered to put on my robe, I hustled her into the kitchen, where I wrapped her in two blankets.

"How long were you out there?" I asked as I filled the coffee maker.

She stared down at the table. "I don't know. Awhile..."

I ground some beans, and when the coffee was ready, I pressed a mug into her cold hands. "Drink this."

Olivia smiled. "Could I have sugar and milk in it?"

"Right. I forgot about that."

She was one of those people who likes coffee with her sugar. I drink mine black and strong, as did Sandra, my ex.

Without asking, I started cooking breakfast, my regular morning job when I still had a family. Olivia expressed no preference, so she got eggs scrambled the way I like them. Even though she'd claimed not to be hungry, she wolfed down the eggs, four slices of bacon and several pieces of toast. I took the opportunity to shower and dress while she finished.

When I came back downstairs, I found her, *sans* blankets, in the living room looking over my shelves of CDs.

"Does Maggie know you're here?"

"She was, um, busy when I left."

"Next time you get here early, please ring the bell. I don't want to find your frozen body on my front steps."

I'd meant it jokingly, but Olivia's expression clearly showed she'd taken me at my word. I'd find later that she often did that.

We spent the morning listening to tunes I thought would be appropriate for her range and expertise. Her sponge-like memory astonished me. She had each song down note perfect after only a few listenings. The bottom of her range was a low F, and none of the songs seemed to strain her upper limits. In short, she could pretty well sing anything she wanted in almost any key.

"Have you taken lessons?" I asked as we enjoyed more coffee and some toast towards the end of the morning.

She shook her head. "I just like to sing."

We had to knock it off around noon so I could go out to Oakville to pick up Kate. We'd planned to buy some bedroom furniture for her at IKEA, a place I was beginning to know well since Sandra had torn our family to shreds.

"You can come early tomorrow before rehearsal to go over these songs again if you'd like."

Olivia shrugged noncommittally.

"It's really no trouble if you'd like to come early," I said as I helped her on with her coat, "but ring the doorbell, okay? It's supposed to be absolutely frigid, and I don't mind getting up."

Twenty-four hours later, I again found her on the steps – this time with Maggie, and it had obviously been her wearing out my doorbell, since her finger was still on it when I opened the door.

She wasted little time getting in my face. "You have no right to badger Olivia the way you do," she snarled. "You should just leave her alone!"

"Look," I said, trying to keep my own anger in check. "I'm simply offering her a way to get off the street. She likes to sing. She's good, and don't you think it's up to *her* to decide what she wants to do?"

So the argument raged back and forth, first on my porch, then in the front hall. Through the whole thing, Olivia just looked on blankly, never asking us to stop shouting, or more importantly, stop discussing her as if she wasn't even there.

Finally, I got a word in edgewise, one that Maggie didn't try to talk over. "What is the big deal about singing in public?"

The venom in Maggie's voice was nearly overpowering. "Don't play games with me! You know goddamn well what Olivia can do with her voice. You just want to use her so she can bring in plenty more customers and save your lazy-ass jobs. Her ability is not going to go unnoticed for long."

I hit her with my best shot. "And why is that so important?"

"Maggie, please," Olivia finally said.

Her friend turned with blazing eyes. "*I* have a stake in this too, you know. *I* took as big a risk as you."

Olivia blanched and looked down at her feet like a scolded child.

"What are you talking about?" I interjected.

But the angry woman had made a decision and turned, her hand on the front door knob. "Do what you want, okay? But when the shit hits the fan, just make sure none of it gets on me!"

With that, she stomped across the porch, down the steps, and hurried off towards Broadview.

I gently closed the front door and turned. Olivia was still standing there, face blank, head lowered. Tears flowed down her cheeks.

Putting my arm around her, I asked, "Hey, are you all right?"

"No, I'm not!" came the answer as she shook off my arm.

Walking into the living room, she sat on my brand new IKEA chair with her head turned away.

I left her alone while I brewed a pot of coffee, hoping that the smell might bring her around. When I brought her a mug, she'd turned the chair around to face the wall and was rocking and humming softly.

She wouldn't acknowledge my presence, and while I went around the house doing various odds and ends, I continually checked on her. The hours ticked by with no change, and I was getting concerned when she appeared in the kitchen doorway as I was reading the paper.

"Can I have some water?"

"Sure," I said springing to my feet.

Olivia took the glass without a word and went back to the living room. I waited a moment, then followed.

The sun had disappeared behind heavy clouds rolling in from the west, leaving the room in near darkness. She was back in the chair still facing the wall, but she wasn't rocking or humming. I sat on the sofa and waited.

"I guess I need a place to stay," she said softly a few minutes later.

"Why was your friend so angry?"

"Because she's right. I'm being foolish."

"What's the 'big risk' Maggie was talking about?"

Olivia turned, but I could barely see her face in the dim light. "I can't answer that, and you must never ask me again."

From her tone, I knew she meant it. So I didn't ask. I seldom asked her anything after that.

I realized now that I should have.

Word was now getting around town that Olivia wasn't singing with us any more, but even so, we had a pretty good house at the Sal that evening, enthusiastic and relatively quiet. Dom had invited a sax playing friend from Montreal to sit in, and Simon had been very impressive on tenor, soprano and flute. We all stayed a bit later than normal, listening to old war stories about the '60s jazz scene as witnessed by Harry the owner and Franco the bartender.

Ronald usually cut out as soon as the gig was over, but he stayed around, primarily to crow about his new computer – as if any of the rest of us cared.

He lived alone, and while he would shack up with the occasional woman, the two passions in his life were the piano and computers. Ronald could make both sing. The few times I'd asked him for help looking up stuff online, I was amazed at how much he knew and how his fingers flew as fast over the computer's keyboard as they did on the piano's. I believed that he could find anything that existed in cyberspace with just the stroke of a few keys.

That night he went on and on about his computer's great processing strength, its storage capacity, how he'd "ramped up his access speed" or some such garbage. Everybody else's eyes glazed over. Didn't he notice nobody cared about any of that except him?

Pain-in-the-ass Ronald was the farthest thing from my mind as I drove home along the deserted streets not much before three a.m.

I share a mutual driveway with my lawyer neighbour, and damned if there wasn't a car parked between the houses. He probably had another sweet young thing over for the night. It would have been within my rights to pound on his door and make the car's owner come down and move it, but I decided to just park behind and make her wait in the morning when she wanted to leave. That's why I entered my house via the front door rather than the back as I usually do.

There aren't any street lights directly in front of my house, so the shrubs, a group of scraggly rhododendrons and other evergreens I'd let get the better of me, blocked off almost all light on the porch.

Tired from the strain of the past three days, fuelled by two scotches I shouldn't have had, I fumbled with the lock and dropped my keys. Bending to pick them up, I noticed the outline of someone sitting on one of the rattan chairs I hadn't bothered to put away for the winter.

"Hello?" I said. "Who's there?"

When I got no answer, I walked the eight or so feet to where the chairs were. Maybe it was Olivia, and she'd fallen asleep waiting for me to return.

Why had I picked this night to come home so late?

I touched the person's shoulder gently and got no response.

"Are you all right?"

Able to see a little better because my eyes had adjusted to the darkness, I could tell the person had their head back, resting it against the house. When I shook the shoulder a little harder, the person slipped sideways and slowly toppled out of the chair.

I'm not ashamed to admit that I had to back away and bend way over to keep from passing out. I didn't have to be very smart to know that something was horribly wrong.

It would have been a simple matter to go into the house and turn on the porch light, but I didn't think of that in my distracted state. Instead I went to the car, and with shaking hands, fished a flashlight out of the glove compartment. I already had it on when I came back up my steps.

It wasn't Olivia, but her friend Maggie – and it looked like she'd been strangled.

The effect of seeing someone lying dead on my porch, her swollen throat a mass of ugly bruising and her tongue fat and purply-red in her open mouth, was made infinitely worse by the harsh, concentrated beam of the flashlight. Maggie's eyes were open, and her expression was incongruously one of surprise, as if she hadn't believed her life was about to end.

Standing up slowly, I clicked off the light and leaned back against the porch railing, telling myself to keep breathing deeply. The first thing that went through my shaky mental faculties was, *What have I gotten myself into?* as I entered the house to call the police.

The two constables who arrived took one look at the body, said something into a walkie-talkie and escorted me to their cruiser, where they sat me in the back. It was only when the door shut that I noticed there were no door handles or window cranks. I'd never before had a twinge of claustrophobia, but I sure felt it then.

I was asked some preliminary questions while we waited for reinforcements, with me leaning close to the plastic divider so I could hear them clearly. My head was still swimming, and I'd started shaking, a delayed reaction to the shock, I suppose.

Three more cars pulled up in short order. Lights bouncing off the neighbouring houses and loud voices talking soon had the first of the curious neighbours on their porches and front walks, staring at the drama taking place on my property.

Yellow crime scene tape was unrolled from the tree at the corner of my property all the way across to the driveway, where there was another big tree, then up to the corner of the house. Towards Broadview, a fourth cruiser parked across the road, sealing it off.

Left alone in my backseat prison, I could only watch helplessly.

Eventually someone in a business suit, obviously more senior, came to the window and peered in. He was a big man, but some of that had gone to fat, and he looked to be not far from retirement.

One of the original constables was with him, and I heard him say, "This is the guy who called it in. That's his house."

"I don't plan on freezing my ass out here talking to him. Take him into the house and get him something to drink. He looks like he needs it. I'll be in to speak with him in a while."

As we walked towards the house, I asked, "Could we go in by the back door? I don't...you know..."

The constable grunted. "That's what I had in mind, buddy," as we continued up the driveway.

To my embarrassment, his hand was on my upper arm when I noticed the street's nosy parker, who lived on the other side of me, step out her front door. I kept my face forward, pretending I didn't see her. The old battleaxe had made it clear long ago that she didn't think much of me or my choice of vocation. This certainly wasn't going to help matters.

Once inside the kitchen, the constable asked me if there was any booze, but I don't have any in the house any more, so he made a pot of coffee. I just sat at the kitchen table dumbly, not even bothering to remove my coat. Through the storm door, I could see people moving around on the porch and the occasional flashes of photos being taken.

We were silently sipping from our steaming mugs when the man who'd freed me from the police cruiser came in the back door.

"Constable, the media has arrived. I want you out front making sure none of them gets past our line. Got that?"

The constable took a big sip of the coffee as he rose and winced as it burned its way down. "I'll get to that right away, sir."

The big man stuck out a meaty paw. "I'm Detective Sergeant Palmer," he said as I got partway out of my seat to shake. "Mind if I join you in a mug of that coffee? It's going to be a long night." He went over to the kitchen door and looked out at the foyer, then shut the door. "You don't mind if we search your house, do you?"

That gave me a twinge, but I couldn't think of a reason to deny the request. A lawyer probably could have given me a dozen. All I wanted at that point was to appear cooperative and above suspicion. I did decide, though, that a prudent course of action would be to not offer any information not directly asked for. I still stupidly had the hope that I might keep Olivia out of this mess.

After filling a mug from the orderly row I kept on the counter, the cop sat down heavily in the seat across from me. "Bet you wish you'd never come home tonight."

I couldn't decide whether the comment was meant to be friendly.

An hour later, I knew it *had* been a mistake to come home. If I'd had even an inkling of what waited for me on the porch, I probably would have *never* come home.

Palmer's questions, while not overtly hostile, were relentless. Quite rightly, he focussed on where I'd been all day, who had seen me, what I'd been doing. I answered everything as fairly and completely as I could, even though there were things I didn't want him to know. I don't think he believed me when I told him I only knew Maggie's first name and that she lived somewhere in the west end. I didn't know where, and I didn't know what she did for a living.

"I've only met her a few times. Actually, she was a friend of the vocalist for the jazz group I play with."

Palmer looked up at that. "And where can I find the vocalist?"

I winced inwardly, realizing I'd just given something up. "I really don't know. She left in the middle of our gig two nights ago, and we haven't heard from her since."

The detective was in the middle of writing when one of the underlings came in and spoke softly into his ear. Palmer whispered something back, and the underling nodded and left.

The detective looked at me for a good twenty seconds, probably to ratchet up my anxiety. It did the trick. "You say you hardly knew the woman on the porch, that she was a friend of your group's singer."

"Yes."

"The singer who's not around."

I nodded.

"But you *are* trying to help."

I nodded again but didn't appreciate the sarcastic edge to his voice.

"Have you reported this singer as missing?"

"She's not exactly missing." I told him briefly what had happened at the club on Tuesday night. "Yesterday, I hired a private investigator to find out what the hell's going on."

Palmer barely refrained from rolling his eyes. "Who?"

"Shannon O'Brien."

His face looked more friendly. "Get her on the phone."

"Isn't it a bit early?"

"Trust me, she'll want to know."

"You know her?"

"Since she was a hotshot young constable. Her dad was head of homicide when I got promoted."

The nearest phone was in the off-limits front hall, so I used my cell. I got an answering service and explained that I really needed to speak to my investigator, no matter what the time was.

"Is this something that can wait until business hours?"

"No, it can't!" I barked. "Something really terrible has happened. I *must* speak to her right away."

The woman at the answering service calmly said she'd relay my message but didn't sound enthusiastic about it.

Two burly cops came into the room, took the last of the coffee after seeing our mugs, and went into a corner to huddle with Palmer. I could only catch words here and there as people began noisily going in and out the front door.

My cell's "Take Five" ringtone started playing, and I snatched it up.

She sounded put out. "Mr. Curran, it's Shannon O'Brien. The answering service said you needed to speak with me immediately. What's up?"

"When I got home from the club a few hours ago, I found a body on my porch." It felt very odd to speak of such violence so matter of factly.

"Whose body? Olivia's?"

"Olivia's friend, Maggie. I haven't seen her since—"

Palmer stepped over and held out his hand. "Give me that. Shannon, it's Guy Palmer... Yeah, it's good to hear your voice, too... Well, the world's a small place. Look, to cut to the chase, your boy came home tonight and found a stiff on his front porch. Strangled... Well, you and I both know these things can get out of hand pretty quickly. What can you tell me?... You will?... Okay, I'll be here waiting. I don't have to tell you the drill... Yes, I'll let them know."

He handed back the phone, and she sounded more friendly. "Mr. Curran —"

"Look, call me Andrew, or Andy."

"Andy – and you call me Shannon, okay? I will get there as soon as I can, less than an hour if the traffic gods are kind. Just sit tight. Everything is going to be all right."

I was beginning to feel a little rough around the edges. "That's easy for you to say. You didn't find someone murdered on your front porch."

"You're right. But I will be there to help. Get some food in your stomach. You'll feel better."

"I don't feel like eating."

"Do it anyway."

I hung up as another plainclothes cop knocked on the back door. "Got a minute, Guy?"

Palmer and one of the cops went out the back door. The third stayed behind to keep an eye on me. Palmer came back in after a brief discussion. It was easy to see from his red face that he was furious.

"Still want to stick to your story about the dead woman?" he asked.

"I've told you what I know."

"Have you?"

"To the best of my ability, yes."

"Then how come the old lady next door told us she's seen her here several times, and on one occasion you had a very loud argument, right out on that porch where she's lying now?"

Looked as if my private investigator was mistaken about everything being all right.

CHAPTER 6

Hell and damn! Shannon thought as she sped through the light traffic of the early morning at a rate considerably over the legal limit.

This job had certainly gone south in a hurry. When she'd gone to bed the previous evening, she'd told her musician boyfriend, Michael, that the case would no doubt turn out to be a simple one of a woman on the lam from some charge in the States who had stupidly stuck her head up into the public light and consequently got hauled back to face the music.

"I'll have this whole thing cleared up within a week," she'd told him confidently.

Why couldn't life ever be easy?

She wished she'd taken Michael up on his offer to spend the night at his downtown loft instead of being the good mom and staying home with her two teenage kids. She'd have had a far shorter drive to get to Curran's house. Of course, Michael had also offered to come out to her place in Caledon. Problem was, she still felt uncomfortable sleeping with Michael in her own house, even if they were doing just that: sleeping. She had to set some kind of example for her seventeen-year-old daughter especially, even though the whole thing was a complete sham. Rachel certainly knew what her mom was doing when she spent the night with her boyfriend.

As she drove, Shannon wondered if something she or her latest recruit had done could have caused the death of this woman. She felt confident that talking to some people at the airport wouldn't have caused any alarm bells to be sounded, but there was no telling what Jackie Goode might have stirred up the previous day.

Swinging south onto the Don Valley Parkway, she had to remind herself not to formulate conclusions without sufficient information. Her experience with the Toronto Police and in her own business had certainly drilled that into her head: get the facts and be thorough. Sloppiness could get you killed.

Now someone *was* dead.

The constable on duty at the end of Curran's street hadn't been informed of her arrival, typical of Guy Palmer. Her dad had said in an unguarded moment years ago that Palmer was a competent enough detective, but he had a "terminal case of the sloppies". He worried about the time he wouldn't be around to pick up his underling's shortcomings. When police detectives made mistakes, innocent people could go to prison – or worse.

By the time Shannon was escorted up the driveway and around to Curran's back door, her mood had blackened considerably.

She found her client sitting at his kitchen table, head down. He looked awful, but she hadn't expected anything else. From all accounts he was a good guy, well thought of by his peers. Murder has a way of hitting people between the eyes with a force they cannot imagine. The better the person, the worse the shock. What she now needed most were some private words with him, but she couldn't think of how she might swing that.

Palmer was on top of her before she was barely in the door, all "hail fellow, well met" as he pulled her into a bear hug against his foul-smelling overcoat.

"Shannon, you look fantastic. How you doing?"

She slid out of his grip and stepped back almost to the door, fighting to keep her expression blank. Palmer stank of cigarettes, coffee and garlic, a lethal combination.

Regardless of the fact that her dad had been a storied homicide detective, Shannon knew most cops distrusted private investigators. Having Palmer on her side could prove invaluable, so she needed to keep everything nice and friendly.

The police detective would be hoping his old boss's daughter might already have information that he could utilize to make his investigation easier. Any time Palmer could find something to save him effort was a valuable thing in his eyes. If she managed things right, she might very well manipulate this situation to her advantage.

Patting Andy on the shoulder, she said, "Sit tight. I'm going to talk with Detective Palmer out on the back deck. I want to get up to speed on where we stand. Is that okay?"

The drummer didn't even look up. "Sure. Fine with me."

"What you got?" Palmer asked as soon as the door shut behind them.

"Curran showed up in my office two days ago, said he wanted to find his band's vocalist, that she'd been escorted out of the club where they play by two heavies. She went without any fuss."

"And you checked up on his story?"

Shannon nodded, fighting the urge to silence Palmer with a loud, "Well, duh."

"Let me show you what *I* got to deal with."

He led Shannon down the driveway and onto the porch. Two techs were hard at work around the body, but Palmer asked them to step back.

She'd been on site after a few murders in her time, but never a manual strangulation. Though she knew from books what it was all about, seeing one up close and personal was pretty intense. There had been enough time for the victim to realize she was going to die.

Shannon turned away, walked down the steps and surveyed the growing crowd at the crime scene tape, all of them eager to know what was going on. They might not be so eager if they knew what the reality actually looked like.

Palmer was next to her. "I know you don't let the dust settle on you. Tell me everything you've found out."

She gave him a concise rundown of what she and her new recruit had found out, which didn't amount to all that much, except that Curran's version of what had happened at the club seemed to be accurate. For the moment, she held back what she'd found out at the airport the previous day.

"Know anything about the stiff on his front porch?" Palmer asked.

"If it's not this missing singer, then no. What did Curran tell you?"

"Well, he made out at first as if he didn't really know the woman. Then we find out from a neighbour that the victim had been over here a number of times, and on one occasion, the two of them had a verbal donnybrook right on the selfsame porch.

"According to him, he left for work at his normal time, about eight. When he came home, shortly before three a.m., he found the body on the porch and calls it in. We've listened to his voice mail to see if she'd called or something before she came here, but other than two hang ups after he left for work, there's nothing. Could have been her, I suppose."

"What does the ME say about time of death?"

"Best first guess is sometime after eight. Your boy's not in the clear." Palmer lit a cigarette and looked into the brightening eastern sky for several moments. "Tell me, do you think Curran's clever enough to have bumped someone off then faked the whole discovery thing? 'Cause that's the way I'm leaning at this point."

This quick decision was part and parcel of the way Palmer worked. He could, of course, be correct, but Shannon's gut told her no, although she'd also gotten a phone report from Goode about her visit the previous afternoon. Jackie'd felt Curran had been on edge. Perhaps it had been the fact that Goode was poking around, perhaps something more sinister.

"What's the dead woman's name?"

"No ID on her. Curran told us it was Maggie. He says he doesn't know any more than that. Of course we're checking it out, but that could take awhile."

Shannon thought for a moment longer. "Think I could have a talk with him – alone?"

"I don't know if I can oblige, Shannon, department protocol and all that. You know how they are downtown these days."

She winked conspiratorially at him. "Since when has that ever stopped people like us? I promise to share anything I get. He might be willing to talk more openly with me. Could be a good shortcut."

"Well, I got stuff around front that needs doing. I suppose I could work it where you'll stand in for one of my boys, short of manpower and all that, you know? It is about time I sent them out to canvass the neighbourhood. But you got to share anything you get. Don't jerk me around on this, Shannon."

They returned to the kitchen, where Palmer gave his men jobs to carry out in order to clear the room. In a matter of moments, Shannon was alone at the kitchen table with her client, a fresh pot of coffee and, comically, a box of fresh doughnuts she'd taken the time to pick up. The friendly dig hadn't been lost on Palmer – but he'd also helped himself to a glazed one.

"Did you eat anything?" she asked.

"I'm not hungry."

"You are, whether you realize it or not." She pushed the doughnuts across the table. "Eat a couple of these; you'll feel better." He didn't move. "Trust me, Andy."

He reached out for the box while Shannon poured two mugs of coffee, and they sat drinking and munching silently for a few minutes.

"I'm in a lot of trouble, aren't I?"

She looked across at him. "Only if you haven't been telling the truth."

"Do you think that?"

"No." She let that sit for a moment before adding, "But I think you've held back information from me."

Curran looked down into his coffee cup as if he thought an answer would magically float to the surface.

"I just wanted to find out if Olivia was okay, find out why she left with those guys." He shook his head slowly and finished in a weary voice, "I didn't think anything like this would happen."

"So you're convinced the death of this Maggie person has a connection with Olivia."

It could have been a question, but it was said as a statement.

"Maggie was her friend. Olivia gets carted off, then her friend turns up dead on my porch. What else could it be?"

"Andy, I could easily come up with several different scenarios. The one thing we need now is all the information we can get. I need you to tell me everything you know about the dead woman." She fished her notebook out of a coat pocket. "And we don't have much time."

♪♯♭·♪♭♭·

The insistent beat of her cell phone's funky ringtone roused Jackie Goode from the depths of a very deep sleep.

Not immediately remembering where she was, she groped around for a nonexistent bedside table before realizing she was sleeping on a friend's sofa. Her cell was on the end table behind her head.

Reaching out and managing to get it open before it switched to voice mail, she croaked, "Yeah, what do you want?"

"It's Shannon O'Brien."

She forced herself to a sitting position. "What time is it?"

"Nearly seven o'clock."

Jackie had finally shut down her friend Carolina's computer when night was just beginning to drain from the eastern sky, sometime after five thirty. Yesterday had been very long.

"You still there?" her boss asked.

Cold, she pulled the blanket up around her. Why did Carolina keep her heat so low?

"I'm still here. Sorry. Just had a late night."

"Well, I've had an early morning. I'm over at Curran's place. Something has come up, and I need you over here."

"How soon?"

"Right away. Where are you?"

"Quite close. I'm at a friend's place up on Cambridge. That's near—"

"I know where Cambridge is," O'Brien snapped. "How soon can you get here?" she repeated.

"If I run all the way, maybe ten minutes."

"Look, you don't need to run."

"I'm just saying I can if you want."

"Just hurry. Bring everything you've got on Curran. The cop at the end of the street will pass you through. Tell him to speak to Detective Palmer if you get any grief."

Jackie was groping for her jeans under the coffee table with her free hand as she asked, "Care to tell me what this is about?"

"Curran found the singer's friend dead on his porch when he got home from his gig a few hours ago."

"Shit. Murder?"

"Yes. And don't talk to anyone about this between where you are now and Curran's house. Got that? No one. Not even Palmer."

"You got it, boss."

Shannon sighed. "Don't call me boss."

Jackie washed up and threw her clothes on in record time, slipping into her runners as she shuffled down the hall to the small home office. Her friend, nearly six feet in height with the slender body of a jogger, was sitting at her desk, dressed in only a short satin robe, no slippers, coffee cup in her right hand and computer glasses poised on the end of her nose as she read through the morning email. How could she not be freezing to death?

"I didn't expect you up this early," Carolina said without looking up.

"Got a phone call. Something's happened."

At Jackie's tone, the tall woman looked up. "Does it have anything to do with what you were using my computer for until all hours?"

"Yes, but I'm sworn to secrecy at the moment." Jackie grinned as she scooped up her notebook from the desk and a sheaf of downloaded documents from the printer. After stuffing everything into her backpack, she started down the hallway for the front door. "Although, if you don't want to wait for me to be able to tell you, I'd suggest turning on the TV. There's probably something there."

Jackie actually *did* run down to Curran's house on Bain Avenue, since she needed to get her blood and brain moving and was also pretty eager to see what was shaking.

Of course, the constable on duty at the end of the street stopped her and an argument ensued, since she didn't look like anyone who would be summoned to a crime scene, unless it was to provide a confession. Unfortunately, he actually said that to her. By the time another constable had trotted down the street to get between them, the media had also closed in, with the result that the argument wound up on the morning news, hard facts about the case being pretty sketchy at that point.

Jackie was close to being arrested when she remembered that Shannon had told her to mention a Detective Palmer if she got hassled. That name eventually opened doors, but not before the two cops had searched her backpack thoroughly and a female constable had patted her down, all of which the TV cameras recorded.

As two constables escorted Jackie along the street, she reflected on the fact that she'd have to do better at keeping her temper and tongue under control.

Once in Curran's kitchen, she found the master of the house, her employer, the fabled Palmer and a junior detective who'd been elected to take notes. As she joined everyone around the table, Shannon flashed her an expression that clearly said, *Keep your mouth shut unless you're asked something specific.*

♪♯♩·♪♭♩·

Shannon's brain felt as if it were made out of cardboard, not a good thing when she needed all her faculties. The situation was far too tricky for an error in judgement.

Curran had passed on everything he knew about Olivia's deceased friend. That wasn't a lot, but it was more than he'd told Palmer originally. It wasn't that Curran had purposefully held anything back, she just had better interrogation chops and possessed an uncanny knack for coaxing memories to the surface. To toss the homicide detective another bone, Shannon had also summoned her new operative to throw in whatever she could about the dead woman – but no more. The PI couldn't see where this was going yet, and she didn't want to give anything away unnecessarily.

While he'd been out of the room, Palmer had shown a bit of initiative and spoken personally to the old lady next door. She'd provided him with the heretofore unknown tidbit that Curran's wife had walked out on him several months earlier. That got Palmer excited all over again.

"And the old lady says you had another woman living here with you," Palmer was just saying when Shannon zoned in on the conversation again. "What do you have to say about that?"

"I didn't tell you because I didn't think it had any bearing on things," Curran shot back. "I told this woman all about it yesterday afternoon when she was here. I'm *not* trying to hide anything!"

He'd indicated Goode, who hadn't spoken up to this point, except for a "What's happening?" when she'd entered.

Palmer swivelled to her. "Is this true?"

Goode had her notebook on the table and read from it. "Yessir. He told me about his wife leaving and indicated that he'd invited the singer to move in. That was shortly after two thirty yesterday, sir."

Shannon couldn't believe Goode was making fun of the homicide detective. She'd have to put a stop to that as soon as she got her alone, or immediately if it got out of hand. No matter that Palmer deserved it. Fortunately, the crack seemed to go right over his head.

"Did he mention anything to you about this Maggie coming over to see him?"

Goode didn't even blink as she said, "No, he didn't."

"And why didn't you ask him why he hadn't bothered to contact the missing girl's friend to find out if she knew where the girl might be?"

Goode feigned embarrassment (and she did it well). "I guess I dropped the ball on that one, didn't I, sir?"

Palmer slapped the table with his hand. "Yes, you did. Now tell me everything you got, and you better not hold back anything!" He turned to Shannon. "That right?"

She had to restrain herself from saying, "Yessir! That's right, sir!"
Palmer could be such an ass.

Eventually, the cops were convinced – at least for the moment – that
Shannon's client was just a victim of circumstances.

They certainly had no grounds to hold him, but Palmer made it clear
that Curran wasn't to go anywhere.

"You mean I have to stay in this house?"

Palmer got up from the table. "No. But I don't want you leaving town
unless I say it's okay."

"I think he means that you're a 'person of interest'," Goode added.

"After all I've told you, you still think *I* might be responsible for what
happened on my porch?" Curran demanded somewhat hysterically.

"Yes."

Shannon shut her notebook and also got up. "Can he at least go to a
hotel or something while your crew finishes their work and the media
loses interest and goes off to the next disaster?"

"I don't see why not – just as long as I know where your boy is at all
times." Palmer looked Curran up and down. "Don't you dare leave town
without clearing it with me."

As Palmer walked towards the front door, Goode pulled her boss's
head down and whispered into her ear, "Tell Palmer you have to use the
washroom. When you're up there, check out the bedroom at the end of
the hall. That's the one I told you about on the phone yesterday."

Shannon came downstairs five minutes later in a mild state of shock.
No, she told herself, *make that amazement.* Having taken psychology in
college, she knew that this Olivia person, while incredibly talented, was
also incredibly screwed up. Did Curran understand just how much?

"Can we take our client and go now?" she asked Palmer at the bottom
of the stairs.

Curran was standing in the doorway to the kitchen. "I'd really rather
not be here right now," he said.

The homicide detective looked at everyone in turn. "Just make sure
that I know where you are," he repeated.

"Can I take my car?"

"No, that's going downtown for examination."

"But it has my drums in it. I need them to work!"

Palmer sighed heavily. "I'll make sure they check those first and let you know when you can pick them up, but it isn't going to be today and probably not tomorrow, either."

"Let's get out of here," Shannon said to her client. "I'll drive you wherever you want to go."

Curran looked pretty despondent. "That's the trouble. I don't know where I should go."

"A hotel is best – unless you have a friend you can crash with."

"I wouldn't wish that on my worst enemy!" he shot back, but with a hint of a smile.

It took about fifteen minutes for Shannon to get her SUV free from the traffic jam of official cars. Curran was allowed to leave with only the clothes on his back, a toothbrush and a few toiletries.

The porch was still draped with crime scene curtains so the forensics specialists could work out of the public eye, but the body had been removed to the morgue. Palmer was pushing for an early autopsy.

Standing around in the front yard was difficult for Curran to bear, since a large group of media and onlookers had gathered outside the police's yellow tape, and several people were pointing at him.

His lawyer neighbour, with his date's car still blocked by Curran's, stuck his head out the door and called. Shannon went with Curran as he walked over.

Pulling them just inside, the lawyer introduced himself. "Robert Bennett. I've heard what happened, Andy. You have my condolences. What a mess." Then he grinned. "Looks like I picked the worst night ever to let someone block your driveway! Any chance you can move?"

Curran managed a weak smile. "You'll have to ask the cops."

"If there's anything I can do to help, just let me know, okay?" He turned to Shannon. "And you are?"

"A private investigator Andrew was consulting on another matter."

"Interesting. Say, Andy, I haven't seen Olivia for a couple of days. Is she out of town?"

"Something like that," he mumbled.

"She doesn't have anything to do with what happened, does she?"

Shannon spoke. "We don't know at this point. Look, I'd rather we didn't say any more."

Bennett nodded. "I understand, but I'm also serious about my offer of help. Here, take my card and call if you need to."

"I know who you are, Mr. Bennett, and we appreciate the offer of help. We'll let you know, okay?"

Shannon's vehicle was now free to leave, so they headed for it, with media people following and shouting questions as they walked. She told her companions not to turn around and definitely not to say anything. Her eyes were on Goode like laser beams as she said the last bit.

Once they were in the car and underway, having decided to go to Shannon's office next, Goode, in the back seat, tapped her boss on the shoulder.

"With all the cops around, I couldn't tell you what I came up with last night."

Shannon looked through the rearview mirror at her employee, who flopped back against the seat and grinned at her. "What?"

"I spent the night surfing the Internet. I thought it might be worth seeing if I could come up with anything on Olivia's past. Seemed to me if bounty hunters were interested in her, there would more than likely be something online. Right?"

"Go on."

"Well, I must have looked at a hundred newspaper, television and radio station websites, but I eventually came up with a fair amount of information."

Curran had turned and was now staring into the back seat. "What did you find?"

"She's from New York, or at least that's where her family's main home is. And her name actually *is* Olivia."

"She's not from California?" Shannon asked.

"Nope, although that's where I think those two guys might have taken her."

"Explain." Shannon caught Jackie's eye in the mirror. "And please don't drag it out."

"All right, boss," she grinned. "We're looking for Olivia St. *James* of the New York St. Jameses. So the name she gave you guys in the band wasn't that far off from her real one, and that made it much easier to find her on the Internet.

"Anyway, the family once owned a large chain of newspapers in the

States. They're now heavily into newsprint and specialty paper. Over the past few years they've diversified into other commodities and have been immensely successful. It's a privately-owned company. They've always kept a low public profile – that goes back to the newspaper baron great grandfather – and they've been even more reclusive of late."

"Why do you say 'of late'?"

"Because six years ago, there was a murder in the family, Olivia's brother, to be exact," Goode said matter-of-factly, but she put her hand on Curran's arm. "I'm sorry to have to tell you this, but there was a lot of speculation in the press at the time that she might be the murderer."

Andy Curran ran both hands through his hair. "Oh my God."

"It gets worse," she added. "The family had her institutionalized because the court found her mentally unsound."

CHAPTER 7

It was lucky I wasn't the one driving when Shannon O'Brien's operative dropped her little bombshell, or we might have been splattered all over the road. The Don Valley Parkway is *not* the place to lose one's concentration, even for a second.

I stared out the window for several minutes, seeing nothing. The two detectives gave me the mental space I needed to begin processing the information I'd just been given. No one spoke until we were passing the York Mills exit.

Shannon broke the silence. "Would it bother you if Ms Goode gave me a rundown on what she found while we drive? We might as well make use of the time, and I have an idea this is going to be a long trip."

"Why?" I asked.

"We have four cars following us. Media types, I imagine, but it wouldn't surprise me if Palmer has given us a tail, too." She grinned. "I don't think he completely trusts me. Don't worry, I can lose them, but it will take an extra bit of time."

Turning again to look at Goode in the back seat, I asked, "Do you have any printouts of what you found?"

Reaching into her backpack, she pulled out a sheaf of papers about a quarter inch thick and handed it to me. "There's more, but this is the best stuff."

The top two sheets had photos of Olivia, one from some sort of family outing. She was dressed in jeans and a T-shirt with a rather rude slogan on it. She looked like any normal teenager, happy and smiling, with her arm around her older brother. The second was of Olivia, a few years older, being hustled into the back of a limo by two large men wearing black overcoats. They looked suspiciously like bodyguards. This time her tear-stained face was a picture of pain and bewilderment. I didn't have to read the caption to know what it was talking about.

I spent the rest of the trip staring at the photos while Goode read from her notes. It all painted a depressing picture of a deeply troubled woman whom I now realized I'd hadn't really known at all.

The St. James family had never spoken to the press about what had happened before or after the murder, so what Goode related came from reporters' interviews with people close to the family, as well as the cops.

Olivia's father, Bernard St. James II, had married late in life, although he had never lacked for female company. It was felt at the time that he had married only to assure the continuation of the family name. The bride had been all of thirty, twenty years her husband's junior. She came from one of Boston's upper crust families.

His wife Lydia had first borne him a son, Bernard St. James III, when he was fifty-two, and Olivia had arrived three years later.

Early childhood for both had been normal enough when you took into account that the family had a palatial home in Manhattan, an estate up the Hudson River in Putnam County, as well as a winter home in Florida near Sarasota – and all the servants to go with them. Their father preferred his children be taught by a succession of tutors or in private schools, since they were children of wealth and privilege.

Young Bernard was tapped from the beginning to take over operation of the family business when the time came, and Olivia was left to develop in whatever way she would. From an early age, she was found to be very artistic.

On the surface, the whole thing sounded dreadfully Edwardian to me: the son counted for everything; the daughter didn't really matter.

In a later interview, though, Olivia's former nanny painted a different picture. "Young Master St. James was a nice enough child, studious, bright, a capable sort, I suppose. But my little Olivia was like a ray of sunshine. Her parents both doted on her, especially her father. She could do nothing wrong and brought joy and light into their lives."

Then, when Olivia was fourteen, her mother had been struck by a car and killed in front of the St. James' mansion. Waiting on the front steps for her mother to cross the street, Olivia had unfortunately witnessed the whole thing. Always a sensitive child, the hit-and-run tragedy had a profound effect on her. As a result, she was reported to have become moody, furtive, and as one unnamed source put it, "distinctly odd".

By the time Goode had gotten that far with the story, we were someplace in Markham, and Shannon's driving skill had lost all pursuers but one. "Probably the cops," she sighed, "but I can beat them, too. The whole thing's stupid, since Palmer's going to guess where I'm taking you, but I *hate* being played like some rank amateur. He should know better. Continue, Jackie."

Goode flipped a page in her notebook. "Let's see...I think we can skip most of the intervening years for the moment, except to say that to everyone's shock, the elder St. James remarried soon after his wife's death. The second wife, a junior lawyer who did a lot of work for the St. James company, was even younger than the first wife had been. The tabloids had a field day with that, spreading the rumour that St.James had been having an affair with her before his wife Lydia's death. Bernard St. James II and his new wife were *not* amused and sued the tabloids, successfully, I guess, because the stories stopped abruptly."

"They also could have been paid off," Shannon observed.

"What happened to Olivia?" I asked Goode.

"That's something I can't answer at this point. I've only been able to find hints and gossip."

"What kind of gossip?"

"A reporter at the time of her brother's murder got some of her acquaintances to blab. I don't know if what they said was true. The family only commented once to deny the story."

I got the feeling that Goode was holding back. "You just better come out and say it."

"After her mother's death, Olivia began running with a fast crowd. Originally it was other students from the girls' school she was attending. Anyway, she got into drugs, bad drugs."

"Like what?"

"The quotes that I saw were along the lines of 'We all smoked a little weed and popped some ecstasy, but when Olivia got mixed up with cocaine and heroin, we drew the line.' The family's denial was along the lines of 'We know nothing of any drug use by our child.' My guess is that they had to know."

I felt pretty certain that Olivia had not been taking drugs when she was with me, but there was something in that dreamy, almost disassociated way she had of speaking, as if she were partially smashed, that reminded me of other former heroin users I'd run into. Heroin? Christ! That was a bad place to be. My past problems with booze paled in comparison.

"Did she get along with the stepmother?" Shannon asked.

"Same answer. We're going to have to dig if we want to find that out."

"Fast forward to the murder, then."

Another few page flips from the back seat. "Okay, so Bernard St. James III has been groomed to take over the family fortune. He's about to turn twenty-four, and Olivia is twenty-one. This is six years ago. The family is at the Florida home for the Christmas holidays.

"By this time, Olivia is behaving very erratically, sometimes inappropriately childlike, withdrawn, moody, by all accounts. It could all be drug-related, but the family denied it. Her mother was snuffed right in front of her, and that had to have left pretty deep scars. Her father is also very ill. Cancer. He was a heavy smoker. She adores her father and brother, has no friends at that point, keeps to herself.

"Christmas Eve. Bernard III announces to the family gathering – including a few aunts and uncles, etc. – that he's going to marry a girl he's been secretly dating in New York. Olivia, highly distraught, causes a major scene. From what I've been able to gather, she felt that he, too, was leaving her. She runs out of the house. Brother follows, saying he wants to talk to her alone, make her understand.

"Neither comes back. After several hours, a search is mounted. Brother Bernard is discovered in a grove of trees down near the river abutting the property, his head bashed in. Olivia is eventually found back in her room in some sort of stupor. The murder weapon, a large blood-stained rock, is found near the body, but there are no identifiable fingerprints or DNA.

"The only thing Olivia can say is that she remembers being with her brother, and they were arguing. Next thing she knows, she's in the hospital. She doesn't even remember going back to her room.

"The cops work on the case for weeks. The only thing they come up with is that a group of kids had been seen partying several times on the property in the vicinity where the body was found. They couldn't be found and didn't come forward, so that was a dead end. No one was ever charged.

"Now here's the kicker: several of the cops believe Olivia did the deed, but fairly quickly, the family has her declared mentally incompetent and institutionalized so the cops can't get at her. Even if they did, would any sort of charge stand up in court when she's already been declared *non compos mentis*? All of this is done out of the media's eye."

"And the father?" Shannon asked.

"Packed it in less than six months after the tragedy. Olivia never saw him again."

"Anything else?"

"In one Bernard II obit, the grieving stepmother vows to manage the family fortune until Olivia is 'once again well and whole'. Professional opinion is that this will never happen." Goode closed her notebook. "Then one night she walks into the Green Salamander in downtown Toronto. I wonder what the hell happened in between."

"You've done some great work, Jackie," Shannon said.

The last tail was long gone when we pulled into the industrial mall where Shannon had her office, but she drove around to the back side of the long building.

"No sense advertising we're here. We'll park at the far end then enter the building through one of the offices. There's a corridor down the middle. We can get into my office without being seen."

"What then?" I asked.

Shannon looked grim as she got out of the car. "We talk. Oh boy, do we talk!"

I saw from the clock that it was nearly noon when I finally sat down at her desk.

The boss handed Goode her laptop and marching orders. "Dig up anything else there is on the murder of Olivia's brother, what institution she was sent to, I want everything you can find on the mother, father, stepmother, any people who were on the scene when the murder happened. Get me names, dates, times, places. Anything you think might be pertinent, I want it. I especially want names of people we can actually talk to. After that, we'll hit the phones and see what they can tell us."

Goode saluted. "Yes, boss!"

Shannon stopped in the doorway of her office. "And I told you not to call me boss!" she said with a sigh, shutting the door. "What are you thinking, Andy?"

I sighed. "A whole lot of things, but mostly that I'm not as surprised by this new information as I should be."

"How so?"

"Olivia's bedroom. I assume you looked at it when you used the facilities this morning."

Shannon nodded. "Those staring eyes. She's a troubled young lady."

"Not as much as you'd think from what she painted," I said stoutly – and perhaps too quickly.

"This case is not going to move any further unless you're willing to lay all your cards on the table. We're in deep water here."

"What do you mean?"

"I need to know everything that passed between you and Olivia, *especially* any mention of Maggie." She stared hard at me. "And I don't think I've gotten that yet."

I nodded slowly. "Where do you want me to start?"

Shannon pulled a yellow legal pad from her desk. "Let's start with this – and please excuse my bluntness – did you sleep with Olivia?"

♪♯ρ·♪♭ρ·

I sat in the living room listening to Olivia and my daughter Kate upstairs in her room, loudly becoming fast friends.

Kate had been begging to come back to stay overnight, since she missed her old bedroom and friends. Sandra had brought her in a few times for a visit, and I tried my best when I wasn't out of town gigging, but I knew the change had been hard on her. I bought a new bed, a dresser and some other things so she could stay with me sometimes for a few days.

Olivia had been living in my house for a week by then, and I had to admit it was nice to have someone around to talk to. I hadn't realized how lonely I'd been. Reading books only adds to solitude, and bars aren't the best place for me to hang out for companionship.

On the other hand, Olivia was a bit of a problem to have around. First off, she really couldn't manage many of the day-to-day things normal people handle with no trouble. She couldn't cook past making toast or brewing coffee or tea. She left her dishes and belongings (what few she had) dropped anywhere in the house. The fridge door would be left open. We won't even talk about the condition of the bathroom after she showered. Basically, I was living with a poorly housebroken fourteen-year-old. Only thing different from an actual teenager was that Olivia hardly slept.

So why didn't I show her the door? She was making enough money now to get her own place, right?

First, she obviously couldn't take care of herself. It was as if Olivia's emotional development had stopped somewhere in her mid-teens, maybe earlier. How had she survived all this time? I couldn't see Maggie playing nursemaid for her.

So I'd taken Olivia on and felt I was stuck with her, for good or ill.

Second reason for her staying was that she just flat-out fascinated me. Okay, maybe it went deeper, but I didn't know that until later.

I delighted Olivia when I dubbed her The Song Sponge. She could hear something maybe twice and have it down, lyrics, melody and style. She also had perfect pitch. Once learned, a song was in the original key, no matter what Ronald would choose. On a few occasions, this led to some rather disastrous (and comical) collisions between vocalist and band. She could read music only rudimentarily and knew nothing about jazz history. Her knowledge started and stopped with the songs she'd learned.

Her phenomenal ear and memory also extended to our parts. It was as if Olivia had a tape recorder in her head. One time early on, she'd floored Ronald by singing note-for-note the beginning of a solo he'd played over a week earlier. It had been by way of a compliment to show how much she'd preferred it to to the one he'd taken that evening, but it was obvious he didn't like what he considered her one-upmanship.

Dom had wryly observed, "You just ought to be glad she doesn't want to play piano!" which caused an even bigger scowl on the pianist's face. Ronald wouldn't talk to any of us for the rest of the evening.

Funny thing was, Olivia couldn't see that what she was capable of doing was freakish in the extreme. She just *did it* and never thought about it.

At an early rehearsal, Dom asked her where she'd learned how to sing.

"By singing for my daddy."

"No, but I mean where? Who taught you?"

"I don't know what you mean."

Ronald glared from the piano. "He means, where are you from?"

Olivia just looked at him blankly, then got up and left the room.

"She's a first class nutcase," Ronald grumbled.

"When someone sings the way she can," Dom shot back, "our girlie can be from Mars for all I care."

That got me thinking, though, so next evening after dinner, as we sat listening to some early recordings of Ella Fitzgerald and Sarah Vaughan, I asked Olivia again to tell me a little about herself. It was all low key, all very friendly.

She looked at me blankly. "I'm a singer. I sing with your band."

"I know, but what did you do before that?"

"I begged for money on the street. You know that."

"You've always done nothing but beg?"

Blank expression.

"You say you learned to sing for your daddy. Where does he live?"

A tear coursed its way down one cheek, followed by several more.

"My daddy isn't alive any more."

"And your mother?"

Olivia sadly shook her head and wouldn't look at me. That's about as far as I ever got with her.

Clearly, she'd suffered some kind of trauma, and I began hoping that if I could give her some normality in her life, it might help.

Another piece of the puzzle had fallen into place recently, at the end of a long rehearsal for a corporate gig. They'd requested a whole bunch of songs Olivia didn't know, and we only had the one rehearsal for her to get them all down.

Ronald had been in a foul mood because he'd felt put upon. He grumbled that there were any number of vocalists around town who could do the gig, and they'd certainly know all the songs.

Dom, ever patient, snorted. "But they couldn't sing them like our girlie here."

She flashed the bassist a huge smile at that.

Ronald made a disgusted face. "Yeah, but she's a total flake! Maybe we should all chip in and get her a good shrink."

He always spoke as if she weren't in the room or couldn't understand what he said.

I was about to light into him when Olivia stuck her face in front of his and snarled, "You're just jealous because I do things you can't. That's what they say down at the club! If anyone needs a shrink here, it's you!"

She stomped out of the room, and from her pounding feet, I could tell she'd gone straight up to her room and slammed the door.

"Out of the mouths of babes," Dom said quietly.

That was the only time I ever heard Olivia really speak like an adult.

"You're ignoring my original question, Mr. Curran," Shannon said, her chair back and the pad on her lap. She was looking at me pointedly. "I can't help you effectively if I don't have the full picture."

She was getting pissed with my stalling, and really, there was no reason *not* to give her an answer. After all, legally, Olivia was far past the age of consent. It was just that I felt guilty about what had happened.

"Okay. Yes, I did sleep with her, but not until right before those guys took her away. It wasn't something she or I planned. It just happened."

"And are you in love with her?" When I didn't answer, she added, "It's really important that I know these things. I'm not prying just to get my jollies or anything. And remember this: Palmer might well be asking you the same questions next."

Looking down at my hands, I said, "It's not easy to talk about. A lot of it is mixed up with the end of my marriage."

Shannon's voice sounded kinder when she answered, "I *do* know what you're going through, Andy. My own marriage fell apart not that long ago. There are still wounds from it, and I'd be a liar to tell you they've completely healed. When my... When my boyfriend Michael and I got together, I was a whole jumble of mixed emotions. It's normal, I guess."

"You're probably right."

"How did your wife take it?"

"What?"

"You and Olivia."

"Oddly, not too well, considering that she's the one who cheated on me then moved out without telling me in advance."

"Your daughter tells me you have a female friend," Sandra said when I rang the bell at Jeremy's house in Oakville one Saturday.

"Is Kate ready to go? I'm sort of pressed for time."

"As always, you won't answer a direct question," my former wife shot back scornfully. "What's wrong with you?"

"Look, Sandra, why are you ragging on me? You're the one who kept the big secrets."

"Well, despite what you said when I moved out, it didn't take you long to find someone. Kate tells me she's pretty and rather young."

"Okay, if it will make you happy, Olivia's just a singer the trio has started working with, and she didn't have a place to live, so I told her she could crash at the house while she gets things together. She has her own room, and we're not involved."

Sandra's expression clearly said she didn't believe me. "Well, at least Kate likes her."

"Yes, Kate does, and I enjoy having someone around to talk to."

Fortunately, our daughter bounced down the stairs with her pink overnight bag and a bulging knapsack, out of which peeked two of her stuffed animals.

"Be good, my little pumpkin," Sandra said as she bent over to dole out a forehead kiss and a hug. "I'll see you Monday evening – at eight," she added pointedly, looking at me. "You have an extra day off, but there's still school on Tuesday."

Kate took my hand as we walked to the car. "I'm bringing Martin the Mouse and Lainey the Lamb to show Olivia. She said she wanted to meet them really badly."

I dragged my mind out of whatever sewer it was scurrying down. "Huh?"

"My stuffed toys, Daddy! Really, you have to pay more attention when I'm talking to you!"

She sounded just like her mother, but when I looked down, the little minx was smiling up at me broadly. Kate certainly knew the right buttons to push on her dear old dad.

Olivia was down in the basement studio when we got home, plunking away on the piano. *Ronald should heed what Dom said*, I chuckled to myself.

Kate disappeared down the stairs, coat, knapsack and all, to show Olivia her fuzzy friends, and in short order I could hear the two of them talking and giggling.

As I got busy with lunch (dialing Kate's favourite pizzeria), the girls passed through the kitchen on their way to Olivia's room. After calling them when lunch was on the table, I could hear them racing down the hall, then the stairs and finally to the kitchen door.

"I win!" Kate screamed.

"So what were you two doing upstairs?" I asked after a couple of slices had disappeared from everyone's plate.

"Olivia and I want to paint her room. We were discussing what we're going to do."

"You don't mind, do you, Andy?" Olivia asked.

I shrugged. "Knock yourselves out. Those old walls could use a fresh coat of paint."

Both girls looked at each other and burst out laughing.

"No, Daddy!" Kate explained. "We want to do a painting *on* the walls."

"Don't forget our plans for the ceiling," added Olivia.

"Would you drive us to an art store after lunch? *Please*, Daddy?"

"Sure," I answered and took a swig from a can of pop. "But why would someone want to do a painting on the walls of a bedroom?"

Kate reached for another slice of pizza. "You wouldn't understand."

"Why not?"

"Because it's going to be an existential statement about the fragility of the separation between conscious reality and universal unconscious."

I must have looked pretty stunned hearing that from my eleven-year-old, because Kate shrieked with laughter.

"And who came up with that description?" I asked weakly.

Olivia dipped her head as she raised her hand shyly. "Uh, that would be me."

"You *are* finding this difficult, aren't you?" Shannon said, but then laughed. "Please, answer my question. We don't have all day."

"No, no, you need to know the background if this is going to make any sense."

I was very grateful for the art project, because it really got Kate excited to the point where she would have moved back home if it had been feasible. That gave me a childish bit of satisfaction, because I knew it really bothered Sandra.

The weekend before Olivia left the Sal with those two men, Kate couldn't visit because Sandra had grounded her over something she'd said to Jeremy. I was dying to find out what that was but restrained myself. Olivia was as disappointed as Kate, and that might have been part of the problem. Olivia seemed to be coming between Kate and her mom – even if it was unintentional.

Olivia's song repertoire was pretty substantial by this point, so we didn't need to rehearse as much. With or without my daughter present, she was spending a lot of time on "the art project", almost as if she knew her time was limited. I hardly saw her, and the door to her room was generally shut.

I have to admit that having her around the house was becoming distracting. There was no sense of a "come on" from her in the slightest, but when she was painting, she would bounce around the house in one of my old shirts, her legs bare, because then she'd only have to hop into the shower to clean up. None of her clothes – even those she wore to gigs – were tight-fitting or particularly revealing, but it wasn't hard to see that she had a very nice body.

So like any red-blooded male, I noticed. I did keep that to myself, feeling more like her guardian, or at worst, a big brother, but it's obvious now that I was beginning to succumb to Olivia's feminine charms.

Two days before she left, she worked all day, only coming down once for tea and toast.

As she sat in my now paint-covered shirt, paint also in her hair, on her face, hands and legs, I thought she looked enchanting.

Down boy! I said in my head. "You really ought to eat a decent meal," I told her.

She looked up at me with those big, dark eyes. "Maybe later. I'm really not hungry now."

I went down to the basement to practise when she disappeared upstairs.

Dinner was a solitary affair, after which I watched the hockey game in my bedroom, followed by the news.

Shortly after eleven thirty, I did a quick hosedown in the shower and went to bed. Sometime in the night, the sound of the shower woke me, but I quickly drifted off again.

Later, there was a light tap on the door.

"What is it?" I asked groggily.

"Can I come in?"

I turned on the bedside lamp and pulled myself up, resting on my elbows as Olivia opened the door a crack. She'd been crying.

"What's wrong?"

She crept into the room a little farther. She had on a knee-length T-shirt, and her hair, combed off her forehead, was still damp. "I'm frightened."

"About what?"

"Things."

"What things?"

"I can't talk about them."

She was standing there in bare feet, shivering, and I did something really foolish.

Pulling the covers back on the empty side of the bed, I said to her. "Get in and get yourself warm, then tell me what's bothering you. The last thing you need is to catch a cold."

Her body was like ice, so I pulled her against me, my front to her back, while giving myself a stern warning that it was only until she stopped shivering.

The effect of that warning lasted all of about ten minutes.

"Next night, she showed up almost as soon as I'd turned out the light, removed her T-shirt and slipped into my bed without asking. Night after that, she was gone."

Shannon's expression looked non-committal as she pondered my words. "So you think sleeping with her had something to do with her leaving with those men?"

"I hope to God not!"

"I don't see why you should feel ashamed about what happened. It's perfectly natural."

"Olivia is like a child in many ways. I know that it shouldn't bother me, but what I did with her just feels wrong, that's all." I sighed heavily. "I was supposed to be watching out for her."

"According to who?"

"According to me."

"That's just unrealistic, Andy."

"You haven't met Olivia. You wouldn't say that if you had."

"Did she seem upset about it?"

"It was certainly awkward. We'd crossed a line and both knew it."

"What did she say?"

I looked down into my lap, embarrassed. "She thanked me for getting her warm. And she wasn't being coy."

At that point, we were interrupted by a knock on the door.

"What is it?" Shannon asked, loud enough to be heard.

Goode stuck her head in. "You might want to take a look at what I found. I think I've hit paydirt."

CHAPTER 8

Shannon was happy to be free of her stuffy office. A glance at the wall clock showed that she and Andy had been talking for nearly an hour.

Jackie and her secretary Janet were behind the desk in the far corner. Strewn over it was an avalanche of paper. Both the fax machine and computer printer were humming away.

The boss stopped with her hands on her hips and nodded. "You two *have* been busy."

"God, I love the Internet!" Goode said, taking yet more papers from the printer.

"So what do you have?"

Janet looked at Jackie. "You tell her. I've just been pressing keys for you."

Jackie, now sorting through the papers on the desk, looked up. "I'm just trying to get this into some semblance of order, but suffice it to say, I think we've found where they've taken Olivia."

"Where?" Curran asked in a choked voice.

"You were right, Shannon: California. I'll bet when you get all that flight information from your guy at the airport, it will confirm it, although New York or Florida are outside chances."

Shannon pulled over a couple of the scarred chairs from the waiting area. "You better explain it all, but take your time. I want it in order."

"This stuff," Jackie began, waving a sheaf of papers, "is information I didn't bother downloading last night. It will have to be gone through for any new tidbits, but it's basically repetition, mostly coverage from the media about the murder investigation and what happened to Olivia afterward – although there's not much about that.

As Janet handed Jackie another sheaf of papers, she continued: "Now this is general information about the St. James family going back to the great-grandfather, although as I said earlier, there isn't much, since they kept to themselves and shunned the media when it didn't suit them."

She handed one stack to her boss and one stack to Curran. "Give me a moment to pull the faxes together."

Shannon began reading the information on the murder. Even though it was pretty sensational stuff, she got the feeling several of the local Florida papers had pulled their punches. Even some of the big national rags had done only a cursory report. Overall, the coverage had not been as massive as she would have expected with a case of this notoriety.

"Janet, make a note to check out who owns these newspapers, will you?" she asked, handing over the printouts in question.

Jackie and Janet pulled together a third grouping of papers, as their boss looked down at a two-page document. It was from another Florida paper, and this one didn't pull any punches. The reporter made her disapproval of the investigation loud and clear. She'd also obviously gone further afield for background information.

One thing leapt off the page: "The death of Bernard St. James III and his sister being found mentally incompetent opens the question of who will control the family's fortune, reputed to be worth more than five hundred million dollars."

Christ! Shannon thought, *this article was written over six years ago. What are they worth now?* She held up the printout. "And I want to talk to the reporter who wrote this."

Jackie looked back over her shoulder. "I'm already working on that. She's moved on to one of the Washington newspapers. I've contacted them, and she's supposed to call us back."

The phone rang. Janet picked it up, listened, then said, "She's right here."

Taking the phone, Shannon heard all the sounds of a police squad room. "Palmer?"

"Hi, Shan. I hear you tried to shake my little escort," he chuckled.

"I don't need babysitters, Guy. If you want my boy, just tell me."

"I want your boy, Shannon."

"Why? What's up?"

"Further developments. First, the dead woman wasn't killed on Curran's porch. Someone dumped her there. Things like that don't happen by accident. I want to know why her body turned up there. Second, the woman was ID'ed by Vice. Seems she made her living on her back. Generally high-class stuff, out-calls and the like, but also a number of steadies coming to her apartment."

"So why do you want to speak to Andy?"

"Wouldn't it make sense that someone deprived of the comfort of his wife might look for a little something to tide him over?"

"Not everyone is like you, Palmer."

"That's hitting below the belt, especially with me trying to play ball with you for the sake of your old man's memory."

"I'm just trying to save you from yourself. This is a pretty stupid line of investigation to follow. You've got a killer on the loose. If she was a hooker, fine, look for one of her johns. I'm confident my boy wasn't one of them."

"Nonetheless, I want to speak to Curran. Are you going to bring him down, or should I send someone to get him? Notice again, Shannon, how nice I'm playing with you, but my respect for your dad has its limits."

"Can I put you on hold for a second?" Shannon looked at her silent companions. "Palmer wants to speak to you downtown, Andy. He's found out that Maggie was turning tricks, and he stupidly thinks you might be implicated. You're going to have to speak to him."

Curran looked scared as he nodded.

"You didn't know this beforehand, did you?" she asked.

"Not really."

"I don't like the sound of that 'not really."

"No, no! I didn't hold out on you. Olivia never said anything directly about it, but I got the distinct feeling that the reason she was panhandling is that she didn't want to hang around Maggie's apartment for some reason. In passing, I thought prostitution might be a possibility, based on the way Maggie dressed and acted."

"It might have been wiser to let the police in on that surmise. They don't take kindly to people who skirt around things. You've done it to them twice now."

"I just didn't think of it."

Shannon reflected that her client was too much of a gentleman by half. "Do you want me to take you downtown?"

He thought for a minute. "No. I'd rather have you stay here and work on this."

"Okay," Shannon said, as she clicked off the hold button on the phone. "He's all yours, Palmer. Send in whoever you've got outside to get him." After hanging up, she turned. "Do you have that card your lawyer friend gave you? I think it would be a good idea to have some representation about now."

Curran blanched. "You think it's that serious?"

"Let's just say I'd rather be safe than sorry. There's another thing."

"What?"

"Maggie wasn't murdered on your porch. Someone dumped her there. Now why would they do that?"

"A warning?"

Shannon tilted her head forward as Michael massaged her tired neck and shoulders. "That feels so good."

The glass coffee table in front of her looked as bad as Janet's desk had earlier in the day: almost completely covered with paper. At least everything was now colour-coded so they could keep track more easily.

It hadn't taken much coaxing for Shannon to stay overnight with Michael Quinn, her lover of just over two years, in his expansive downtown loft. It had been a case she'd taken on for him that had brought them together, and while it had been one of the most difficult and dangerous ones of her career, it had also been one of the defining moments of her life.

Now the owner of a successful musical instrument rental business, Michael had also been a keyboard player of note with one of the seminal rock bands of the early 80s. Back then, he'd also been her high school crush, and that had really complicated things in the early part of their relationship.

"Are you through for the evening, luv?" Michael asked in his gorgeous British accent. She couldn't understand why he thought it was so ugly, but then most people from England seemed to think the same thing about a Birmingham accent.

"Not really, but toughing it out might do more harm than good. I'm sure to miss something."

"Can I get you a drink?"

"Yeah. Make it a double," she said as she turned her head and kissed the back of his hand. "I need it."

Now, after eleven, Shannon felt every minute of her very long day in her tight muscles and aching brain.

When Michael sat down, she leaned against him, feet curled next to her, and took a long sip of the bourbon she favoured. The warmth radiated out from her belly.

"Oh, that's nice."

"I've haven't seen you this involved with a case since that day I walked into your office."

"If I'd had any idea where this one was going, I'd have run away screaming."

"I've seen Andy Curran play a couple of times, you know. He's quite good. And a couple of weeks ago, someone was in the shop, raving about this singer you're trying to find."

Taking another sip of her drink, Shannon shook her head at the perversity of life. Michael's band had reformed on a part-time basis, and she was in a relationship with the man she'd worshipped as a seventeen-year-old.

"What are you thinking about?" he asked as he stroked her hair.

"I wish you didn't have to go to England next week to rehearse."

"The tour is staring us in the face, and I've put the lads off as long as I dare. At least it's only twenty-two shows."

"Yeah, I know, and at least five of them will be in Canada."

"This is why I hate going on the road."

"You'll have fun. Rolly and the others have grown up now, and you have a million-selling CD to support."

"You could come, if you'd like. Chuck the business and run away with me."

"You know I can't do that. Besides, there's the kids."

"As if they would mind!"

"My mother..."

"Bring her along too."

"Yeah, right! I can just see her riding herd on Rolly and Lee. 'Don't forget to wear your rubbers, boys. There are lots of diseases out there, you know.'"

They both laughed, and Shannon turned her face up to be kissed.

Eventually, Michael said, "Do you want to take this to the bedroom, O'Brien?"

She sat up. "Lead the way, Quinn."

"I thought you were tired."

"Never!"

Sleep didn't come easily afterwards, though, at least for Shannon. Michael rolled over and was snoring within minutes. *Men!* she thought, but her smile was fond.

Slipping out of bed and into her robe, she went back to the living room. The pile of papers looked as daunting as ever.

Turning to pick up the two nearly empty whiskey glasses, she spotted the CD Curran had handed her when she'd dropped him at the Holiday Inn near Yorkdale Mall. Palmer had not given him an easy ride, but in the end hadn't made anything stick. She'd wanted the info first hand, so she'd offered to drive down and fetch him. In the middle of rush hour, it hadn't been a pleasant journey, but it had given them time to talk further about Olivia.

"Listen to it," Curran had said as he'd stuck his head back inside her car. "It will explain a lot."

Someone had written on the CD "Olivia demo #1".

Crossing the wide room, Shannon slipped the disc into the player, turned the volume down low and sat back on the sofa to listen. Absentmindedly, she took a sip from one of the whisky glasses.

After a short piano introduction, Olivia's voice glided out of the speakers in a deeply moody rendition of the Joni Mitchell song "A Case of You", done here as a ballad. The lyrics, brought alive by Olivia's voice, came across with such painful intensity that Shannon could scarcely breathe. This was *exactly* the way she had felt when her marriage had begun to fall apart, and she was desperately trying to decide if it was worth saving. Halfway through the song, she realized she was weeping.

The song disappeared into the mists, and Shannon hit pause to recover her self-control. *I've heard this song many times before,* she thought, *but it's never hit me with such intensity. It felt like Olivia was singing about me.*

Starting the CD again, the next song had the same sort of effect, and the next. Every song reached out to touch her in some personal way. It was as if Olivia could cut right through the music and lyrics, grab you at a very visceral level and not let go. Each performance had tremendous emotional impact.

Lost in her thoughts, Shannon almost didn't hear the muffled ring of her cell phone. Sliding to the other end of the sofa, she fished it out of her shoulder bag. "Shannon O'Brien."

It was her answering service. "Sorry to bother you so late, Ms O'Brien, but you said we should. A Ms Stein just returned your call. She said you can call her now if you like. If not, then tomorrow after ten a.m."

There would be other nights to get a good sleep.

Pulling her notebook and pen toward her, Shannon dialed.

"Stein. Whaddaya want?" Even though she'd worked in Florida and now in Washington, the reporter's accent sounded right out of New York City.

"This is Shannon O'Brien."

"Oh, yeah. Sorry. I thought it was the night desk calling to bug me about a story I'm doing."

"If this isn't a good time to talk..."

"Nah. It's fine as long as we don't go on too long. They'll get my damn copy when I'm good and ready to give it to them." There was the soft clicking of a computer keyboard in the background. "You don't mind if I continue working while we talk, do you?"

"No, that's fine. And thank you for calling back."

"So this is about Olivia St. James? That's an old story to be bringing up."

"Would it surprise you to know that she was recently singing with a jazz trio in a Toronto club?"

"*What?*"

Shannon gave the *Reader's Digest* version of the situation, and at the end, Stein responded with a low whistle.

"Well, knock me over with a feather! So what can I do for you?"

"I need information. After having read all the accounts of what happened in Florida six years ago, I think you're probably the best person to give it to me."

"That obvious? It's one of the reasons I'm in Washington now – not that I'm complaining."

"I don't understand."

"One does not mess with the St. Jameses, my dear, and I had the temerity to do that. So, like I said, I'm working to deadline. Hit me with what you really need to know, and we can always talk again another day."

"Okay. First up, the last of your stories said that Olivia was institutionalized somewhere in California. Do you know exactly where?"

"Not off the top of my head, but I can put my hands on the inform-ation without much trouble. Give me your email address, and I'll fire it off to you."

"Great. From your articles, it's pretty clear you had sources other reporters didn't."

"No, I had sources other reporters didn't bother to cultivate. They just toed the party line. That's not my style."

"Would any of those sources speak with me?"

"They might, but I'll have to check with them first."

"Lastly, what's your take on the St. James murder? Reading between the lines, I think you did have to pull your punches, at least a little."

"You can't imagine," the reporter laughed. "Cutting to the chase, the whole thing stank. To my mind, the girl was guilty as sin, and they did a lot of fancy stepping to prove that she was mentally incompetent. Odd? Definitely. But mental? I'm not so sure. The drugs might have been a contributing factor. She was a pretty heavy user. But it fits with the way that family does things to get her shuffled off to some institution rather than have to face the public scandal of a murder trial."

"They had enough clout to do that?"

"I think so. Anyway, I'm not that against what the outcome was, except for the manipulation part. After all, what's the difference? She gets sent away for good, the state doesn't have to foot the bill for incarceration or the cost of a trial. Everybody wins."

Except Olivia, Shannon thought. "What if she wasn't guilty?"

"Unless you know something I don't, there's no way that's possible. Although no one actually saw her clobber her brother, she's the best bet. Two of the investigating cops told me that off the record. Now I get to ask you a few questions, okay? This situation you're describing in Toronto sounds worthy of a follow-up story, and where I'm working now, the St. Jameses can't touch me."

"I'd rather you held off on any story for the moment. I don't want anyone to know I'm poking around – especially after what you've been telling me. I *will* feed you anything I find, though, before anyone else gets it. You have my word on that."

"Fair enough. I'm too busy at the moment with a brewing lobbyist scandal, anyway. So, any idea how our Olivia turned up in Canada?"

"I don't think they let her out of her cage, if that's what you're asking. My guess is she escaped and managed to make it this far. Then, because she started singing with the jazz trio, she got some press. The people in California were on the lookout and sent two bounty hunters to nab her and bring her back."

"A jazz vocalist?" Stein said with a raucous laugh. "I wonder if the cops in Florida know about this."

"That's one thing I want to check. An easy guess, though, is that this institution, or the St. James family, or both just wanted to get her back without anyone knowing she'd been gone."

Next morning at six, though she'd only had four hours sleep, Shannon had left Michael's apartment before he'd even crawled out of bed. She wanted to get to the office and hopefully finish her day by mid-afternoon. Luckily, he was used to her behaving this way when she was hot on a case, teasingly calling her Miss Monomania.

After talking to Stein, she had decided she'd like to speak to Olivia's nanny – sooner rather than later. With two other cases on the go for O'Brien Investigates needing at least a bit of her attention, she had a full dance card, and it wouldn't get any shorter if she did what she really wanted to do: head home to Rachel and Robbie. With the business going crazy lately, she'd been away a lot, and the guilt weighed heavily on her. Better to start early, and if everything worked out, salvage a bit of downtime with her kids. Maybe she'd treat them to pizza and a video. That was, if Rachel didn't have a hot date. Shannon had hardly seen her the past two weeks.

Having called Jackie Goode about an early start, she picked her up at the corner of King and Jameson, and they circled around the bottom of the city on the Gardiner Expressway before hitting the Don Valley Parkway north.

"Sorry to drag you out so early on a Saturday," Shannon told her new recruit.

"Not a problem," Jackie yawned, "but I'm afraid I didn't get a lot done last night. Guess I finally hit the wall."

"Well, I had a bit of a busy evening."

As they drove past downtown, Shannon related the phone conversation with Ellen Stein as accurately as she could remember it. Little by little, she was beginning to regard Goode as an associate rather than a raw recruit on tryout. The work Goode had done so far was solid and businesslike.

Shannon pulled into the Tim Hortons on Woodbine for coffee and muffins. Even though she'd made a quick cup before leaving Michael's, she could feel herself drooping already from lack of sleep. Goode looked as if she could use a jolt of caffeine, too.

Back in the SUV, they cracked open their steaming coffees and sipped gingerly. Even though cars and trucks were blasting up and down Woodbine, somewhere nearby Shannon could hear a robin singing, the first one she'd noticed. She suddenly felt the pull of the outdoors and wanted to chuck the whole thing, grab Michael and take to the paths through the woods near her farm.

On the other hand, there was work to be done and a suddenly hot investigative trail to follow. As she turned the key and the engine roared to life, Goode spoke. "I'm beginning to think this whole situation stinks."

Shannon glanced over as she put the vehicle in gear. "In what way?"

"Everything is just too damn convenient. The mother's dead, the father's dying, the son is poised to take the reins of the family fortune, and the mentally weak daughter falls apart. From what you've told me, Stein's thoughts headed in the same direction."

"Not really. She seems quite firm in her belief that Olivia did the deed and got what she deserved. The fact that a trial was short circuited didn't make that much difference to her, since the cost of Olivia's incarceration would be borne by the rich family rather than the state."

"Hmmm. Perhaps we should take the time to look at other stories Stein has covered."

Shannon smiled. Good instincts, or considering how insightful her new recruit was proving, should she start thinking of it as Goode instincts? "I've already done that. Stein definitely leans left on the matter of the rich paying their own way. Perhaps she allowed this to colour her opinion. Her writing can be pretty strident."

Not wanting to disturb the flow of their conversation, Shannon pulled into her parking space in front of the office and shut off the engine. Rolling down her window, she heard another robin singing at the top of a nearby pine. Again the call of the wild...

Goode broke off a piece of her bran muffin and popped it in her mouth. "Friends will tell you that I have the unfortunate tendency to see conspiracies behind every bush, but considering what we now know, don't you have any misgivings?"

"In regards to what?"

"Let's put it this way: I'd really like to find out more about this stepmother. Everything seems to have worked out pretty damn well for her, don't you think?"

Now it was Shannon's turn to fall silent. That possibility hadn't occurred to her. She'd want a lot more information before heading down that road.

Jackie continued, "How about I tackle the hit-and-run on the mother? Going back that far, not every story has made the newspapers' online archives, or I may have missed something."

"Your time would be better spent tracking down how Olivia got herself out of the institution in California. We also need to make sure she's been taken back there. We're only assuming that's the case. And after all, that's what we're actually getting paid to do. Looking for bogeymen behind every tree isn't the way to go about this. We have to keep our eye on the ball."

She got out of the SUV and unlocked the door to the office. Jackie followed.

Inside, the message waiting light was flashing on Janet's phone. Crossing the floor, Shannon picked up the message but played it back on the speaker phone, when she realized it was from Ellen Stein.

"Hello, Shannon. It took a bit of doing, but I finally dug out my notes on the St. James thing and figured it might be best to talk on the phone. Assuming that they haven't moved her someplace else, Olivia St. James was institutionalized at Sunnyvale. It's in a pretty remote location near the California/Nevada border. Nearest town is Portola, and the nearest city with an airport is Reno. Sunnyvale specializes in lushes and dopers of the rich and famous, with a few crazies thrown in. Hope this helps. Oh, and don't forget: I got dibs on anything you find. You promised. Get in touch if I can be any further help."

Jackie had a sour expression when Shannon turned to say, "Well, there are your marching orders. Could you start checking out Sunnyvale for me? But be discreet. I don't want them to know we're nosing around. It may not make a difference, but you never know."

Shannon went into her office, shut the door and got to work catching up on the other cases her business was handling. One of her other operatives was due in at ten for a briefing, and if she didn't hop to it, she'd have nothing to give him.

Shortly before noon, Jackie stuck her head in the door. "I've just had a very interesting phone call. Want to hear about it?"

Shannon stopped making notes on the client report she was putting together. "What do you have?"

"First, some background. Sunnyvale is a very chi-chi place, only the best of the best need apply. Check out their website. You'd think it was a resort where you go to get fit – not fixed. But some of their methods sound downright weird. It's also not the kind of place you can check yourself out of. You have to sign a commitment to stay there for a certain length of time. They won't just let you walk away if you feel like it. Anyway, I decided to call them up and see if she's there."

Sighing, Shannon asked, "Do you think that was wise? I asked you to be discreet."

"We weren't going to get any useful information poking around that way. This place is *très exclusif.*"

"Better come in and tell me about it."

Jackie entered the office and perched on the end of the client chair. "I pretended to be from one of the Florida papers, you know, following up on the tragic story after six years.

"Got put on to an assistant director who probably couldn't answer a question straight if his life depended on it. At first he stonewalled me, saying that it was policy not to give out any information on their 'residents', as he called them. He wouldn't even say if she had ever been there.

"Intimating that I'd got the information about her being there from a reliable source within the family, I asked again how she was doing. After another round of stonewalling, I decided to pull his tail to see if I could shake anything loose. 'I've gotten a very interesting call from a colleague in Toronto claiming that Olivia St. James has been seen in that city. Care to comment?' He nearly dropped the phone.

"He put me on hold for about five minutes and—"

"Let me guess," Shannon said, rather annoyed that her instructions had been ignored. "They told you that she was indeed there and has been there continuously since put into their care."

Goode looked a little bit crestfallen that her thunder had been stolen. "Was it that obvious?"

"What else would you expect him to say? But at least we know where she is."

CHAPTER 9

The sound of my cell phone ringing was about as welcome as finding the tax man at the door with two Mounties standing behind.

Rolling over with a groan, I picked up the bedside clock radio and held it in front of my face.

Even though it was only quarter past ten at night, I'd already been asleep in my hotel bed for nearly an hour. It felt like a year since my life had gone into the garbage can. It hadn't even been a day yet.

Reaching for my cell, I only succeeded in knocking it onto the floor. Managing to find it before it switched into voicemail, my voice came out as a croak. "Andy Curran."

"You idiot!" my ex-wife screamed at me. "How could you have been so goddamned stupid?"

I rubbed my free hand through my hair. I really didn't need this right now.

"The cops were just here hassling Jeremy and me. You can't imagine what it felt like to find out someone has been murdered on our front porch! You could have at least phoned to tell me. And where the hell are you? I called the house just now, and there was no answer."

"First of all, Sandra, it's not your house any more. Remember?"

She was right, though. I should have contacted her, but every time I'd thought of it was the wrong time to make a call. After the police had interviewed me for the second time, the only thing I'd been able to think about was a nice, soft bed with fresh sheets and closing my eyes. I didn't know when I'd ever been this weary.

I don't think she even noticed my opening salvo. "It's all about this little chickie you took up with, isn't it? I knew the moment I heard about her what a sleazebag she was. And you allowed *our daughter*—"

"Back off, Sandra! I'm not in the mood for any of your sanctimonious crap. I've had a *really* bad day, and if you can't talk to me reasonably, I'm going to hang up, and you can do your screaming at the dial tone."

There was silence for a moment, then she said with a lot less heat, "Tell me what happened."

So I told her.

"And your girl has gone off. That's really quite pathetic, Andy."

Her voice had a distinct sneer to it. How had we grown so far apart in so short a time?

"Thanks for being so understanding. And for your information, she's not my girl." The next part would increase the friction again, but I decided to plunge ahead anyway. "How's Kate?"

"Not very good. I can't imagine why, but she was very fond of this Olivia woman."

Something struck me. "How did Kate know she was gone?"

"She called Kate on the phone."

It felt like my eyes were bugging out of my head. *"When?"*

"It might have been last night. I'm not sure."

"Can I talk to Kate?"

"No. I don't think that's a good idea."

"Goddammit, Sandra, I need to talk to my daughter!"

"She's upset enough about your friend leaving and what's happened at the house. You can't talk to her. And with all the trouble you've gotten yourself into, Jeremy feels I should get the custody agreement changed. I don't want Kate staying with you any more."

I lost it at that point and said some very nasty, regrettable things before ending the call. Too late, I realized that Sandra might have been taping the conversation, and if that was the case, I'd really put my foot in it. Leave it to bloody Jeremy to think of that.

With sleep now miles away, I flopped back on the bed and switched on the TV – just in time to catch the coverage of the crime that had taken place on my front porch.

It was a lovely end to a lovely day.

My eyes felt gritty from lack of sleep when I got up next morning.

Something was nagging at the back of my mind, and it suddenly came to me in the middle of a hot shower that I had a gig to play that evening. Only problem with that was I had no drums. They were in the back of my impounded car.

We had to drive to London in the early afternoon, and that didn't leave much time to get something pulled together.

Reaching out of the shower, I grabbed my watch off the sink. Nearly ten. I had two more drum kits in the basement of my house, but I didn't know if the cops would hassle me about removing anything. I also didn't know if I could face seeing the front porch.

I finished my shower in record time and dialed Dom. He lived in Unionville, and that had given me an idea.

"Dom? Andy. Look I've got a prob—"

"Andy? What the hell is going on with you? I'm sitting here reading the paper, and you're all over the front page!"

"Wonderful. Things just keep getting better and better. You should have seen the TV coverage last night."

"I took the kid to the hockey game last night and didn't see any of the boob tube. Man, oh man, what's going on?"

"Read the damn paper, Dom."

"You still doing the gig tonight?"

"Yes," I said wearily. "Only problem is I don't have any drums. They're in the car, and the cops have impounded that to check for evidence."

"How can I help?" Good old Dom was standing up to be counted when I really needed him.

"Can you meet me at Quinn Musical around one? I'll rent a kit there. We can drive out to London together."

"It'll be a tight fit with my bass, but we can manage it. Quinn's at one. Got it."

I called Ronald next. He didn't have a television and had spent the previous day and evening rehearsing the fill-in vocalist, so he probably didn't know about my problems either. I think the vocalist might have decided to spend the night, because he seemed rather distracted and really didn't ask much in the way of questions, and that surprised me.

After assuring him I would be at the gig, I pulled on my now rather grungy clothes, left the hotel and crossed Dufferin Street to Yorkdale Shopping Centre.

I couldn't go to the gig looking like I did.

When the taxi pulled into the industrial mall where Quinn and O'Brien had their businesses, I was surprised to see Shannon's SUV out front. I hadn't figured she'd work Saturdays.

Being a bit pressed for time and not sure how long it would take to get drum rental paperwork done, I went to the far end of the building to Quinn's. Dom had arrived five minutes earlier.

The boss, Michael Quinn, was in that day, surprising since he's once again a hot commodity in the music business. I'd met him years before and was flattered that he remembered me.

"Actually, your name came up last night."

I cringed inwardly. He'd seen the news on TV. "It hasn't been very pleasant," I said, hoping to deflect any further comments.

"So Shannon tells me."

"Oh, you know Shannon O'Brien?" I responded, too late noticing that Dom, standing behind Quinn, was gesticulating wildly.

Quinn seemed a bit embarrassed now. "We are, um, we've been seeing each other for a couple of years. She was at my flat last night."

So now we were both standing there feeling awkward.

Dom said, "Andy, it's getting pretty late. We have to hit the road."

"Right," Quinn and I both said in unison, then laughed.

I'd told one of his employees over the phone what I needed, and it was all ready to go. I expected to see some paperwork, but Quinn told me there wasn't any.

"Why not?"

He smiled. "Because Shannon would kill me if I charged you. You can just bring them by next time you're up this way. I don't get much call for the rental of jazz kits anyway."

It took a while to get the stuff loaded. Fortunately, I'd been carrying my stick bag to the house when I'd found Maggie's body, so we were all set to head down the 401 to London.

The phone rang and Quinn listened for a moment, then said, "Actually he's here right now, borrowing a drum kit. I'll tell him." He covered the mouthpiece with his hand. "Can you drop in and talk to Shannon?"

Dom was tapping his watch, impatiently signalling our need to leave. "Can I call her later?"

Quinn passed that on, then stood nodding for a few moments. "Right, I'll tell him. Yes, he does look like shit," he laughed before hanging up. "She says it can wait until you get back. She's got a lot of news, some of it very good. The main thing is that your friend Olivia is apparently back in California. She said you'd know what that means."

We headed off to our gig with me in a much better frame of mind. I tried the O'Brien office twice but couldn't get through, so I left a message that said I also had a bit of new information. The rest of the trip was taken up with me telling Dom what had happened since I'd walked into the O'Brien office the day after Olivia had been driven off in that car.

That night at the corporate function in London, Ronald's replacement vocalist was pretty B-flat, but got through all her tunes relatively unscathed. The guy who'd hired us, though, was unhappy that we'd showed up with someone other than Olivia and let Ronald know it.

"Didn't you tell him ahead of time?" I barked at Ron between sets.

"One vocalist is as good as another for these sorts of things."

"Like hell they are!" I continued at higher than my normal volume.

Dom pulled me aside. "Relax. I think that was a good thing to have happen. Our Ronny needs to be cut down occasionally, and an employer has better effect doing it than you or I would." Then he clapped me on the back. "Plus it's nice when someone reminds him just how much we should be missing Olivia."

After our short break, I played better than I had in quite a long time. Anger always helps one focus.

Sunday morning started with another phone call. This time I was at least half-awake, so I managed not to knock my cell off the night table.

"Daddy?" came a tremulous little voice.

"Katy?" Judging from the fact she was whispering, I had to ask the next question. "Does Mom know you're calling?"

"Um, no. One of my friends snuck me her cell phone. I'm grounded," she added disgustedly.

"You have friends who have cell phones?"

Her more normal voice came out in her answer and dripped with

'Boy, are my parents in the stone age'. "Of course they do. I'm about the only kid I know who *doesn't* have one."

"Tell it to the Marines," I teased her back, and she giggled.

"Why is Mommy so mad at you?" she said.

I didn't want to get into it, but I also didn't want to lie to her. "Something happened the other night and—"

"You mean Olivia's friend Maggie getting capped?"

"What did you say?"

"That's what all the kids in school call it," Kate answered warily, as if a parental tirade was imminent.

"No, no. How do you know about Maggie?"

"You know my friend Jennifer who lives on Pape? She called and told me. Mom wouldn't let me watch the news."

I took a deep breath to try to slow down my racing heart. "No, Kate. That's not what I meant. How do you know who Maggie is?"

"She came over a couple of times when Olivia was babysitting. I didn't like her. She made Olivia sad, but I'm sorry that she died."

You could have knocked me over with a feather. Talk about the unaware parent!

"Do you know what they talked about?"

"Olivia always made me go to my room, but I'd crawl back to the top of the stairs and listen. Maggie wanted Olivia to stop singing with you. She said it was too dangerous. What did she mean, Daddy? Is that why Olivia had to go away?"

"I don't know, honey. I'm trying to find that out."

"Olivia called me, you know."

"Yes, your mom mentioned that. Do remember what day it was?"

"It was on Wednesday after school. Mommy was still at work, and I got to the phone before the babysitting dragon could."

When we were still together, I was normally around when Kate got home from school. Since both Jeremy and Sandra worked downtown, my ex had needed to hire a sitter. Kate didn't like her, hence the name. I kept my nose out of it, but I did think it was pretty funny.

"What did Olivia say, Kate?"

"She told me she had to go away and that I should take care of you."

"Did she tell you where she was?"

"No, but she sounded scared. She spoke so soft I could hardly hear what she was saying."

"What else did she say?"

"Well, she said that she missed me very much, and..." Kate sounded a little weepy. "She said she was sorry that she had to leave without saying goodbye. She told me I should keep painting, that someday I'd be really famous." Now Kate was crying. "Daddy, why did she have to go? I miss her so much!"

"Shhhhh, shhhhh, little Katy. Daddy's trying to help her come back. I'm trying my hardest, sweetie; I promise."

When she calmed down a bit, Kate asked when I'd be coming to visit her. I skirted the issue by saying that my car was in the shop, but I hoped I'd be able to make it next weekend.

"But I want to come to the house and work on our painting. Olivia told me I could."

"Maybe next weekend, honey. We'll see."

"You always say that when you don't want to tell me no."

"You have your old dad figured out pretty well, don't you?"

"Well, yeah," she shot back in a pretty decent Valley Girl imitation. "Gotta go, Dad. Mom's calling me. I love you!"

With that, she clicked off, leaving me feeling as if the whole world was spinning out of control.

I'd never thought of asking my daughter about Olivia, but it was logical that she might know something, since they'd spent so much time together. Now that we were off the phone, a thousand other questions I might have asked her flooded my brain.

One thing was for certain, though, if the cops found out Kate knew anything, they'd want to question her, and that was something I had to keep from happening at all costs. Sandra would hit the roof, and I might be left with all sorts of access problems because of it. Kate didn't need that. Her life had been upset far too much when Sandra had moved out and had only recently begun getting back on an even keel.

And how in heaven's name was I going to explain to Kate that Olivia might have murdered her own brother?

Picking up my cell again, I dialed O'Brien Investigates. I needed to find out what I should do, and I needed to find out fast. The old battleaxe might possibly spill the beans to the cops about Kate and Olivia. Everyone in the neighbourhood knew we could always count on her sticking her nose in where it didn't belong.

♪♯♪·♪♭♪·

Jackie was getting restless with all the phone and Internet jockeying she'd been forced to do. She hadn't gotten into investigating for that. She wanted to be out doing things, not talking about them!

She did understand that the Internet had changed things in detective work, as it had in many other arenas. Perhaps more, since you could now get information at the click of a mouse that would have taken weeks to get with old-fashioned footwork. Still, she was five days into the first real case she'd worked on and there had only been one face-to-face interview plus those tidbits she'd picked up at the Salamander from her visit there.

It surprised Jackie that her new boss could be so pedantic about how she did things. Sure, she was thorough, but things moved so damned slowly.

It was perfectly obvious to her that something dirty had gone on in the St. James family. Why couldn't her boss see it?

From everything she'd learned about Olivia so far, she certainly didn't sound like someone who'd bash her brother's skull in with a rock. Even though the evidence against her looked conclusive, no one knew better than Jackie that lies could be made into fake truth pretty easily.

Absentmindedly, she rubbed the scar on her left shoulder.

Not able to relax, even though it was Sunday, she rolled things around in her head. She suddenly had a hot idea involving a bit of extra sleuthing, and if she hit pay dirt, she'd be able to drop it in Shannon's lap first thing in the morning. Jackie knew she needed to rack up points if she wanted to be taken on steadily by O'Brien Investigates. Switching off the TV, she reached for her cell on the coffee table.

"Hey, Carolina, feel like some company?"

"I'm going to a concert this afternoon, but if you want to use the computer, come on over."

"What makes you think that's the reason I'm calling?"

"Well, let's see. How about because the last four times you've called, you wanted to use my computer?"

Jackie bristled. "That's not the only reason I come to see you."

"Oh, so you don't want to use my computer?"

"Look, if it's so much of a hassle, I can always go to the library."

"Relax, Jackie. I'm just yanking your chain. Come on over."

As she put on her coat, Jackie looked over the wreck of her one-room apartment. One of these days she really should give it a thorough cleaning. Grabbing her backpack, she headed out. Today wasn't that day.

Maggie, or Margaret, she thought as she waited for the streetcar, *I'm gonna find out just who the hell you were.*

Trouble was, Jackie would *again* spend her day on the Internet. At least she hoped it would be profitable.

♪♯♩·♪♭♩·

The phone rang only once, but it caused Shannon to open her eyes, stretch, then notice that the sun was rather bright outside. A look at the bedside clock told her she'd actually slept in until ten past nine. How had her mother kept her son Robbie quiet for so long?

There was a light tap on the door, and Rachel stuck her head in. "You awake, Mom?"

Shannon smiled at her daughter. "I am now."

"Sorry about that." She came into the room with a mug of steaming coffee, its fragrance heavenly. "That was the answering service. One of your clients called for you."

The detective groaned as she sat up. Couldn't they leave her alone for one day?

"Do you know who?"

"Someone named Curran. He said that it's really important."

After a sip of coffee, Shannon said, "They *all* say it's really important. This one, though, probably is. Do you have the phone number where he can be reached?"

With a grin, Rachel pulled it out of her jeans. Now that she'd grown out of the goth thing, she'd become quite the looker, all dark wavy hair and luminous eyes. Her daughter was destined to break more than a few hearts. She pulled her other hand from behind her back and produced a muffin. "Grams said I should also bring this up to you, but you've sogged in bed so long, I don't know if you deserve it."

Shannon had said the same sort of thing to her daughter many times in the past – mostly on school days.

She laughed as she took it and peeled off the paper. "Thanks, honey. I'll take care of this call and come down as soon as I have a shower. Tell everyone how grateful I am for letting me sleep in."

After Rachel shut the door, Shannon took another sip of coffee and a bite of the warm muffin. Thank God for her mother. Without her, the O'Brien household would grind to a halt within a day.

With a heavy sigh, she picked up the phone. Perhaps this wouldn't mess up her whole day, but she had a bad feeling it might. Just as long as it didn't get in the way of Sunday dinner with Michael and the family. Her mother had promised her favourite: roast beef with Yorkshire pudding. Missing that would really irritate her.

The call connected with the familiar, "Andy Curran."

"Shannon. What's up?"

"I just spoke to my daughter. It was stupid, I know, but I never expected that she'd know anything."

"Stop. Andy, I have no idea what you're you talking about."

He sounded tense. She needed him to get a grip so he could tell his story in an orderly fashion. She also wasn't happy that she hadn't thought of talking to the child herself.

Once calmer, Andy laid out his previous phone call succinctly. Shannon felt as he did, that keeping the child under the police radar was a good thing, but she was eager to talk to Kate herself.

"I'd like to interview her, Andy. Today if possible. Can you arrange that?"

"Things aren't very good between her mother and me at the moment. The cops have already been over to hassle her. She's going to be hard to convince." He hesitated for a moment. "There's also the fact that my daughter made the phone call to me secretly. Sandra grounded her, and she's not supposed to talk on the phone. I don't want to get her busted."

Shannon thought for a moment. "We can skate around that. I think the best thing would be to just go over to the house. We'd be a lot easier to blow off if you phone ahead."

"Well..."

"Look, the worst she can do is deny us access. I have a few cards to play there. Are you still at the Yorkdale Holiday Inn?"

' "Yeah."

"Expect me in an hour."

Andy had told Shannon that no one could glower like his former wife, and judging by the woman's expression as she held the door partially open, the PI believed him.

"No, Andy, this isn't a good time. Go away!"

Lending moral reinforcement was "the other man" standing behind her, glowering almost as darkly. Lanky, balding and not all that handsome, Shannon couldn't see why Sandra, a stylish blonde with smouldering good looks, had taken up with him. She knew that there were a lot of other dynamics at work in marriage breakdowns, but outwardly, both parties had gone on to radically different choices in their new loves. Olivia was dark, open, childlike. Both Currans had moved on to their opposites.

· Shannon stepped forward. "You may not believe us, but we're here to help you. Your daughter has information the police will want to know. Sooner or later, they're going to realize that. When they do, they'll be standing on your doorstep, and you won't be able to tell them no. Would you rather talk to them or to us?"

"How can you keep the police from questioning Katherine?"

Shannon indicated the bag she was holding. "I brought video equipment. I'll record the entire interview. If there's anything the police should know about, I'll show them the tape." She smiled in an engaging manner. "I know what I'm doing. I used to be a cop myself."

Sandra said, "If you'll excuse us for a minute," and shut the door.

Inside could be heard some rather heated words between the ex and her boyfriend.

"How do you think it's going?" Shannon asked.

Unexpectedly, Curran grinned. "Knowing Sandra, she's made up her mind to keep me out. Perhaps good old Jeremy will be able to convince her otherwise."

After a three-minute wait, the door opened again, but if anything, the wife's expression was darker. "I'll give you half an hour. We're very busy today."

Figuring she could get more time if it was needed, Shannon nodded and squeezed through the partially-open door. This woman's feelings were quite easy to read.

She was told to set up in the living room. With not so much as a pillow out of place, the space looked like something straight out of a home decor magazine. *All probably the work of a very expensive interior decorator and a weekly cleaning woman*, Shannon reflected, thinking of her own rumpled but very enjoyed living room. This room looked as if no one ever so much as walked into it.

Kate was called downstairs but stopped in the doorway, the broad smile sliding from her face as she saw who was waiting, clearly fearing she was about to get yelled at over her forbidden phone call.

"Daddy?"

Curran crossed the room and picked her up in a strong hug. "How's my girl?"

Shannon noticed he was looking over Kate's shoulder directly at Jeremy. The testosterone level in the room rose dramatically.

"Daddy, what's going on?"

He walked over to Shannon. "Kate, this is Shannon O'Brien. She wants to ask you some questions. Would that be okay with you?"

She had a very wary expression. "About what?"

Andy smiled. "About Olivia. This is the person I've hired to find her. You want to help with that, don't you?"

"Daddy, why are you talking like a dork all of a sudden?"

Sandra leaped to her feet. "Katherine Grace Curran! I have told you about speaking that way many times!"

She glared across the room, but it was clear the anger was aimed at her husband. Obviously, the woman hadn't spent much time in schoolyards lately.

"Okay, kid," Curran said, pretending not to notice the outburst, "I've brought this here private investigator to grill you about the missing woman caper. How's that?"

Kate wiggled from his arms and walked over to Shannon with her hand extended. "Are you really a PI?"

"Yes, I am."

"I thought all PIs were men."

"You're right. Most are."

The girl's expression turned mischievous. "Are you going to close the curtains and shine a bright light in my eyes and scream at me?"

Shannon grinned at her cheekiness. "We only do that to bad guys. You're not a bad guy, are you?"

"No. What do you want me to do?"

"Why don't you just sit here on the sofa with me, and we'll talk. Okay?"

Kate was obviously unhappy about her mother and Jeremy insisting on remaining in the room, but there wasn't much to be done about it.

Working slowly and methodically, the investigator took the little girl through her relationship with Olivia and her contact with Maggie. It went pretty much the way Curran had told her over the phone earlier.

"So how many times do you think Olivia's friend Maggie came over when you were there?"

The little girl looked up. "Three. She came over three times. Sometimes Olivia babysat me if Daddy had to go out to play, and it wasn't with the trio."

Sandra shifted in her chair and looked as if she might interrupt, but Jeremy put his hand on her arm, and she didn't.

"So Maggie and Olivia got along well together?"

Kate shook her head. "Every time Maggie came over, Olivia was very sad afterwards."

"What did they talk about?"

"Olivia always sent me out of the room, but I'd listen."

"Why?"

"Because Olivia was my friend, and I wanted to protect her. I didn't like it when she cried."

"So what sorts of things did they talk about?"

"Maggie said that Olivia owed her, and she was being very stupid singing in my daddy's band."

"Did she say why Olivia owed her?"

"It was something about getting her out, getting her to someplace far away, and if she was smart, she'd keep her head down, otherwise they'd come and get her."

"Who?"

"Maggie didn't say. I thought it was about money, because Maggie always made Olivia give her money. I think Olivia just did it so she would leave. My daddy didn't like Maggie being over at our house, that's why she came when he was out."

"Is there anything else you can remember them talking about?"

"Once Maggie said that she'd saved Olivia, and if she had to go back, they'd get her good, and Olivia started crying."

"When you saw Olivia last, how did she seem to you? Was she happy? Sad? The same as always?"

"She was very quiet. I'd say things, and she wouldn't hear them." Kate looked over at her dad. "I think she was going to quit Daddy's band and run away again."

"Why do you say that?"

Kate shrugged. "She told me I could finish painting the room for her if I wanted. She'd sketched out all the forms, and I could colour them in. She says I'm very good at doing that."

"So she ran away?"

"No! Those men came and took her before she could get away. Now she's back where she was, and she's really scared."

The room was still and Shannon's voice, though gentle and soft, sounded almost strident in the silence. "How do you know that, Kate?"

"She called me on Wednesday after school."

"This is really important: do you think you could tell me exactly what she said?"

"It was hard to hear her because she was whispering. She said she was sorry she had to leave without saying goodbye. She also said to tell my daddy she was sorry, and I should take care of him."

"Sorry about what?"

"She didn't say. That was right at the end of the phone call. Something banged really loud, then there was shouting and the phone went dead." Kate looked over at her dad with a troubled expression. "Olivia's all right, isn't she, Dad?"

CHAPTER 10

Shannon's SUV was charging east through Mississauga on the 403. I got the feeling we'd spent more time talking to Kate than she'd wanted.

"So where do you think we stand?" I asked.

"What? Oh yeah. Sorry. I was just tossing something else over in my head."

"What?"

"You puzzle me. You only seem passionate and committed about two things: your daughter and Olivia. To be honest, music appears to come a distant third. It's been my experience that musicians are passionate about their art almost to the exclusion of everything else in their lives."

"Michael's like that?"

"When he's 'working', as he puts it? Sure. Nothing else in the universe matters."

"I've always been a musician. Well, at least since age nine. That's when my dad got me into the same drum and bugle corps he'd been in as a kid." I thought about what she'd said. "You know, I fell in love with the drums because I was very good at it. I didn't have to be shown things over and over. My teacher always said I just 'got it.'"

"But a lot of people play instruments when they're young, and they become quite good. Then for some reason, they move on to other things. Surely you must know, must have played with people like that. Why are you still playing at your age? Not to be insulting, but you can't be making all that much money."

"It's what I do," I answered simply. "Maybe the difference between Michael and me is that I don't compose. I don't aspire to be anything more than a jobbing musician who's very good at his craft – and I am."

"What would you do if you had to stop playing drums?"

"I don't know. I like to read. If I didn't have to make a living, I'd probably spend a lot more of my time reading."

When we pulled off the 401 at Dufferin so she could drop me at the Holiday Inn, I added, "I can't imagine *not* playing drums, if that's what you're getting at. I'd be pretty unhappy if I couldn't."

♪♯♩·♪♭♩·

Shannon was at work early the next morning, feeling really energized for the first time in weeks. Yesterday evening had been just the tonic she'd needed: her mother's excellent dinner, a nice bottle of wine, then the whole family had watched a couple of movies. She'd even let Robbie stay up well after eleven – to his amazement.

Later, she'd also asked Michael to stay, and that had been all right, too. That morning, there had been no disapproving glares from her mother when they came down to grab a piece of toast and tea before heading their separate ways.

Also spurring her on was the fact that the Curran case had reached the point where her blood was always stirred. The next step they might take would be the equivalent of releasing the bloodhounds: getting into the field, talking, improvising, taking chances, and hopefully in the end carrying the day. This was where she could still love her job.

Even though it was only just eight o'clock, Jackie was already sitting on the office doorstep with her own cup of coffee. A proprietary arm lay over her bulging backpack.

"You're here early. I was hoping for some quiet time to catch up on a few things." She stuck her key into the door lock. "Curran isn't due until ten. He's down springing his car from the cops."

"I know. I just got off the phone with him."

"Why were you talking with him?" Shannon asked over her shoulder as she switched on the lights.

"I wanted to ask him some questions."

"About what?"

"About what I'm going to show you."

"Okay. Come into my office, and let's see what you've got."

While Goode laid out yet more computer printouts and her notes, Shannon checked her email. Another of the agency's jobs was coming to a conclusion nicely, while the just-completed one was only waiting for her to finish the report to the client. Cheques from both would be good and fat. A returning client wanted several security checks on prospective employees carried out. Business was certainly booming.

"Ready?" Jackie asked, as she sat down in the chair on the opposite side of the desk.

Shannon turned away from the computer monitor. "Fire away."

Jackie slid a photo across the desk. "Take a look at this."

The photo was of a girl, maybe in her early twenties, good looking, dressed in a gorgeous ball gown, and on the arm of an older man in a tux, presumably her father. Judging by the hair and clothing, the shot had been taken maybe twenty years ago.

"Who is this?"

"Margaret Joy Allan Springfield of the Baltimore Springfields. This is from her coming-out party."

Margaret. Maggie. Shannon had only seen her after being strangled, but now that she knew, there were some echoes of the fresh young thing beaming out of the photo in the contorted and bruised face she'd seen on Andy Curran's front porch.

"How did you come up with this?"

"By working twelve hours yesterday, mostly on my friend's computer. I also ran up a pretty hefty phone bill and some Internet search charges, by the way."

It was always heart-wrenching to see a hopeful young face, knowing that they're going to finish their life on the killing floor, the subject of police crime scene photos, media speculation and endless heartbreak to those who loved them.

"So tell me what you've got on her," Shannon said, putting a damper on her emotions.

Jackie scanned down her notebook. "She was born into a well-off family. Dad was a lobbyist in Washington, mother was a university professor, both from old money, both now deceased. At the time of her death the other night, Maggie was forty-three and seven months. She has a brother and a sister, both younger, and from what I've found, she had a fairly normal childhood, assuming you include summers in

Europe, skiing in Colorado, safaris, cruises and country club membership a normal part of life. The rot didn't begin to set in until she was in her mid-teens.

"The parents had her in a private boarding school. First inkling of anything being wrong is when she got summarily booted out, apparently for drug use.

"They put her in the local high school, where she again got into trouble. This time it included skipping classes and minor stuff like smoking. Her first arrest was at age sixteen for shoplifting, followed by one for assault on a classmate.

"At this point, the beleaguered parents put Maggie into a full time program for problem children, and from the little I could find out on that, she straightened up and flew right, and finished off her high school years okay. Next hit I got was in university. This time it definitely was drugs. She got busted by the cops in a campus raid. First rehab stint for her. Are you beginning to get the picture?

"Well, with what I've been able to find out about her life, it's pretty much the same after this: she gets in trouble, parents bail her out, she does all right for a year or two then backslides. Cycle repeats."

Shannon was pleased and impressed. "Obviously, a good bit of this information didn't come off the Internet. Who did you talk to?"

"I worked on the assumption that Maggie and Olivia started out from the same place, namely Sunnyvale. Then I asked myself where they might have gone first. The nearest decent size town is—"

"Reno, just across the border in Nevada. Right."

"Now, if you ran this institution, and you found out one of your more important patients had got away but had the help of someone else, *and* you didn't want the word to get out on that, what would you do?"

"I'd get police help to catch the unimportant one. They'd be pretty sure Olivia wouldn't strike out on her own."

"After that, it didn't take me long to come up with Maggie's real name. The Plumas County Sheriff's office put out an APB on one Margaret Springfield last October. From what I found out, our Maggie stole a car, drove to Reno and disappeared. The bulletin said she might have another patient with her. Her name was given as Olive Saint, incidentally. Once I had that, I was halfway home."

"How did you finally run her down?"

"Basically, I figured she might have had other brushes with the law and that they'd have been reported in the papers. Car thefts rate pretty low in the scheme of things – unless you're a celebrity – so it took awhile. I just searched back until I found out she was from Baltimore. After that, I looked up her graduating class on that online classmate service, found a friend who was willing to talk, and that led me to her brother."

Shannon's face fell. "You talked to her family?"

"Sure. Why the look?"

"Palmer and his crew probably haven't gotten this far. They don't know yet that Maggie started out from California. The family most likely doesn't know that she's dead." She looked at Jackie. "Or did you tell them?"

Jackie looked uncomfortable. "I, ah, skated around that."

"What did you say?"

"I told her brother that she was involved with something here in Toronto and that I was trying to find her before the police did."

"Jesus! How could you? What do you think is going to happen when they get the news she's dead? I have a good reputation with the police, and they're going to know it was us. How could you have been so stupid?"

Jackie's face coloured. "I guess I didn't think it through."

"Damn straight you didn't think it through!"

"Look, I'm sorry, okay? I took a shortcut, and I shouldn't have."

Shannon shook her head disgustedly. "We have to share this information with Palmer, you know. I told him I wouldn't hold out on him, and I keep my promises."

Both women were silent while they thought about the situation.

Jackie spoke first. "Do you think it's wise to tell Palmer about the California connection?"

Shannon made no immediate response. "You're assuming that being involved with Olivia was the reason for Maggie's murder. From what I've gathered, Palmer is going with the prostitution angle. If he's working that, then he's looking for a john she might have been shaking down, or one who was worried she might be indiscreet, or maybe just some crazy. That's assuming the idiot isn't still trying to pin it on Curran."

"But if we use my hypothesis, then telling Palmer about Sunnyvale and its connection to Maggie could put Olivia in danger."

"Why would the people running Sunnyvale want Maggie dead?"

"I don't have an answer for that."

With a heavy sigh and shake of her head, Shannon said, "I *hate* these moral dilemmas."

"Why don't we see what Curran wants to do before calling Palmer? If he decides he knows all he wants to know, then we're off the hook."

"He's already given us the go-ahead to keep working on this. Sure, I can warn Palmer about protecting Olivia, but will he do it? He'll go for the arrest if the trail leads there, and that will be his sole concern, if I know him." She shook her head again. "Shit!"

As she fumed over what Jackie had done, Shannon also decided to use the conference area of her office for the meeting with Curran. Trouble was, it was a mess. Since she was already angry with Jackie, she told her to clean it up.

After that was done, she threw Jackie her car keys. "Go to the restaurant down the road and get them to make up a tray of sandwiches. I don't think I could face another Timbit. I want some cream for the coffee, too. Edible oil won't cut it today, either. And don't forget to wash out three coffee mugs when you get back. They're looking pretty disgusting."

As her employee went out the door, Shannon said a few rather unladylike things under her breath.

"So that's what we've come up with as far as Maggie goes," Shannon said as she sipped a rather good mug of coffee. Jackie had taken it upon herself to find a decent roast. Where in this industrial wasteland, she had no idea.

The meeting had been going on for over an hour, during which time Shannon had laid out everything they now knew. Curran, staring at the wall above her head, seemed lost in thought. "It certainly makes me feel a lot more sorry for her than I did," he finally said. "Maggie had a pretty awful life."

Shannon remained silent until her client looked at her. "Andy, how far do you want to take this?"

"What do you mean?"

"When you came to me, you said you just wanted to find out what happened to Olivia. I think we've answered that question pretty thoroughly. Do you really want to go on? This is the point where it's liable to get real expensive, real fast."

She let him think about that while she got busy gathering up the papers on the table while Jackie laid out the food.

Finally, he spoke. "I can't get rid of the vision of those bastards shoving Olivia into that car, taking her back to somewhere she doesn't want to be. Despite what you've found out, I think she's a good person. Do you remember the last thing she said to my daughter when she called was, 'Tell your daddy I'm sorry'?"

"I remember."

"When I first came to you, I said I was ready to borrow against my house if necessary. That offer stands."

"In that case, how much money you spend depends on what results you want."

"What I want..." Curran repeated, then zoned out again as he looked vacantly down at a paper he'd picked up.

Jackie, after a nod from her boss, poured more coffee. "So what's the verdict, Andy?" she asked impatiently.

Shannon looked at her sharply but nodded at Curran when he looked up at her.

"I just want to make sure that Olivia is okay," he said almost to himself. "From all I've heard, she probably needs to be in that institution."

Goode shifted uncomfortably. "Can we be certain of that?"

"Jackie," her boss said warningly.

"No, I think this needs to be said. I've looked at all the documents over a dozen times, and I have questions about what happened. First and foremost, though, the whole thing is just too damn convenient. The mother dies, the father dies, the son is murdered and the daughter is committed. Who wins in that situation? The stepmother. Am I the only one bothered by that fact?"

Shannon held up her hand. "Don't you think the police investigating the brother's murder would have considered it?"

"With the amount of money up for grabs, don't you think people can be bought off?"

Shannon, sticking up for law enforcement, answered tightly, "Things don't necessarily work like that."

The effect of her words on her junior operative was galvanic. "You don't know shit!" she snarled, then turned on her heel and walked right out of the building, flinging the outside glass door shut with enough force that Shannon thought it might shatter.

Clearly, something was very wrong, but that didn't excuse the way Goode had behaved in front of a client. A lot of the excellent work Jackie had done on this case had just been wiped out by her inability to control her temper. An operative who couldn't keep a lid on personal issues was worse than useless. She was dangerous.

"I'm sorry about my employee's outburst," she said to Curran and covered for Goode with a bit of a white lie. "She's been under a lot of pressure lately."

Whether he believed that or not, Curran nodded. "We *should* find out if Olivia was given a square deal."

The detective felt as if she needed to be blunt. "I fully realize there's a romantic complication to this situation. If riding to Olivia's rescue is the motivation behind your decision, I should warn you it's a bad reason to go down this road. I've read the same reports Jackie has, plus I spoke to the one reporter who aggressively went after the murder story. My conclusion is that Olivia is a very troubled person. You should get yourself ready to be very disappointed."

"Do it anyway." He sighed. "You're right about her being troubled. I know that. Really, I do, but there's also what she can do with her voice. You listened to the CD I gave you?"

Shannon nodded.

"And what did you think?"

"It was...overwhelming."

"That sort of talent deserves to be shared, not locked away in some institution." He stood up. "I also firmly believe Olivia's calling to me for help. And I won't let her down."

So there they were, her marching orders. "I'm going to need more money from you. As I said, this is where it's going to get expensive. Someone is going to have to go to California, New York and maybe Florida."

"I can write you a cheque for four thousand, but that'll clean out my bank accounts. Will that cover it for the moment? I'll go see my bank manager tomorrow about a loan or a mortgage, if needed."

"Four thousand will do just fine." She got up, then noticed the sandwiches. "I guess this meeting got a little sidetracked. Want to take one for the road?

Curran took three.

Musicians, she thought with a shake of her head. *No matter what, you can always count on them taking free food.*

Working on the hunch that she hadn't gone far, Shannon found Jackie Goode about three blocks away, sitting on the curb, head down. She pulled up, crossed the road and sat down next to the woman.

"Want to tell me about it?"

Goode didn't look up. "I got screwed by the cops once, totally hung out to dry. I never talk about it to anyone, just try to keep it out of my mind, but my father...he was a real piece of work. A man's man, they all called him."

"He abused you?"

"Oh, yeah. Used to beat all of us up, too, when he felt like it. I finally worked up the courage to take it to the local RCMP detachment. They didn't believe me. I was stunned. You see, they all knew my father, didn't think he was capable of something like that. Next thing I know, he's down at the cop shop, and *I'm* getting grilled as if I'd done something wrong! It was sick." She had her arms wrapped around herself tightly, rocking. "I've never been so scared."

"How old were you?"

"Fourteen."

Shannon put an arm around her. "I'm so sorry I made this all surface."

"It's not your fault."

"And your father?"

"Dead. Heart attack. Serves him right."

"And the rest of your family?"

"Mom's dead, and my brother ran away, too. I never heard from him again."

"Friends? A significant other?"

"Three friends. Two of them have moved away in the last year." Jackie sniffed once. "I really blew it, didn't I?"

Deciding that bluntness was best, Shannon answered, "Yes. I've got to be able to trust the people who work for me, Jackie. You know, 'all for one' and all that bullshit."

"I really wanted this job." She sniffed again. "Me and my goddamn big mouth..."

Shannon stood up. "Come on. My bum is getting cold sitting on the curb. Let's go back to the office." Jackie still didn't get up. "Okay?"

Goode shuffled across the street, head down, and once in the SUV, sat with her body twisted towards the side window.

Inside the office, Shannon handed her a sandwich and commanded, "Eat. You'll feel better."

Jackie looked up and managed a wan smile. "You sound like a mother."

"I am. Got two great kids. Robbie's thirteen, and Rachel is about to be eighteen going on thirty." She looked into the distance. "I had a husband once, too. I thought he was the love of my life. Found out he liked sleeping around on me. I actually caught him in one of our investigations, and it was damned painful."

"But now you're seeing Quicksilver," Jackie said, using Michael's stage moniker.

"You *have* done your homework, I see."

"I remember reading it in the paper. Kit Mason is one of the friends I mentioned. She told me all about him."

"It never fails to surprise me how incestuous the music business is." Picking up half a tuna sandwich, Shannon took a bite. "I told Curran one of us is going to have to go to California."

Jackie's eyes registered shock. "You're not showing me the door?"

Shannon met her eyes and held them. "Not yet, but I'm going to have to give this a lot of thought."

The other woman nodded solemnly.

That night, instead of putting in some much-needed time on her business's books, as she'd set out to do, Shannon wasted most of the evening mulling over how best to skin this cat that was Curran's case.

Around ten, her mother came into the kitchen to find her daughter drumming her fingers and staring off into space.

"Would you like a cup of tea, dear?"

"As long as you're making one for yourself."

After putting the kettle on, her mom sat down across the table. "Troublesome case?"

"I just can't make up my mind which way to jump on this one," Shannon said disgustedly, "and it's driving me nuts."

"What's the problem?"

"Not so much *what* to do as *who* should do what."

"And the issue is?"

"I've taken on a new operative, and she's turning out to be a bit of a loose cannon. I don't know if I can trust her to exercise good judgment all the time."

"Can you use one of your other people?"

"They're all busy with their own assignments, and I can't move them. To top it off, one is about to leave on vacation. My problem child is the only person I can spare."

The kettle's shrill note interrupted, and Shannon watched her mom prepare the tea, always done with a proper teapot and china cups.

"Which is the more critical thing that needs doing?" the grey-haired woman asked over her shoulder.

Shannon was at least clear on that. "Interviewing people involved with the family at the centre of the case and poking around in a six-year-old murder investigation. That part would be pretty delicate."

"You should handle that." Mother handed daughter a cup and saucer then pushed some bank statements aside to place a small plate of homemade cookies between them. "What's the other job?"

"Go out to California and poke around at an institution that specializes in problems of the rich and famous. It could possibly be dangerous. I might be way off base, but someone employed by them could be responsible for that murder in the east end last week."

"This loose cannon you're speaking about, I once knew a young lady whose father described her in exactly those terms and was constantly worried about her, God rest his soul." The older woman smiled. "And look how she's turned out."

"Yes, and her bad judgment almost got her children killed, not to mention herself and her boyfriend."

"We all make mistakes."

"But in this business, they can turn deadly in a second."

"Just trust your good sense."

"That's been in short supply lately."

Shannon flashed a tight smile as she came to her decision. After Jackie had ticked her boss off this morning, it was certain she would be doubly careful next time out. But what if she weren't?

ᒍᔨᑉᐧᒍᑊᑉᐧ

As she sat at the kitchen table in her tiny apartment that night, Jackie felt like crawling into a hole and dying. She couldn't remember having endured such a bad day in a long, long time.

With a bottle of beer getting warm on the table in front of her, Jackie sat thinking about what had happened that morning – and why.

She could have sworn she'd put aside the traumas of her childhood, but today's outburst had shown that to be a crock. Where had it come from? Her mouth had been in gear before she'd even had a chance to realize what she was saying.

The most logical explanation was the way Olivia had been taken advantage of, since she was incapable of defending herself. Because of her own background, that sort of thing had always made Jackie's blood boil. Coupled with the fact that her boss seemed to be blindly accepting of what the cops had concluded about Olivia's brother's murder, Jackie had just lost it.

What really frightened her was that she had no control over it.

Picking up the beer, she turned it in her hand, staring but not seeing it, then swallowed a mouthful. It tasted like cat piss. She slammed the bottle down, then swept it off the table, where it shattered all over the floor.

"Ah, fuck it!" she said and put her forehead down on her arm.

A few minutes later, her cell phone rang. Retrieving it from her coat pocket, she flipped it open. "Yeah?"

"Jackie, it's Shannon. Is your passport up-to-date?"

CHAPTER 11

It felt quite strange being back in my house, knowing that numerous strangers had trooped through it in my absence. Everything in the kitchen was exactly the way I'd left it, though, including the carton of half and half, which reeked and came out as lumpy sludge when I dumped it into the sink.

While getting my drums out of the car, I ran into Bennett, who was just arriving home, a different beautiful lady on his arm. What was this guy's secret?

"Andy! I was wondering when you'd show up again." Turning to his lady friend, he handed her his keys. "Karen, how about going inside and getting comfortable? I'll only be a minute."

"Don't be long," she said.

"How'd you make out with Howard?" Bennett asked.

Howard Heller was the lawyer he'd hooked me up with when the police decided they wanted to pry into my life.

"He did the job," I answered, weary of everything and aware Bennett wanted to know more. "Thanks for your help. Now, if you'll excuse me."

He clapped me on the back. "Sure, sure. Anyway, I have to be getting inside," he added.

Back in the kitchen, I took just about everything out of the fridge and dumped it in the garbage. Tonight, I'd order out and do a big shopping trip in the morning.

Later, I poured myself a large snifter of brandy that I'd bought on the way home and sat in the living room, lonely and very blue. None of my favourite musical companions – Coltrane, Brownie, Lennie Tristano – had anything to say to me.

By ten o'clock, tired of sitting in the dark, I went upstairs, another large brandy in my hand. Warning voices told me I shouldn't be doing this, but tonight I felt I had to. Instead of going to my own room, I went to Olivia's and lay down on the mattress on the floor. With her reading lamp focused on the wall behind me, I looked up at her starry sky, arms under my head. By some trick, she'd managed to make the stars seem like they were twinkling, or maybe that was the effect of too much brandy. I didn't know, and I didn't care.

For tonight, it was enough that they twinkled.

Next morning, I woke up in my own bed with a head the size of a bass drum, and a throbbing backbeat to drive the point home. Before taking the pledge, I'd woken up many mornings feeling like this, not sure how I'd gotten into bed. Somehow, back then it hadn't seemed quite so bad. I thought that it was because I was out of practice, but knew I could never go down that path again.

If anything could be said to have sent Sandra looking for comfort with another man, it would have been that. The really ironic thing about the collapse of our marriage was that I'd stopped drinking a good six months before it had happened.

Shortly after ten, Shannon phoned. "I'm at the airport, waiting to board a plane for New York. Jackie is heading out to California later today. I figure I'll be gone two, maybe three days."

"And Ms Goode?" I answered in what I thought was a neutral tone voice, but she immediately sussed out the way I felt.

"Look, Andy, that incident yesterday was unfortunate, but I now know where she's coming from. I don't want to go into it, but there are good reasons for her overreaction. Her job on the west coast is just to sniff around the place where Olivia is being held, nothing more. We can trust her to do that."

"Have you looked at Sunnyvale's website?"

"Actually, I've only had time to look at a few downloaded pages. It's at the top of my to-do list."

"After I left your office yesterday, I went over to my bass player's house, and we looked at pretty well everything on the site. We don't think this is the place for Olivia to be. Their approach seems positively cultish in some ways. You should check it out."

She sounded embarrassed when she answered, "Okay, I have my laptop with me, and I'll do that at my first opportunity. Thanks for the heads up."

"Good hunting."

"You'll be hearing from me."

"I'd appreciate that."

Late in the morning, the other two members of the trio showed up for rehearsal with yet another singer to audition. She was better than the one we'd used on the weekend, but still a far cry from Olivia. Ronald had stupidly told her about what had taken place on my front porch, and she seemed clearly uneasy. After her departure, we kicked around the idea of taking on a sax or trumpet player instead of a new vocalist but couldn't come to a decision.

Dom, at my request, had brought copies of the local newspapers' coverage of Maggie's death. After they left, I opened a can of pop, took the papers to the living room and went through everything. There was not much that I hadn't heard already, but it amazed me how much my neighbours knew of the comings and goings at my house – and I'm not talking about just the old lady next door.

A plan had been formulating in my mind since the day before. My hired guns were off doing their things, but one piece was being left out of the puzzle.

What had Maggie known that the murderer didn't want getting out?

♪♯♠·♪♭♩·

Carolina had borrowed her mother's Mercedes to take Jackie out to the airport, and that was proving to have been a bad idea.

Her mother had been late getting home with the car, Carolina had been even later getting down to Jackie's apartment in Parkdale, then they'd found the Gardiner at a dead stop right across the bottom of the city. Forced to take back streets they really didn't know in Etobicoke, Jackie was literally chewing her nails as the minutes ticked away. Carolina, as always, seemed completely unconcerned, talking away as she drove at a more sedate pace than the situation demanded.

Jackie felt like smacking her in the head, chucking her in the back seat and taking over behind the wheel to make some actual time. It would be a total disaster if she wasn't on this flight. She knew her job counted on it.

Finally, she'd had enough. "Carolina, just shut up and drive like you mean it. My plane leaves in little more than an hour."

Her friend looked shocked by the outburst. "I'm going as fast as I can."

"Are you? At this rate, we might as well turn around and go home. We're not going to make it!"

"And you're saying it's my fault?"

"Damned right I am!"

An odd expression flicked across Carolina's face. "Well, in that case..."

She went through the next stop sign as if it wasn't there. She ran the next two lights, honking and flashing her lights to warn people.

Glancing at the speedometer, Jackie saw that they were going along Dixon Road at nearly one hundred clicks.

"Are you nuts? You're going to get us pulled over!"

"And you're going to say next, 'And then where will we be?' Problem is, you have no faith in the power of good karma."

"What the hell are you talking about?"

"I had a dream this morning that I'd get you to the airport on time, and that you wouldn't thank me."

Jackie knew enough to just shut up and hold on tight.

Carolina was weaving in and out of traffic, and miraculously, everyone was getting out of her way. By the time they took a squealing left turn into the airport, the car only barely on its inside wheels, Carolina had run five lights and broken at least half a dozen other laws of the Ontario Highway Traffic Act.

Once in the airport proper, Carolina floored the car. Not one RCMP cruiser made an appearance, and only a couple of people looked up as they screeched to a halt outside Terminal One.

"Told you," Carolina said, "and you've still got fifty-five minutes!"

"Hell with that," Jackie said as she reached into the back seat to grab her suitcase and backpack. "I'm outta here!"

She was through the doors and twenty feet into the terminal before she realized that she hadn't thanked her friend for the lift. *How the hell does she do that?* Jackie wondered as she searched for the ticket counter.

They were already boarding passengers when she eventually raced up to the gate. In a further stroke of luck, the plane hadn't been over-booked, and Jackie still had her seat, but she didn't dare relax until she'd clicked the seat belt around her waist.

The man in the window seat took in Jackie's best jeans, tailored blouse and tidy hair now back to its original dark brown. His smile was overly friendly, so Jackie leaned back, shutting her eyes as the flight attendants began their safety spiel.

Jackie had picked up a cop's flip-up notebook like the one her boss used. It wasn't a "sucking up" purchase, but one designed to make her look more professional to any cops she might meet. She was making notes in it when the refreshment cart came by.

"Can I buy you a drink?" the guy by the window asked.

After the ride to the airport, she felt as if she needed one. "Sure."

When she'd received her Bloody Caesar, the guy patted the seat between them. "Why don't you slide over?"

Jackie didn't have to be much of a detective to see the mark of a recently removed wedding band on the hand patting the seat and wanted no part of that scene, regardless of the fact she wasn't even remotely tempted.

"Actually, I have some work to do," she answered after thanking him for the drink.

"What do you do?"

"I work for the CRA."

"CRA?"

"Canada Revenue Agency. I'm going to Reno to bust a Canadian businessman for tax evasion. This is going to be fun!"

Her comment had the desired effect on the guy; he shrank away and pretended to look out the window. *Maybe I should find out who he is and turn him in*, she thought with a chuckle.

Getting her backpack down from the overhead bin, she spent the rest of the flight to Salt Lake City, then the connecting one to Reno, going through her notes for about the twentieth time.

The air was decidedly cool when she stepped out of the terminal building in Reno, and she was glad she'd packed some heavier clothing.

Her original plan had been to get a good night's sleep at one of the airport hotels, but she was so wired from actually being out in the field that she decided to drive through to Portola, which was only an hour away. The night was clear, and she had plenty of time to watch the desolation of Nevada eventually giving way to the tall pines and hills of the High Sierras of California.

Portola proved to be pretty small and a bit rough around the edges, at least along the highway.

I should fit right in, Jackie thought as she pulled into a gas station. She pumped a couple of bucks worth of gas and went inside to pay. A scrawny kid with pimples and an attitude was behind the counter.

"Know of a good place I can get a room for the night?" Jackie asked.

"I got room in my bed," he smirked.

Beginning to feel tired and a bit cranky, Jackie fired back, "Won't your mommy have something to say about that?"

"Fuck you."

"Not a chance," she leaned forward and exaggeratedly made note of the name on his tag, "Brian. Now are you going to tell me the name of a place to stay or not?"

"There's a motel back on the right down the road," he said grumpily. "You'll like it. It's nice and cheap."

Adding a bag of Fritos to her purchase, Jackie paid and left.

The kid was right: the place was rather rundown but the room was reasonably clean, and she'd slept in worse places.

Setting her watch's alarm to seven thirty, she stripped, took a shower and climbed into bed, suddenly weary.

Tomorrow morning would find her poking her nose into Sunnyvale's private business.

♪♯♪·♪♭♪·

Shannon landed at Westchester County Airport right on schedule. Turbulence had made the trip from Toronto on the small plane way more exciting than she would have liked. Even smooth flights made her uneasy, and she'd gripped the seat arms the entire time.

The rental car was ready and waiting, and she was soon on her way to her first interview, a map of greater New York spread out on the seat next to her.

Now she *did* owe Ellen Stein one, something the reporter had reminded her of once again when they'd spoken on the phone that morning.

"You had a quote in one of your articles from Olivia St. James's nanny. I'm heading down to the States to do some nosing around. You don't happen to know how I can reach her?"

"After your call the other night, I pulled out all my notes on the St. James murder, and I've got them right here. Let's see... Her name is Jeffries, Darcy Jeffries. She's retired and living with her people in a small town on the Long Island Sound."

Shannon had her notebook out. "Name?"

"Mamaroneck. Want me to spell it?"

"No, I believe I passed through there a few years back."

Here's to good hunting, Shannon thought as she parked on a side street in an area of mostly old wooden houses and small apartment buildings. Shannon was feeling in a positive mood, since she'd made the complicated thirty-minute drive with nary a mistake.

Obviously, this part of town would be considered the "other side of the tracks", but the address she walked up to was a two-storey wood frame house that was freshly painted and tidy. The entire front yard was a garden, already with a good showing of spring bulbs.

A young black woman answered the bell.

"I'm here to see Darcy Jeffries."

The woman smiled. "That's my granny. She's in the back garden. Come on through."

The rear of the house had a porch extending its narrow width, and the backyard contained a postage stamp-sized lawn surrounded by fruit trees and tilled earth waiting for vegetables to be planted.

In the middle of the groomed grass on a chaise lounge sat a tiny, elderly woman wearing a flowered dress and partially covered by a blanket against the chill of the day. In her hand she held a white cloth umbrella to shield her from the sun. Next to her was an empty lawn chair.

"Granny, here's your guest from Canada," the young woman said.

Darcy Jeffries held out her hand. "Please excuse me if I don't get up. It's not so easy getting these old bones to move any more." She smiled. "And please take a seat. Would you like some tea?"

Shannon didn't feel in need of tea but decided it would be rude to decline. "I think I might enjoy a cup."

"Suzanne, honey, would you bring out tea? Please use the best china for our guest!"

As the younger woman went back into the house, Darcy Jeffries looked at Shannon for a long moment. "I haven't talked about my poor little dove for many years," she said in a voice that was weak and quavered slightly, "but not a day passes when I don't think of her. Why have you come?"

As usual, in these sorts of situations, Shannon was flying by the seat of her pants, well aware that one wrong step could bring an interview to a halt. It was always best to go in with a goal, but to feel your way along to it, rather than sticking to a prearranged agenda.

"The reporter who gave me your name said you knew Olivia well."

"Well? I was with her from the moment she came home from the hospital! Mrs. Lydia entrusted me with the care of that child, and I took my duties seriously. I do not think anyone knew Miss Olivia better than I."

"Will you tell me about her?"

Shannon heard pretty much what she expected to, given the old woman's obvious devotion. Her words painted a picture of a happy, inquisitive child in her early years, but prone to daydreaming. Her schoolwork wasn't particularly distinguished, but this was due more to inattention than poor mental acuity.

"All that child was interested in was drawing and singing. Her parents refused to see it, but she was cut out for the artistic life. I still have some of her pictures in the house if you'd like to see them."

Tea was served with some marvellous homemade ginger cookies. "My favourites," the old lady smiled as she held out the serving plate.

Picking up the conversation again, Shannon said, "But something happened."

"My land, something did indeed. It was a great tragedy. Poor, poor Mrs. Lydia, and my poor angel for having to witness it."

"You weren't there?"

"I was just inside the house, talking with the butler. Miss Olivia was standing on the steps waiting for her momma. She was growing into quite the independent young lady at the time. Her parents didn't like her being out of the house by herself, even if it was only on the steps, you know. They fretted so!"

"So what happened?"

"The outside door was open, and I heard the squeal of tires and a muffled thump. For a moment I feared that something had happened to Miss Olivia, but then I heard her scream, and we both came to the door. It was an awful sight! I can see it to this day. Miss Olivia was in the street holding her momma's poor, broken body and screaming enough to make you fear for her sanity."

"I understand she was much changed afterwards."

"Wouldn't you be?"

"Certainly, but perhaps I should have said, how did she change?"

The old woman thought for a moment. "Moody. Daydreamed more than ever, poor lamb. Her drawings became darker, more angry. And she stopped singing. Only person she'd sing to was her daddy, and then he practically had to beg her."

"I don't know how to bring this up more delicately, but there are reports of drug use."

For a long moment, Shannon wasn't sure whether she'd blown it, but there had been no sidestepping the issue. Mrs. Jeffries looked up at seagulls circling overhead. Nearby, a train raced through town, and someone leaned on their car horn.

Finally, the old woman fixed a hard gaze on Shannon. "Why do you want to know about these things?"

"I'm trying to help her. You have to believe me about that."

"Those are easy words to say."

"But they are true, nonetheless."

"What is the reason you came to see me? You dodged that question earlier."

"As I told you on the phone, I'm a private investigator, and I have a client in Toronto who is interested in her case."

She waggled a wrinkled finger. "You're still skating around your answer, young lady."

Shannon smiled. "My client is a musician. There was a singer in his band. She was a street person. No one knew anything about her. It's turned out that she was Olivia St. James."

"But that's impossible! Miss Olivia is in California, locked away in that horrible institution."

"We don't know all the details about what happened, but it appears she escaped and made her way to Toronto."

"Is she there now? How is she? Oh glory be, is she better?"

"The answer to all three of your questions is tied up in why I'm here. Two men came and took her away. She apparently went willingly. Again, we don't know for certain, but she's back at Sunnyvale now. As to how she is, I really can't answer that."

"This is all very startling, but you have given me hope, my dear, and for that, I will be frank with you.

"After the death of her poor momma, I'm afraid that Miss Olivia went rapidly downhill. She still had friends she would socialize with back then. They turned out to be very bad people. Being around her as I was, I couldn't help but see that something was wrong. Finally, I discovered some pills in her sock drawer and some marijuana."

"What did you do?"

"I confronted her. I told her it would break her daddy's heart to know, so I wouldn't tell him, but she had to stop with this immediately. She cried and carried on some, but she agreed. I later found out that all she did was hide it better."

"Did her father notice anything different?

"You would have had to be blind not to see it. She told him she was depressed."

"Did he seek any psychological help for her?"

"Yes, but I don't think it helped much, and Mr. Bernard's attention had strayed by that time."

Even though Shannon figured she knew the answer, she asked, "Why was that?"

The old woman's disgust was apparent on her face even before she spoke. "Because he had taken up with *that* woman!"

"You're speaking of Maxine St. James, his second wife."

"The very one. I don't like to speak ill of the dead, but never did Mr. Bernard make a bigger mistake than to get involved with her."

"Please tell me about her."

"What is there to tell? She came in and took over. She is a very strong-willed woman."

"So you didn't like her."

"I don't think anyone on staff did. She is focussed on herself and herself alone. She made life...difficult."

"Did Olivia get along with her?"

"She did and she didn't. By the time Mrs. Maxine came along, my girl was growing more and more detached. Her stepmother, of course, figured she knew what was best for Olivia, changed psychiatrists, but not much good came of it."

Now came the really sticky part. "Were you there the night Olivia's brother died?"

Darcy Jeffries got very emotional and couldn't speak for several minutes. Shannon got up and tried to comfort her, but her efforts were waved away.

The young girl stepped out the back door, obviously having kept an eye on her grandmother. "Is everything all right?"

"Yes, Suzanne," the old woman answered. "We're just digging around in some bad old memories."

Shannon had poured more tea, and the old woman gratefully took a sip. "You're so kind."

"I'm sorry to have to bring it up, but it's, well, it's important."

"I understand." Darcy took another sip of tea. "That was the worst day of my life, with the exception of when my Clement passed away so long ago. Miss Olivia's tragedy, now that's much fresher in my mind.

"What is there to say? The family was in Florida for the holidays, even though Mrs. Maxine was really the only one who wanted to be there. She would have got rid of me by then if she could have, but Mr. Bernard insisted that his daughter needed me. I'd stopped being her nanny by then, of course, and had become more like a maid to her. To be honest, I felt he wanted me to keep an eye on her. I guess on that sad, sad night, I didn't watch her closely enough."

Now was the moment. "You had to have heard the whispering, maybe even the police spoke to you about it: do you think it's possible Olivia St. James murdered her brother?"

"You do get to the point, young lady."

"I'm sorry to have been so blunt."

"No, no, that's quite all right. Old ladies tend to go on sometimes." Darcy Jeffries wouldn't look at Shannon while she answered. "At first, even though I couldn't say it out loud, I thought she might have done it. Her drawings and paintings had been growing more hateful for several months. I didn't enjoy looking at them any longer.

"After they took her away, it was my job to pack all her belongings away for storage, and I found something."

"What?"

"A journal. I'd never seen her with it, but since I'd confronted her about the drugs, we hadn't been so close. I guess she decided to confide to empty pages rather than to her old Darcy. Anyway, it was hidden in the back of her closet."

"And what did the journal say?"

"Many, many hateful things. I don't like to think about most of it."

"I'm sorry, but it might really help to know."

Her face looked pained as she began speaking. "First of all, Miss Olivia hated herself. She felt she was to blame for her momma's death. She could have called out or run to her, pushed her out of the way. She *saw* that car coming for her. That's what she said. She also knew that heroin was driving a wedge between herself and her family."

"Heroin *is* a pretty major drug to be taking."

"Perhaps she used it to dull the pain, but why didn't she come to someone who loved her, come to *me* for help?" Her face crumpled in anguish. "I would have done *anything* for that child!"

"The last entry was the night before her brother was...her brother died. Miss Olivia felt that everyone was leaving her, that she would literally be left all by herself. She blamed Mrs. Maxine. She said things about her stepmother that make me blush just to think of them. I don't know where she learned about things like that!"

"What happened to the journal?"

She looked down at her hands. "I don't know."

"Are there friends of hers whom I can speak to, people she may have confided in?"

"There were bad folk she 'hung out' with very occasionally, but somebody you or I might call a friend? Not really. She preferred being by herself. I think that contributed to her problems. I even spoke to Mr. Bernard about it once. He told me not to worry."

"So, after reading this journal, you felt Olivia did not murder her brother?"

"That's right."

"Why?"

"Because there were many beautiful things in it, as well. They were surrounded by filth, but even a beautiful flower can grow in a dung heap. It was as if my poor darling was at war with herself." The sun had gone behind a cloud, and the woman shivered, "I'm afraid it's getting late, and an old lady like me needs her nap in the afternoon."

"You've been most generous with your time."

Shannon got to her feet, then helped the old woman to hers. By the side of the chaise were two canes. Mrs. Jeffries leaned on one, but the detective also offered her arm as they made their way slowly to the house.

"I have one more question for you: does the name Margaret Springfield mean anything to you, or Maggie?"

Mrs. Jeffries shook her head. "Why do you ask?"

"We think she also left Sunnyvale when Olivia did."

"I'm sorry. I never heard that name before." As they got to the porch, she looked up at Shannon and asked, "And you say my little dove was singing in a band?"

"Yes, and I've heard a recording. It is very, very good."

"I would dearly love to hear that!"

"I'll send you a copy as soon as I get back to Toronto."

Once in the kitchen, Mrs. Jeffries sat heavily on a chair, clearly taxed. "Where are you going to next, dear?"

"New York City. I'm hoping to speak with Mrs. St. James."

Darcy's expression became very hard. "Would you ask her for me where *she* was when young Mr. Bernard was murdered? I told the police they should ask her that, but you know what it's like. Who listens to an old Negro woman?"

CHAPTER 12

Just before leaving the Jeffries' house in Mamaroneck, the old woman decided that the P.I. should speak with the St. James's long-time butler, who lived nearby. Since it was barely mid-afternoon, this seemed like a good idea. Shannon could tackle her New York itinerary the next day.

A quick phone call got it all set up. James Davis would see her as soon as she could get there.

"Jim can certainly give you more up-to-date information than I can," Mrs. Jeffries said at her door. "He's a good man, but be truthful with him. He doesn't suffer deception lightly, especially where his former employers are concerned."

Shannon was now threading her way back across Westchester County to Tarrytown. This time she wasn't so lucky. Between traffic and confusing road signs, she managed to get lost once and almost ended up crossing the Hudson River on the Tappan Zee Bridge. To avoid that, she had to make a white-knuckle cut across two lanes at the last minute, barely making the exit ramp in time.

James Davis was living in a retirement home off the town's main street and right down by the river. The sun was getting low against the hills rising from the opposite shore, lighting up the water and dazzling Shannon's eyes as she crossed the small lobby. A tall, grey-haired black man in a three-piece suit and spit-polished shoes rose from one of the couches when she told the person behind the desk why she was there.

"It's me you're looking for, ma'am," he said, his voice deep and rich.

Shannon took a few steps, holding out her hand, then watched as it disappeared into one of the biggest hands she'd ever seen. "Shannon O'Brien. Thank you for seeing me."

"James Davis, but you be sure to call me Jim, young lady. Everyone around here does, right, Shirley?" he said, winking at the woman behind the front desk. "I thought we might have some coffee in the dining room. It won't be busy for another hour and I'd like you to see my river."

"Oh, it's your river?"

"I've lived by or near the lordly Hudson all my life, so I feel like I own a little part of it."

By that time they'd entered the dining room, and the view of the river was truly magnificent. Davis helped Shannon into a seat with practised form.

"Now what do you think? Isn't she beautiful?"

"Absolutely. The river is quite wide here."

"This is the Tappan Zee. The area was settled by the Dutch. They used to catch some big fish out there, even sturgeon in years past."

A waitress came over.

"Coffee, please, Irma, for my guest and myself."

As she walked away, Davis confided in Shannon, "I still haven't gotten used to not getting it myself." When the coffee was served, he took a sip, then said, "I want to make it clear to you that the reason I've agreed to speak with you is mostly because of my long acquaintance with Mrs. Jeffries."

Mostly? Shannon thought. *That's a very interesting choice of words.*

She didn't pursue it, however, not wanting to jeopardize the voluntary interview. Sometimes she missed being a cop and being able to throw her weight around a bit when needed.

"So what is your visit all about?"

Shannon had decided to use her digital recorder so that her mind would be more free to frame questions and watch for small nuances in facial expressions and body language.

"Do you mind?" she asked, indicating the recorder. He nodded his assent, so the detective began her gentle interrogation. "You worked for the St. James family."

"Two months shy of sixty-five years." At Shannon's obviously surprised expression, he added, "My daddy got me a job with the St. Jameses when I was fifteen. I went on to serve as their butler for over forty years."

"That's an impressive length of time."

Davis nodded and took another sip. "You mentioned something on the phone about Miss Olivia."

Shannon laid out the story of the singer at the Green Salamander who turned out to be Olivia St. James, leaving out the part about her friend's murder.

Davis listened intently, nodding on occasion, but not interrupting. "And you're sure this was Miss Olivia?"

"Absolutely, but it took some digging to discover her identity. It came as quite a shock to my client. She would never tell him anything about herself."

"It comes as quite a shock to *me*. Does the family know?"

"That's something I can't answer. According to the institution itself, she is there and has never left. I know otherwise. If you want my opinion, now that they've got her back, they're trying to cover up the fact that one of their patients was missing for over six months. What can you tell me about Olivia's, ah, troubles?"

Davis nodded. "I've tried to put that whole awful year out of my mind. First Master Bernard, then Miss Olivia and finally Mr. Bernard. The whole family just crumbled in front of our eyes." He shook his head sadly.

"I've got Mrs. Jeffries' opinions and views on the family, especially about Olivia, and I was hoping you'd give me yours. I'd especially like to know what's been going on since she was sent to Sunnyvale."

"Anything I say would be two years out of date. I've had no contact with them since I retired."

"I need any information I can get."

"What is it you're looking for?" he asked.

"To be honest, I really don't know yet."

"Darcy Jeffries has told you that she doesn't think Miss Olivia murdered her brother. Is that it?"

"I'm keeping an open mind on everything. All I want is your input."

"I think that you should know that Darcy was let go right after the murder. She'd been with the family for over twenty years. I guess they felt someone had to take the blame, in a small way, for what happened. But the firing has weighed heavily on her ever since. It might have coloured what she's told you."

"Fair enough."

"Why don't you just ask me questions, and I'll answer them as I see fit, okay?"

Shannon nodded. "Would you describe Olivia to me? I'm looking for a gut reaction. Don't think too much, just talk."

Davis ignored her and looked out the window at the Hudson. Over to the left, the bridge, a huge, brooding presence when seen from up close and below, dominated the scene.

"She was...is a very complicated person. I personally found her strange, even as a child."

"In what way?"

"She kept to herself a lot but didn't seem unhappy. She constantly drew and sang, and often seemed to be in a fog, quite frankly. I don't know what her parents expected from her, but they weren't happy about her lack of application to her studies. She didn't have many friends.

"Then there was the horrible death of her mother. I can see now it was the defining moment in her life. After that, everything seemed to fall apart for her. It must have been tough, but her father, in his own grief, was very distracted."

"How did she change?"

"You spoke about all this with Darcy Jeffries?"

"Yes, I did."

"You have to understand, Ms O'Brien, that the St. James family was very good to me over the years, and I still owe them a great deal of loyalty. Darcy doesn't feel quite the same as I do."

"I know that she has a problem with the current Mrs. St. James, but her loyalty to Olivia is certainly great. She confirmed what I'd already heard from other sources about the drug use, if that's why you're hesitating."

Davis looked down at his empty coffee cup. The waitress was nowhere to be seen.

"There is that, yes. As I said, Miss Olivia kept to herself. That's not quite the right way to put it. It's more that she was secretive. No one knew about the drugs for quite a long time, and they might never have if it wasn't for the time she overdosed."

This was something new. "And how old was she?" Shannon asked, as if her recollection of this event had failed.

"Let's see, she would have been seventeen. Her brother found her collapsed in her bathroom. The doctor figured she'd gotten a supply of heroin that was stronger than she was used to. I heard all this from Mr. Bernard. He came to me because he didn't know who else to talk to."

"You must have felt honoured."

"Over the years we'd become a little more than employer and butler. I'd known him all of his life. The poor man was horrified, of course, and blamed himself for not seeing it."

"It was all hushed up very well."

"That was one thing wrong with that family, if I may be so bold. Except for the week she had to be hospitalized, there was no discussion of Miss Olivia being treated anyplace other than home. But they not only hushed things up to the outside world, they hushed it up among themselves. What happened to Miss Olivia was never mentioned by the family in my hearing. It was as if it had never happened."

"They got her help, of course."

"Certainly. Now that I knew about her difficulties, I kept a very careful watch, and there were several times I thought she seemed to be 'under the influence', shall we say. I couldn't get any proof, and Mrs. Jeffries never saw the girl without clothes any more, so she couldn't check for needle marks. She always wore long sleeves and jeans or slacks, if that's any indication."

Shannon thought that it might be. "How did Olivia get along with her stepmother?"

"Again, I can't really say. Outwardly, things seemed fine, although they hardly ever spoke. The only time I personally heard them have words was over her wanting to talk to her daddy and Mrs. Maxine saying that he couldn't be disturbed."

"Do you remember what was said?"

"You have to realize that Miss Olivia was maybe nineteen at the time, and a lot of children have trouble with parents at that age."

"What did she say?"

"Miss Olivia said she was unhappy with the way her stepmother treated her. She didn't want to be told when she could and could not see her own father. Actually, I was shocked to hear her speak this way. She was usually so docile and quiet."

"Tell me about Olivia's mother, the first Mrs. St. James."

"She was a loving, caring parent and wife, always ready to help others. Mrs. Lydia was the person responsible for me getting more education, and for that I will always be grateful. It was a real tragedy when she died. We all suffered from that loss."

"And the current Mrs. St. James?"

Davis looked troubled, and Shannon felt that his professed loyalty to the family might be getting in the way. It also meant that she really needed to hear the former butler's assessment.

"Believe me," she said as earnestly as she could, "that anything you say will be in the strictest confidence. You have my absolute word on that."

"Please don't take this wrongly, but I don't know you."

"I understand. Is there anything you can tell me about her?"

"Mrs. Maxine is a very complicated person, very capable, intelligent, but she can also be very hard. She is not afraid to say what she thinks, and sometimes this creates friction in her relationships with people."

"She was originally a lawyer, I believe."

"She still is, although she doesn't take on clients. I do believe she manages the St. James holdings as well as Mr. Bernard did and probably better than his son would have."

"Did she love her husband?"

"Now that is an odd question! Of course she did. She nursed him herself in his last months, and made his passing as easy as possible."

"Was she a good wife?"

"I believe she was exactly what Mr. Bernard needed when he married her." Davis got to his feet. "I don't want to seem rude, but there is a TV show I like to watch at this time every day." He smiled. "For so many years, my time was very seldom my own, and I am enjoying having that freedom for my remaining years."

Shannon also got up and shook his hand. "I appreciate you meeting with me. You've been very generous with your thoughts. One last question, though?"

"Certainly."

"Do you think Olivia St. James could have murdered her brother?"

He frowned. "She was certainly acting irrationally those last months. Some of it was no doubt due to her father's worsening medical condition. He didn't hide the fact that he had only a short time to live. Miss Olivia was taking drugs again, although where she was getting them was a mystery. She barely left the house, and never without being accompanied by either Mrs. Jeffries or the chauffeur."

"Whose idea was that?"

"Mine. I thought it for the best."

"Do you think Mrs. St. James would speak to me?"

"I doubt that very much. Now, if you'll excuse me."

He turned and left the room.

Getting behind the wheel of her rental car again, Shannon felt that there had been a lot more information to glean. It was her experience that servants heard and saw far more than their employers realized and far less than they would admit. James Davis had struck her as an intelligent and proud man who would have been an exemplary butler, and therefore probably knew pretty well everything that had gone on in that house.

But he was still far too good an employee to talk about all of it.

Before starting the engine, Shannon used her cell phone to call her office for messages.

"Let's see, boss," Janet said as she noisily flipped through some pages.

"Not you, too," Shannon answered wearily.

"Okay, b... I mean, Shannon. A Mrs. Jeffries called to say she'd like you to call her. And Jackie got off okay."

Before making the call, Shannon decided to find a place to stay for the night. It didn't take long, being so close to the New York State Thruway, but she did have to pay more than she wanted.

Once inside the room, she got on the phone.

"Thank you for calling back," Darcy Jeffries said in a tired voice. "This afternoon I was not completely truthful with you. I was brought up to regard 'untruths' as a very bad thing."

"Mrs. Jeffries, you shouldn't—"

"No, no. Please hear me out. I know that you're attempting to help my angel. Heaven knows, she needs the help of someone." She sighed loudly. "I'm too old to do much, but that doesn't mean I should do nothing."

"Is this about Olivia's journal?"

The old woman gasped then, surprisingly, chuckled. "I guess I didn't do very well trying to fool you. Why didn't you say something?"

"I figured I could always swing by later on. Do you know where the journal is?"

"I have it. I can't tell you why I took it, and I haven't looked at it since – until after you left today. I think you should have it, even though my entire family is against it. I've also spoken to James, and he's not happy about it, either. He doesn't want to stir up any more trouble for the family. But I can be a stubborn old woman when I want to be." She chuckled again.

"May I come over to get it now?"

"Tomorrow morning would be better."

"I guess that would work for me," Shannon answered, not happy about the delay. "I'll be there at nine a.m."

Later, at quarter past eleven, Shannon laid her laptop next to her on the bed, leaned back against the pillows and rubbed her eyes wearily.

For nearly five hours she'd gone through every single page of the Sunnyvale website, then compared it to websites for similar facilities, and what she'd learned left her feeling decidedly uneasy.

Curran was right. Sunnyvale did sound cultish in its approach. They had all sorts of levels that "Seekers" could attain over a course of "study", which included the usual things like group therapy, one-on-one work with their "Teachers", but they also utilized things like "Responsibility Sessions", a term that gave Shannon a chill.

One of the first pages trumpeted, "The core of our program is helping our Seekers to take Complete Responsibility for all their Actions and any Consequences that come as a result. Everyone is expected to follow our very strict Regime at all times. We believe it is our 'tough love' approach that allows everyone entering our program to make progress far exceeding what other facilities are capable of producing. We tackle the most difficult cases and can boast that our graduates' extraordinarily low recidivism rate is second to none."

To Shannon's mind, this did not seem like the sort of place a person like Olivia belonged. Yes, she had some of the types of problems Sunnyvale was set up to handle, but would a drug addiction normally require a six-year stay? Something didn't quite fit here. Jackie's scenario seemed to be taking on more credibility.

After sending emails to Rachel, Robby and Michael, Shannon took a shower and went to bed.

Sleep was a long time coming and was not very restful.

Next morning, arriving early at the Jeffries' house, Shannon found her way blocked by a police car. Her heart sank, and she pounded her hands on the steering wheel in frustration. If anything had happened because of her prying...

This exact scenario had run through her dreams the previous night, and she found herself unnerved. Parking her car a few blocks away, she walked back to the head of the street.

"What's going on?" she asked the cop, even though she could see fire engines ahead on the street.

"There's been a fire overnight. They're cleaning up now, but it will still be a little while."

"I have an appointment with someone at nine o'clock." She gave him the address but dreaded what he'd say.

"Oh, that's just this side of the fire," he answered, taking out his walkie-talkie. "I'll see what's going on for you."

"Thanks."

Shannon couldn't believe she'd caught this break. All the way over, she'd worried that something would have happened overnight. It's one of those things you always see in mystery stories: the detective doesn't jump on a key piece of evidence, and it's destroyed or stolen or people die. Thankfully, that hadn't been the case this time.

The cop finished his conversation and told Shannon she could go down the street.

Neighbours were still out on the street, watching the firemen going through the wreckage at the back of the house two doors down from the Jeffries. Suzanne Jeffries was out in front, talking with a group of women. She turned when she saw Shannon approaching, but her welcoming smile was tentative, at best.

"Looks as if you had a lot of excitement here last night. Was anybody hurt?"

Suzanne shook her head. "Come on inside. Granny is waiting for you."

Mrs. Jeffries was in the living room, watching an old show on TV.

"You had some excitement here last night," Shannon repeated.

"More than I want. Our poor neighbours!"

"Do they know the cause of the fire?"

"Arson," the younger Jeffries said. "Somebody lit a fire under the back porch."

The old lady cackled. "I thought it might have been started because I told you about the journal."

The granddaughter rolled her eyes. "Granny! Isn't that a little—"

"But I fooled 'em," Darcy continued, still smiling. "When we went out to look at the fire, I took the journal with me. Hid it under my coat!"

Suzanne looked at her unhappily.

"They'll probably find it was kids," Shannon said.

"I think it was *her*." She held up a brown leather-bound book about the size of a novel. "This must have something in it she doesn't want us to know."

Shannon pointedly looked at her watch, not willing to let the conversation continue. What the old lady was suggesting was pretty ludicrous. "I really have to be going, Mrs. Jeffries."

"You will keep this very safe?"

"Absolutely, and when I'm done with it, I'll make sure you get it back, if you'd like."

"I want you to give it to Miss Olivia."

"That may not be possible."

"It will be. I feel certain you will succeed." Darcy Jeffries made a point of getting to her feet in order to hand Shannon the journal. "Remember now, I'm counting on you."

Shannon hustled back to her car, still somewhat unnerved, but she had the journal, and perhaps it would have something useful in it. Thinking back to what Jim Davis had said the previous afternoon, she wondered whether something wasn't quite right with Mrs. Jeffries. She was old and perhaps going a bit senile.

Once back in her rental car, Shannon checked for messages. There was one from Janet back in Toronto. "Shan, call me immediately. Something big has come up."

CHAPTER 13

On her first morning in Portola, Jackie was jolted out of a deep sleep by a transport truck driving through her room – at least that was the way it sounded. It had been a mistake to open the window for a little fresh air. Now she understood why the motel had been so inexpensive.

Hopping into the shower, she wasted little time. It was going to be a big day for her.

She dressed in her tightest jeans and a new flannel shirt on which she left the top two buttons open. Well-worn hiking boots finished off her cover as an outdoors type. Looking in the mirror after putting on make-up – no make-up being her general rule – she felt satisfied with the way she looked, but slightly unhappy to be resorting to what she considered cheap tricks. At this point, though, success was the only thing that mattered.

"Ready as I'll ever be," she told her reflection.

Having scoped out Portola from Toronto using Internet maps, she knew exactly where a lot of useful places in town were: stores, cop shop, post office, library. Since the day was looking to be fine and warm, she slung a light jacket over her shoulder and headed out.

Portola wasn't large, but had once been an important railroad town. Most of the shops were located along the state highway or on a short main street that ran south of the old railyard. The pine-covered hills rising up everywhere she looked were quite spectacular, and the air smelled fresh and wonderfully clean after Toronto. Spring had come early, and everything already glowed in soft greens. While the ground was still pretty wet, Jackie couldn't see any traces of snow.

Feeling the need to stretch her legs after the long flight and drive of the day before, Jackie walked around looking for a restaurant, one that served up a good, basic breakfast – and the best in local gossip. She chose Dee's Station Café close to the railyard.

A slender redhead, her hair pulled tightly back, looked up from behind the counter across the back of the room as Jackie threaded her way through the tables.

"Morning."

"It *is* a good morning," Jackie replied confidently.

She found a place at the counter and looked around. The café was about half full, mostly older gents dressed casually. All were giving the newcomer a blatant once over. In keeping with the railroad heritage of the town, one wall was decorated with lots of photos of railroad activity and the picture window at the entrance had a large locomotive model.

"Nice place," Jackie said as she picked up a menu.

The woman poured a cup of coffee and smiled. "Thanks. I'm Dee, by the way."

"Pleased to meet you. I'm Janice."

Even though she really didn't have any sort of accent, Dee immediately made Jackie as a non-local. "Where you from, honey?"

"Lethbridge, Alberta, ma'am," which was close enough to the truth. "I'm just passing through. Going to LA to see what there is to see."

"So what brings you through Portola?"

"I was in Reno for a few days and remembered that I have a friend from university who's around here someplace."

"Whereabouts?"

"A facility called Sunnyvale. Have you heard of it?" Jackie dropped her voice a bit. "Jennifer got herself into some trouble with drugs. Her folks are worth a pile, and they sent her to Sunnyvale for help a couple of months ago. Know anything about it?"

Dee's face became hard to read, but one thing was clear: it wasn't as open and friendly as it had been.

"They're west and south of town a ways. They keep to themselves and don't take kindly to people messing with their business, if you know what I mean. One thing I can tell you for certain, you won't be allowed in to see your friend. No one in their program is allowed visitors, not even family except under special circumstances." She pulled out her order pad. "Now, what'll you have?"

Jackie ordered the breakfast special and ate the rather good meal in silence. The conversations going on around her contained no references to Sunnyvale.

The rest of the morning was spent working her way down the main street, casually asking questions, but always with a slightly altered background story: she was hoping to get a job there, her brother had stayed there, anything but her real reason for asking.

Some of the townsfolk were cautious about talking to a stranger about Sunnyvale. A few were openly hostile about the place, and they provided the more valuable information.

A woman working cash at the local drug store really got herself worked up. "*Those* people, the way they *act*, you'd think they *own* this town. My son works out at the airstrip back along the highway in Beckwourth. A lot of private planes with Sunnyvale people land there. It's all big SUVs and 'stay away from us, boy. We're your betters'!"

"They don't actually say that, do they?"

"As good as!"

"But I've heard that a lot of famous people go there for treatment. They probably want to keep it a secret."

"That don't give anyone the right to lord it over others, does it? Then there's the place itself. You can't hardly get within a mile of it. My son says they got cameras in the woods, and men with dogs. It ain't good for our town."

Jackie paid for her pack of gum and left the store. Time she went up and scoped out Sunnyvale. She knew now that it was no good trying to get in by the front door, and after talking to the woman, going in through the woods would be tricky. Perhaps all the negative things she'd heard had a good explanation.

Perhaps not.

Jackie hadn't been able to find the location of Sunnyvale on any of the online map sites, and the Sunnyvale website only gave a phone number and post office box, so she walked to the town's visitor centre, just past her motel at the east end of town.

She gave a variation of her cover story to the pleasant, older woman on duty inside, who quite happily told her she could find Sunnyvale a few miles out of town on County Road 40.

"You'll see it just past that new hotel, the Chalet View. Runs off to the left down to Clio. Used to be impassable in winter, but the Sunnyvale folks keep it open at least as far as their place now. Sunnyvale's several miles down. Haven't ever been in there, though. Not many of us have."

As Jackie pushed open the little gate in the picket fence in front of the visitor's centre, she caught a break. A large, bright red pickup, looking as if had just been washed and hand-polished, drove right by. On the door in gold letters was the logo and stylized font of Sunnyvale.

She took off running as fast as she could while trying to see where the pickup was going. At the light down the road, it turned left, probably heading for the main street. Jumping in her car, Jackie cut off a cattle truck as she screeched out of the motel's driveway. It was a fingers-drumming-on-the-steering-wheel three minutes before the traffic light allowed her to turn left.

The pick-up wasn't parked on Commercial Street, so she swung by the post office on Gulling, and there it was in the parking lot. Jackie pulled onto a side street and stopped under some trees. From there, she had a good view of the parking lot, with the red pickup right at the back.

Five minutes later, a tall man in boots, jeans, regulation flannel shirt, cowboy hat and aviator-style sunglasses came out the side door and walked to the pickup. He held the mail in one big hand and had a large cardboard box under his arm.

Jackie started her engine, waited a good five seconds before moving, and began following her quarry at a leisurely pace. With so little traffic in town, she had to play it very cool.

The guy made two more stops: at a hardware store Jackie hadn't visited, then backtracking to the café where she'd eaten breakfast. All she could hope was that Dee had gone off duty or wouldn't mention her snooping. The man came out after only a minute, carrying a styrofoam cup.

From half a kilometre behind, Jackie shadowed the red pickup as it drove west on Highway 70. As hoped, it turned south onto County Road 40. Keeping well behind, Jackie followed it down the dirt road.

She traversed several more winding kilometres, splashing through puddles in various places and kicking up gravel if she went too fast. The red truck wouldn't stay clean in this very long. The tall pine trees grew close on both sides, but since the trunks went far up before the branches started and undergrowth was sparse, she got a good view of the surrounding countryside which rose and fell quite steeply. Trees were everywhere, and the road passed no houses she could see. It was a pretty lonely place and perfect for what Sunnyvale required.

Eventually the road dipped, then turned sharply left to descend rapidly. She could see fairly far ahead because of the slope, but there was no sign of the pickup. Instead of stopping, Jackie continued on for another four kilometres, stopped for several minutes where the road widened, then turned around. By the time she traced her way back at a slower rate, fifteen minutes had passed. If he'd suspected anything, the guy would have dropped his guard by now.

Approaching the top of the steep hill where she'd lost the pickup, she slowed and looked around. Just below the crest, well hidden behind some trees, a narrow asphalt drive swung off and disappeared where the road turned down the steep incline. From this direction it was hard to spot, but from the other, nearly impossible, since you'd be looking at the turn. The only marker by the road was a small post, coated with dust but with red and gold stripes clearly painted at the top.

Bingo! she thought.

Continuing back to the highway, Jackie pulled onto the narrow shoulder and consulted the detailed topographical map she'd bought in town. There was no marking for that drive leading off into the bush.

Back in Portola, she went to the library, logged on to a computer and looked at satellite photos of the area. Around six kilometres off the road, she could clearly see a large, nineteen-building facility on the flat bottom of a narrow valley. The topo map told her it was surrounded on all sides by very steep hills, good to observe from, rotten to get up in a hurry.

Four kilometres east of Sunnyvale's drive, she spotted a logging track, heading off into the trees. It would suit her purposes well. Half an hour later, she discovered the track was little more than a light scraping of the sandy soil with a whole lot of water-filled ruts and stones. The bottom of her car scraped ominously in several spots as she backed down it, her idea being that facing out, she could make a quicker getaway if needed.

A kilometre from the road, the track dipped into a gully, effectively hiding her from any eyes.

It was at this point she realized that no one knew where she was. That was downright stupid and dangerous. Once in the heat of the chase, she'd completely forgotten about the need to take care of that safety measure.

Taking a flyer, Jackie pulled out her cell and waited a couple of minutes while it searched vainly for a signal. "Damn!" she said, stuffing it back in her pocket, well aware that any screw-up would mean her job.

Shoving the map into the small pack she'd prepared back in Toronto, Jackie headed into the bush on foot.

She'd just have to make sure she didn't make any mistakes.

An hour and a quarter later, she was lying on her muddy stomach under a bit of scrub, overlooking Sunnyvale, which lay spread out on the valley floor fifty metres or more below her.

It was lucky she'd heard about the surveillance cameras, because she certainly would have stumbled within range of them. They were cleverly hidden high in the trees. One missed camera, and she was toast. The lack of scrub under the trees made approaching the compound doubly hard, and she had spent a lot of the time on her stomach, crawling through mud and the carpet of pine needles.

Her binocs showed manicured grounds, where a few dozen people were strolling around or sitting in groups. The buildings were of varying sizes, and except for the three largest ones, all were a single storey. More ominously, surrounding the place was a tall, chain-link fence with razor wire at the top, the mainstay of Sunnyvale's "superior security". A large grass-covered berm had been constructed inside the fence, concealing it from those within, but also leaving more than enough room to stop somebody from climbing over unobserved – if they decided to brave the razor wire. Poles around the perimeter bristled with further surveillance cameras.

Was it meant to keep the public out or the "Seekers" in?

Scanning the grounds several more times, she noticed there were two distinct sets of clothing. Everyone seemed to be wearing jeans or sweatpants, with runners for footwear, but the shirts or jackets were either red and orange or blue and green, the latter for staff, the former for patients, judging by the numbers. She also saw three big men in reddish-brown pants and jackets. These had to be security.

Over the next three hours, Jackie circled the enclave, always at a safe distance, and always with her eyes and ears open for anything signalling that she'd been detected. They'd probably just escort her away from their property, which seemed to extend several hundred metres from the fence line, judging by the cameras in the trees, but she didn't want to chance that. One look inside her backpack would make it pretty clear she was more than a casual hiker.

Jackie didn't learn a lot more, except that everyone seemed to take part in outdoor exercise at three p.m. Buildings emptied, and roughly one hundred people gathered in a large centre quadrangle. At each corner of it, poles with loudspeakers blasted out directions and music. Although more than two hundred metres away, Jackie could make out the occasional word when the wind blew in her direction.

She spotted three women who could be Olivia, but with all the moving about, Jackie never could manage to see clearly enough to be certain.

She packed it in around four thirty, knowing that darkness descended quickly up in the hills. The last thing she wanted was to be stumbling around in the bush after dark.

Her surveillance hadn't gotten her much in the way of new information, except that if Olivia and Maggie had escaped by scaling that fence, her hat was off to them.

On her way back to town, Jackie kept trying for a phone signal strong enough to use. It wasn't until she was about two kilometres away that she got anything decent. She decided to return to the motel, take a hot shower to get the sweat and dirt off, then phone Shannon to give her the bird's eye lowdown on the little she had – and also to pitch her idea for the next step, one she was sure would upset her boss.

♪♯♪·♪♭♪·

My two hired guns had been gone for twenty-four hours, and I hadn't gotten very far on my own project: Maggie. I'd found out pretty quick when I'd phoned Palmer the day before that the cops only want to speak with you when *they* want to speak with you. Unless you have something they want, don't even bother trying to engage them in any sort of conversation. The Toronto detective had as much as told me that, before hanging up on me.

The papers and TV news had been little help. Their lack of new information led to endless looping of the events on my front porch. The police tape was still up, and that kept most people away, but wackos still had to be chased off the porch and out of my yard at all times of the day and night.

Palmer was *so* helpful when I complained about this. "Hire yourself some security company to keep the curious away. That's the only way to do it."

"But I don't have that kind of money."

"Not my problem."

When it got out that Maggie had been turning tricks, Sandra, of course, went ballistic. "You bring whores to our house?"

"Don't say *our* house," I snapped, "and I didn't bring her anywhere. As a matter of fact, I tried my best to *discourage* her from coming around."

"You weren't very effective, were you? Your own daughter ratted you out on that one! I'll bet your girly was cut from the same cloth."

I felt like throwing the phone through the window but somehow managed to keep my voice steady. "Sandra, you're overwrought, so I'll excuse that. I need help to get through this mess."

"You expect *me* to help?"

"No, I expect you not to make it more difficult than it already is."

That at least got through to her. Up until I'd invited Olivia to live at the house, we'd gotten along reasonably well. Always a control freak, Sandra probably felt I was finally slipping away from her. I know that sounds perverse, considering she'd walked out on me.

"May I talk to Kate?" I asked after a few seconds of silence.

"Yeah, sure, I'll get her." She put down the phone noisily, and I could hear her yell, "Kate! Your dad's on the phone."

The little devil picked it up way too fast not to have been listening to our conversation from the top of the stairs.

"Hi, Daddy? Have you found Olivia yet?"

Whether she was trying to get her mother's goat or was simply being an unaware kid, the phone downstairs was hung up far harder than it needed to be.

"The detective I brought over on Sunday is out looking with one of her assistants. Have you remembered anything else about Olivia that you think she should know? Any help from you might get her back even faster."

The line was silent while Kate thought. "We mostly talked about our painting. She said she was glad I was there to help her with it. She also liked living at our house. She said it was so friendly. That's sort of a weird thing to say, isn't it?"

"I'm writing it down, Katie, and I'll tell P.I. O'Brien."

"It's pretty cool that you have a lady detective working for you, Daddy. All my friends are jealous."

I smiled at that. "I'm going to take you out for burgers and a movie on Sunday. How does that sound?"

"Great! But are you sure Mom will let you? I mean, you should see her whenever a news report comes on. She throws a hairy fit."

"I'll talk to her when we're finished, honey. I think I can make her understand."

"Then we're finished. I'll tell her, okay? Love you, Daddy!"

The Salamander was packed that night, and it wasn't people who'd be disappointed that Olivia wasn't singing, either. Nor were they there to hear our new vocalist, who did the job okay, although she just couldn't hold a candle to Olivia; no one could. They were there to check out the guy who'd found a stiff on his front porch. I've never had so many offers of drinks in my life. If I hadn't been firm in my commitment to stay on the wagon, I could have gone on quite a bender without leaving the club.

"Any news on our AWOL singer?" Dom asked when we had a moment alone.

I really didn't want to tell him very much. He had liked Olivia a lot, teasing her like a kid sister, but I wasn't sure how he'd respond to what Shannon and Jackie had found out about her.

"That investigator you connected me with has sent someone out to look for her at Sunnyvale."

"Yeah, weird place. Hard to think of Olivia being there. Ronald was talking to me about it earlier."

"How does Ronald know about Sunnyvale?"

Dom shrugged. "Search me. You know how he spends half his life on the frigging computer."

Halfway through the third set, two women came in and took an empty table off to the side. Dom pointed them out to me, and it didn't take much perception to peg them as ladies of the night. We did get the odd one in occasionally, looking to dig up a little business on a cold night, but Harry usually gave them the bum's rush pretty quick. He didn't want trouble with the cops. If they came in on the arm of a male, that was a different matter. Those girls were traditionally welcome in a jazz club.

They were staring at me as they talked together. When they noticed that I'd caught on, they didn't look away embarrassed, but their expressions didn't lead me to think they were interested in me in a business sense either.

The last set was mostly instrumental, and Ronald was in the mood to cook. When his interest was piqued, the man could blow with the best of them, and that was a pleasure to be part of. Off the bandstand, the only thing keeping us together was the fact that he hustled gigs, good paying gigs, which made up for most of his multitude of shortcomings. It doesn't cast Dom and me in a very good light, though. I guess people would call us lazy. We'd both be broke if we had to rely on each other for work.

We got a good round of applause after our last tune of the night, and Ronald even acknowledged my drum solo to the audience, a rare occurrence. But it was one of my better efforts. I'd spent the entire afternoon practising to ease my frustration at the way my life was going.

With a towel around my neck, I was putting all my sticks back in the leather bag I use for them, when one of the "ladies" walked up to me.

"You the guy who found that girl on his porch?"

I straightened up, thinking, *Great come-on line.* "Yeah, that's me."

Her companion was right behind. "You got time to talk to us?"

God forgive me, but my first thought was that Sandra was trying to set me up. I actually looked around for a photographer or cop. "May I buy you ladies a drink?"

We went over to the band table. Dom was making an early evening of it, and Ronald had to take our new singer, Julia, home. We'd have a bit of privacy. Loraine took our order with nothing more than a comically raised eyebrow at my companions.

"Now, what can I do for you?" I asked, once the drinks had been served.

"We been talking about this a lot," said the one who'd first approached me. She was a tall, obviously dyed blonde.

Her companion, shorter, with faux red hair and enormous breasts, added, "Yeah. We knew Maggie. We don't want to talk to no cops, but we thought somebody should know what she told us."

CHAPTER 14

"I will expect you at twelve thirty, then, Ms O'Brien. Luncheon will be served, and we can chat."

"Certainly, Mrs. St. James," Shannon said into her cell. "That will work well for me."

She couldn't believe the turn of events. Since leaving Toronto, she'd gotten useful information, certainly, but it wasn't enough to lead to any firm conclusions. Then the one person she really needed to see – and had been told she couldn't – called her office out of the blue, inviting her down to Manhattan for lunch, supposedly to help her understand Olivia's situation with the family.

"I don't want you relying on specious information. That could hurt all of us," she'd said. "Let me set the record straight for you."

Shannon didn't believe for a moment that there wasn't an ulterior motive.

The railroad serving Mamaroneck ran on a raised bed not far from the Jeffries' house. She stopped next to the large, red brick station at ground level, grabbed a timetable and asked directions for someplace nearby where she could get photocopying done. The timing was incredibly tight, but she managed it and got to the platform just as the train rounded the bend.

At Grand Central Station, Shannon flagged a cab, which took her to the St. James mansion on the Upper East Side, just off Third Avenue. Built in the early part of the twentieth century, it was an imposing grey stone building, three storeys tall, now uncomfortably flanked by nondescript high rises. The four steps up from the street were covered with a bright red carpet. This was where Olivia had been brought up.

Hard to imagine a person from such a background begging on Toronto streets.

The bell was answered almost immediately by a large man in a dark, impeccably-tailored suit. Despite this, he looked more like a bouncer than a butler. The quality of the staff had gone downhill since the retirement of James Davis.

"I have an appointment with Mrs. St. James," Shannon said, looking way up.

"You are expected. Please come in."

Relieved of her light spring jacket, shoulder bag and laptop case, she followed the butler into the depths of the house to a room at the back. The front rooms had been all dark woods with heavy draperies, carpets and furniture, but the one for their "informal luncheon" was light, airy and decorated in whites and yellows. The windows provided a view over a small, exquisite backyard, with a redbud in full spring glory at its centre.

The lady of the house, coiffed, manicured and elegantly dressed, rose at Shannon's entry.

"I'm so glad you could come to meet with me," she murmured, extending her hand.

Her grip was firm like a man's, and she held Shannon's eyes for several seconds.

"It's my pleasure," Shannon replied, squeezing even harder.

"Today is so beautiful and warm, I thought the breakfast nook would make a better place for lunch than the dining room."

She picked up a little bell, and a maid appeared, carrying an ice bucket. White wine was poured to accompany a clear broth, then the maid served the main course of lobster crêpes and salad, followed by coffee and miniature pastries. The meal was superb.

While they ate, Shannon's brain was working overtime, trying to observe the smallest details and detect the tiniest nuances in the vapid conversation, which pointedly stayed away from anything to do with the real reason for this meeting. The widow of Bernard St. James II was very beautiful and knew it. Blonde and in her mid-forties, she obviously made a great effort keeping herself trim and fit. Shannon had already learned from Ellen Stein that she hadn't remarried and wasn't seeing anyone. Maybe the super-sized butler was there for reasons other than butling?

After the maid had poured a second cup of coffee for each woman and withdrawn, Mrs. St. James looked across the table. Her deep blue eyes glinted. "I've heard that you're investigating my family."

"From James Davis," Shannon answered, pointedly not posing it as a question.

"As you know, he was with us for almost sixty-five years. He still thinks of himself as a loyal employee."

"Obviously."

"I understand my stepdaughter turned up in your city not that long ago."

"Did you also know that she was nabbed by two bounty hunters and returned to California?"

"Of course. Olivia needs to be in the facility where she was placed. If you've met her, then you know she is a very troubled person." Maxine St. James took another sip of coffee. "I asked you here today to make certain you haven't been getting, ah, *suspect* information and drawing wrong conclusions from that."

Shannon leaned back in her seat. "Why don't you set the record straight then?"

"Olivia, quite frankly, lives in a dream world. Her parents spoiled her completely, and her considerable psychological needs were swept under the carpet. My late husband just could not bear to face the issues."

"But you could."

"Of course. I was not emotionally tied to the problem. After the tragic death of her brother, Olivia's grip on whatever reality she still retained crumbled completely. When I finally convinced Bernard that she needed help we could not provide at home, she was little more than a walking vegetable. Quite sadly, her condition has not improved over the years."

Shannon leaned forward. "Couldn't a portion of her problems be put down to her drug addiction? Surely that situation has improved."

"Ms O'Brien, I am aware of everything you discussed with Jim. To answer you, yes, that has been taken into account."

"Mrs. St. James, what exactly is wrong with Olivia?"

"Well, not being a trained psychologist, I can only tell you what I've been told. She is in a dissociative state. The doctors we brought in – and only the best of the best, incidentally – feel that the horrible experience of seeing her birth mother killed in front of her eyes drove her into this state. Her brother being murdered just put the final nail in the coffin."

"Is she examined by these experts on a regular basis to see if there have been any changes?"

"Of course. They travel to California once a year to examine her. In the six years my stepdaughter has been at Sunnyvale, there has been no change in her condition. As a matter of fact, they feel she's deteriorating."

"Really? That wasn't the experience of the people who met and interacted with her in Toronto. Yes, she did seem rather odd in many ways, but she managed to hold down a job singing in a band and was quite good at it, I've been told."

Maxine's eyes narrowed. "That is very encouraging news indeed. It would be wonderful to be able to welcome her back home – *if* what you say is actually the case." It was abundantly obvious from her gestures and tiny changes in her expression and voice that the *last* thing this woman wanted was to welcome her stepdaughter home.

It was at that point that Shannon's thoughts on where this case was leading took a dramatic turn. "Does the name Margaret Springfield ring any bells?"

Maxine's look of puzzlement was nearly convincing, but a slight change in her eyes gave her away. "I can't say that it does."

"She was also at Sunnyvale. Margaret was the woman who helped Olivia escape."

Bingo! Shannon thought. *That was a bit of information you didn't know I had.*

Shannon had to hand it to her. This woman was darned slick, but that last volley of information had definitely caught her off guard.

Maxine got to her feet. "You'll have to excuse me, but I have several appointments this afternoon. Based on what you've told me, I will certainly be following up with Sunnyvale."

Shannon rudely stayed put. "I'd like to know when you were aware that Olivia had checked out of Sunnyvale."

"Well, frankly, this is a bone of contention. Naturally, they don't want it widely known that a patient had, ah, left. They neglected to inform me for nearly two weeks. I've taken the situation up with their directors, and we have yet to reach a settlement."

Her parting salvo fired, Shannon also rose. "Thank you so much for a lovely meal – and the information."

As they walked down the main hall, Maxine said, "We are a quiet family, Shannon – may I call you Shannon? – and we value our privacy. I will certainly act on what you've told me. Please let us handle things from here. I appreciate your concern for poor Olivia, but it's really best that way."

The butler helped Shannon on with her jacket and handed back her bag and the laptop case. With one on each shoulder, she ventured out onto the street.

"The least they could have done was call me a cab," she grumbled.

Walking towards Park Avenue where she had her best chance of flagging one, she looked up at the trees, already showing quite a bit of leaf compared with Toronto.

At Lexington, she was about to cross when someone pushed her very hard in the centre of her back, causing her to crash painfully forward onto her knees. Her addled wits registered that the strap of her shoulder bag was being sliced by a knife, then the thief was off.

Gathering her wits, Shannon managed to yell out, "Stop! Thief!"

Not very original, but it did get action. A man partway up the block had seen the whole thing, and as the thief ran by, he calmly stuck out his foot and sent the bastard sprawling. Shannon's bag spilled open from the force of the impact, spewing its contents all over the sidewalk. By this time, she was struggling to her feet and registered that the thief had grabbed something. He was off like a flash, disappearing around the next corner.

Shannon made her way stiffly to the man who was bent over, picking up her belongings.

"Thanks," she said.

"Don't mention it. I was mugged about a month ago, and I sure wish someone had bothered to do what I did. You wouldn't believe what I had to go through getting all my ID changed."

Fortunately her wallet was intact, not that she wasn't experienced enough to stow the really important things in different places, but the wallet had all her money in it, except for the one hundred dollar bill folded inside her passport in the money belt around her waist.

"I'm afraid the guy took your agenda."

"My agenda?" Shannon asked, puzzled, then realized he was talking about Olivia's journal. "Well, that's a piss-off."

"You should do like me," he answered, tapping the side of his head.

"I keep it all up here. Can't steal that, now, can they?"

The knees of her suit pants were ruined, and there was also some blood. Her Sir Galahad insisted on flagging a taxi for her, leaving her sitting on a nearby doorstep.

So Mrs. Blonde and Beautiful wants to play rough? she smiled grimly. *This time she may find she's bitten off more than she can chew!*

If she'd had someone to wager with, Shannon would have put her hundred down on what she'd find when she got to the rental car parked near the railroad station in Mamaroneck.

One of the rear windows had been smashed in, and the package of photocopies she'd placed on the seat was gone. Her reaction might have astounded an onlooker; she merely shrugged, got in the car and drove off. First stop was the photocopying place she'd visited that morning.

"Do you have those other copies I left with you?"

"Sure thing, ma'am," the kid behind the counter said, "although why you didn't take them is beyond me."

"Just call it a little insurance policy that paid off big," Shannon said over her shoulder as she went out the door.

Back in the car, she rang her office. "I may return tomorrow morning, or I may take a run down to Florida. Could you check on flights? I'd prefer to fly out of the same airport, if possible."

"Sure thing," Janet replied.

"Has Jackie checked in?"

"Only the call when she landed in Reno."

"When she does bother to call, tell her I want to talk with her right away. She's got to keep in touch better. Tell her that, too."

"How are you doing down in the Big Apple?"

"Let's just say I've had a very interesting day."

Shannon next called Ellen Stein, leaving a message. "Hi. It's Shannon O'Brien. You mentioned to me the other day that you knew of a former colleague of Maxine St. James who might be willing to speak to me about her. Could you set something up?"

She decided to find a different hotel that night, something nearer the airport in White Plains so she could get out easily in the morning. Also, it was now obvious that someone was around keeping pretty close tabs on her movements. She'd feel better if they didn't know where she was, considering the strangled woman back in Toronto. She also took the time to pick up some replacement slacks for the ones that had been ruined. White Plains had some nice shopping.

Maxine St. James had played a pretty ballsy game with her that day, Shannon reflected, as she cleaned up the scrapes on her knees. She knew the investigator wouldn't go to the police. People get mugged all the time in New York. Cars get broken into in parking lots with the same frequency. Nothing could be proven against old Max, even if the perps were caught. There was also a message being sent: don't mess with me; I play to win.

"Well, I do too," Shannon said to the hotel bathroom mirror, "and now you've got me angry."

Wanting to get started reading the photocopies of Olivia's journal, she ordered a burger and fries from room service. Her health-conscious daughter would have been appalled, but the meal tasted damn good.

Janet called back near six o'clock to say that she'd found flights to Toronto and Tampa. "You have until nine tonight to confirm one or the other. I've emailed all the details."

"Got it already, Janet. Thanks. Any word from California?"

"Not a peep. I've been trying her cell every fifteen minutes. Do you think she's okay?"

"She'd better be, or she's fired," Shannon shot back with a bit of gallows humour.

Fifteen minutes later, Ellen Stein called. "I spoke to my guy. He'll talk to you. Phone okay?"

"Sure. I got the side window of my rental smashed in today, and I really don't feel like driving anywhere."

"That sounds interesting. In regards to your little project?"

"Yes."

"Care to tell me about it?"

"Not just yet, but soon. Okay?"

"I'm trusting you, Shannon O'Brien. Don't shut me out of this story."

"Oh, believe me, I'm positive you and I can work something out. I owe a few people a bit of payback."

Shannon got the phone number with instructions to call after nine.

Pulling over the sheaf of photocopies again, pen in her mouth, she began numbering, reading and sorting. One thing had become clear early on: the book was not chronological, but if there was a method to the sequencing of the entries, she couldn't see it.

The spelling and punctuation were atrocious, proof that Olivia had not excelled in her schooling. The handwriting was big and loopy throughout, very much like a little girl. One early entry could be pegged to when Olivia was fifteen, and if one were to assume that there were entries up to when she was twenty-one, the handwriting would have changed, become more streamlined as the girl changed to a woman. If anything, it had become bigger and loopier.

Some of the entries describing her stepmother were quite interesting. The girl's hatred leapt off the pages, visceral and raw but juvenile. Reading between the lines, Shannon could see that Olivia blamed Maxine for increasing the distance between father and daughter. She wrote several times about "not feeling like his little girl any more". If what Shannon was now thinking turned out to be true, Maxine's plans had been well-laid and executed.

Shortly after eight, her cell buzzed again, bouncing all over the night table next to her. Expecting a call from Michael, she grabbed it fast and flipped it open.

"Hello, lover. About time you called."

The phone at the other end was silent for a moment. "You sound like you could use a cold shower."

A blush crept from Shannon's face right down her body when she realized the caller was Jackie.

"Uh, sorry. I thought you were someone else."

"Obviously."

"How come it's taken you so long to check in?" Shannon demanded more forcefully than needed because of her embarrassment.

"There are extenuating circumstances. Things happened fast this afternoon, and once I got into the hills, I couldn't get a decent signal on my cell."

"You'll have to do better than that, Jackie. You're out there on your lonesome, and if I don't know where you are and what you're doing, I can't send anyone to help if you get into trouble. You've got to make it your business to keep me in the loop."

She had another reason for saying this. Shannon did not want her loose cannon doing any improvising – especially this far from home.

♪♯♪·♪♭♪·

Jackie had been on a real high. Always one who liked to walk the edge, she felt energized and positive about what she'd accomplished that day.

Her boss's admonition about keeping in touch brought her down in a big hurry. Shannon was right, of course, but Jackie couldn't help feeling as if someone had sucked half the air out of her balloon.

She made up a quick excuse, but it didn't make the situation any better. Shannon obviously sensed the lameness in it. "So what did you come up with?" she asked.

Jackie had made a few notes before calling and gave a concise report to her boss, hoping it would make up for her communication gaffe.

"So you might have seen Olivia?"

"They were doing exercises outdoors, like some freaking gym class. Even with binoculars it was hard to see people clearly from that distance. I'm fairly sure I saw Olivia, but I wouldn't be prepared to swear to it in court."

"I've looked thoroughly at their website. I find it disquieting she was sent to a place like Sunnyvale. I also wonder how many other people have been stuck there as long as she has," Shannon commented.

"The people in town have a hands-off attitude towards the place. I couldn't get many to talk about it. What I saw out in that valley today could certainly be mistaken for a jail." Jackie took a swig of the cold beer she'd bought at the store down the road. It rolled down her throat quite nicely. "What've you found out?"

"I may have stirred up the hornet's nest. I actually got invited to lunch at chez St. James today. The stepmother is a formidable woman."

Jackie then got a pretty amazing story about Shannon's luck in getting her hands on the journal and her bad luck in losing it.

"As evidence, it might not amount to much, since I haven't read anything that directly incriminates Maxine, and it could always be fobbed off as the ravings of a lunatic. There's enough evidence of that. Since Maxine moved so fast to get her hands on what she thinks are all the copies of the journal, it's best to let her believe she's beaten me. It may lead her to underestimate us in the future."

"It sounds like you've come over to my way of thinking about this."

"Let's say more than halfway. She came right out and told me that she orchestrated Olivia's commitment to Sunnyvale. Reading between the lines, she's more than happy to have Olivia stay there. We need to find out why."

"That could prove difficult."

"I'm well aware of that. As I said, she's a formidable woman."

"Okay, I've scoped out the opposition. What do you want me to do next? Do I stay out here? Come home?"

Shannon thought for a moment. "I'm worried Maxine may try something out there. If she *has* pulled a fast one with her stepdaughter, she could try to solve her problem once and for all."

"Why didn't she try it sooner, then? Like in Toronto, for instance."

"If they'd found her still panhandling, that might have been the case. Things got more complicated when she took up with Andy Curran and the trio. Maxine St. James is a lawyer, and a good one from what I gather. She'd know that taking Olivia out would have been very risky."

"Well, she'll expect us to move against her legally, probably through Andy. He would have cause to try to prove that Olivia isn't as nuts as Maxine's shrinks say."

"That would take far too long – and remember, there's a big border in the way."

"Could one of the people you've interviewed down there help?"

"The only likely one for that would be Darcy Jeffries. The retired butler proved what side he's on. We still have the problem of time – and expense. This would cost a bundle."

Jackie decided to go for broke. "So you're worried about Olivia?"

"Concerned is a better word – until we have more facts."

"You need to get someone on the inside."

Shannon saw exactly what her new employee was suggesting. "I'm going to have to give this some thought, Jackie. It could be dangerous."

"Dangerous? How? I go in posing as someone with a drug problem. You could pull me out anytime."

"I'm going to have to think this over," Shannon repeated.

"So what do I do tonight?"

Her boss's reply had a smile in it. "Take the night off after a good day at work. I'll call in the morning at eight o'clock your time. By the way, that was an example of how to communicate. Just thought I should point it out in case you weren't noticing."

Her boss clicked off, and Jackie flopped back on her bed. She hadn't gotten an immediate no to her idea, and that was something.

She got dressed in her other pair of jeans but with a cropped T-shirt this time. She'd be damned if she was going to spend the evening with her feet on the bed watching lame-ass TV shows.

No, she was going out to do a little prospecting. In Reno.

CHAPTER 15

I realized my stomach would probably hate me in a few hours, but the cheeseburger was tasting awfully good, and by the way the two "ladies" with me were scarfing down their food, they felt the same. If you want a great burger after three in the morning in Toronto, go to Fran's at College and Yonge.

Having decided that the Sal was not the place to talk about the subject they'd brought up, we'd driven around the downtown streets for the previous two hours. Taking a cue from Shannon O'Brien, I'd just let them talk. It had been very enlightening. They didn't stay on topic very well, but even the digressions had been eye-opening. I now knew far more than I ever wanted to about what it was like making your living on your back.

Shelley, the redhead, appeared to be the instigator of their little excursion and took the lead once we were in my car.

"Did you know Maggie well?" she asked.

"No. And quite frankly, I don't think she liked me very much."

The blonde, Donna, piped up from the backseat. "That's what she said. Called you a dickhead for talking her mousey friend into singing with your group."

"How do you two know Maggie?"

Shelley spoke. "Once you been in the business, it isn't hard to find out where us working girls hang. It's always a good idea when you're new in town to find out the lay of the land before you put out your shingle. Take for instance the fact that prostitution ain't illegal in this province. Streetwalkin' is, though."

"We hang in some of the better hotel bars," Donna added.

"What did Maggie do?"

"She worked out of her place, mostly. Occasionally did some outcalls."

I must have looked confused, because Donna said, "Don't you know nothin' about hooking?"

"Consider me an empty page."

"What's that supposed to mean? Oh, I get it! That's cute."

Next to me, Shelley rolled her eyes. "Know those adult ads the free weekly papers in town run? They're for girls who work like Maggie. Personally, I think she was spooked out of working in public. Probably had a bad experience."

"Maybe she wanted to stay out of the way of the cops," I said. "Did she ever say anything to you about being on the run?"

"Not in so many words. But then there was that oddball girl with her."

Playing along, I said, "Yeah, I can't figure out how she fits into all this."

"Me neither," chimed in Donna. "She was a strange one."

"She didn't turn tricks, too, did she?"

I couldn't afford to look right at Shelley, but I could hear the sneer in her answer. "Nah. She was a goody two-shoes. I don't think she'd ever even had sex. Maggie told me a couple of times when she had a john over and the girl was there, she actually hid in a closet! But I don't think Maggie woulda been too happy if she'd started turning tricks. She was awfully protective of her."

Now, I wouldn't consider myself a Casanova or anything, but when I was single and playing in a bar band, I'd taken home my share of young ladies. I only had one experience that I knew of with a virgin, and Olivia didn't strike me as one during the two nights we'd slept together. I didn't think she had a ton of experience, but she certainly knew her way around.

"I saw her panhandling at Union Station. When did that start?"

"About two weeks after they hit town. She had to pull her weight somehow, and since they were both illegals, they couldn't get regular jobs."

"They were saving up to go to Europe or something," Donna added.

"Really?"

"Yeah, that was their goal. Go to Europe and start over."

"Wouldn't Maggie have been making a good buck? It wouldn't take long to save up for a couple of plane tickets."

"Boy, you don't know much! When they got here, they had the clothes on their back, and that was it. We had to take them in until they got on their feet."

"That's how come we know so much," Shelley added. "We turned them on to an apartment in a building near ours. We didn't socialize much once they moved in, but we were over there a couple of times."

"The cops admitted to me that she had some high-class clients. Surely she'd charge them accordingly."

Donna and Shelley looked at each other. Shelley spoke. "We don't like to speak bad about a dead friend, but a good bit of her income went up her nose. She tried hard to stop with the toot but kept falling back."

"But how much do a couple of plane tickets cost?"

"Think, buddy! They had no ID. You try crossing borders without good ID, you're gonna get nailed."

"How did they get into Canada then?"

"They never said."

"Did they say where they crossed the border?"

"Not that I remember, but I got the impression it was someplace in the middle of nowhere."

"And they arrived in Toronto in..." I led.

Donna again. "Musta been the end of November. We'd had that big dump of snow the night before. Right?"

Shelley thought for a second. "November twenty-first."

"What can you tell me about the way Maggie and Olivia got on?"

"Even when she was real strung out, Maggie looked after the kid."

"Yeah, there was some weird bond between those two," Donna added. "They were so different. Olivia hardly said boo, but you couldn't shut Maggie up, especially when she was high."

"Olivia never did any drugs?" I asked.

"Not that I saw. She was like a mouse most of the time. She'd sing along with the radio if she didn't think anyone was listening. She did have a real nice voice. Sort of gave me the shivers, though, when she sang. It felt like she was crawling around inside my head."

I pushed my plate away. My stomach felt like I'd swallowed a bowling ball. "So Maggie worked at home most of the time. Did she ever have any trouble?"

"Once or twice a client tried to get a little rough, but she could handle herself. She kept a knife between the mattress and the box-spring. Knew how to handle it, too."

A rare flash of inspiration hit me. "Did she also carry a knife on her when she went out?"

"She would have been stupid not to, considering she did outcalls. Yeah, she had a sweet little switchblade. Got it from a punk on Yonge Street."

"In her handbag or on her person?"

Donna guffawed. "You sound just like a cop when you say that. Cops get a hard-on saying things like 'on her person.'"

"In a sheath she'd sewn on the inside of her boot," Shelley answered.

How had Maggie been strangled with no struggle if she had a knife and apparently knew how to use it? Or had she hurt someone, and we didn't know? I'd certainly heard nothing about a knife from the cops.

"So the cops haven't talked to you?"

"The cops don't even know we exist. So far, neither of us has been busted in this town, and we want to keep it that way."

It was getting late, and the conversation had meandered several times into long discourses on the problems of sex trade workers – as both ladies called themselves. That's when I'd suggested a bite at Fran's, hoping it would focus our discussion.

Shannon O'Brien would have been much better handling this. Maybe I could get Shelley and Donna to talk to her. Obviously, some of the information had to get to the police, and she would know the best way to do that.

Donna ordered a refill on her Coke. Shelley looked like she was ready to split.

"You said when we were down at the Salamander that you knew something the cops didn't, and you wanted to tell me. What is it?"

Shelley said, "First, you can't tell no one where you heard this. I don't want some whack job coming after us. And I don't trust the cops as far as I can throw them. Not even the lady cops. They're sometimes worse than the men."

"Believe me, I am honoured that you came to me. My lips are sealed."

Donna giggled. "Ain't you the gallant?"

Shelley frowned. This time it was directed at me. "The night before she was murdered, she came to the bar I was working. Fortunately I wasn't occupied. She was in a real state. Olivia had called. Somebody had found her and taken her away. I didn't know what the hell Maggie was babbling about, and she seemed really wasted to me."

"Did Maggie say when Olivia called?"

"I don't know. Sometime that afternoon, I think."

"And you?" I asked, indicating Donna.

"I was *occupied,* so I didn't see her."

"Did Maggie say anything else?"

"Only something about if they'd got Olivia, they'd be coming after her because she knew too much."

"About what?"

"How the hell should I know? She was almost incoherent. Said she wasn't going home, that she had someone who could help her. I guess she meant you."

"Did she mention my name?"

Shelley raised an eyebrow comically. "Not unless you can think of another 'asshole drummer' she knew."

That figured. "Was there *anything* else?"

"Only that if something happened to her, we should make sure you knew to go after some guy named Sonny Vale."

♪♯♩·♪♭♩·

Shannon woke up feeling as if she'd gotten hit over the head with something hard and heavy. Her brain was throbbing, and her eyes felt as if someone had thrown a handful of dirt in each.

It had been a long, tough night, after a long tough day. Following her call from Jackie, she'd called the number Ellen Stein had supplied.

The phone rang three times, and a woman answered. "Hello?"

"May I speak to Joseph Menotti, please?"

"I'll see if he's free." Her hand muffled the phone, but Shannon could hear talking. "Who's calling?"

"My name is Shannon O'Brien. I was told to call after nine."

A male voice came on the line. "What can I do for you?"

"Good evening, Mr. Menotti. I really appreciate you agreeing to talk with me. Did Ellen Stein give you any background?"

"Call me Joe. She said you wanted to talk about Maxine St. James."

"That's right." Shannon wrote the date and time on a fresh page in her notebook. "In what context do you know her, Joe?"

"We started our careers at the same law firm."

"And that was?"

"Nineteen years ago. The firm was Holden Westerman."

"Can you describe Maxine St. James for me?"

"Her name was Kingman in those days. Let's see...more ambitious than any two people I know – and I know some pretty ambitious people – smart, good legal instincts, quick to adapt. That woman could turn on a dime. Have you met her?"

"This afternoon."

"Then you also know how beautiful she is. Maxine did not hesitate to trade on that in order to get ahead. When we started out, the salary was not all that great. You know, you've got to get an apartment, nice clothes, things like that. Well, I think she spent half her salary on clothes the first year – not frivolously either. She dressed to be noticed at all times. It was pure class, but you were also very aware she was a woman. Do you know what I'm trying to say?"

"Yes, I do."

"She could also deliver the goods. Pretty early on, old man Holden put her on the St. James account as a junior, doing the things requiring legwork, nothing glamourous, but she made the most of the opportunity. Within a year she was the go-to person for anything to do with St. James."

"Ellen told me she thought Maxine had been having an affair with Bernard St. James. Did she get that from you?"

Menotti laughed. "That's a journalist for you. All I told her was that they would meet together a fair bit, more than you might expect. Although as history proved, they got married awfully quickly after the death of his first wife."

Now came the meat and potatoes of the interview. "I'm going to make some statements, and I'd like you to agree or disagree with them. I'd also like you to elaborate if you'd care to."

"Or refuse to answer. Tell me something, Ms O'Brien, do you have any legal training?"

"Only what you'd get to become a cop. That's what I did before I went out on my own. Why do you ask?"

"Oh, what you're suggesting is a pretty interesting tactic, that's all."

Reading between the lines, Shannon knew that Joe wanted her to know that he was no fool. She'd have to handle this just right.

"Your questions?" he prompted.

"Maxine would do whatever it takes in order to get what she wants." No hesitation. "Yes."

"Even if that might involve operating in grey areas of the law."

"Possibly."

"No elaboration?"

"No."

"People were surprised when she married Bernard St. James."

"Not many."

"She changed after she married him."

"She hardened. She left the law firm immediately, of course. Bernard would never allow a wife of his to work."

"And did it surprise you that she acquiesced?"

Menotti laughed again. "Please don't take this the wrong way, but I didn't know private eyes used words like 'acquiesced.'"

"I grew up with my nose in books. I was planning on being a librarian at one time," she shot back with amusement.

"Touché! To answer your question, I don't think Maxine stopped working. She was more involved than ever in the St. James fortune."

"To the point where she might have been calling the shots?"

"You have to understand that I wasn't involved in anything to do with the St. James account. I'm only aware of things through hearsay."

"Good hearsay?"

"I'd say so. In any event, nobody ordered Bernard St. James to do anything. He had a very commanding personality."

"Even after he became ill?"

"Maybe he backed off a bit then. Maxine certainly would have been the one to turn to in that case."

"Another statement: Maxine has handled the family fortunes well since the death of her husband."

"Yes."

"Do you think close family members would have gotten in her way?"

Menotti thought for a moment. "Are you speaking of the son or the daughter?"

"Let's say both."

"Strike the daughter off. From all I've heard, she's a flake. As for the unfortunate son, I met him once or twice at functions. He seemed capable enough."

"Better than his stepmother?"

"I'd have to say no, but he was young when he died so tragically. No telling what he might have become. But to respond to your question, he would certainly have given Maxine trouble. His father had groomed him to take over."

"Do you have any knowledge of the contents of Bernard St. James's will?"

"If I did, I wouldn't tell you. Next?"

Shannon got that little message loud and clear. "Maxine made out awfully well in the way things turned out. Maybe too well."

Again silence, then, "Possibly."

"Maxine might have had something to do with the murder of her stepson."

"I won't respond to that."

"She could have had something to do with the death of Lydia St. James."

"That's really stretching, Ms O'Brien. I find it surprising you want to go there."

"Okay. She had something to do with the institutionalizing of her stepdaughter."

"Of course she did. That's common knowledge."

"But she might have manipulated the situation."

"I told you, the daughter is a flake. I don't think anything would have to be manipulated. Has someone told you that might be the case?"

"My client thinks so."

"And that client has met her?"

"Olivia St. James had been singing with a jazz trio for several months in Toronto until last week."

"*What?*"

"That's the same response I've gotten from everybody," Shannon said. "I find that interesting, don't you?"

Menotti's response was thoughtful. "Very."

"Would it surprise you that Maxine St. James insists that her stepdaughter's condition is no better than it was when she was institutionalized six years ago?"

"In the face of the previous statement? Yes and no."

"Yes and no?"

"The yes is obvious. But the no side of the equation... You've insinuated a few things, Ms O'Brien, that I find very disturbing. If what you're saying has any basis in truth, then these are very serious charges indeed. Did you voice any of this to Mrs. St. James today?"

"Not really. But as it turns out, she has already made some moves against me."

"That is very telling. What are you going to do next?"

"I'm going to be careful."

Menotti laughed. "I'll bet you are. And I think that's wise."

"I just want to go back for one more statement: you only knew Maxine Kingman through work."

"Stein didn't mention anything to you?"

"No. Why?"

"Because I was engaged to Maxine for three months. She called it off, then about a year later, she was married to Bernard St. James." He yawned. "It's getting late. Is that it?"

"If you had to tell me one more thing about Maxine St. James, what would it be?"

"Watch your step."

Sitting in a booth in the airport's coffee shop, Shannon was faced with a conundrum.

Her brain told her that the next logical step for her to take would be to go to Florida to talk to the cops down there about the St. James murder. What she might find out could solidify some of the suppositions she was forming.

But after her lengthy conversation with Jackie the previous evening, she felt she also needed to pay attention to what was going on in California. Maybe her next move should be out there.

Overriding all of this were several things needing her attention back in Toronto. If she was going to California or Florida, they had to be taken care of that day.

Looking at her watch while she emptied her coffee cup, she saw she'd have just enough time to call Andy Curran before her flight back to Toronto. She definitely needed to talk to him face to face before the end of the day.

It wasn't even eight o'clock yet. Curran had played the previous evening and probably hadn't gotten home until after two at the earliest. She hated to bother him.

Her worst fears were confirmed when the phone rang five times before a very groggy voice croaked, "Hello?"

"It's Shannon. I'm sorry to wake you, but we need to speak."

"Give me a minute." He was as good as his word and sounded more together when he came on the line again. "What can I do for you?"

"I'm still in New York. I need a little guidance."

"Have you had any luck?"

"Quite a bit, but I don't have time to go into it now. Will you be home this afternoon? We need to talk."

"I'll be home. I've got a couple of students late in the afternoon."

"Good. I'm going to drop by and lay everything out for you. I'll call first. Gotta run. Bye."

Westchester County is a tiny airport, and the plane that day was one of those little puddle-jumpers. She put the flight to good use, writing up all her notes on the laptop, which helped her organize her thoughts. So focussed was she on this task that she didn't have time to be anxious about being up in the air.

Once the plane had landed, she called home to let her mom know she'd be around for dinner, then headed to her office.

Traffic was a bit heavier than she'd hoped, so she didn't pull in at the headquarters of O'Brien Investigates until nearly eleven thirty. Flashing past Janet's desk with a wave, she dropped into her seat and picked up the phone in one movement.

The line rang twice before Jackie picked up. "You're late," she said cheekily.

Shannon looked to the heavens for strength. "I just got in from New York. Traffic was murder."

"And?"

"If I could be assured that it would be useful, would you be willing to go into Sunnyvale to check up on Olivia?"

"Yes."

"That's pretty definite."

"I've been thinking about it, too. I can't come up with any other way to make sure she's okay. Doesn't sound as if they or her stepmother would throw the doors open wide, and going through the courts would take too long. Let's do it."

"Not so fast. This has to be planned out. I'm going to catch a flight out tomorrow and also bring in some local help."

"Why?"

"Because you're in the United States. I don't think they'd take kindly to any of this snooping, especially from Canadians. We're already on the windy side of the law since we don't have licenses to operate in California. I know someone in Oakland who will help us. Stay close to a phone today."

"You want me to do anything in the meantime?"

"I want you to keep your head down. If they suspect a thing, we're dead in the water. Stay in your room. We don't know who in town works at Sunnyvale. Got that?"

"Yes, ma'am!"

"All I've got to do is come up with some way to get you in there."

"I've already got that in hand."

"Great! What's your angle?"

"You don't want to know."

CHAPTER 16

Someone was on my porch, moving around quietly. Jumping to the window, I saw Shannon. Why hadn't she rung the bell?

Hitting mute on the stereo, I went out. Other than scuttling in and out as quickly as I could to grab each morning's *Globe and Mail*, it was the first time I'd been on my porch since the previous Thursday.

I found her leaning back against the railing, looking down at the chalk outline, still horrendously vivid on the weathered wood and flaking paint.

"Communing with the dead?" I asked.

She looked up, her face showing her fatigue. "Something like that."

"Are you ready to come in? I'll make coffee. You look like you could use some."

"In a minute. I'm just trying to get my bearings. Maggie was a big part of this mess, and I really haven't stopped to consider her."

I turned and looked out at the street. A car was going slowly by, and even though I'd taken down the yellow police tape, it slowed and the driver peered out curiously. I stared back, heartily fed up with the notoriety.

"I hadn't either. I couldn't see past our mutual animosity towards each other."

"I'd like to know how she fits into all of this."

"I think I can tell you that."

We spent the next hour going over what I'd learned the previous evening from the two "working girls".

Shannon looked at something on the three pages of notes I'd given her. "I'm glad you took the time to do this while it was fresh in your mind. It will be very helpful."

"What do you think we should do about what the ladies told me?"

"Meaning Palmer?"

I nodded. "Shelley and Donna don't want hassles. I'm sure Palmer, using that charm only he possesses, will come down like a hammer on them."

"I'm sure you're right. Unless we've completely misread what happened to Maggie, Palmer's been barking up the wrong tree for several days now, and knowing the way the department runs, the boys above him are beginning to get antsy at the lack of results. Oh, he'll pounce on them all right."

"So how do we get the information to Palmer without involving the women?"

Shannon pursed her lips and silently considered. "I don't see how we can, but there are two reasons we may not want to."

"What are they?"

"These," she said as she reached into the open briefcase sitting next to her on the sofa. "This is a report of what I found out on my trip to New York. And this is a report Jackie Goode dictated from California to my secretary. She's still out there waiting for instructions. You read them while I make a few phone calls."

She left the room, heading for the back door, which closed quietly behind her. I was just about finished when she came back. Even though she had only briefly mentioned her encounter with the man who tried to steal her purse, I noted how awkwardly she was walking.

"Knees okay?"

She sat back down on the sofa. "Just a bit stiff. No lasting damage."

"These reports read like a mystery novel."

Shannon smiled. "Mystery novels seldom get it right. What you've read is what an investigator does, private or public. While getting knocked down on the streets of New York is no fun, it happens. It could always have been a bullet to the back of the head, so I don't feel too bad about banged-up knees."

"You think things are that dangerous?"

She shook her head. "No. Maxine St. James is not stupid. The police would be after her in a heartbeat. She just wanted what I had and used a perfect opportunity to get it. She knows I won't go to the cops about what happened, though. Unless whoever stole the journal and broke into the car was caught and then confessed as to who put him up to it, no one could connect her with anything."

I was outraged. "So we just have to take this?"

"For the moment," she yawned. "Sorry. What Maxine gave us yesterday was a wake-up call. I picked up a tail when I picked up the journal, and the bad thing was, I didn't catch on. I now know she heard about me from the retired butler, but I should have been more on my guard. I will be from now on, and I suggest you do the same." She let that sink in, then asked, "Any questions on those reports?"

"This report from you," I said, "says that you've read Olivia's journal. Did it contain anything useful?"

"Hard to tell. There's a lot to wade through, and some of it's pretty dense. It has given me one lead, though, which I haven't been able to follow up yet."

She again reached into her briefcase, pulling out a thick manila envelope. "This is the journal."

I chuckled. "Wouldn't Ms St. James be annoyed to find out you'd hoodwinked her."

"We have the advantage as long as she doesn't know I still have a copy." Shannon leaned over and handed me the sheaf of papers. "Look this over for me."

"It's Olivia's handwriting all right."

I stopped on the third page, where there was a stunning little sketch of a cat asleep on a bed. "The style is very different from what's upstairs on the walls of her room. I've got some of her doodling in the basement, if you'd care to see it. While I'm up, would you like more coffee?"

Shannon smiled. "Absolutely."

When I returned to the living room, she wasn't there. "Shannon?"

"I'm upstairs," she called. "Be right with you." The old staircase creaked comfortably as she made her way down. "I was just looking at the room again. It really is amazing."

"Communing with Olivia this time?"

She picked up the dozen or so sheets I'd brought up from the studio. When Ronald, Dom and I would stop to discuss some arcane musical point during rehearsals, Olivia would often get bored and pick up any piece of paper lying around to sketch something, usually one of us. They were all a bit irreverent, as she'd catch us in some slightly unflattering way. Ronald was the one most lampooned.

But some of the sketches were of things like a beach or mountains. She'd also drawn Kate curled up on the sofa with a book, and had not only caught her likeness quite well, but also the look of intense concentration she gets on her face when she's reading. Whether Olivia had done it from memory at a rehearsal or from life, I didn't know. I wanted to get it framed for one of the bare spaces on the living room wall.

Shannon studied the sketches while I skimmed the photocopies of Olivia's journal. At times the entries sounded quite lucid, but sadly there weren't many of those. A great deal of it was troubling. Very little of it reminded me of the Olivia I'd known.

"You'll notice that she mentions the name Jack quite frequently," Shannon said, "and there is also someone called Taggart, usually written about in unflattering terms. I believe it's the same person."

"Yeah, there's one on this page. She calls him her saviour here."

"Look on page twenty-two."

I read the entry, then looked up. "Jesus! This is over the top."

"The person she usually reserves that kind of venom for is her stepmother."

"What do you make of it?"

"Taggart was the one who brought her heroin," Shannon said.

"You know that for sure?"

"Call it an educated guess. I'm sure in the back of her mind she was worried someone might find the book. The fact that she uses euphemisms for her drug dependency seems to confirm that. It's the one thing she would never want anyone to know."

"And the way she talks about her stepmother?"

"I don't think she cared about that. And I'm also pretty certain Maxine St. James knew about her feelings without reading the journal."

"May I keep these?" I asked. "I might spot something you wouldn't."

"Do you have someplace safe you could put it, a place no one could find – for certain? If Maxine St. James discovers I made that second copy, we lose our advantage."

"Haven't you made more?"

"Of course, but she'll figure that out."

"Do you honestly think she'd have someone break into my house?"

She looked at me seriously. "There is the outside possibility, just to make certain she's not surprised by anything we might have that she doesn't know about. They could have searched here already, for that matter. I'm sure she'd hire the best, and those people don't leave any trace. But no, I don't think you have much to worry about."

"Is it safe to bring Kate over here?"

"Have you been concerned about that?"

"I did think that maybe Maggie was dumped here as a warning."

"I think she was dumped here to make trouble for you."

"So where do we go from here?"

"You're up to speed now on what Jackie and I have been doing. Now we have to make the hard decisions."

"Like?"

"There's no question you have information that should go to the police. Withholding it is a crime."

"The way you just said that, I'm thinking you're going to give me a better reason than protecting those two women to keep us from contacting Palmer." I smiled. "Just a wild guess."

"Maxine wasted no time in going after me. Obviously she had someone look in my shoulder bag when I was at her home. I was baiting her by bringing the journal into the house with me. I also left one photocopy I'd made in plain sight in my car. She rose to the bait with alarming speed. I wasn't even a block from her house when that guy was on me, and I'm sure she already had the photocopy from the car by that time. She also thinks I never got a chance to read much of it.

"If we take all we've learned and stir in a bit of conspiracy theory, Maxine St. James could have been responsible for the murder of her predecessor, Lydia St. James, and her stepson, had Olivia committed and ordered the murder of Maggie."

I was surprised. "You honestly believe that?"

Shannon shook her head. "I just don't know, but it's not a theory we can throw out, either. Tell me, Andy, you lived with her for several weeks. Do you think Olivia should be institutionalized?"

"She is very odd, but no, definitely not."

"But yet they've had her at Sunnyvale for six years, and the experts examining her say she should stay there. I'm concerned about Olivia's wellbeing. If we're right on any of the suppositions I've made, *especially* if we're right on *more* than one of them, she could be in big trouble. In that sort of high stakes game, Maxine has a lot to lose."

"And if something happens to Olivia, the whole problem just disappears," I said, finishing the thought for her. "Jesus... Why not just go to the cops with all this? Let them handle it."

"Two reasons," Shannon said. "One, we've got almost no concrete evidence. Yes, we can lead them to Sunnyvale because of Maggie, but then we have to lay all our other cards on the table, and that could totally screw up what we're trying to do. Two, once Maxine gets wind of anything, we're forcing her to make a move we may not want – at any cost. And don't forget, we've also got a very thick border in the way. That slows down police investigations considerably."

"So what choice do we have?"

"One I personally don't want to make. We have a person on site whom the bad guys don't know. If we get her into Sunnyvale, we can accomplish two things: we have a way to get more information, and we have somebody who can keep an eye on Olivia."

"Why are you so worried about sending Jackie Goode in there?"

Shannon sighed. "Because she just started working for me. I don't know if she's up to it – and it could be dangerous."

"Why don't you go?"

"Because I've already played my hand with Maxine. They know who I am."

"So we have no choice?"

"We have no choice."

"You look tired, honey," Shannon's mother said as her daughter hung her jacket on a peg by the back door.

Judging by the smells coming from the oven, dinner was well in hand – a good thing, because if dinner had been up to Shannon, everybody would have been eating take-out pizza.

"Is that beef stew I smell?" she asked, giving her mom a hug. "When do we eat?"

"About a half hour."

"Good. I have a couple of phone calls to make."

Her mother poured a glass of wine. "Take this. You look like you could use it."

Shannon smiled. "Thanks. I do need it."

Glass of wine in hand, Shannon went into the small room off the kitchen that served as her home office.

Taking out her laptop, she turned it on so she'd have all her data at hand. With a quick consultation of her phone list, she dialed a number in California.

"Bump City Security," a female voice said.

"I'd like to speak to Roy Moody, please."

"I'll see if he's available. Whom shall I say is calling?"

"Shannon O'Brien."

"Shannon!" A deep voice, sounding as if it came right out of the earth, blasted from the phone a moment later. Shannon was ready and had the receiver a good two inches from her ear. "How long has it been since we last talked?"

"Four years next month."

"That long? Man, I'm feeling old."

"We all are."

"So, how ya doin'?"

"I'm fine, Roy."

"And that ne'er-do-well husband of yours?"

"*Ex*-husband."

"Oh." A pause. "I'm really sorry to hear that."

"Shit happens."

"Yeah, don't I know it."

Shannon had first met Roy when she and her husband had attended a convention in Las Vegas just after they'd quit Toronto Police Services and struck out on their own. Roy had recently done the same thing with the Oakland force.

"Built like a door" had been Shannon's first assessment of the huge black man with the shaved head, the ready smile and the quick comeback. The three ex-cops had bonded and spent a good weekend learning the ropes about what was new and hot on the PI and security scene as far as equipment, methods and business practices went.

Roy was unmarried, and twice over the years, they'd helped each other out on jobs, the last time being four years ago when the O'Briens were trying to get information on a scam being run out of San Francisco. Their friend's knowledge of the area had proved invaluable and had saved them days of leg work.

"I suspect this isn't a social call after all this time."

"Got a bit of a sticky situation in your neck of the woods."

"Bay area?"

"A bit east. Portola, to be exact."

"That's not exactly near here, Shannon."

"It's a hell of a lot closer than I am."

"So what's it about? There isn't much around Portola other than fishing on Lake Davis. Nearest thing of any consequence is Reno and Lake Tahoe."

"Ever hear of a rehab-slash-psychiatric institution called Sunnyvale?"

"Sure thing. They do big business with Hollywood types who wander too far into substance abuse. You running with that chi-chi crowd on this one?"

"Yes and no. While there is a substance abuse aspect to my case, it goes much deeper than that." She stopped, her natural cautiousness poking up its head. "At least, I *think* it goes deeper."

"How can I help you?"

"Use your connections. All I know about the place, I've gleaned from their website and a few other mentions on the Internet. I need the inside scuttlebutt."

Roy chuckled. "You think I run in the rarified atmosphere of those circles?"

"Doesn't everyone in California?" Shannon shot right back. "I'm sure you have sources you can call on."

"How quick you need it?"

"ASAP."

Shannon had to move the receiver an additional two inches from her ear because of his laugh. "I got a lot of things on the go at the moment, girl."

"I'm really glad business is good, Roy, but I'm in a time bind. I stirred up something in New York the other day, and I'm worried about some sort of violent reaction in California."

"How violent?"

"The worst kind."

"On you or one of yours?"

"On someone in Sunnyvale."

"Nothing you can go to the cops with?"

"Not at this point, but I'm working on that angle. This is a devilishly tricky one."

His decision was characteristically swift. "I'm on it. Where can I reach you?"

"I'm flying out tomorrow morning. I can be reached on my cell, except when I'm in the air, of course."

"I'll do what I can tonight, but it's more realistic you'll hear back from me tomorrow."

"Roy..."

"We always got each other's backs; you know that. Nuff said."

"Regardless, thanks."

Shannon needed to be at the airport by seven the next morning. When she called him after dinner, Michael insisted on driving her.

"I hardly get to see you lately," he said when she objected. "Besides, if you're not back in three days, I'm not going to see you at all. I'm in the UK rehearsing as of the weekend."

"I wish I didn't have to go. You know that. It's just how it is."

"Then let me drive you to the airport," he repeated reasonably.

She knew when she was beaten. "Okay, Michael. Maybe I'll get this thing in California cleared up in record time. I could come back early and I wouldn't necessarily have to tell the family. We could make a night of it."

"This job isn't dangerous, is it?"

"I don't think so. As I said, I'm hoping I can get what we need and get back home before you leave town."

After hanging up, she sat for several minutes, hoping she hadn't brought the devil down on her head with that last comment.

"Welcome to Reno," Jackie said in the falsely hearty delivery of a tour bus operator. "Our only goal is to make your visit as enjoyable as possible. Don't forget to gamble as often as possible."

Shannon just wanted to get the hell away from the airport, with its slot machines everywhere you turned. She pushed ahead through the revolving door, making no response to the wisecrack.

Once in the rental car and out on the highway, she relaxed, but only a little.

"Bad flight?" Jackie asked.

"Every flight is bad. Anything new to report?"

"Not a thing. I did just as you asked and kept my head down."

"Good." Shannon checked her cell phone's signal strength for the fourth time since landing. She really needed whatever information Roy could dig up. Swivelling to face Jackie, she said, "Now tell me this plan for getting into Sunnyvale."

Jackie shot her a sideways glance. "The only sure way to get in is to pose as a patient, right?"

"I suppose."

"There's no way we're going to jump their fence, and the front gate is manned twenty-four/seven, so a bold frontal infiltration is out."

"I'd like to scope out the place anyway."

"Suit yourself." A silent mile or two later, Jackie said, "I figure our best bet is for me to go in with a substance abuse problem."

"Alcohol?"

"I'd have to admit to a long-term problem, and I don't think the physical effects of that could be faked. They'd spot it."

"Same goes for drugs, then."

"Not crack."

"Where are we going to get some of that?"

"I already have it."

"What? You bought crack?"

"Relax. There's drugs to be had in Reno with little trouble. I scored all I'll need the other night."

Shannon didn't like it, and they argued about it over the miles to Portola, but she was fighting a losing battle. Jackie had obviously done her research.

"That's certainly the admin building by the front gate," Jackie said, pointing, "and the big building to its left seems to be a recreation centre."

Shannon put the binocs to her eyes again and scanned the very large compound that made up Sunnyvale.

Barely stopping to change in Jackie's motel room, Shannon had wanted to hit the ground running. Hidden by low scrub, they were lying on their stomachs underneath some pines near the top of a high hill.

The day before, and contrary to what she'd told her boss, Jackie had reconnoitered the area, finding a better route into Sunnyvale, although it meant a longer hike. Parking a car so near the entrance hadn't seemed like a good idea.

"I've been studying some of those Internet map sites that include satellite coverage. There are nineteen buildings of varying sizes. The other day I counted eighty-three people doing exercises. If I'm correct about the colour coding, staff and patients both take part."

"What about security?"

"I don't think so. See anybody wearing brown? I believe that's them."

Shannon moved the binoculars to the right. "There are two at the front gate talking to someone who just drove up. They're wearing brown."

"I checked one of their vehicles in town. It had extra heavy duty suspension. My guess is they can manage pretty well in the backcountry. The woods around here are crisscrossed with fire roads and the like."

Putting down the binocs, Shannon rolled onto her side, facing Jackie. "What are you getting at?"

"In case I have to clear out in a hurry."

Before packing it in for the day, Shannon took a whole flash card of photos, from long range to extremely close. As they got ready to back away from the somewhat exposed hillside, the exercise period started, with people trooping out of nearly every building.

Shannon slowly scanned the assembly. Nothing could be heard from the loudspeakers, since the wind was at their backs.

"That's her," she said finally. Handing the binoculars to Jackie, she picked up the camera and clicked off a few shots. "She's on the right side, near that bench. See her?"

"So that's our problem child. She seems okay from what I can see."

"No way to tell for sure from this distance. Let's get going. I'm waiting for a phone call."

Once they got back into cell phone range, Shannon got her call. It went on for quite some time, with a lot of head nodding and one or two word answers.

After hanging up, Shannon was quiet until they got back to the motel.

"So what's up?" Jackie asked when she could bear it no longer.

"That was my friend Roy. He asked around and managed to speak to a few 'graduates' of the Sunnyvale program."

"And?"

Shannon piled a few pillows on one of the beds and lay back against the headboard. "They all spoke pretty positively about the program. It was tough but effective."

"Did this Roy guy ask them about Olivia?"

"Not in so many words. We don't want anything to get back to anybody, do we? He did ask about people who were there for something other than substance abuse problems."

Jackie sat down on the bed. "And what sort of answers did he get?"

"He was told those people are kept by themselves most of the time. Some of them are apparently pretty troubled. They have their own programs and their own activities."

"Any idea how many there are?"

"Not more than a dozen, Roy said."

"This could complicate matters."

"Just what I was thinking." She turned her head and looked at Jackie. "The people at Sunnyvale can be very tough when they have to be. They don't fool around. It's all part of this 'tough love/you have to face up to your faults' thing that's the basis of their program."

"I'm ready," Jackie said confidently.

"Are you?"

CHAPTER 17

Shannon was uneasy. She never liked investigations that kept posing new questions at a faster pace than she could discover answers. A week into this one, the answers she had would barely fill a postcard; the questions would – and did – fill a notebook.

"And you're sure your friend Kit knows what to say if Sunnyvale calls her?" she asked.

Jackie was lounging on her bed, looking completely unstressed as she watched TV.

"Yup. She's going to say that I'm her best friend – which I am, incidentally – and she's just looking out for me. My crack addiction is completely out of control. Relax. Kit's got a good head on her shoulders."

Shannon hoped the coolness was all an act. Being too certain in any situation could be highly dangerous, especially when you didn't have much experience.

It was late morning on her second day in California. Roy had told them he'd be making an early start, and she tried to keep herself from glancing yet again at the bedside clock or her watch in an effort to make time go by more quickly.

"And you're clear on what I need you to accomplish at Sunnyvale?"

Jackie muted the tiny TV and looked over at her boss. "I am very clear on what you need, most important of which is not to put myself or Olivia in any danger. If I have any concerns about that, I will get in touch with you immediately. You can count on me, Shannon. I won't do anything stupid."

Roy Moody had one bed half-covered with equipment he'd brought.

"You're lucky I'm not using this stuff so much lately. You got some pretty specialized equipment here, *and* hard to get."

Shannon laughed. "You always were a gadget junkie, Roy. Admit it."

Actually, she was really glad he'd brought all that he had. Having to cross a border, she'd been able to carry next to nothing. Too many questions would have been asked, and she didn't have a license to operate in California. She'd never skated so close to the edge before.

Jackie, too, had confirmed herself a gadget junkie as she dove right in, asking questions and trying things out.

"The big problem," Roy said, as he pulled up a chair, sitting backwards on it with his head resting on his arms, "is to get this stuff into Sunnyvale. The two sources I spoke to told me they take everything away from you, and the body search extends to cavities. These guys don't fool around. Too many people have tried to smuggle in their junk."

"I'm sure they're even more careful since they lost our girl and her friend a few months ago," Shannon said. "We're going to have to watch our step."

"That's why I brought this," he said, indicating a shallow box on the bed. Roy tossed it over with a grin. "This is the latest thing."

"It looks like a clear plastic box."

His smile was expansive. "Until you put something in it."

He took a pen out of his pocket, opened the box, put it in, shut the lid and handed it back to Shannon.

The box still appeared to be empty.

"It's a riff on an old magic trick. Got it from a friend of mine. He's one of those spooks, but I can't say for who. With a little bit of adhesive, this baby can sit on the inside of a toilet bowl or underneath a sink, and you'd have to be looking awful hard to spot it. This'll be your girl's care package. Everything a good little spy needs: radio communicator, GPS transmitter, digital camera that you can hide, um, wherever you might want to hide it, laser light for signalling and a small knife – just in case, you understand."

As he enumerated each item, Jackie tossed it over and into his magic box it went.

Shannon sighed. "All that remains is to hope nothing goes wrong. If somebody finds this stuff, we're screwed."

"Nobody's gonna find it. I'll excuse myself to use the washroom and hide it when I'm in there. If we don't hear from your girl—"

Jackie made a face. "I *do* have a name, you know."

Roy laughed. "You got an attitude on you, Jackie Goode. I like that."

I don't, Shannon thought.

"Anyway, if we don't hear from Jackie by the next night, wc know something's wrong, and we pull her out."

"And for opening doors?"

Here Roy reached into the inside pocket of his sport jacket. "I got these little babies." Handing them across to Shannon, he said, "I know the company that put in the security systems at Sunnyvale. Believe me, one of those five cards will work on any door lock in the place."

"Cool," Jackie said. "How did you get your hands on these?"

"Let's just say I don't know and leave it at that." Roy picked up a few last things. "Some surgical tape to put our goodies on your body when you leave the washroom, a bit of bubble wrap to keep everything from rattling around, and extra adhesive to reattach the empty box and you should be good to go, girl...Jackie." He reached forward, grabbing a black box half the size of a cigarette pack, which he handed to Shannon. "You have to put this within one thousand feet of wherever they have Jackie. Inside is a digital recorder that her transmitter will activate."

"And that's how I get her reports."

"Exactly. All you have to do is open this little rubber door, and you can stick in this flash stick to download the info. You can also listen on site through headphones plugged in here. It's totally weatherproof. Jackie will also be able to receive short messages from you."

Shannon shook her head in wonder as she went over to the window and pulled back the curtain to look out for about the tenth time, a totally futile gesture.

"FedEx will get here when they get here," Jackie laughed. "Relax."

The previous evening, they'd burned up the phone lines pulling the money end of this together. The fact that Roy's business had moved heavily into concert and tour security had suggested to Jackie that her friend Kit Mason, blues guitarist extraordinaire, be seen to have sent her to rehab. That way Roy would also be a logical person to show up with her at Sunnyvale.

"My photo's even in two spots on Kit's website," Jackie had said, in her effort to convince her boss. "It'll work."

Shannon kept getting the feeling she was being railroaded. "And your friend Kit is cool with fronting you this kind of cash? Curran says he can't come up with it for another twenty-four hours at least."

"Relax. Kit has more money than God these days. She's done really well for herself. The cheque is no big deal for her."

"Shannon?" Roy said, "do what your girl says: relax. We got everything worked out here."

If someone told her to relax one more time, she was going to scream. Forcing herself to sit down, she said nonetheless, "I can't help thinking we haven't taken something into account."

♪‡ŗ·♪♭ŗ·

Jackie breathed a huge sigh of relief as the nurse? orderly? security guard? shut the door to her room.

She was in.

It had been a huge strain keeping her nerves under control for the past two days around her boss. She guessed that if she'd shown the slightest hesitation, the tiniest flutter of apprehension, the whole thing would have been called off.

Now she was inside Sunnyvale, and her real work could begin. First order of business was to check for any surveillance in the room. She'd done a fair bit of studying over the past few months on that sort of thing, and Roy and Shannon had coached her with additional tips and tricks, but she knew darn well that nothing was foolproof. In the digital age, it was easier than ever to spy. Their best hope was that Sunnyvale had no real reason to spend a lot of money spying on their clientele.

The intake session had gone well, with the interviewer seeming to suspect nothing. Roy had aced his part, playing to perfection the bored security heavy fed up with a useless babysitting job.

He'd tipped her the wink as he'd left the washroom and she was being led into the examination room.

Never a big user of drugs, she'd done the occasional line of coke and smoked crack a couple of times when she'd bombed out of university after her aunt died. Shannon appeared taken aback by Jackie's knowledge but later actually admitted to smoking weed, "two or three times" while in college. "And if you ever tell my daughter or son, I'll cut out your liver with a dull spoon!"

The effect of the crack she'd smoked the evening before had blasted into her skull with the force of a freight train; it was high-grade stuff and Jackie had spent a very interesting evening getting totally wiped. That morning she'd done the same, to make sure the level of the drug in her bloodstream would be alarming. The whole ordeal had left her nerves frayed and ragged, her brain lethargic but curiously on edge. She kept that information to herself. For the necessary time, she'd be able to play her part without much effort.

Shannon had decided it would be best for Jackie to seem to be there under duress.

"Make out like your friend Kit strong-armed you into rehab," she had said just before Roy drove Jackie up to Sunnyvale that morning, "and that your thinking is to play the game so you can stay in her good books. We also need you to appear pretty far gone. Quite often crackheads suffer from hallucinations and paranoia. I suggest you use that."

Jackie grinned. "Since when did you become such an expert on the long term effects of crack?"

"Since last night on the Internet while you were so out of it. You had me worried."

"That's why I stay away from the stuff. It's really addictive, and its effects are highly seductive."

Shannon gave her a hug as she was leaving. "Just be careful, Jackie. Play it smart; play it safe."

The intake session at Sunnyvale had been quite an experience with Jackie switching back and forth between sullen and snarling. Once in the examination room she had thrown a few things around for extra effect. A doctor had hustled in soon after.

"I'm Dr. Smith, and I'm the director here at Sunnyvale," he said, as he surveyed the damage.

Jackie studied his face carefully. The smile did not extend to his eyes.

"Now, Ms Goode, Nurse Simpson here will help you off with your clothes and do the first part of your examination. I'll see you at the other end. Please refrain from any more histrionics."

Simpson held out a gown. "Take off your clothes, and put this on." She wasn't smiling.

"No."

"Look, dear, either you do as I ask, or I'll get two strapping assistants to help me. You wouldn't want that, would you? If you're going to be successful here, you have to learn to do as you're asked."

"I don't want to be here."

"That's not what your friend said when she called us."

"She's full of it. I don't have any problems."

"That's what a lot of our Seekers say. When you prove to us you don't have a problem, you'll be free to leave, okay?"

While Jackie took off her clothes, Simpson went over some papers Dr. Smith had handed her, all the while keeping a careful eye on her charge.

Simpson did the usual things: height, weight, blood pressure, and she also took several blood samples. Then then came the cavity search, something Roy had warned her about, not that it made it any less unpleasant.

"You'd be surprised what some people will try to do, dear. We want to give you the best chance of beating your problems."

When she was handed over to Dr. Smith, he not only went over the results of the physical, but wanted a detailed history. Jackie, Shannon and Roy had decided that this could be dangerous, since details could easily be forgotten, so she resorted to being uncooperative.

"You're only hurting yourself, Jackie. If you want to discover how to heal yourself, you're going to have to cooperate."

When she was finally shown to her room, it was near sunset. She was given her "Sunnyvale outfit": sweatsuits, jeans, T-shirts and a jacket, all of them either blue, green or a combination, but she had no chance to get into the washroom where Roy had left his package.

Nurse Simpson accompanied her to her room. "We want you to stay by yourself tonight. Dinner will be brought to you in a few minutes. If you need us, we're just a ring away," she finished, pointing to a red button on the bedside table.

There was a ceiling-mounted TV, a clock radio and a reading light over the bed. A small table and chair finished off the decor. The only window overlooked the central courtyard.

"How long do I have to stay in here?" she demanded.

Simpson stopped by the door. "Someone will talk to you tomorrow.

It's mostly up to you how quickly things happen around here."

The door clicked shut behind her, the sound of the lock turning was decisively loud in the quiet room.

Jackie flopped onto the bed and stared up at a camera mounted in a tamper-proof case on the ceiling to the right of the TV.

She had to find some way to get into that washroom, and she didn't have long to do it.

♪♯♪·♪♭♪·

Roy headed back to Oakland almost immediately after returning from Sunnyvale.

"I got work to do," he told Shannon, "and the place never runs well when the bossman's away. You know that."

She gave him a big hug. "I'm just glad I have you to count on. You have no idea how much help you've been."

"Oh, I do, I do," he chuckled, and squeezed her back. "That's what friends are for. And by the way, your husband's a fool."

"That's putting it mildly."

"You happy?"

"Yes. I have a great new guy. He's a musician. My kids love him. Even my mother likes him."

"Oh, spare me!" Roy pulled back and looked at her. "But you do look happy. Tell that musician, he doesn't treat you right, he's got me to deal with."

"He's a good man."

"Better be. Now, I'm only a phone call away. You know what you're doing, but if things get out of hand, you know who you can count on."

"We'll be fine, thanks to all your gadgets."

"You going up there tonight?"

"Late this afternoon. I don't know the terrain well enough to risk being out at night yet."

"Then you need some night-vision goggles."

"Don't tell me," Shannon said, laughing as Roy began rummaging in his bag.

He handed her the bulky contraption. They always reminded her of some sort of torture device.

"Let me know when you hear from your girl. She may have a hard time getting into the can where I stashed her goodies. If she can't manage it, we'll have to go to Plan B."

"What's Plan B?"

He smiled. "Search me. I haven't thought of it yet."

Shannon spent her evening on the phone and the Internet, trying to keep all the balls in the air. At least the three-hour time difference made it a bit easier.

Everything was quiet on the home front. The business was easily handled by a short discussion with Janet, who was a careful and steady worker. Shannon had come to rely on her over the past five years.

She reached Andy as he was heading out the door to his gig at the Salamander. "I just wanted to let you know that everything went well today. Jackie is inside Sunnyvale."

"Any word from her yet? Has she seen Olivia?" He sounded anxious.

"No, but I'm pretty sure I saw Olivia yesterday when we were observing the compound from a hillside."

"How did she seem?"

"Andy, I was at least seven hundred feet away! Relax. The moment I know *anything*, I'll be in touch. Just sit tight."

Hanging up the phone, she grimaced. He sounded pretty strung out, and that was never a good sign in a client. What this job needed most of all was patience. Shannon felt like somebody who was fishing: she had her hooks in the water, and sooner or later she'd get a bite.

With that thought in mind, she retrieved her notebook from the top of the TV and a photocopy of Olivia's journal from her laptop case. Leaning back against the pillows on the bed, she began reading and taking notes. Eventually, she opened her laptop and went online again.

"Let's see if we can find out what's become of you, Jack Taggart, and why Olivia's journal entries about you are so conflicted."

ᐧᕕᑉᐧᑌᕕᑉᐧ

Jackie made sure she stayed fidgety her first evening in Sunnyvale, certain that they'd be observing her. One of the primary effects of crack addiction is restlessness, as well as irritability and moodiness. Jackie was a past master of all three, so it was no stretch for her to fake it.

She did not like being locked in her room, so she just amplified those feelings and let herself go. Flipping around the TV channels, pacing the room, even trying to open the sealed window, she thought she put on a pretty convincing show.

Finally, she allowed herself to doze a bit. Around nine thirty, a smiling orderly knocked on the door, then unlocked it without waiting for a reply. Behind him in the corridor was a cart with "healthy" snacks and fruit juices. She really wanted a burger and fries with a beer chaser.

"When am I going to be let out of here?" she demanded harshly. "I don't like being locked in."

"It's not up to me," he looked down at his clipboard, "Jackie."

"Who said you can call me by my first name?" she looked at the nametag on his red polo shirt, "Frank?"

"Relax. Everybody's on first names here. It's all part of the casual atmosphere."

"Do you call being locked in 'casual'?"

Frank shrugged. "It has nothing to do with me. Start behaving yourself, and you won't be locked in. It's for your own safety, anyway."

"What do you mean 'start behaving myself'? What have I done?"

His eyes flicked over to the window. "Nothing."

"You're spying on me! I don't like it!"

The friendliness was wearing off. "Like I said, Jackie, it's for your own safety. You wouldn't be here if you didn't have a big problem. We can help, but only if you help, too."

Jackie had her hands on her hips and watched as Frank's eyes dropped to take in her body. "Well, thanks for the pep talk. Now get the hell out and leave me alone!"

As the spring-loaded door eased shut behind him, she picked up the clock radio and hurled it. It shattered with a satisfying crash, just as the lock clicked. She looked up at the camera and gave it the finger.

Sitting on the bed, Jackie put her head in her hands, pretending to cry. After a few minutes, she flopped onto her side and curled up into a ball.

Eventually, she dozed off again.

The next morning, a female orderly opened the door sometime after sunrise. The smashed appliance crunched as she walked over to the bed.

"You awake, honey?"

"I am now," Jackie grumbled as she peered around the blanket she'd pulled over herself during the night.

Surveying the damage, the orderly said, "Looks like you had a bad night."

"I feel like a pile of shit." Sitting up, she added, "Are you going to let me out of here?"

"All in good time. Doc Smith wants to talk with you some more, and you're going to be introduced to the Teacher who's been assigned to you. After that, we'll see."

"When's all this excitement going to happen?"

"Soon as you've had your breakfast. You must be hungry. You haven't eaten since you got here."

Jackie was absolutely famished. The things she'd do for her job...

"What can I have?"

Doris – according to her nametag – listed off a bunch of yogurt flavours, fruit, juices, smoothies and cereals. All sounded far too healthy, when what Jackie craved was eggs, bacon, home fries and toast with lots of butter.

"What? No pop tarts?"

"One of the things we teach people here is how to make smarter choices in what they eat," Doris told her patiently.

Staying in character, Jackie waved her hand dismissively. "Bring me whatever crap you want."

The food, when it came, was good quality. The show biz crowd would expect no less. After that it was a shower (supervised by Doris) and a meeting with Dr. Smith and her Teacher, Barry, a wiry guy with a big nose.

Judging by what she heard, they'd swallowed her story, and the blood tests had backed up the results. A complete program was mapped out; it would start immediately. She feigned disinterest throughout, keeping her arms folded across her chest and looking away.

"We're only trying to help you, Jackie," Barry said, "and I guarantee you'll do much better if you improve your attitude."

"I'll improve if you let me go to the can right now, unless you want me to do it here. Fruit always gives me the shits."

Barry got up, keeping his face suitably blank, but Smith's was easy to read: disgust.

Just down the hall, Barry stopped and inclined his head. "In here. I'll be waiting outside. Don't flush. We need a stool sample," he added as he held up a plastic cup and tongue depressor.

Once inside, Jackie moved fast. Sitting down on the toilet backwards, she prayed she could provide the sample needed.

Carefully lifting the lid on the water tank, she felt around inside. Shit! No box. She searched again wildly, making sure she hadn't missed it, cursing under her breath. If someone had already come across it, this operation was toast – or worse.

Trying to keep down the rising panic, she picked up the lid with shaking hands. She didn't drop it. She didn't make a sound as she replaced it. Then she felt around underneath the tank.

And there it was.

Turning right way around on the seat, she pulled down her sweats and did what she'd come in for while she also quickly emptied the box, taping various articles to her stomach and underarms, relying on the bulky sweatshirt she'd put on to hide it.

Barry pounded on the door. "You gonna be much longer in there?"

"Almost done!" she called out as she closed the case and reattached it underneath the toilet. Slouching out the door moments later without the cup, she said to Barry, "All yours, buddy. Knock yourself out."

As he went inside, Jackie smiled broadly. That had been almost too easy.

CHAPTER 18

The motel bed was too hard, and consequently, Shannon's back was complaining the next morning. Groaning, she turned over and looked at the clock through one eye. Not even six. It felt as if she hadn't slept.

There was work to be done. Rising, she turned on the coffee maker, already loaded with both of the pouches that had been supplied. Maybe she'd be surprised this time, and it would actually be worth drinking.

It took a good ten minutes, luxuriating under the warmth of the shower, to get some of the kinks out of her back.

The coffee proved disappointing, but at least it was hot and gave her a desperately-needed caffeine jolt.

Slipping into her muddy jeans and hiking shoes, she puzzled over what top to wear. It might be best to opt for layers. The weather report was for clear and sunny, so rain gear wasn't necessary, but the day, while cool now, promised to be hot later. She grabbed yesterday's jacket, since it was already dirty. No sense messing up something else.

Her plan was to go out, check again for word from Jackie, then come back to sort out her other big problem.

After a thorough Internet search, she hadn't found any trace of Jack Taggart after Bernard St. James III had been murdered.

She had a pretty good idea what had become of him.

♪♯♩·♪♭♩·

First thing on the agenda for Jackie that morning was an acupuncture treatment.

The treatment room was light and airy, with two small supply tables against one wall, a couple of chairs, and a wheeled cart with an electrical gadget on it. Dominating all was a waist-high treatment table in the centre. Soft synthesizer music with nature sounds mixed in played from speakers in the ceiling, and several charts of acupuncture points on the body were mounted on the walls.

Jackie eyed everything warily. The nice music and pleasant surroundings didn't hide the fact that they stuck things in you. She hated needles of any kind.

Doris took a short gown from one of the tables. "Put this on."

"Do I have to take off my clothes?"

"Yes. You can leave your bra and panties on if you want."

This was *not* good. With all her gadgets taped to her body, what the hell was she going to do?

"And just why do I need someone sticking needles in me?"

"It will help control your cravings," Dr. Smith answered as he walked into the room. "Now get those clothes off, the gown on and hop onto the table. I'll be back in a few minutes."

"I'm not going to take my clothes off while *she* watches." Jackie indicated the orderly with a flip of her head.

Smith looked at Jackie for a moment, then said, "Wait outside the room, Doris, but don't go far."

Jackie slipped her clothes off in record time, then used some of the tape to fasten everything underneath the lowest shelf on one of the small tables. Just as she climbed onto the examining table, Doris stuck her head in the door. Five seconds earlier, and it would have been all over for her little operation.

Smith was brisk and businesslike, giving Jackie a short lecture on the philosophy of acupuncture and what she could expect from it.

"Acupuncture is a large component of our program at Sunnyvale. It allows us to accomplish a number of objectives without resorting to pharmaceutical medications. We're very against that sort of thing. Our treatment generally relies on natural medicine.

"I'm going to do two things today. One is to give you what we call an ear tack. If you feel any craving for crack, I'll show you how to manipulate the short needle it contains to make those cravings recede. I will also do what we call a general tonic to tune up and balance your internal organs. Your tongue indicates that your digestion is not good. This will help."

"I don't think it's necessary."

"I'll be the judge of that. Now lie down."

The hair-thin needles didn't hurt particularly going in, but the physical effects they produced were quite startling. Inserted in various points on her body, the needles throbbed and seemed to grow hot. One needle often caused a reaction in another, which was also disconcerting.

"Now this is a new part of our treatment," Smith told her when he'd inserted about a dozen needles. "I'm going to connect some of the needles to this little machine and put a low electrical current through them. This will cause the acupuncture points to activate electrically. We find it speeds up treatment considerably."

Until then, things hadn't been too bad, but having groups of muscles contracting because of the electricity was definitely *not* a pleasant feeling. First, it took quite some time to get the machine adjusted, and Smith turned something up too high at one point, causing an agonizing muscle contraction in one leg.

Jackie cried out in pain and surprise.

"Sorry about that," Smith mumbled as he worked. "You seem to be very susceptible to the current."

With a little more fiddling, he finally had everything adjusted to his satisfaction.

Smith walked to the door and switched off most of the room lights. "I'm going to leave you for about half an hour. Just lie here, relax and enjoy the treatment."

The last thing Jackie did was relax – or enjoy it. She did not like the idea of being a human pin cushion, and even though nothing really hurt, it all felt very strange. That jolt of mis-adjusted voltage had also completely unnerved her.

Later, when Smith had finally finished with her and left, she slapped her goodies to her body again and practically ran from the treatment room.

The rest of that first morning was spent keeping Barry happy.

Jackie could not get a handle on the guy. He seemed concerned and caring but also unnecessarily harsh in his appraisal of her. If she had honestly had an addiction problem and low self-esteem, he might have done some lasting damage. It was all probably part of a well thought-out program, but it would have been hard to take.

She'd decided that if she was going to be allowed to mingle with the other Seekers, she'd have to appear a little more compliant – at least for the moment. Now that she had her toys, she also needed to get out of the room they'd assigned her. The fisheye lens on the camera covered practically every bit of it. She doubted the regular rooms would have CCTV surveillance. Hollywood types would not put up with *that*.

"Can we go outside?" Jackie asked, after about an hour. "I seriously need some fresh air."

Barry thought about it for a moment, then answered, "Sure. I could use a bit of air myself."

Outside the building, he walked her towards a small grove of trees with unoccupied picnic tables under them.

The day was clear, a bit cool, but pleasant. Feeling the wind on her face was a big improvement. Across the compound was the high hill where Jackie had taken Shannon two days before. She parked herself in a spot where she could be seen easily if her boss was up there watching.

Barry set down his papers and a small recorder he'd been using. Realizing she'd start sweating if she stayed out in the sun as she was, Jackie got up and moved to a shadier spot. She could not afford to take off her sweatshirt at the moment and didn't know how securely Roy's tape would hold if it got damp. Most of it was being used for a second time.

Trying to relax, she focussed on what Barry was saying. It was all about how the program would serve her if she would let it. "I'm not saying it will be easy. You are going to have to face a lot of things about yourself that you won't like, but if you do face them down, you'll be building an inner strength that will carry you through the worst situations."

Playing along, she asked, "And your program works for everybody?"

He nodded. "If the person *really* wants to get better and beat the failure that's been dogging their steps, we can help them do it. If they truly want to get better, they *will* get better. I have never seen it fail."

Jackie could tell that Barry believed everything he said.

She really wanted to ask him why Sunnyvale had failed Olivia so miserably.

Since Jackie had been a good girl, Barry rewarded her with a new room by mid-afternoon – one with no camera. It was also in a building further towards the centre of the compound, which meant it was nearer the hill Shannon would probably be watching from.

As she put down the armful of clothes she'd carried over from the other building, Jackie immediately noticed the empty bookcase in the corner. She turned to Barry. "How come it's empty? You don't allow people to read here?"

"No, we *encourage* everyone to read. You have to earn the right to have books, just like everything else here." He turned and walked to the door. "We have exercise period in twenty minutes. You might want to change into something lighter. Do a good job exercising, and we'll see about a book. Same goes for the TV and things like that." He looked her squarely in the eye. "But don't forget that the pendulum can also swing in the opposite direction. You can *lose* things, too."

As soon as the door clicked shut behind him, Jackie sprang into action. It took ten minutes to be as sure as she could be that she wasn't being monitored.

Once that was done, she stripped off her outer clothes and removed all of Roy's goodies.

Where to hide them was a problem, since she couldn't be sure the room wouldn't be searched. She decided on using the back of the padded reading chair next to the bookcase.

She sliced four inches along the bottom seam with Roy's little knife, then stuffed each item in one at a time. It would be tricky to get them out in a hurry, but unless the chair was turned over, her hiding place would be hard to detect.

She just had time to get her T-shirt back on change into some shorts before Barry returned for her. It was hard to keep the smug grin off her face as she followed him to the quadrangle.

"This is the rest of my current Family," he said as he indicated four other people. "I'll leave you to introduce yourselves. I have a meeting with the director, but you'll see me this evening."

One of the group was a pop diva who'd lately had a string of cancelled concerts as well as TV talk show appearances where she'd been slurring words and forgetting the lyrics to her forgettable songs. There was a mom of three who had developed a painkiller dependency after the birth of her third child (now seven years old), a businessman who drank too much and a young punk with an attitude problem who'd been sent to Sunnyvale by a judge in exchange for a suspended sentence for stealing his father's car and wrecking it.

Except for the punk, everyone seemed friendly enough and quite happy to talk about their problems. The punk brazenly stared at Jackie's body to the point where she thought he could do with a little roughing up.

More people joined the growing crowd on the grass of the quadrangle. Eventually, a perky young blonde with a face just aching to have a fist slammed into it stood in the centre and did her thing, a combination of aerobics, dance movement, stretching and the usual predictable exercises done in gym classes around the world. Her chirpy, enthusiastic voice and music that was at least fifteen years out of date made Jackie want to scream.

It didn't escape Jackie that one of the few contemporary songs was by her litter-mate, the pop diva, who basked in the glow of her meagre fame as she sang along with it. No wonder the girl had self-esteem issues. Kit could wipe the floor with her.

Everyone bought into the exercising with enthusiasm – with the exception of the punk, who did the very least he could. Using the fact that she was the new kid on the block, Jackie purposely screwed up so she would have a better chance to stop and look around. Eventually, she spotted Olivia in a far corner of the quadrangle, with a man and woman in brown near her. Seeing that gave her pause. Could Olivia's nasty stepmother be on the lookout for something?

During a short pause, when everyone had a sip of water from bottles that were handed out, Jackie sidled over to the mom in her group. "Do we have to stay with our Family?"

"No, but why would you want to move?"

"The punk keeps staring at my butt."

"Randy's harmless. He just needs his attitude rearranged. That's really why he's here."

"I still don't like it."

"They encourage us to be together. Since you're new, I can't be sure how Barry will feel about it."

With this exchange as a possible excuse, Jackie moved farther back in the crowd so she could use the remaining time to observe Olivia better.

Her face looked more gaunt than it had in the promo shot Jackie had been shown. But it was the faraway look in her eyes that made Jackie feel most uneasy. Did they have her on drugs?

A few other people near Olivia seemed a bit strange, too, and all of them seemed to be kept apart from the others. If this continued to be the case, Jackie's job would be a lot harder.

She sighed as she did yet another stupid exercise. What she really wanted to be doing was running hard and lifting weights. Bullshit group aerobics were not her thing.

♪♯♩♪♭♩·

Up on the hillside, Shannon was watching. She too had located Olivia, and once she'd made sure Jackie was on the quadrangle, she spent most of her time watching the girl. Even through binoculars, it was easy to see that she moved awkwardly, as if they had her on some kind of drug. Could they be on to Jackie, or did they just want to make sure Olivia wouldn't escape again?

There had been no word from Jackie yet, but at least she was out exercising and seemed to be okay. She'd moved towards Olivia, but not too near, Shannon noticed with satisfaction.

When exercise period was over, Olivia was led off with five other people, so Shannon kept tabs on Jackie, who went back to talk to the group she'd been with at the beginning of the exercise session. Then she walked slowly off to a building in the middle of the compound and went inside. This must be where she was being housed. Shannon scanned the rest of the compound, but Olivia had already disappeared.

An LED on the side of Roy's receiver/transmitter began flashing, so Shannon plugged in the small headset he'd also supplied.

Reception was not great, but Shannon was relieved that everything seemed to be working. Jackie was in mid-sentence.

"...so that's what I saw. I'm going to—"

"Jackie, it's Shannon. I'm here."

"I was hoping you would be. You on the hill?"

"Yes. That's where I thought reception would be best. I saw you going into a building after exercise period. Is your room in there?"

"Yes."

"So what's up? You'll have to speak louder. There's a lot of noise on your transmission."

"That's because I'm in the bathroom with the shower on. I checked the room for bugs, but you never know."

"What side of the building are you on?"

"Your side. Just a minute. I'll go open the curtain so you know which room it is."

Moments later, a curtain pulled aside, and Jackie appeared in the window for a few seconds.

"Got it?" she asked.

"Yes. I don't think we should be on too long. Do you have anything for me?"

"Did you spot Olivia?"

"Yes."

"How did she seem to you?"

"Spaced out."

"Me, too. I'm still feeling my way around, but I'm going to try to get closer to her, maybe talk. We all eat in that large building at the eastern end of the compound."

"Just don't take any chances. We only want to find out what her situation is. Once you accomplish that, we'll have to reevaluate where we're going with this."

"Is Roy around?"

"No, he's gone back to Oakland."

"Tell him he did a good job."

"I'm sure he knows that."

"I'm going to sign off. We have something called a 'responsibility session' before dinner, and I still need to figure out the most effective way to play this: cooperative or uncooperative. The bullshit in this place is enough to make me puke."

"Leave me a message before you go to bed. I'll pick it up in the morning at the latest."

"Gotcha. Over and out."

♪♯♪·♪♭♪·

Jackie glared at everyone in the circle around her. Group therapy had never been a thrilling concept for her, and being the new kid on the block, everyone had been having a go at her. The fact that they were the ones who were actually screwed up, and she was only play-acting didn't make it any easier. Barry just sat back after telling everyone her background and let them have at her.

As she put up with the amateur-hour psychologists, Jackie was busy trying to figure out how to get closer to Olivia without arousing any suspicion. The punk hadn't taken part in much of the dissection of her fake problems, even though Barry had tried to draw him into the conversation.

She tried not to get angry – difficult under the circumstances. "How long have all of you been here, and do you think you're better off now than when you arrived?"

Mary, the mom, gushed, "I *am* a lot better. I can't believe the progress I've made in a month. I see things really clearly now."

David, the businessman, said, "I know I'm always going to have trouble with booze, and I'll have to be around it a lot, too, because of my job, but I think I'll be able to handle it now. That's not bad for six weeks."

The pop star, Alycia, declared she was beginning to understand how all the bad things had happened to her. "There are people who will hang on you for the good times. They're facilitators, and I have to be on my guard against them. I don't think I'll be ready to leave for at least a month."

At this, Randy the punk spoke up scornfully. "That's about the amount of time it will take your manager to get you a new record deal, I seem to remember you saying a few nights ago."

Alycia glared at him.

He continued. "You're all completely full of shit. This whole place is full of shit. And I am *so* tired of listening to the three of you whine."

Getting up, he stomped out of the room and slammed the door. Barry sighed loudly and scribbled on his note pad.

"He's an angry young man," David said, shaking his head.

Mary added, "He won't make any progress until he opens up. I still say you should put him in another group, Barry. He needs to be with kids his own age."

"We'll be the judge of that, Mary," Barry said surprisingly firmly. "We've had this discussion before."

Jackie saw an opportunity and grabbed it. "Well, I think Randy has the right idea. It's bullshit to sit with a bunch of people who have more problems than I do and have to listen to them tell *me* what I'm doing wrong. Who made you the experts?"

"We're coming from the same place you are," Mary said, with what she probably hoped was a reassuring smile.

"It's all bullshit. I'm outta here!"

She stormed out of the room in much the same way Randy had – except she slammed the door so hard the glass in its window cracked.

It was hard not to smile.

Randy was by himself under a tree at the far end of the compound. Jackie went over and sat down next to him. It was several minutes before he spoke. "So did they send you out here to get me?"

Jackie laughed. "Hell no! I basically told them the same thing you did."

They were silent for awhile before he asked, "Is it true you know Kit Mason?"

This was from left field. "Yeah, and I wish she'd kept her nose out of my business."

"What's she like?"

"Why do you want to know?"

"No reason," he said, shrugging. "I just like her music."

"You got any of her CDs?"

"Yeah. She says it like it is. She's also a bitchin' guitarist," he added, sounding more like a teenager.

Jackie smiled. "So you're a fan."

He shrugged again. "Yeah, I guess I am."

She pretended to consider for a moment. "How about you show me the ropes around here, and when we blow this place, I'll introduce you to Kit?"

After pretending to consider that, Randy said, "Okay. First thing you should know is that they're going to take something away from you for what you did. That's what they call 'the System'. I've been sleeping on the floor for the past week."

He said it as if it was a badge of honour.

"Why don't you just play the game and get yourself out of here?"

"Tried that. They seem to know when you're bullshitting them. It's kind of spooky."

"Tell me about those people who were way off by themselves during the exercise thing. I thought this was supposed to be one happy family."

"The space cadets? They're all nuts. A couple of them have been here for years. Good for a laugh sometimes, though."

The dining hall was large and noisy. Barry was waiting for Jackie at the door, along with Dr. Smith. Both eyed her ominously.

"I'm told you had a bad session this afternoon," Dr. Smith said.

She shrugged. "Depends what you call bad."

"I've told you, Jackie, good behaviour is rewarded and bad behaviour is punished. You know what that means."

"No, I don't, but I'm sure you're going to tell me."

"There will only be juice and crackers for your dinner tonight, and we've removed the pillow and bedding from your room. Since you're new, it will only be for tonight. Jackie, you have to understand we can only help you if you're willing to help yourself."

Randy had informed her she was supposed to sit with people she didn't know at meals. That was supposed to bring Seekers "out of themselves," or some such ridiculous thing.

"You mean I can sit with the pop stars and other show biz people?"

Randy had rolled his eyes. "They never sit out with us. Their claim is that the rest of us hassle them. They have a special dining room. That's where Smith and the upper guys eat, too. Sort of shows their program's built on lies, doesn't it?"

At first Jackie sat down at a table looking angry. Eventually, she wandered off to the food line, where she was handed a glass of some venomous smelling green-coloured liquid and a cellophane bag containing four whole wheat crackers.

Being one of the last to get her meal, she came out and stood looking over the crowded room. At the far end was the table where the six "space cadets" sat with their handlers. One seat at the round table remained empty, and it was right next to Olivia.

Nobody said anything as she sat down.

Some of them ate normally. One had only a spoon, and the weirdest of the lot ate sloppily with just her fingers. Jackie stared straight ahead, her face blank.

After about five minutes, she picked up the crackers, looked down at them for a moment, then slowly closed her hand, crushing them to crumbs. All eyes were on her, but still no one spoke.

Olivia, with a bowl of tomato soup in front of her, leaned against Jackie and asked in an exaggerated whisper, "Since you don't seem to want them, can I have your crackers? They never give you enough here."

Jackie turned and looked at her, then grunted, "Sure."

She managed to gag down the green glop so her stomach wouldn't be screaming at her all night, but that was about it. The red shirts talked quietly among themselves, but the space cadets remained silent throughout the meal, other than Olivia, who hummed constantly.

In those few brief seconds she'd looked into Olivia's eyes, Jackie had been shocked. They were dull and didn't seem to be tracking properly.

Smith definitely had her on something.

♪♯♩·♪♭♩·

Ronald, Dom and I looked at Harry blankly.

"It's a business decision, pure and simple. When you had Olivia, things were really looking up. Now they aren't again, and I need to get this place at least half-full just to break even. Weekends haven't been too good lately, either. Something had to give, and I'm afraid it's you guys. I feel bad about it, but that's the way it is. If business still doesn't pick up, I'm going to be forced to close. Live jazz is going down the toilet in this city."

Ronald was incensed. "So you're firing us, just like that?"

Harry shrugged. "Like I said: business is poor."

For a moment I thought our pianist was going to go ballistic, but suddenly he just sagged back in his seat.

"Thanks for being honest, Harry," I said, then added, glancing pointedly at Ronald, "We appreciate the week's notice. It will give us a chance to look for another gig."

Harry excused himself, and we sat silently for several moments, each lost in our own thoughts.

It hadn't been a good night all around. If we'd had twenty people at any one time that evening, I would have been surprised. With such an empty house, we'd hardly been able to get it up ourselves and had produced three pretty mediocre sets.

I looked at my companions. "Any hot ideas?"

Dom looked at me blankly, but Ronald's face was scarlet. Was it anger – or something else?

"What's eating you?" Dom asked.

"Nothing!" Ronald answered.

"Harry's just being honest with us. We've had a good run and—"

"We've got to get that damn girl back! She's the one who queered the whole deal. I shouldn't have..."

He stopped short, and his face got even redder, if that was possible.

"Shouldn't have what, Ronald?" I asked.

"I shouldn't have been so hard on her. She might have stuck around."

"Leaving was not her choice."

"How was I to know she was an escapee from some funny farm in California?" He looked at his watch. "Hell. I got to get out of here. Sorry I can't help with the equipment. We'll talk, okay?"

Ronald had his coat on and was out the door in less than minute. Dom and I watched him go.

"There's something Ronald's hiding from us," Dom said.

"Yeah, and I have a bad feeling I know what it is."

I'd never told the pianist about Sunnyvale, or the fact that it was in California.

CHAPTER 19

Unable to sleep, Shannon got up in the middle of the night, dressed quickly and drove out to Sunnyvale. The long walk in through the trees and scrub was greatly simplified by the night-vision goggles. They were bulky and she knew she looked ridiculous, but they did the job. She arrived on top of her observation hill shortly before three a.m.

Thick fog, luminous in the light of a nearly full moon, had flowed down to the valley floor, making most of the compound invisible. The peaks of the smaller buildings poked through like rocks in a slowly undulating grey sea, and the upper storeys of the larger buildings appeared to float majestically like ships.

The fog also strangely magnified any sound in this otherwise silent world. A door slammed, a dog barked and someone coughed loudly, but because of the impenetrable blanket, the noises seemed to come from everywhere and nowhere.

Shannon shivered and cursed softly as she lay on the damp ground. The previous day, she'd fastened the transmitter/recorder by means of cable ties to the middle of a thick bush on the edge of the hillside, giving it a clear opening to the compound below. Faced with cold hands, wet hardware and reaching up awkwardly through the branches, she was having a hard time popping off the protective cap that covered the headphone jack. Standing up to accomplish this more easily was not an option.

Finally the cap gave up the fight, but not before Shannon had scratched her hands and split a nail to the quick.

This had better be worth it, she thought as she fumbled with the headset.

Jackie's voice flooded into her ears, sounding cool, calm and collected. "Hi, Shannon. I'm sending this at ten fifteen at night. This place shuts down pretty early, since they don't encourage us to fraternize. It can lead to 'temptation', as they put it.

"I had to act out this aft in order to get some information, so they took away my radio, my bedding and my pillow. All I have left is one blanket. So all in all, it's been a pretty dry evening.

"I managed to sit with our quarry at dinner. It's not something I can do on a regular basis, but I thought I could risk getting close once in public. You should see her eyes. If she isn't spaced on something, I'm a horse's ass. I've been sitting here trying to think of a reason they'd be so obvious about it. Any dough-head could spot it a mile off.

"After dinner, I watched where Olivia and the other space cadets – that's what the other inmates call them – were led off to, and it's the building just to the north of the admin building. It's probably hidden from where you are, but you might want to check it out.

"If I'm going to get any decent info, I have to find a way to talk with her alone. That might mean getting into her building after dark. The staff members with the space cadets all have key cards on their belts, so if Roy stays on his roll equipment-wise, I should be able to get in there with one of the master key cards he gave me. Keep your fingers crossed.

"That's it. One thing I've got to say: when I get out of here, you owe me the biggest honkin' steak dinner with all the trimmings. The food here is macrobiotic, lo-cal, organic junk, for the most part. Fresh fruit and vegetables I can live with, but I don't want them all ground up together and looking like green slime in a glass.

"Sorry for the bitching, but I hadn't been counting on crap food. I'll catch a couple of hours of sleep, then see if I can do a bit of a reconnoitre of the grounds. And yes, I'll be very careful.

"What's up in the real world? Leave a short message so I know this gadget is working. Over and out."

Shannon pulled down the mike arm on her headset and pushed a button on the transmitter. It glowed red, showing it was on. "Jackie, got your report. Thanks. You're doing a great job. If you get a chance – and be really careful about this – ask Olivia about someone named Jack Taggart. I'd bring it up very gently. She gets pretty emotional about him in that journal of hers, so I don't know what her reaction might be, but I'm really curious to see what she says. Only do this if you won't compromise your cover. Job one is to keep your head down. Over and out."

She'd barely stuffed the headset back into her pocket when she heard a twig crack nearby. In the stillness, it sounded like a rifle report.

Taking stock of her surroundings, she slowly curled up her legs so the bush covered her completely. Then she waited. How loudly had she spoken? Sound carried amazingly. Crap! If she'd queered this business, she was going to be *really* upset with herself.

Five minutes, ten minutes. A rock was digging into her side. She barely dared to breath.

Then someone spoke. "See anything?"

"No. I reckon it was another false alarm."

"Third one this week. If this keeps up, the boss is going to have us camping up here."

"That won't do. What do we tell him?"

"How about deer? Or a bear? Renaldo swears he saw one up here a few months back. The boss might swallow that."

"Okay. We'll tell him we found bear tracks."

Shannon lay there an additional ten minutes just to be sure, then slowly backed out from under the bush.

They must have motion detectors, since she'd been ultra careful about the cameras. Infrared would have shown her outline. It was lucky the ground was dry up here, and she was taking care to walk as much as she could on dry pine needles under the trees. Footprints would have clinched it.

She soon found three detectors nearby, placed six metres up in the pines. Pretty cagey of someone. Make the cameras fairly obvious, then hit them with motion detectors while they weren't expecting it.

Now that she knew where they were located, she could take steps to avoid them, too. Only luck and the laziness of the staff had saved her.

As she sped back to Portola with the sky brightening to morning, Shannon wasn't sure which had been more unnerving: almost stumbling into trouble or possibly stumbling into a bear.

♪♯♪·♪♭♪·

Jackie woke just after three. The thin blanket did nothing to keep her

warm, even with a sweatsuit on and two pairs of socks, but she'd really
conked out for a while after transmitting her report to Shannon. Her left
shoulder was sore from having slept on it for several hours. Ten minutes
spent stretching all the kinks out made her feel as if she could move
without actually creaking.

Pushing the curtain aside, she looked out the window. Only half the
lights from earlier were on, leaving generous swathes of darkness. She
didn't think it would be a good idea to actually go into Olivia's room
and possibly frighten her. This little stroll was best suited to seeing just
what was possible and what needed to be worked out.

Earlier in the evening, Jackie had stepped out the door of her
building and found that the light over it was on a motion detector, so
leaving that way was wouldn't work. Her room's one window was the
slider type, and with a bit of fiddling, she managed to get the screen off.
Leaning out far enough to see how much light was around her side of
the building, she decided to risk a quick reconnoitre.

After a few minutes of watching in all directions, she slipped the hood
of her sweatshirt over her head and hopped onto the sill, then dropped
to the ground and rolled back towards the building. A further two
minutes brought no cries of alarm or running feet, so she crawled on
her belly to the end of the building, finding a space in the shadows there.

So far so good. The dark colours of the clothes she'd been given
certainly helped her clandestine journey, but she wished now she'd thought
of adding silk gloves and balaclava to Roy's care package. Light skin was
surprisingly easy to see. The building Olivia was housed in was on the
same side of the compound as Jackie's, but being closer to the admin
building, there was also more light. If there were going to be staff members
out and about at night, they'd probably be found in that general area.

Away from the buildings and pathways, there was no artificial light,
and Jackie noticed with satisfaction that fog was beginning to roll down
the hills on both sides of Sunnyvale. The site had probably been chosen
as being nicely secluded because of the surrounding terrain, but it also
lent itself to mists and fogs on nights such as this.

She worked her way from one pool of darkness to another, and was
less than halfway to her goal when the fog began obscuring everything.
In a few minutes, it was so thick, she could walk where she wanted.
Unless she went right under a light or actually bumped into someone,

they'd never know she was there. Still, her ears strained to catch any hint of sound that might mean danger.

One unexpected problem did arise, though: she was no longer certain which building was which and almost blundered into the side of what must have been a staff building, because she could hear people inside talking and laughing loudly, along with the unmistakable clink of beer bottles hitting together.

So, she thought, *when the mice are asleep, the cats play. Interesting...*

She reached what she was pretty certain was the building housing the space cadets. It was built lower to the ground than the building she was staying in, since it was on a flatter part of the site.

Jackie was poking around, trying to see into the rooms when she heard the sound she'd been dreading: rapid footsteps coming toward her on the walkway from the admin building.

She threw herself down in the wet grass facing the building, hoping the shadows would hide her.

The footsteps went right to the door, where the motion detector switched the light on. Jackie could make out the burly man she'd seen in town the other day swiping his key card and entering the building.

Deciding she'd tempted fate enough that night, Jackie got to her feet and was preparing to slip away when a voice spoke just to her right.

"What are you doing out there?" The female voice was soft, but intense.

Jackie froze, cursing her stupidity.

"Don't worry, I'm not going to tell anybody. Do you like the fog like I do?"

By now she realized the sound was coming from the window near her right shoulder, not from outside the building. One of the space cadets was talking to her.

"Yeah," she whispered.

"What are you doing out there?"

"It's a game I sometimes play, sort of like one of those video games, but in real life."

"Don't you know you'll get in a lot of trouble if they catch you out of your room?"

"That's all part of the game."

"Cool. I'd like to be out there with you, but we can't get out of our windows any more."

Stringing her along, Jackie asked, "Why not?"

"They've screwed them in place. I suppose I could break through, but I'd have no way to hide that, and they'd get pretty angry. I don't want to have to sleep on the floor."

With that information, Jackie decided to take a chance. "What's your name?"

"Olivia."

Bingo!

Realizing that whoever had come over from admin to this building could easily discover the two of them talking, Jackie decided to cut the conversation short.

"I gotta go now."

"That's too bad. I never have anybody to talk to when I sit here at night and look out."

"Oh, I might drop by another night when I'm playing my little games."

"I'd like that."

A sound at the front door and the light coming on made Jackie flit around the corner. All she needed was for Olivia to call out, and she'd be screwed. Fortunately, nothing happened, and she relaxed as the person walked off towards the admin building. She wasted no time getting back to her room, but her scrabbling entry through the window was anything but quick and graceful. Because of the slope behind her building, the sill was about five feet off the ground.

Jackie lay on the floor, wet, tired but very exhilarated by her excursion. She knew she'd been lucky with the fog and the dark night and actually speaking to Olivia, but it's said that luck is the residue of hard work...and taking chances.

♪♯♩·♪♭·

Dom and I had stayed up past four talking about the Olivia situation, first at the Sal, then, when Flo and Loraine gave us the boot, at the Mars Restaurant on College.

As a result of more booze than I'd had in nearly three years and several coffee chasers, I wasn't in top form when I woke up near noon.

Unburdening myself had felt good, since I'd really had no one just to talk to since Sandra had left. Olivia would have looked at me as if I'd fallen out of a tree if I'd said some of the same things to her. We'd parted as the sky was beginning to lighten the east.

Clapping me on the shoulder, Dom said, "This thing with our girlie is a lot more complicated than I thought. At first Ronald and I were sure she'd been spirited away by some manager who'd previously signed her. Man, you wouldn't believe the scenarios we came up with!"

"I'm glad you kept it from me. I probably would have popped you both in the nose. This has *not* been a good week for me."

"I think Ronald is now seeing the value of having Olivia working with us. If you want my opinion, he was jealous of the attention she was getting."

"Look, we're all pretty good players, especially Ronald, but Olivia is just plain special. Of course she was going to get the lion's share of the attention."

"You know that and I know that, but Ronald, well...he's Ronald. He's a hell of a player, Andy, not just good. With his skill and our backup, no telling how far we could have ridden on Olivia's coattails. Now we're faced with losing our steady gig."

"It's no good talking about it. We'll only get more depressed. I'm going home and hitting the sack. Kate is coming over this weekend, and I've still got fingerprint dust all over the house. I don't want her to see that. Tomorrow's going to be a busy day."

Lying in bed, I was working up the energy to head for the shower when someone started pounding on the downstairs door. Earlier in my musical life, I'd shared a house with the guys in my band, and when you have a bunch of musicians and parties till all hours, you learn pretty quickly how cops knock on doors.

This was definitely a cop, and he clearly was not in a good mood. I threw on some clothes and hustled down, fully expecting to see dents on my front door from the law enforcement knuckles.

"Andrew Curran?" one of two uniformed officers asked.

"Yes."

"Please come with us."

"What's this about?"

"I can't tell you that, sir. We've only been instructed to bring you downtown."

"Look, I just got out of bed. Can't I have some breakfast and come down later?"

His expression clearly showed he thought I was a complete moron. "I'm sorry, sir, but it doesn't work like that."

"Can I at least get my goddamn socks and shoes on?"

One of them actually followed me upstairs and waited outside my bedroom while I put on clean clothes. They even let me brush my teeth.

Of course, the old busybody next door was out on her porch to see me escorted down the driveway to the cruiser. At least they hadn't used handcuffs.

♪‡ρ·♪♭ρ·

Shannon got back to the motel, crashed for a few hours and rose as Portola came to life. First order of business was a nice hot shower.

It sounded as if things were going well at Sunnyvale. She only hoped her inexperienced operative wouldn't get overconfident. The memory of those livid knife scars Jackie had shown her had been the result of getting cocky. She hoped Jackie had learned something from that.

Shannon's goal at the moment was finding out exactly what had happened to this Taggart guy mentioned so many times in Olivia's journal – mentions ranging from saint to devil. It had not been hard to read between the lines. The retired butler, James Davis, had admitted that everyone in the St. James family had been completely stunned that Olivia was so deeply involved with drugs when she'd overdosed. Both he and Darcy Jeffries had told Shannon that they couldn't understand where she'd been getting the drugs.

She was willing to put money down that Jack Taggart was the one responsible, although why no one else suspected him was beyond comprehension.

Drying off, Shannon wiped the steamed-over mirror and studied her reflection. Part of her was still smarting over the way Maxine St. James had tried to play her for a fool. She'd been so smug about her little game as they'd eaten their civilized lunch, all the while thinking that she was about to put something over on the private investigator. Even though Shannon had the last laugh, she didn't take kindly to being thought a fool.

Wrapped in a towel, she went out into the room and flipped open her laptop. In short order, two emails told her that overnight searches by firms she'd utilized many times in the past to trace people had turned up nothing on Jack Taggart except his last known address in Brooklyn, something she already had.

The world was still a big place, but it was shrinking daily due to the omnipresence of the Internet. Yes, Taggart could be anywhere, living under an assumed name, and it might take weeks or even months to run him to ground, but there were ways to find nearly anyone these days.

But Shannon knew in her gut this wouldn't prove to be the case with Taggart, because she was betting he was no longer in this world, and *somehow* she was going to tie that fact to Maxine St. James.

Picking up her cell phone, she speed-dialed Roy's personal number.

"Moody."

"Roy? It's Shannon."

"What's up, gorgeous? Your girl doin' okay in Sunnyvale?"

"Looks like it, but I've got a bit of a problem."

"How can I help?"

"I need to go to New York to do some poking around, and I don't have anyone I can spare to hold the fort here while I'm gone. You got a likely candidate?"

"Let's see..." She could hear him rustling papers. "Yeah, I got just the guy. I'll call my man Marvell and tell him to hustle on up there. Is tonight okay?"

"Yeah, sure. I'll hopefully be in the Big Apple by then, so maybe it would be best for me to speak with him before I leave. He can use this motel room. When can I expect his call?"

"You'll hear from him shortly."

"I'll also inform Jackie. And Roy..."

"Yeah?"

"You're charging me for all this. I want to make that clear. This is not a freebie."

"I wouldn't think of insulting you."

"I'm not kidding, Roy. I expect an appropriate bill."

He sighed. "I know better than to argue with you. But you have to let me give you the bill over dinner."

Shannon couldn't help smiling. She'd always suspected Roy was sweet on her. With Rob, her ex, out of the way, he probably figured he finally had a chance.

"We'll see."

By the time Shannon hit the road, she'd done a quick trip out to the surveillance position to leave a message bringing Jackie up to speed. There she'd received the welcome news that Goode had made contact with Olivia the previous night.

Marvell had been told what was expected of him. She'd left the map that she had annotated, showing the location of the motion detectors and the cameras she and Jackie had found – and the route to follow to avoid them. On the phone, he had seemed experienced and competent. She hoped it proved to be true. She was leaving him with a big responsibility.

As her plane lifted off, however, she felt confident she had everything in hand.

CHAPTER 20

Music from the speaker in the ceiling flooded Jackie's room at half past six the next morning. If she'd had a pillow, she would have jammed it over her head and tried to continue sleeping.

"This is worse than being at some goddamn summer camp," she mumbled as she struggled to sit up on the bare mattress. The stiffness was back in spades.

Even with several layers of clothes, she was still chilled to the bone. Maybe they'd also turned off the heat to help drive home their point.

Getting in the shower, she'd only managed to soap up her hair when the water went cold.

Pounding on the tile wall with her hands, she yelled out, "You bastards!" knowing that if anyone were listening, they'd know they were ahead on this round. She didn't care.

Having to rinse off with ice cold water didn't improve Jackie's mood one iota. At breakfast, she sat with her Family, but for two very different reasons. First, she didn't want to be too much on the radar of the people running the camp, but also, feeling so cold and groggy from lack of sleep, she needed to be able to get a decent breakfast in her stomach. Deciding that playing ball was the way to go this morning, she joined the line and let them serve all the food her plate could hold.

Randy grinned at her across the table. "Looks like somebody didn't have a very good night."

"Piss off."

Mary, sitting next to Jackie, shook her head disapprovingly.

Barry wandered over and sat on the empty chair to Jackie's left, forcing her to move over a bit. In his hand he had a metal thermal coffee cup. It looked as though it could hold about a quart. He was also wearing baggy shorts and flip-flops, completing his head counsellor ensemble. She gritted her teeth and kept on shovelling in the food.

"You seem pretty hungry this morning, Jackie. Is your appetite returning?"

She fixed him with one of "those" expressions. "My appetite never went away."

"You probably had a pretty rough evening. Do you understand why we did what we did?"

"I have no idea how taking away my bedding and making me freeze my ass off all night is going to help me kick a drug habit I don't think I have."

"Jackie, Jackie. It's all part of helping you understand that there are consequences for everything you do. Part of facing up to the problems we all have is understanding the concept of consequences."

"Barry," she said without looking up, "why don't you go peddle your bullshit somewhere else and let me finish my breakfast in peace?"

Ten seconds later, two guys in brown appeared on either side of Jackie, lifted her up bodily and carried her out of the dining hall. The place went silent as they moved through the room.

Once outside, they put her down on the grass and walked back to the building, but stayed at the entrance. Clearly, they weren't going to allow her in again.

"The things I do for my job," she grumbled as she started down the walkway leading to the building where her room was.

Partway there, she paused, then took a walkway going off to the right, towards the building where Olivia had her room.

With her hands shoved deep in the pockets of her sweatshirt, she went along slowly, kicking at small stones and sticks in her path as if she were deep in thought and very unhappy. She was positive someone would be watching.

Thinking she might need to get into Olivia's building unobserved, it was best to see the place in daylight to get some idea of how that might be accomplished. She was going to use this golden opportunity to try to find out all she could.

The rest of the morning was a giant snore: a one-on-one session with Barry and some woman who sat there nodding like a bobble-head doll and scribbling notes at a furious pace any time Jackie spoke. Coming up with enough BS to fill the two-hour session was surprisingly easy once she realized that even if she changed stories later on, it would just be put down to her mental or psychological state. The more erratic they thought she was, the better.

After that she underwent another session with the acupuncture needles.

Lunchtime found Jackie chowing down on a very good chef's salad, the first decent meal they'd served as far as she was concerned. She made doubly sure to keep her mouth shut because she was so hungry.

Having arrived at the dining hall early, she was the first to sit down at the table in the back corner the space cadets seemed to favour. The room was beginning to fill up, but there was no sign of them.

A short, heavyset man slid right into the seat Olivia had used the evening before – and the one Jackie hoped she'd use again.

"Mind if I join you?"

Jackie wanted to snarl, "Yes! I do mind!" but didn't know if that would get her removed again.

For the next five minutes, he tried to start up a conversation. She answered monosyllabically, not needing some jerk trying to make time with her and possibly queering the deal if Olivia showed up. That thought made her decide to take action. "Look, Mac, I don't play your side of the field. Know what I mean? If you want to get your ya-yas, go someplace else."

He tried to make out that wasn't what he was after but picked up his tray and left when Jackie refused to even answer with grunts.

A minute later, the first of the cadets came to the table. Jackie kept her head down but her eye on him. The rest straggled in, Olivia being the last.

She immediately showed more interest in Jackie than previously and struck up a conversation as soon as her bum hit the chair.

"You were here yesterday evening."

Careful not to look up, Jackie answered softly, "I was a lot of places yesterday evening."

"You also did something bad."

She froze. "What do you mean?"

"You annoyed your Teacher at breakfast, and they made you leave."

"How do you know? You weren't even here."

"Everyone was talking about it. Patty," Olivia indicated the guard across from her with a toss of her head, "said that you were a troublemaker, and they had their eye on you."

Just great, Jackie thought. *That's the last thing I need.*

Olivia continued. "My friend Maggie was always a troublemaker too. She got me in *a lot* of trouble. Maybe I shouldn't be sitting with you."

Jackie felt the same, now that she knew. She had to get out of the room and not outwardly show any further interest in Olivia, but she also felt she had to move her contact with Olivia along – without frightening her.

The girl began picking out every piece of red onion in her salad, carefully laying them around the rim of the plate. Taking a few more mouthfuls, Jackie thought about what she might do. Time to trust her luck again. She stumbled a bit getting up and let her empty juice cup fall off the tray. Putting it down on the seat, she knelt just as Olivia leaned over to help.

As their heads dropped below the table, Jackie said into her ear. "I enjoyed talking to you last night at the window of your room."

"You?"

"Yup. If you don't tell anyone about it, I'll come over again tonight."

Carrying her tray to the front of the hall, Jackie thought to herself, *C'mon fog!*

Somehow she made it through the afternoon. Jackie had always resented people trying to crawl inside her head. These people wanted to know *everything,* and even if she were strung out on crack and at Sunnyvale for real, she wouldn't have poured out her guts to just anyone.

Barry seemed to sense this and kept after her to unburden herself so she "could begin to heal". The only thing that kept her from telling him where to stick his healing was her memory of the frigid night she'd just spent.

Later, when everyone came out to do exercises, Jackie kept a watchful eye on Olivia. She'd seemed less spaced out at lunch and was now going through the stupid routines as if she meant it.

Just before dinner, Jackie checked for any messages from Shannon. There were two, but it was the second that gave her pause. She could see why a trip to New York was important, but the news left her feeling vulnerable. Putting her trust in someone she didn't know was not comforting.

On the other hand, Shannon was also indicating her confidence in Jackie, and that wasn't a bad thing.

That evening, one of the inmates gave a concert in the dining hall. He was a rocker who'd been with a legendary band in the late sixties but was notorious for having a big ego and a bad attitude. After one more hit about twenty years ago, he'd vanished from sight. He told the audience the concert was to help with his rehabilitation, but Jackie felt the poor slob just wanted to validate himself and show off. Strumming an acoustic guitar and singing, he wasn't half bad, but she wouldn't have put down good money to hear him.

Towards the end of the set, he asked if there was anyone else who might want to come up and sing something, probably hoping that one or two of the other entertainers she'd seen around Sunnyvale would lend some of their glitter to his performance.

Jackie immediately swung her eyes over to Olivia, who was down near the front. She'd had a look of concentration on her face during the performance, but Jackie couldn't tell if she was enjoying it or hating it. From all she'd heard, Olivia could blow the guy out of the water.

Would she or wouldn't she?

"Isn't there *anyone* here who'd like to sing something with me?" the guy cajoled.

His eyes widened noticeably when Olivia stood up and said in a hesitant voice, "I'd like to sing."

There were a few titters from around the room and more than a little sad head-shaking. Patty, the guard, pulled Olivia's head down and said something into her ear, but Olivia shook her head and said, "No! I want to sing."

The guy looked truly sorry he'd asked as Olivia made her way down to the front. This was obviously *not* what he'd had in mind.

Olivia put her head close to his, and they talked softly, with a lot of head-shaking on his part. Maybe he was trying to play dumb about knowing how to play any of the songs she'd done with the trio back in Toronto, but there was also little chance he'd know those.

Finally he nodded reluctantly. Olivia hummed something while he hunted for the notes, then he nodded again and turned to the mike. "My friend and I will be singing 'Summertime.'"

He played a few chords, and Olivia didn't come in. After a few more he stopped. At the back of the hall somebody guffawed. Jackie was pretty sure it was Randy.

Everyone else looked uncomfortable.

Olivia turned to the guy and said loud enough for most to hear, "Too fast."

He said something back, and she shook her head violently, snapping her fingers to show him the tempo she wanted.

His face looked pretty ugly for a brief moment, then he got control of himself, shrugged and started again. The strumming was a little more jazzy and a lot slower.

Olivia opened her mouth – and the world just fell away. Even though the song was unrehearsed and a bit ragged around the edges, her performance was absolutely stunning. The opening verse she sang very low and throaty, almost as if she was humming to herself. In fact, the first note started out from a sustained hum.

The second verse she sang up the octave in a soprano that sounded cool and clear as a stream on a sweaty hot day.

Where there might have been a solo in the middle of the song, Olivia leaned into the mike and hummed, first high where she'd just been, then down low as in the beginning, playing with the melody, brilliantly teasing out some notes and rushing over others.

Repeating the first verse, Mr. Music pushed her off to the side and foolishly took over. The audience visibly sagged, even though he did a decent enough job. Olivia began accompanying him with a bit of vocalizing, no words, just delicate little flutters of melody around the man's voice.

While no musician herself, Jackie could still tell complete mastery when she heard it. They hadn't been kidding about this strange woman's talent.

The song ended, and for a moment no one made a sound. Then everyone remembered to breathe at the same moment, and erupted in applause, with several people leaping to their feet.

Olivia looked like a frightened animal as she looked out at them, then she ducked her head and started moving toward the exit.

"Sing something else!" someone called out, but she didn't stop, even though the applause hadn't finished.

Mr. Music didn't ask if anyone else wanted to sing.

♪‡ρ·♪♭ρ·

After raking me over the coals for at least five hours, the damn cops hadn't even offered to drive me home. As a matter of fact, Palmer had told me disgustedly, "Get out of here, Curran. You're lucky I don't lock your sorry ass up."

At least the weather was nice. Needing to clear my head, I decided to walk home.

Cutting through Cabbagetown so I could use the footbridge that crossed the Don Valley Parkway, connecting the east and west sides of Riverdale Park, I tried to enjoy the end of a beautiful spring day, but I couldn't get past what I'd just been through.

Detective Palmer had known everything Shannon had discovered about Maggie and Olivia, and he hadn't gotten the info from her, because he'd cursed her out soundly several times during my ordeal. Someone had ratted us out.

What made me sad was that from the beginning, I knew it had to have been someone in the trio, because only Dom and Ronald could have known.

It had taken a long time to go through everything, then Palmer and his fellow detectives went over and over what I'd said, trying to trip me up. I suppose I could have demanded the lawyer I'd been using, but I had the feeling they'd lock me up overnight and start fresh in the morning if I insisted. That would have done me in with Sandra.

Immediately after getting out of the police station, I'd gone to a pay phone, having forgotten to grab my cell that morning, and called Shannon's office.

"She's somewhere in transit between Reno and New York," Janet said. "I can't get hold of her at the moment. The cops were waiting when I got here this morning, but they wouldn't tell me why they wanted her. What's going on?"

"Tell Shannon that Palmer knows pretty well everything about Olivia and Maggie. I'm guessing it was one of the guys in my trio who ratted us out. She should speak to me as soon as she can. I'm on my way home now and don't have my cell, but she can try me after five. I'll be home all evening."

"Boy, we've sure landed in the soup this time."

"You can say that again."

I made it home by quarter after four and used the time to take a shower and get something into my stomach. Thank heaven for frozen dinners. With the plastic tray pushed away and a second cup of coffee in front of me, I sat staring at my cell phone.

I was about to pick it up when it rang.

"Andy?" Dom asked. "Where the hell have you been? I've been calling you all day."

"I know. I didn't have my cell with me, but I noticed you rang a bunch of times."

"So what's up?"

"Why did you do it, Dom? Do you have any idea how you've fucked things up?"

He was silent for too long before he said, "What are you talking about?"

"I'm pretty sure I know why you did it. You were hoping that by putting the cops on the scent, we'd be able to get Olivia back sooner. That *is* it. Right?"

He sighed. "Yeah."

"I thought it was Ronald at first, especially after he acted so weird last night, but the detectives knew things that I'd only told you."

"Are things really that bad?"

"I don't know. I can't reach the PI who's handling the case. If nothing else, you've got the cops really steamed at her, because she'd promised to share anything she came up with, and she hasn't. That is definitely *not* a good thing."

"I'm really sorry, but—"

"No, no. The reason we didn't say anything is that we were afraid of putting Olivia in danger. There's something very wrong with all that's happened to her, and we wanted to find out what that was before we laid everything we've discovered on the cops. Now that's totally blown."

"Christ, I'm sorry. I just got worried with what Harry told us last night. We can't afford to lose this gig. *I* can't afford it."

"What about Olivia? Aren't we responsible for her? You may have just put her out on a big limb and handed somebody a saw. I only hope I can reach Shannon in time."

"Where is she?"

"I thought she was out in California, but apparently she's en route to New York City again. Something must be up."

"Is there *anything* I can do?"

"No, Dom," I said quietly. "You've done enough already."

ↀ#�·ↀᑊᑊ·

If she'd had her gun, Shannon would have been tempted to pull it and demand to be let off the plane ahead of everyone else.

She'd had to endure two late and very rough flights, plus a two-hour stopover in Denver that was scheduled to be only one.

In Denver, she'd dialed the answering service, since it was past the time when Janet would have headed home.

"Janet has left three messages, Ms O'Brien. She wants you to call her at home before you do anything. She stressed the 'anything.'"

Janet never wanted to be bothered at home unless the shit had *really* hit the fan.

Ten minutes later, Shannon put the cell down on her lap and rubbed the bridge of her nose. A whole herd of cows had done their thing in front of the fan, and the results were covering everybody, but mostly her. Why the hell did this have to happen now?

Janet had told her about Andy Curran's call and Palmer's men showing up at the office looking for her. She knew she needed to speak to Andy next, but not before calming down. It's never good to yell at clients – even when they've managed to screw things up completely.

The smartest thing to do would be to get on the next plane to Toronto and try to patch things up with Palmer. When he was angry – and it sure sounded like he was now – he tended to think even less than normal, and that could be dangerous to everybody. If he wanted to, he could have her licence for this – at the very least. Obstruction of justice charges were probably already underway.

But Shannon's instincts told her she needed to stay after Taggart. She spent the Denver/New York leg of her trip trying to figure a way out of this awful mess. By the time she got to the cab stand at Kennedy, it was nearly midnight, and she felt as if she'd been thrown down a flight of stairs. During the stopover in Denver, she'd managed to book a hotel room in Brooklyn that wasn't far from the last known address of Jack Taggart. All she could think about was getting there and collapsing into bed.

Hopping into the first cab in the line, she gave the name and address of her hotel and sank back into the seat, closing her eyes.

"Hey, lady, we're here," the cab driver said, rapping sharply on the plastic screen behind the front seat.

She opened her eyes with a groan. It had been such a nice dream: just Michael and her on a rug in front of a fireplace. The cabby could have driven her to Timbuktu and back while she'd been asleep, but the fare didn't look too out of line, so she paid it without grumbling.

Once she'd checked in, Shannon plugged her cell in to recharge. The hot shower that beckoned would have to wait a little longer. Business first. Even though the hour was late, she called Andy to get filled in on the extent of the bad news. Perhaps tomorrow would be a better day.

$$\partial \sharp \Gamma \cdot \partial b \Gamma \cdot$$

Because the weather had been the same as the day before, the hoped-for fog rolled down the hillside towards Sunnyvale right on schedule. Jackie had dozed for a few hours after returning to her room but had been too much on edge to fall asleep completely. Time dragged. Whenever she allowed herself to look at the clock, only five or ten minutes had passed.

As she again climbed out the window of her room, the fog wasn't as dense as she had hoped. Knowing that this trip might be longer than the previous one, she decided not to wait until it was thicker. For all she knew, a wind might come up and blow it all away. Better to move now.

Since she knew where she was going, Jackie made better time and arrived quickly at Olivia's window.

"I didn't think you were going to come," Olivia said, seemingly right next to her. Jackie nearly jumped out of her skin, even though she'd been expecting to hear the girl.

"Where are you?" she asked, staring through the screen into the room. Olivia stepped into view. "Who are you?"

"I'm a friend."

"I don't have many friends."

"I know, and that's why I'm here."

Olivia pulled up a chair and sat with her chin resting on her arms, which she'd crossed on the sill.

"Is it nice out there tonight?"

Jackie moved closer to the screen until her lips were almost touching it. Sound carried on the still night air, so she needed to keep her voice low.

"It's very nice. Quiet. Lonely. A bit chilly. Do you know if the guards walk around much?"

"Yes, but they don't like to come out on nights like this. They're lazy. You should be okay."

"I enjoyed your song tonight."

"I shouldn't have done it," she said quietly, but her anguish was plain. "I promised myself I wouldn't do that ever again."

"Why?"

"Because it made a friend of mine die."

This revelation caught Jackie completely by surprise. How the hell did Olivia know about that? "Do you mean Maggie?"

The girl caught her breath and pressed her face against the reinforced screen. "Did you know her?"

"Is it Maggie you're talking about?" Jackie persisted.

The answer came out more like a hiss. "Yes."

"And do you know who killed her?"

"Why are you asking me this? I don't want to think about it."

Jackie leaned forward until only the thickness of the screen separated her lips from Olivia's ear. "Listen to me. I'm here to help you, Olivia. I came from Toronto—"

"Did Andy send you?"

"Yes. He's—"

"You have to tell him to stop. They said they'd kill him. You must go away! "

"Who told you that?"

"I can't tell you!"

Jackie decided to push her even more. "Did they also kill Maggie?"

"I can't tell you," she repeated with a sob.

"Why not? We can help you, if you'll let us."

"No, you can't. No one can help me."

"Let us help you."

"No!" she practically shouted, and both women froze. Then she whispered, "You have to go."

"Will you be here tomorrow?"

"No."

"I'm going to come anyway. Are you happy they killed your friend?"

"Of course not!"

"Then I want you to think about helping us. We can get them. Get them for Maggie. Get them for you."

"I'm scared."

Olivia had turned her head to the side, still pressed against the screen.

Jackie whispered directly into her ear, "So am I," then slipped off into the shadows.

The fog wasn't the only thing swirling as Jackie made her way back to her building.

What Olivia had told her was nothing short of explosive. If she did indeed know who killed Maggie, the situation had suddenly become very dangerous for both of them. Jackie was under no illusion that people who have committed one murder wouldn't hesitate to commit another to save themselves.

She had to tell this Marvell character immediately what Olivia had said, so he could pass it on to Shannon. Maybe it was time to get herself *and* Olivia out of there.

As the fog thickened, Jackie sprinted for the back of her building. The moment she slipped back safely through the window of her room, she was scrambling to get the transmitter out of its hiding place in the back of the chair. She'd be the first to admit she was worried.

CHAPTER 21

By the time Shannon got off the phone with Andy Curran, she was about as depressed as she'd ever been. Even though a hot shower would have felt great, she lacked the energy to do anything about it.

A few minutes later, her cell chirruped happily, *not* reflecting its owner's state of mind.

It was Michael. "How's my globetrotter?" he asked.

"Today I trotted about a mile up shit creek."

"That bad? Or are you just tired?"

"I'm worried *and* tired, goddammit!" she said with more heat than she'd intended.

"Tell me about it, luv," he answered soothingly.

She did, leaving nothing out and giving herself a good verbal butt-kicking for not stressing to Curran before she left town to keep his mouth shut.

Michael, as he often did, saw right to the heart of the matter. "What will get the coppers off your back?"

"Bringing in whoever killed this Maggie woman."

"Do you have any idea who it was?"

"Sort of, but I've got enough on my hands. I can't do Palmer's job, too."

"I didn't say you should, but couldn't you get someone else to do it for you?"

The image of a very large black man floated into Shannon's mind. "You just might be on to something."

"In any event, you can't return now. If you do, this Palmer bloke will very likely keep you here. That won't do at all, will it?"

"No."

"Right. Then just proceed as if nothing is wrong back here. Put it out of your mind and get on with the job." His voice changed. "Now, is there anything else I can do?"

She finally grinned. "Don't leave for the UK until I can give you a proper send-off."

"You've got until Saturday then. My plane leaves at five o'clock."

"I'll try really hard to be there, Quinn."

"I'm counting on it, O'Brien."

When she hung up, it was well after one, too late to do any work on Taggart. Shannon picked up the phone to make two last calls: one to Roy and one to his employee, Marvell. At least she didn't have anything to worry about with Jackie. She appeared to have the situation at Sunnyvale well in hand.

Talking to Roy on the phone did a lot to settle Shannon down. He just sounded so confident as he took down the information he needed. "I should be able to get you something on this by tomorrow afternoon. Is that okay?"

"Perfect, Roy. How are you going to handle them? From what I heard from my contact at the Toronto airport, these charter companies don't like to give out information."

"Hey, babe, give your man some credit here. I just have to put the fear of God in them. Believe me, the last thing they want is to be dragged into a murder investigation. I can make them spill the information. Trust ole Roy. Tomorrow I'll have the names and addresses of those two bastards for you."

"What about Marvell? I couldn't get him on the phone just now."

"He's probably out checking your trapline. You worry too much."

"Sometimes I think I don't worry enough," she said.

"Get some rest. You'll feel better tomorrow if you do. Just put everything out of your mind."

Shannon stared at the cell phone in her hand after the call ended, considering Roy's words. "Easy for you to say," she said disgustedly as she headed for the shower.

Next morning, Shannon was on her way by eight thirty. This time she had her eye on the cabby to make sure he didn't take the out-of-towner by any circuitous route.

Sleep had come more easily than she'd expected, and even though she'd slept in, there hadn't been enough of it to do the job. She was left feeling groggy and out of sorts, a bad thing when she really needed to be at the peak of her game.

"This is it, lady," the cab driver told her as he pulled up in front of a three-storey brick apartment building that clearly had seen better days. "Want me to wait?"

"No. I may be awhile. Thanks for the lift."

The money and receipt had barely changed hands before the cabby was doing a tire-screeching U-turn in search of his next fare.

Sizing up the building and offering a silent prayer, Shannon started up the front walk with as positive an outlook on the day's prospects as she could muster. *Yesterday's in the past*, she told herself firmly. How come she didn't believe it?

The super wasn't home, but she spoke with his wife, a plump Hispanic whose accent made her speech nearly indecipherable. Even so, after a few minutes it was clear the woman didn't know anything about Jack Taggart.

"How long have you been here?"

The woman thought for a minute. "*Cinco años.*"

Not good enough. Taggart hadn't been around for over six years, as far as she'd been able to discover.

"Is there someone who has been living here longer than that?"

A look of puzzlement crossed the woman's face, then she turned on her heel and stomped off down the hall, throwing some rapid-fire Spanish back over her shoulder. It had the sound of something like "Wait here," so Shannon stayed put.

A few minutes later, the super's wife was back with a grey-haired woman in tow. Thankfully, her English was perfect, though heavily shaded by her obvious Brooklyn heritage.

"I'm Nancy Morris," she said as she came to a halt. "Maria tells me you have some questions she can't answer."

"Shannon O'Brien. How long have you lived here?"

"Nearly twenty years now. I used to teach Spanish, so Maria comes to me when she needs help."

"I'm looking for information on a man named Jack Taggart. Does that name ring a bell?"

She pursed her lips in concentration, then shook her head. "Do you have a description of him?"

Shannon shook her head. "Sorry, no. He was an artist, you know, paintings and the like. He would have lived here about six years ago."

"I think I remember him. Big man. Full of himself."

"Do you remember the last time you saw him?"

"Search me." The woman must have seen Shannon's shoulders sag a bit, because she reached forward and patted her arm. "But I do know someone who can help you. She's been here even longer than me and had the apartment next door to the man you're looking for."

Sadie Parker lived in a third-floor apartment filled to overflowing with plants, mostly orchids. She was a tiny woman whose entire body seemed to be one giant mass of wrinkles. Although hard of hearing, her bright eyes showed that her brain was still completely in gear.

"Sadie," Mrs. Morris shouted, "this woman is asking about the artist who lived next to you several years ago. Remember him?"

"Jack Taggart? Of course I remember him!"

Shannon held out a business card, which the woman carried over to her living room window to look at in better light.

"So you're a private investigator – from Toronto, too. Why in the world would you be interested in Jack?"

"It's part of a missing person case I'm working on."

Sadie offered Shannon tea but pointedly didn't offer any to her neighbour. "Thank you for bringing this young lady up, Mrs. Morris. I'm sure you have any number of things to take care of." Once the door was shut, Sadie smiled. "She's a very nice lady, but the worst gossip in the world. I'm sure you don't want all of Flatbush knowing your business."

Tea was served with butter cookies. They sat at a small table near the window.

"I haven't thought about Jack Taggart in years," the old woman said as she picked up a cookie.

"When did he move out?"

"Move out? He never moved out. He just suddenly left the country."

Shannon had found if she leaned forward and spoke close to the old woman's ear, she could make herself understood without having to shout. "When was that?"

"Let's see. It was just before my Sam passed away, that's over six years ago now."

"It's important that I nail down the exact date."

"Just a minute." Sadie left the room and came back with a photo album. "My daughter visited from England the week before. That's the last time she saw her father alive. Let's see…" She thumbed through several pages. "Yes, here it is. This is Sam and my grandson Nate. Jack Taggart took that photo."

The photo was a good one. Taken in black and white, it perfectly caught the merriment in the departed Sam's eyes as he looked at his grandson. The granddad looked gaunt and ill, though. Shannon knew all too well what that meant. She'd seen it in her own father as cancer had sucked his life away.

"It's a nice photo," she said with a forced smile. "And do you remember the date?"

"The date is on the back, I believe. Jack was supposed to do up a large print of this for me, but then he just took off."

"The date?"

"Let's see." She lifted the clear plastic sheet covering the page and turned over the photo. "January third."

That date fit right in with Shannon's timetable. Olivia's brother had been murdered nine days earlier.

"Did he say where he was going?"

"Jack tended to brag. He told us he was about to come into some money and was going to travel, go to Europe and just paint."

"Did he say where the money was coming from?"

Sadie shrugged. "He said he was getting it because he knew 'how to play the game'. That's the way Jack talked. He was nice enough, but a bit conceited. Told Sam he wasn't going to have to teach any more."

"So he had a lot of students."

The old woman laughed. "To hear him talk, you'd think so, but I only knew of one: a spoiled rich kid in Manhattan. Jack bragged about how much he was charging her parents for lessons. Sam, God rest his soul, was impressed by things like that."

"Do you know anything about Jack Taggart being mixed up with illegal drugs?"

Silence descended on the apartment, and Shannon became aware of all the noise of a huge metropolis like New York that had been going on just outside the window.

"I...ah...oh dear..."

Shannon was surprised by Sadie's response, trying to guess what it meant. "Mrs. Parker, I'm not the police. I'm only interested in Jack Taggart, and anything past that I don't care about. You can trust me."

"You seem like a nice person," she said, "and I suppose it doesn't make any difference now. My husband was very sick in his last months. They tried everything to keep him alive, and it only made him feel worse. Jack suggested he smoke marijuana to ease the nausea, and it did help. It was a godsend, actually."

"I'm talking about more harmful drugs."

Sadie was quiet again for a moment. "I don't think so, but I do know that Jack had some unsavoury friends. He used to hang out at that bar around the corner, O'Reilly's."

"Is it still there?"

"Oh, yes."

"Tell me about when he left."

"As I said, he went away. They didn't do anything with his apartment until three months had passed. Then all his things were carted off. I don't know what happened to them."

"Did he say goodbye to you or your husband?"

"No. One morning, he just wasn't there. He did stick a short note under our door, saying he'd get in touch when he got to where he was going, but he never did. That upset Sam something awful. The poor dear didn't have any more of his 'happy smoke' as he called it, and had no idea where to buy any. A few weeks after, I had to put him in the hospital."

"You wouldn't have a photo of Taggart, would you?"

Sadie shook her head.

"Can you tell me anything else? It might be just a small thing to you, but you never know; it could help."

Sadie Parker thought for nearly a minute. "No. I was somewhat preoccupied in those days. Please forgive me."

Shannon took the old woman's hands in hers. "You have been extremely helpful, Mrs. Parker. There's nothing to apologize for." Getting to her feet, she added, "Thank you very much for the tea and cookies."

Sadie got slowly to her feet. "I don't have much to do these days, just caring for my flowers and visiting with my few remaining friends, so it's nice when someone comes and visits."

"Please keep my card on hand, and if you remember anything else, the smallest thing, don't hesitate to call."

Shannon had her hand on the doorknob when Sadie called out, "Oh! I can't believe I didn't remember that. I only look at it every day."

"What?"

"Come with me, young lady. I want to show you something."

She led Shannon towards the back of the apartment. Just past the bathroom was a small room fixed up as an office.

Entering it, she turned and said, "This was my Sam's room. I've kept it exactly the same since the day he left me. Come in and look at this. Jack Taggart drew it, and Sam liked it so much, Jack sold it to him. I was uncomfortable with it at first, but now it's like an old friend."

Shannon stood in the doorway. On the opposite wall was a framed pencil sketch, done in a vigorous, masculine style. The subject was Olivia at maybe twenty years old, sprawled on a sofa. Her face had a faraway, dreamy expression, and a shy smile flickered around her mouth.

She was also naked.

$$\partial \ddagger \rho \cdot \partial b \rho \cdot$$

I spent four hours on Saturday morning, cleaning the house as best I could. My feeling is that I make a pretty thorough job of it, but on several occasions women have gone into a bathroom I'd just cleaned and spent an hour cleaning it again.

Sandra had called the evening before to say that she and Jeremy had to drive into town anyway, so they'd be happy to save me the trip out to Oakville.

It all sounded reasonable enough, but I was pretty certain she simply wanted to check out whether everything was kosher at the old homestead: no police, no gawkers – and no bloodstains on the porch.

The previous day's events at the cop shop had knocked me for a loop. Shannon's call in the evening hadn't helped in the least, since it was abundantly clear she was very upset. I didn't blame her. *I* was very upset.

Palmer was going to haul in the two hookers who'd told me their story, and they'd blame me for getting them dragged into the mess. Imagining them showing up at the house simultaneously with Sandra and Jeremy made me break out in a cold sweat.

Shannon had asked for every detail of my meeting with Palmer. Since she hadn't let me know what was happening at her end for nearly two days, I hadn't been able to tell Palmer anything about her trip, which had infuriated him even more.

"I did have to tell him who Olivia's family is," I told Shannon.

"Did you tell him about the journal?" she demanded.

"No. I haven't had a chance to look at it yet, and it just slipped my mind. Is that bad?"

"No, it's very good. The *last* thing we want is for him to tell Maxine St. James we have copies. I'm sure he'll get in touch with her now. Does he know we have Jackie out at Sunnyvale?"

I smiled. "Somehow that slipped my mind, too."

"A small miracle, as well."

"Once my bass player made his call, Palmer knew he had me by the balls. He told me I had to answer his questions or go to jail."

"Why didn't you call that lawyer?"

"He caught me off guard. I didn't have time to think anything through."

"And now he's going to come after me – and rightly so. I'm also worried about what he's going to stir up with his blundering around. The man makes the bull in a china shop look graceful." She sighed. "I'll keep in close touch with you. Anything happens, I want to know – day or night. Understand? Here's my cell number, but make sure *no one* else gets it. The last thing I need is Palmer calling me up, though I suppose he can always get the number by other means. Let's just not make it easy for him."

"I'm really sorry this happened."

"To be honest, Andy," she'd said tiredly, "I am, too. I have enough problems."

I'd just finished house cleaning and was sitting down with a cup of reheated coffee when I heard a car pull in.

Hurrying out the back door, I met Kate and Sandra as they were getting out of the car. Jeremy wisely decided to stay put. He was not welcome in my house.

Sandra had bought Kate a suitcase, a snazzy leather one – something we never would have wasted money on in the past. As we walked up the driveway, I noticed Kate casting sideways glances at the porch. I'd carefully washed off the chalk marks, drawn the blinds in the living room and planned that they'd stay shut all weekend. The front door was also going to be off limits. Whether Kate might have nightmares regardless was a question I couldn't yet answer. All I could do was be there for her if she did.

Sandra didn't stay long. It was the first time she'd been in the house since walking out on our marriage, and it was clearly making her uncomfortable. She did want to use the bathroom, and Kate and I went along to dump her suitcase in her room. I'd already shut the door to "Olivia's room", but I think both of us wanted to make certain Sandra didn't see it.

"And you'll have Kate home on time," she said at the back door, prior to leaving.

"Absolutely."

Kate gave her mother a hug. "Thank you for letting me visit Daddy. I really appreciate it. Have fun with Jeremy while I'm gone."

Sandra's eyes went wide for a moment, then she shook it off, thinking that her eleven-year-old daughter couldn't have meant what she'd thought. I wasn't so sure. Kids grow up far too quickly these days, and I'd noticed a big difference in my little Katy the past few months.

Once the door shut, Kate turned to me. "So should I get to work, or are you going to take me out to lunch?"

"Who said anything about lunch?"

"You should have," she said with a mock pout. "After all, I don't come to visit every day."

"If I were to agree to take you out to lunch, where should it be?"

"I'd like some Greek food, and they have some of the best up on the Danforth, you know."

"But you don't like Greek food."

"I'm trying to broaden my horizons."

The spell was broken when she began to giggle. "Relax, Daddy. I was just pulling your leg. Pizza is fine."

"Oh, *now* I see. Asking for Greek food was just a ploy to get me to order pizza."

She rolled her eyes. "Would I try something like that on my own father?"

♩♯♪·♩♭♪·

O'Reilly's Grill and Tap House, despite its grandiose name, looked like a dive. The first clue was the two missing letters on the sign over the door. The finishing touch was the erratically flashing neon beer sign in one of the grimy ellipsoid windows that flanked the door.

Shannon took a deep breath and went in.

Conversation stopped when the denizens saw what was silhouetted against the daylight that streamed in behind her.

The place had about a dozen customers of varying ages, all of whom looked rough around the edges, and all of whom were staring intently at the intruder.

With more confidence than she felt, Shannon walked over to the bar.

"You O'Reilly?" she asked the bartender.

He laughed. "Are you kidding? There ain't been an O'Reilly in this dump for twenty-something years."

"Are you the owner?"

"I might be. What do you want?"

Shannon looked around. Inside, the place didn't seem quite so bad, except for the stench of stale beer and cigarettes. Two seats down, an old man was hunched over a plate stacked with what looked like a rather nice pastrami sandwich and equally good-looking fries. Even though it was far too early for lunch, her stomach grumbled in response.

"How about bringing me a beer and what my neighbour down the line is having?"

"We got lots of beers, lady. Which one?"

She smiled. "I'll let you pick."

Shannon was aware of a buzz in the room. She didn't have to ask who it was about.

While the bartender walked down to the small serving window connecting with the kitchen, then served a few customers, she looked around a bit more. All three TVs hanging from the ceiling were tuned to the Yankees pre-game show. By a quirk of fate, they were playing the Toronto Blue Jays that day.

Observing the patrons more closely, she saw that nobody seemed less than forty. The chunky, balding bartender looked pretty close to retirement, so the chances were good he'd been here for awhile.

"Here you go, little lady," he said, plunking down her beer. "Food will be up in five."

"So *are* you the owner?" she asked.

"Are you a cop?" he shot right back.

"Do I look like a cop?"

"You sure do. Smell like one, too." He tapped his nose. "I got good senses."

"Well, you're right and you're wrong." She reached into her shoulder bag, taking out the leather case with her PI identity card and sliding it across the bar. "But I *used* to be a cop."

"Ontario, huh? What brings you to New York or, more specifically, into O'Reilly's?"

"I'm looking for information about someone. You been here long?"

"I've *owned* this establishment for twenty years. My name's Matt Hughes," he said as he stuck out his hand.

"Shannon O'Brien. Pleased to meet you."

"So who you looking for?"

"Jack Taggart."

"Jack Taggart?" He shook his head slowly. "Man, I ain't thought about Jack for years."

"He used to come in here a lot, I understand."

"He practically lived here."

"Tell me about him."

"Why you looking for Jack?"

"To tell you the truth, I think he's no longer among the living."

"When did he die?"

"When did you see him last?"

The bartender raised his eyebrows but said no more, because the cook called out through the window, "Pastrami up!"

Hughes actually dusted off a jar of Dijon mustard for her, and after pouring a beer for himself, leaned his forearms on the bar.

"You have my attention."

Shannon worked her interview in around the sandwich and fries as best she could. It had been over twenty-four hours since her last meal.

"Tell me about Taggart."

"Jack had a big mouth that occasionally got him in trouble, and he thought he was God's gift to women, but let me tell you, he was friggin' great company. I never met anybody who could tell a joke like Jack. Most nights he ate his meals here, had a few beers, a few laughs and went home to work. I got a great portrait of my wife that he painted. Traded it for three months' worth of dinners."

"He disappeared six years ago."

"Yeah. We all thought it odd he didn't stop in to say goodbye. I got a postcard a few days later, or I might've called the cops."

Shannon didn't have the heart to tell Matt that the card probably hadn't been from Taggart and had been sent for precisely that reason.

"Did he ever say anything about a girl he was giving art lessons to?"

"The rich brat over in Manhattan? He didn't say much about her, but he went on and on about her stepmother."

"Really?"

"Oh, yeah. Bragged to all of us about how he was nailing her every chance he got."

CHAPTER 22

Jackie had behaved well enough the previous day that she was allowed to use the extensive gym for an hour the next morning, after which she enjoyed the best massage she'd ever experienced. There had to be something at Sunnyvale to justify the hefty price tag.

Barry met her just after she'd left the Physical Building, as everyone referred to it. Whether it was planned or an accident, Jackie couldn't tell. She operated always on the assumption that every move she made during the day was carefully monitored. Nighttime appeared to be another matter.

"Did you have a good sleep last night, Jackie?" he asked.

Jackie shrugged by way of an answer.

He pulled her to a nearby bench, where he sat partially turned to her, a leg tucked up. "And how are you *really* doing? Having any physical effects? Any problems in the night?"

She struggled to keep her face blank. Did they suspect something, or worse yet, know something, or was this just an innocuous question?

"Well, Barry, my head hits the pillow, and the next thing I know, it's morning."

"Really? People with a crack addiction usually have trouble restoring their sleep patterns. Quite odd..."

Jackie could have smacked herself in the head. Of course, she knew that. What the hell had she been thinking? "I've never had trouble sleeping. My friend Kit took me to a doctor, actually the guy who recommended this place, and *he* found it hard to believe. I guess I'm just an oddball that way."

Barry looked at her with an expression that was difficult to read, then got up and walked off.

She kept her head down for the rest of the morning, hyper-aware of how one slip could scuttle this whole operation, taking her job with it. Her gaffe also hardened her conviction that it was time to pull out. She also stayed well away from Olivia but noticed how the girl stared at her during breakfast. She'd have to point out how dangerous that could be if she visited her again in the night.

Just before exercise period, Jackie extracted the transmitter from its hiding place in the back of the chair for the third time since sunrise to see if there was any response from Marvell to her message about what Olivia had said. Roy's gadget remained obstinately silent.

Where the hell was he?

Moving over to the window, she looked up at the hillside. Could Marvell be up there right now? It was really beginning to creep her out that she hadn't heard a thing.

"Marvell, you there?" she said into the mike. "I *really* need a little contact with you about now. We need to get O and me out of here."

"I don't think that's going to happen," a voice behind her said.

Jackie's guts turned to jelly.

In the doorway to her room stood Dr. Smith and two men she'd never seen before: one short and one tall.

The receiving unit from up on the hill dangled from the larger man's hand.

$$\mathcal{J} \text{♯} \rho \cdot \mathcal{J} b \rho \cdot$$

Shannon faced a real dilemma: she needed to be in four places at once.

As part of her original trip east, she had wanted to speak to the lead cop in the St. James murder investigation in Florida six years earlier. She'd contacted him the evening before and tentatively made an appointment with him for the next day. It might not lead to anything startling, but it would give her background she was lacking.

"I have all the time in the world these days," he'd said on the phone. "Not much to do except fish."

"How much of the case do you remember?" Shannon asked.

The old cop's voice suddenly didn't sound so friendly. "I'm retired, *not* senile."

"I'm terribly sorry. That's not what I meant at all. I used to be a police officer, and my dad was the head of homicide in Toronto. I know how complicated these cases can get. I may have some pretty obscure questions, that's all."

"Well, I'll be at home," he answered, still sounding miffed. "Give me a call when you land."

Shannon felt she'd have to handle this one with kid gloves.

She was also toying with the idea of contacting Maxine St. James again. It might prove interesting to see what she'd shake loose by letting old Max in on a few of the things she'd learned on her trip to Brooklyn. It was pretty obvious by now that she was deeply involved with what had happened to Olivia, her brother, and possibly even their mother. Shannon was also itching for a little payback for that stunt with the journal.

Immature? Maybe, but also very overdue.

Next, there was a possible trip back to Toronto. Michael had been correct that Palmer might already have a warrant out for her arrest, but at this point she wasn't sure she had enough bait to dangle in front of the cop to get her out of that mess. Her professional career, not to mention her freedom, depended on making the correct call on this one.

Lastly, maybe it was time for a face-to-face talk with Olivia, but could she be counted on even to be coherent?

Sitting in the hotel lobby with her bags next to her, Shannon had a decision to make: which way to jump. She flipped open her cell phone to see if Marvell had gotten in touch. She wasn't particularly worried about Jackie, but with everything that had been happening, she was getting good and spooked.

The last thing she needed was another screw-up.

♪‡ρ·♪ḃρ·

Kate and I shared a really terrific day, the best one yet.

After we polished off a large pizza with pepperoni and green pepper (a vegetable first for my daughter), we sat talking about school and some of her classmates in Oakville. I'd noticed with some sadness over the past month or so that her local friends had begun fading into the past. This is what happens with kids as they move on with their lives, but I was sorry to see it happening to my own child.

Moving her straw along the bottom, Kate hoovered up the last of the Pepsi from her second can and got up from the table.

"Time to get to work."

"No, time to clear the table. You know the rules."

I could tell from her expression that she'd been testing me again. Soon she'd be rolling her eyes at these types of requests, then would come arguments. By seventeen or eighteen, she'd hopefully be normal again. It was something neither Sandra nor I had looked forward to, and now we'd have to face it separately. That thought filled me with trepidation.

After reading my current book for an hour with some Lennie Tristano in the background as accompaniment, I wandered upstairs to see what my offspring was up to.

Kate had moved a work light to the right side of the window on the one unfinished wall. Jars of paint surrounded her, along with old yogurt containers of water to clean her brushes, and in her hand was Olivia's favourite palette. She had on an old dress shirt I'd given her that hung below her knees.

"How's it going, pumpkin?"

She turned her paint-streaked face to me. "Hi, Daddy. Do you like what I'm doing?"

"As far as I can tell, it looks great. Olivia will be very pleased."

"I'm pretty sure I'm doing what she wanted." She looked down at the floor. "I think I'm going to need more of this ultramarine blue. We should get it before the art supply store closes."

"You're a painty mess, Katy. By the time we get you cleaned up, we might not even make it. Why don't we run the errand tomorrow?"

As she turned back to the wall, I walked over to look at the lines that had been pencilled on the white base coat. Unlike the earlier walls, these sketches were done with smooth confidence. Olivia had become increasingly sure of herself as her project had expanded.

Since there wasn't much room to stand where Kate was painting, I moved to the other side of the window. The rest of the room was so overwhelming that I'd never looked at the sketches on this blank wall.

Three minutes later, my hands were shaking as I realized what Olivia had intended. Turning around, I looked at the three finished walls. All the eyes in the room were subtly turned towards this side of the window, seeming to stare at the scene which had yet to be painted.

Though they were only preliminary drawings and would certainly have been more clearly defined as a finished painting, what Olivia had sketched there was completely devastating.

"Kate, I think we should go and get that paint now. The stores might not be open tomorrow."

She had one brush crossway in her mouth and another in her hand as she turned to me with an exasperated expression.

"Dad..."

"Come on, Kate. Hop in the shower and get cleaned off."

"Okay, but you'll have to close up the paints and at least get my brushes into some water."

She scooted out of the room, and I breathed a sigh of relief. I did *not* want her to see what was sketched on the left hand side of that wall, but Shannon needed to know about it right away.

$$\text{᠌ᢠᑊ-᠌ᑊᑲᕐ·}$$

As her cab sat in a line of traffic on the Grand Central Parkway just short of LaGuardia, Shannon decided to call Roy and give his cage a rattle. He was late getting her the information he'd promised.

"What's up?" she asked when she got him on the phone.

"It took a little longer than I would have thought to pry the info out of the flyboys in San Diego. I actually had to *fly* down here. The old telephone intimidation thing didn't work. I only just walked into the office five minutes ago."

"I'm sorry this has been such a pain."

"It's what I get for shooting my damn mouth off. Never yank the tails of the gods. Anyway, I have the name of your two boys who showed up in Toronto."

"So give."

"Dave Haggerty and Rich Colville, and guess what? They aren't bounty hunters – at least they aren't *registered* with anybody as bounty hunters. I'm willing to check around more for you, but it will take time."

"That would be really helpful, Roy. Thanks. Have you heard from Marvell? I've tried him twice so far today and haven't been able to raise him. It may be that he's out at Sunnyvale and can't call. The reception is lousy up in those hills."

"That's not good." Her friend suddenly sounded concerned. "I told Marvell to take our satellite phone with him. He can call from practically anywhere on the planet."

"Shit. Look, I'm practically at La Guardia. I was going to hop a plane for Florida, but I don't like this. Something's happened; I can *feel* it. I'll be on the next plane to Reno. I'll call as soon as I'm booked. Can you meet me there?"

"If Marvell's in some kind of trouble, you can bet your girl is, too – *and* that other girl you're so interested in. Do you want me to call the Plumas County Sheriff?"

"Let's not panic. Marvell may just be having equipment problems. I wouldn't want to blow this whole thing for no reason. Call if you hear anything."

The cab arrived at the airport.

"What airline did you say, lady?" the cabby asked.

"Just drop me here."

She jumped out of the cab, threw too much money at the cabby and raced inside the building. It took almost two minutes to find a pay phone.

The next call was trickier and needed to be made from a New York exchange. Getting out her notebook, Shannon found the number she needed and dialed.

A woman's voice answered. "St. James residence."

"Yes, this is Mr. Menotti's law office. He used to work with Mrs. St. James and would like to have a word with her."

"I'm very sorry, but she's not taking calls at the moment."

"This is a matter of some urgency."

"I am most happy to take a message."

"Mr. Menotti will be dropping by this evening with those photos they'd been talking about a few days ago. Is nine o'clock suitable?"

"I'm sorry, but Madam will not be at home this evening."

"Just a moment, please." Shannon covered the phone with her hand for a moment. "Mr. Menotti informs me that he is expected this evening."

"I am sorry, but Madam does not have Mr. Menotti's visit entered in her agenda."

"It was probably just an oversight. Would this afternoon be more suitable? This is a rather delicate situation that needs to be resolved with alacrity."

"Madam was called out of town unexpectedly. She is on her way to the private plane now, and should be returning tomorrow if you'd like to call then."

"I'm sorry to have bothered you."

Shannon hung up, wondering what sort of trouble had been stirred up.

ᏗᏉᎵᎭᏉᏆᎵᎭ

Even travelling at supersonic speed, the flight to Salt Lake City would have been too slow for Shannon's liking. When she landed, she had Roy on the phone before she'd even disembarked for the sprint to the connecting flight.

"Talk to me, Roy."

"Still no word from Marvell. I'm maybe an hour from Portola, two from Reno."

"I should be landing in Reno right around then."

"What do you want me to do?"

Should she play it fast and loose, or conservatively?

"There's a little airport just outside of Portola. Can you think of any way you can find out if Maxine St. James landed there or is scheduled to land there? I'd be willing to bet the ranch she's headed for Sunnyvale." Shannon wiped her hand across her face. "If she's not there yet, you pick me up at Reno. I'm certain they won't do anything until she gets there."

"And if she's already there?"

"Get the Plumas County Sheriff on the line. They'd be our only hope."

"You got it."

"The connecting flight for Reno doesn't take off for forty-five minutes. Call me if you get a chance."

Roy's call came at the last possible moment. Shannon was literally taking her seat on the plane.

"I'll be waiting for you in Reno. Look for me right outside arrivals. I'm driving the Hummer today. It's black."

"So is the owner," she laughed. "I'm sure I won't be able to miss either of you."

"Very funny. You may be happy for a dark vehicle before the night is over."

"I'm happy I've got you on my side. Be on time. I'm not going to bother picking up my bag. It'll be faster."

"So how'd you know this Maxine St. James person was on her way out here and would land in Portola?" Roy asked.

Shannon opened her eyes. The way Roy was driving, dodging trucks and slower vehicles, she really didn't want to see what was happening.

"It was only a lucky guess. When I phoned her home and the person who answered said she'd been called out of town unexpectedly, I figured she had to be coming here. I couldn't take the chance it might have been something else. From what I've found out the last few days, she could have—"

Muffled as it was by her shoulder bag, Shannon barely heard the ring of her cell phone.

"Talk to me," she barked as soon as she'd flipped it open.

"Shannon? This is Andy Curran."

"What is it? I'm kind of pressed for time right now."

"I discovered something about two hours ago. You know the room upstairs that Olivia was painting?"

"Andy, I'm in California again. We think that Jackie's cover may have been blown at Sunnyvale. I'm on my way there now to make sure she's okay. This really isn't a good time."

"Just listen to me for a moment, okay?" Curran sounded angry and frustrated.

"Make it quick."

"Did you look at the pencil sketches on that one blank wall in Olivia's room?"

"I didn't realize there was even anything on it."

"They're not very noticeable unless you're right in front of it. I hadn't looked at that wall, either. The rest of the room is so overwhelming, why look at anything else? Well, I looked at it today. On the left side of the window are three figures. One is crouched down, hiding her face. I'm pretty sure that one is supposed to be Olivia."

Shannon's pulse quickened. "And the other two figures?"

"A man and a woman. The woman is standing behind the man, and she's got what looks like a rock in her hand. She's bashing the poor guy's skull in. It's really gruesome."

"Jesus!" Shannon said, and Roy looked over at her sharply. "Do you remember any of the photos from the information Jackie culled off the Internet? Does the woman look like anyone whose photo you've seen?"

"I don't think so."

"How is she dressed?"

"She appears to have pants on. It's hard to tell because it's only a rough sketch."

"Long hair or short?"

"Longish hair. About the length of Sandra's."

A thought occurred to Shannon. "It couldn't be you and your wife in the drawing, could it? I mean that would sort of make sense, given what happened between you."

Curran was definite. "No. It's not me. I'm certain of that. Olivia sketched me a few times. Mostly playing drums, but the male figure on the wall is not me. The woman isn't Sandra, either. Olivia never laid eyes on her."

"You've got Internet access, don't you?"

"Yes."

"Get online and search for photos of Maxine St. James. They shouldn't be hard to find. She's involved in a lot of charity work and the like. Just search using her name. Call me back when you've compared her with the image on the wall. Okay?"

"Okay."

"And make it snappy. Once we get up into the hills, the phone reception gets pretty dodgy."

Shannon quickly sketched out for Roy what Curran had just told her. She also mentioned what she'd uncovered about Taggart apparently sleeping with his student's stepmom.

"She sounds like some piece of work," Roy said.

"She's dangerous. Swiping that journal from me proves she's willing to play a high-stakes game. Maxine probably never saw it before it was given to me but couldn't take the chance it didn't contain something explosive. Some comments about Taggart in the journal are making a lot more sense based on what I just found out in New York. For one, I believe Taggart was also screwing Olivia. I saw a hell of a nude he did of her, and if she doesn't look post-coital in it, then I don't know anything about the subject."

Roy looked at his watch. "St. James should have just landed at Portola, if the info I got was correct."

"How far are we?"

"We're going to be about fifteen minutes behind her – if we decide to go in by the front door."

"That's the big question, isn't it?"

Shannon's cell phone rang. It was Curran, but the reception wasn't good.

"I've looked at...pictures and it...her."

"You're fading in and out, Andy. Say that again."

There was no answer.

"Crap!" she said. "I lost him. Goddamn cell phones!"

"Reach into the back seat. I brought another satellite phone with me," Roy said.

"Thank the Lord," she answered as she got up on her knees and turned around.

"You honestly think you're going to bring this woman to justice with just her half-nuts stepdaughter testifying against her?"

"It's a wedge, Roy, it's a wedge. Using it, who knows what else can be pried loose?" She found the phone and resumed her seat, switching it on. "Keep your foot on that accelerator, Roy. We don't want to get to Sunnyvale too late."

CHAPTER 23

Jackie had been trussed up with duct tape and stuffed in one of the big laundry bags housekeeping used at Sunnyvale, but she'd gone down fighting. She'd neutralized the small man with a boot to the groin, and Smith was going to have a nice shiner after two quick jabs to the eye. The big guy, not standing on ceremony, had decked her from behind with a chair, and it was soon over. They hadn't been gentle after that, but she'd given as good as she'd got.

When they'd eventually dumped her unceremoniously out of the bag, Jackie had still been confident she'd get out of this mess. They'd taken her to the acupuncture treatment room, which was at the very end of the administration building and farthest away from the rest of the camp.

The weasely-looking guy bent over Jackie and grabbed a corner of the duct tape covering her mouth. He ripped it off so violently, she yelped without being able to stop it, and lay there glaring at him, half-expecting to see her lips clinging to the tape.

He smiled. "Not so tough now, huh?"

"Fuck you."

Turning her head, she saw a skinny black guy lying on his side in the corner.

She forced her face to remain blank as she realized it must be Marvell. His shaved head had a big, bloody knot on it where somebody had slugged him. Observing his shallow breathing, she knew he was still part of this world but definitely out of the battle. They'd tied Marvell's hands and feet with his shoelaces. The big man bent over him with the roll of duct tape and proceeded to wrap his arms and legs more securely.

"Who's he?" she asked belligerently.

The smaller guy laughed at her. "Come off it! We already know you two were working together."

"I've never seen him in my life."

The little guy shrugged. "Suit yourself. He told us a lot before he 'fell asleep'. Thought he was tough like you. And now *you're* going to tell us everything you know."

Doc Smith came into the room with an ice bag held against his face. She saw with satisfaction when he adjusted it that his right eye was swollen shut.

"Did you speak to her?" Little Guy asked.

"She's at the airport now, waiting for the pilots to show up, and she is *not* happy," Smith answered.

"What about the girl?"

"Locked in her room. I gave her another injection, so she'll be out of it for quite awhile."

"Do you think that's wise?"

"Relax. She'll be fine when the time comes."

"What should I do with this one?" Big Guy asked as he tossed the tape onto one of the tables.

"Leave him there, Dave," Little Guy said. "We can deal with him later. Go search this one's room."

Smith gave Jackie a not-too-gentle poke in the ribs with his foot. "And her?"

"She's a real problem. We need to find out how much she knows. This is a lot more serious than when the girl got away the first time."

Smith took the ice pack off his eye and looked down at Jackie with a sigh. "I don't suppose it would do any good to ask you to just tell us."

Jackie decided to give it one last try. "I don't know what the hell you wackos are talking about. When my friend Kit finds out what—"

A resounding slap across the face from Little Guy shut her down in mid-sentence. "Don't waste our time," he snarled. "We already know you're a plant. We listened to your pleas for help on the radio after we clobbered your friend over there." Then he smiled, but it wasn't the kind that warms a person's heart. "Are you going to answer our questions the nice way – or the not nice way?"

Jackie had faced a killer before and seen that kind of expression: the smile of a predator.

The last thing she needed them to know was how petrified she was. "Drop dead," she answered as calmly as she could.

The last thing she needed them to know was how petrified she was.

Little Guy slapped a fresh piece of tape across her mouth then patted her cheek. "That was your one chance, missy. Too bad you blew it." He straightened up. "Well, Doc, our orders are to get information. What would you suggest? We can beat it out of her, I suppose."

The good doctor looked unhappy. Obviously, he didn't have much stomach for the rough stuff, and Jackie hoped she might be able to use that to her advantage.

Throwing himself into one of the chairs, Little Guy put his hands behind his head. "Of course, we might ask Dave to break a few of her bones. That would work with what we have planned for later."

"No, Richard. I think we can be a little more creative than that," Smith responded. "I have some things to attend to. We can deal with this later. She won't be here until this evening. It also might be better to wait until the office staff has gone off for the day. Things could get a little noisy before it's all over."

Jackie did *not* like the sound of that.

♪♯♪·♪♭·

I couldn't believe that I'd lost my connection with Shannon's cell phone in the middle of trying to answer her question. A subsequent call had not worked, either.

Katy couldn't understand why I didn't want her working on the painting, and as I couldn't come out and tell her, we had quite a fight. When she called me a moron, I had no choice but to send her to her room. She demanded that I call Sandra to come and take her home.

This was not the way I'd wanted our weekend to go, and I knew the situation would have to be dealt with before my daughter fell asleep.

The phone rang, and I heard Katy's feet as she ran to my bedroom to answer it. Another infraction to be dealt with. She probably thought it was her mom.

I went to the front hall and picked up the receiver.

"...so could you please get your daddy on the phone?"

"He's downstairs. I'll call him."

She only partially covered the phone with her hand. "Dad! It's the lady detective on the phone!"

"I've already got it, Kate," I answered. "You can hang up and go back to your room. I'll be up in a moment to talk to you."

"All right," Katy said, sounding rather disheartened.

I waited for the phone to click off. Little ears didn't need to be on the line.

"Did you hear anything I said during that last phone call?" I asked.

"Not the important bits," Shannon answered. "Is that sketch on your wall Maxine St. James or not?"

"I'm not sure. It could be."

"You can't do better than that?"

"Do you want the truth or the answer you want to hear?"

She sighed. "The truth."

"What should I do?"

The line was silent for a moment. "Call Palmer. Tell him what you've found out. It might help the situation. Tell him I'll call as soon as I have the situation out here secured."

"Is Jackie Goode okay?"

"We haven't had any contact since yesterday, but I don't think she's in any serious danger. They probably just busted her."

"And Olivia?"

"Her stepmother flew out here just ahead of me. *That* I don't like the sound of. I don't know if Palmer has been in touch with her, or if something else has stirred her up, but I am concerned. We're on our way to Sunnyvale right now. We'll make sure Olivia's all right, too."

"Let me know, please."

"I'll do that. Now call Palmer."

I hung up, then stood there thinking.

"Katy," I called up the stairs. "I know you were up there listening. Would you come down here, please?"

There was no answer right away, then I heard a small, "All right."

We went to the living room and sat down on the sofa.

"It's not good to eavesdrop on phone conversations. You know that."

She hung her head and nodded. "I know." Then came a few sniffles. "I'm sorry I called you a moron."

"I'm sorry I got angry." I pulled her against me. "I don't like it when you make me play the heavy." I kissed the top of her head. "The lady detective wants me to let the police know something."

"Is this about the man on the wall getting his head bashed in?"

I couldn't believe what I'd heard. "It's, um..."

Kate looked up at me. "I saw it this afternoon when I first went up to the room."

"You did?"

"Yes, and I also noticed you freak when you saw it. What does it mean?"

"Did Olivia tell you anything about it?"

"No. She must have done it after I was here the weekend before she went away. I only saw her draw the stuff I was painting today. I have no idea how she wants to paint that side of the wall." She was speaking about it so matter of factly, I began to doubt my sanity. "Why do you have to call the police about it?

"Because of something bad that happened to poor Olivia many years ago."

"Did she see someone get killed?"

"We don't know."

"Was it her brother?"

Now I really *was* freaked out. "How did you know that?"

"Because the guy getting bashed with the rock looks like Olivia. Didn't you notice?"

"I guess not."

♪♯♩·♪♭♩·

Shannon and Roy blasted through the motel room in all of a minute. There was no sign of Marvell, but also no obvious sign anyone else had been there. On the bedside table they found notes Marvell had made about his trips out to Sunnyvale.

"Take these, and we'll read them on the way," Shannon said. "I'll drive. I know the way better than you do."

It was pretty well dark as they took off down Highway 70.

Roy had the notes on his lap and had unfolded the topo map Jackie had bought when she'd first arrived in California. He studied both for several minutes.

"I'm thinking we should go to the front gate. The other way will take far too long and still leave us with the problem of getting in."

"We don't know how many security people they have or where they might be in the compound. We have to know those answers before we do anything. What good will it do anyone if they nail us, too?"

"I've been inside, Shannon, and my money is on them using the admin building for any hanky-panky. They can't risk having the regular inmates know anything is going on."

"Okay. So how do we crack this nut?"

"How soon before we have to decide?"

"Six, maybe seven minutes."

"Let me finish Marvell's notes. They may give us a clue."

As Roy read, Shannon thought about what had set the bad guys off. If Jackie or Marvell had blown it, that wouldn't be a reason for Maxine to hustle across the country. A thought flitted across her brain. Had Jackie found out something particularly dangerous to her? Then the real issue sat up and screamed inside her head.

She pounded the steering wheel in frustration at her own blindness.

"What's up?" Roy asked.

"Christ! Why didn't I see it before? Sunnyvale has been helping Maxine all along. If it got out that they were drugging their charges or keeping people there for no real reason, they'd be in a lot of trouble. I figured she was just paying them a lot of money to do what she needed. What if it goes deeper than that?"

"Oh shit. A classic case of not being able to see the forest for the trees. We're both dunces."

"Either Maxine has some super strong hold over them or—"

"She owns the goddamn place!" He smacked his forehead with his palm. "If that's the case, we could already be too late. How much time to the turn-off?"

"That's it up ahead, Roy."

"Stop the car."

Shannon did, and Roy opened the satellite phone.

"Who are you calling?"

Roy clicked it on and waited for it to find a signal. "Two places. The sheriff's office and Sunnyvale. I just had a brainstorm."

♪♯♩·♪♭♩·

Jackie had spent too many hours on her stomach. Her legs and arms, pulled up tightly behind her, had been cramping, and she was having trouble breathing. Every time she rolled onto her side, one of the two men kicked her back onto her stomach. If anyone had bothered to ask her, she would have freely admitted she was scared shitless.

Marvell had finally come to, sort of. He'd done a lot of moaning and rolling around of his head, but it wasn't until maybe an hour before that he'd stopped and opened his eyes.

The big guy, Dave, was watching them at the time. "You're awake, buddy, and don't think I don't know it. Just be a good boy, and we won't have to hurt you again. Got it?"

Dave really was a big man. She and Marvell would have a hard time with this guy –even *if* they could get themselves free.

Think! Jackie told herself for about the millionth time. *There has to be a way out of this.*

Despite the fact that Doc Smith was involved, Richard seemed to be the one in charge. When he strolled back into the room, he had all of Jackie's other surveillance toys.

"Looks as if you didn't search the room all that well, my friend," he said to Dave. "I found these stuffed into the back of a chair."

Dave coloured and looked down while his friend laughed at him. "Relax. It was a pretty good hiding place." He dumped the stuff on one of the tables. "You got some first-rate equipment here, girlie. I just checked these pass cards, and one of them opens every door I tried. Not bad. How did you smuggle this stuff in here? I'll be interested to hear the answer."

Smith came into the room. "I just spoke to her, and she's really upset. Her jet will be landing in half an hour. It will be another half hour to drive here. I sent Renaldo to pick her up."

"Then I'd suggest we get our butts in gear and get some answers to the questions she's gonna have. Might shut her up a bit."

The doctor nodded. "This one first," he said nodding at Jackie. "She's the inside person. Put her up on the table. I'll be right back."

Dave picked Jackie up with about as much effort as a sack of groceries. Dumping her on her front, he put a meaty paw in the middle of her back and pushed down hard enough to make breathing even more difficult. She knew there was no point in trying to struggle.

Smith returned in a matter of minutes. He handed Richard a razor knife. "Cut her clothes off. I think it would be good to have her naked."

Taped up and with the big guy leaning on her, she was helpless as the other man went about his work with obvious pleasure. If she ever got him alone, she'd make sure he paid in full. She thought they might leave her the dignity of her underwear, but that came off with two swipes of the knife. Jackie tried to hold back the flush of shame flowing down her body.

They would pay.

Smith, who'd been standing off to the side, told them, "Turn her over but take the tape off her hands. I need her arms at her sides."

Jackie shut her eyes so she wouldn't have to watch them looking at her.

Smith had brought in several heavy nylon straps, the kind used to hold things on roof racks. As Richard and Dave held her down, he looped one strap around her left wrist, then over her stomach around the other wrist and then underneath the table. Once buckled, she was completely pinned down. A second strap was wrapped around her ankles and a third over her upper chest. All were pulled extremely tight.

"Put some tape on her mouth," Smith said. "It could get noisy while we soften her up."

Jackie's eyes got big as the doctor wheeled over his little cart with the packages of acupuncture needles and his electronic gadget on it.

"What you gonna do with that?" Dave asked.

"I think it's best to get our information without leaving a trace. Any marks will be so tiny you could go over the girl's body with a microscope and still not be assured of seeing anything. She'll tell us in short order what we want to know."

Even though it was completely pointless, Jackie struggled as hard as she could. The straps made it impossible to move more than a few inches. What pushed her rage to the very edge, though, was Dave guffawing at her efforts.

Richard chuckled as he noticed her murderous eyes. "If looks could kill, my friend," he said nudging his partner.

"Hold down her left leg," Smith ordered. "If she's moving around, I can't put the needles in."

Smith put in a total of twelve needles: two in each leg, two in each arm and four in her chest. He was not at all gentle as he inserted each one, after carefully measuring off the correct spots. The needles bit deep, right into the heart of the trigger points, and this time it *was* painful, the reaction intense as he moved each needle roughly to get the spot "heated" up. Her heart was already racing even before he began connecting wires from his black box to each one.

Smith looked down at her with all the feeling of looking at a bug before squashing it with his foot. "She seems to be particularly sensitive to this. That's why I thought of it. Now for the application of a little current."

Over against the wall, Marvell must have been struggling, because one of the small tables suddenly crashed down.

As he took a blackjack from his pocket, Richard said, "If he doesn't stop, hit him with this and put him out again."

Smith's eyes dropped as he switched on his machine, then began slowly rotating dials. "I've got to be careful. I don't know if too much might stop her heart."

At first, it felt pretty much like it had the first day she'd been at Sunnyvale.

Then Richard said, "Nothing's happening. Better turn it up."

Jackie felt as if she would have levitated right off the table if it hadn't been for the straps holding her down. The pain was unimaginable. As the power cycled back and forth between pairs of needles, the nearby muscles completely seized up. It felt as if they were ripping themselves to shreds.

With interested expressions, the three men watched her writhe, straining against the straps for a good thirty seconds, which felt like three days. She couldn't scream because of the tape over her mouth.

Smith turned off his infernal machine, and Jackie went limp, her skin slick with sweat. Reaching out, Richard yanked the tape from her face, leaving the skin around her mouth feeling even more raw and tingling.

His face hovered right over Jackie's. "How do you feel now about telling us why you're here and what you've found out?"

"Fuck you!"

"Doc, why don't you turn on the juice a little higher and let her toast a little longer? We'll see if she's still uncooperative after that. Okay?"

"No, don't..." Jackie moaned, panting uncontrollably.

"Too late. Remember, you do not get a second chance with us. Hit it, Doc."

This time Jackie did scream, loud and long, pleading with the men to turn the machine off. It felt as if she was dying.

She held out longer than she would have imagined.

Dave had wanted Doc Smith to turn the current up even higher, but he refused, because he couldn't be certain what might happen.

"She dies now, so what? She's certainly going to die later."

"No, you dummy!" Richard snarled. "We need answers." He looked at Jackie. "You gonna tell us something now?"

It was the third jolt she'd gotten since they'd taken the tape from her mouth, and she'd screamed herself hoarse. Her voice came out in a shaky whisper. "What...do you want to know?"

"Who you're working for," said a voice from the doorway, a woman's voice, and it did not sound happy.

Everyone turned as three more people entered the room. One was a woman dressed in an expensive business suit, not a hair out of place. Jackie recognized her at once: Maxine St. James. Close behind were two large men, each wearing dark suits and looking even more menacing than Dave.

"What is going on here, Smith?" Maxine demanded.

"Ah, Mrs. St. James," Smith answered soothingly, looking nervous, "we didn't expect you so soon."

"That's obvious."

"We're getting information from this woman. She's the one I told you about. Unfortunately, she wasn't being cooperative, so we've had to resort to harsher means."

"And what have you found out?"

"Nothing yet. She is very stubborn."

Maxine moved around the table and spotted Marvell. "And this one?"

"Her accomplice."

Richard's face was suddenly hovering over Jackie's. "You heard the lady. Who are you working for?"

Her throat felt like she'd been swallowing sandpaper. "May I have some water?"

"No. Answer the question or you'll get another jolt."

"I'm from Toronto. The people I work for were hired by—"

Jackie's voice dropped away. She just couldn't speak any more.

"Oh, for God's sake, give her some water," Maxine said, "or we're going to be here all night."

Doc Smith and Richard both stared pointedly at Dave, who shrugged and left the room, returning a moment later with a water bottle. Richard snatched the bottle and poured some water down Jackie's throat, so fast she started choking. That only made her throat feel worse.

"You've had your drink. Continue," Maxine said, taking a seat on one of the chairs against the wall.

"The man in Toronto who lived with your stepdaughter hired us."

"Why are you here?"

"To make sure Olivia is all right."

"And what do you know about my precious stepdaughter?"

Jackie played her one remaining card. "Everything."

The response was laughter from Maxine. "Oh, I doubt that very much. Olivia is a shifty little creature. For instance, I'll bet she's told you that I killed her brother, which is totally ridiculous, of course. It was actually me who shielded her from the police. There would have been a trial; she would have gone to prison – or worse – if it hadn't been for me."

Jackie swallowed a few times, attempting to ease the pain in her throat. "Then why did her friend Maggie have to die?"

"I have no idea what you're talking about."

Jackie had been watching Dave when she'd asked that, and his eyes betrayed him. He, for one, knew what she was talking about.

"Why haven't you had Olivia murdered?"

"Murder my own stepdaughter? Preposterous!"

"No, Maxine, not preposterous."

Jackie managed to turn her head far enough to see Olivia standing in the doorway. She didn't seem very steady on her legs, but the pistol in her hands was steady enough.

"Tell her why I can't die."

CHAPTER 24

Racing up the long, winding drive to Sunnyvale from the county road, Shannon couldn't help crossing herself while saying a silent prayer. Roy's idea probably wouldn't work – and it could go drastically wrong, but it was the only plan they'd had time to come up with.

Reaching into the back seat, Roy retrieved a metal box. "You use a cop-issue Beretta, right?"

"Yeah."

He slipped out the clip to check it, then slammed it home and put it on her lap. "Safety's on. Here are four more clips."

She stopped the car momentarily to put the clips in her pocket and stick the pistol under her right leg, where she could reach it easily. Having to concentrate on driving, she couldn't see what he took out of the case for himself, but it was big, and knowing Roy, it would have a lot of stopping power.

"The front gate is right around the next bend. Don't stop too close to it," he said. "All set?"

"I'd feel better if we had the cavalry right behind us."

"That ain't gonna happen. It's us against the house, girl."

Shannon nodded. "I'm ready."

Since turning off the road, she'd had the high beams on. Roy also had roof-mounted lights, and as she swung the Hummer through the last turn, she flipped them on, hoping to get that much more cover by blinding whoever was on duty.

"Don't let the nice decorations fool you," Roy said, "That is one strong gate."

The span of both halves of the gate was about fifteen feet, almost the same amount in height, and the decorative points looked as if they might be pretty sharp. On both sides were substantial brick pillars leading into ivy-covered, brick walls.

"My bet is there's glass or spikes embedded in the top of those walls," Roy said, "but they also have to preserve their country club appearance for the gentry. They'd tell you it's to keep the media out."

A uniformed man stood in the small guard house to the left of the gate. Shielding his eyes with one hand, he used the other to motion them to stop.

"Here goes nothin'," Shannon said, as the guard stepped out of the hut and walked towards them.

"He's carrying," Roy told her.

"And he's got communication on his belt. This is not good." Rolling down the window, she said in her best cop voice as the guard stepped up, "Plumas County Sheriff. We got a call that there's been trouble up here."

He looked at her suspiciously. "Since when does Plumas County have Hummers?"

Roy leaned over towards the window. "Since the FBI got involved in some funny business going on here. Open the gate!"

"I need to see ID," the guard said stolidly.

Now it was change to Plan B, so Shannon, while keeping her eyes straight ahead, said out of the corner of her mouth, "Sorry about this, Roy."

She floored the Hummer.

The vehicle's tires squealed and didn't get any traction for a moment. Then it shot forward twenty feet to the gates. They actually held for a moment before Roy and Shannon went through with a horrendous sound of shredding metal. Slouching down low in case the guard unloaded on them, they sped forward as fast as they could. A golf cart went spinning as they slammed into it.

"Stay to the left! Stay to the left!" Roy shouted as the drive divided. "There's a parking lot ahead, and the door into the admin building is on your right. You'll see it in a moment."

"Let's hope there aren't armed guards pouring out of it," Shannon answered tightly as she accelerated up the drive.

The lot was nearly empty, and she yanked the wheel right then left, executing two screeching turns before jamming on her brakes right in front of the glass doors. The roof lights flooded the reception area just inside. Another guard was at the main desk with a phone in his hand.

She hoped there wasn't a gun in the other.

"Bail out your side," Roy yelled as he threw open his door.

Shannon grabbed her pistol, opened her door, hit the ground and rolled. She left a fair bit of skin on the pavement, but in her keyed-up state, she didn't even feel it.

Scrambling to the side of the building, she inched toward the glass doors. Roy was on the opposite side, waiting.

As the seconds ticked away their advantage in surprise, she began making motions to indicate that the guard inside might not be able to see much because of the headlights and spots on top of the Hummer blinding him. Roy nodded his agreement. He poked his head forward to look inside, then pulled rapidly back, gesturing to indicate that the guard was coming, and Shannon would have to take care of him.

The door pushed open and the guard stuck his head out cautiously, looking left at Roy. He had a walkie-talkie in one hand and a pistol in the other.

Shannon used the opportunity to step forward and put her gun to his head. "Move slowly. Drop your weapon and the walkie-talkie, and you won't get hurt. Do it now!"

He did as he was told. "What the hell do you people want?"

Roy moved forward and picked up the two things the guard had dropped. "Get him inside. We make too easy a target out here."

They hustled the man inside and around a corner. Roy stayed back to keep a lookout.

"Did you call the Sheriff's office?" Shannon demanded.

"Well, yeah," the guard said in a how-can-you-be-so-stupid tone of voice. "Wouldn't you?"

He looked amazed when Roy said, "Good. Maybe they'll hustle their butts a bit more."

"Some people arrived here about twenty to thirty minutes ago," Shannon said. "Where did they go?"

"I...I don't know."

"That's bullshit. Are they in this building?"

"No," the guard said, but his eyes gave him away when they flicked momentarily over Shannon's shoulder to the corridor beyond.

"Roy! Any signs?"

"Not yet."

She looked down at the guard's belt, where a ring of keys hung. "We're going to lock the front door. Move it!"

He wasn't moving smartly until Shannon jammed her gun into his back.

"We got to move, girl," Roy called out. "There's probably another way into this building."

They hustled the guard into a nearby closet and locked him in, then sprinted down the dark hallway.

The walkie-talkie chirped. "No sign of them outside the front of the admin building. They must be inside. Frank, you there? Talk to me, Frank."

"Good," Roy said to Shannon as they moved forward. "Not knowing if he's a hostage will make them move more cautiously."

At the far end of the broad corridor were double doors. The sign on one said Treatment Suite. As they pushed through, lights went on.

Both froze in crouched positions, eyes and weapons on the move, looking for sources of danger.

"Motion detection lighting," Roy sighed. "I hate those things."

On either side of the area there were rooms with names indicating their use for various new-age treatments: aromatherapy, candling, homeopathy. None seemed to be occupied.

At the end of the corridor, they found a stairway going up. There was also a door to the outside. They made sure it was locked.

Roy crept up a few steps on the stairway and leaned out, looking up, then came back to Shannon. "There's a light on up there. I'm assuming it's turned on for a reason. It's not bright enough to be corridor lights."

She smiled grimly. "Nowhere to go but up."

At the landing, they could hear voices.

Shannon crept forward, crawling the last few steps so that her head barely cleared the floor at the top. Looking to the left, she saw a similar layout to the floor below, but at the end room on the left, the door was open and she could just make out the back of someone standing just inside. This room was also the source of the light.

"Tell her why I can't die," a woman's voice said. The words seemed to come from the person in the doorway.

Shannon backed down a few steps to Roy. With her mouth against his ear, she outlined the situation. He nodded his understanding.

They silently crept forward. At the top of the stairs, she moved left, flattening herself against the wall while Roy went right, sliding along the end wall toward the opposite side of the corridor to spread out the targets if anyone got stupid.

She slipped forward another fifteen feet, then stopped. Should she bust in on them or wait for more information? Lives could hang in the balance of her decision.

ᎠᏉᏓᎣᏈᎠ

"Put down the gun, Olivia," Dr. Smith said, sounding more in control of himself than he had all evening. Perhaps his stunted professionalism was finally kicking in.

Jackie saw that Olivia's eyes were moving all over the place. Whether it was drugs or nerves, she couldn't be sure, but it didn't bode well for the situation.

"No!" Olivia's voice was definite, defiant.

"Where the hell did she get a gun?" Richard asked in amazement.

"Dr. Smith keeps one in his bottom desk drawer."

"Give the gun to Dr. Smith, Olivia," Maxine said, sounding completely unconcerned. "It's dangerous to be waving something like that around."

"Tell Jackie why you can't kill me!" the girl repeated, swinging the pistol back at Maxine.

"I would never want to kill you, Olivia," Maxine answered. "You're my stepdaughter."

"You started killing me when you had me locked away in here!"

"It was for your own good. You know that."

"No, it wasn't, and *you* know it! You needed me alive so you could stay in control. I'm not as stupid as you think I am. I figured it out. My daddy said he would look out for me, that he would set things up for after he was gone.

"He wouldn't have wanted me to be here, rotting. They were giving me drugs. You had them do that, didn't you? You made it so I would never get out. My daddy loved me. He'd never have allowed this to happen to me. He told me what he'd planned. There could only be one reason why you were doing this and why I'm still alive."

Maxine made no response, but she'd gone pale.

"You know what the really funny thing is, Maxine?" Olivia laughed, and it had an ominously hysterical edge to it. "I don't want the damn money. I never wanted it. You can have it for all I care. If you'd just bothered to ask me, I would have told you that."

"Put down the gun, Olivia, and we can talk, if that's what you want. I can see now that I was wrong about you."

"It's too late for that. You've hurt people." The gun swivelled to indicate Richard and Dave. "These men did more than come to fetch me back, didn't they? This big man didn't fly back with us. He stayed in Toronto to deal with Maggie. You knew I would have told her everything, and that's why you had her killed, wasn't it?"

"That's preposterous!"

But it was easy to see from Maxine's face that it was true. Dave also had a pinched expression. Regardless of how this discussion would end, Jackie knew she had to get free.

"Olivia," she croaked as strongly as she could, "can you undo these straps with one hand?"

When the girl's eyes swivelled to hers, one of Maxine's big men began slowly moving his hand towards the opening of his jacket.

Olivia saw it, too. "Don't you dare! I'll shoot you."

With some training, Olivia would have known that her best bet for controlling the situation would have been to keep her gun trained on Maxine. Everyone in the room worked for her and wouldn't risk something happening to their boss.

The treatment room was too wide, and the bad guys too spread out for the girl to spot every movement. Even Jackie didn't notice big Dave making his move until far too late.

"*Olivia!*" she yelled with more voice than she knew she had.

Two nearly simultaneous shots rang out, deafening in the confined area.

And all hell broke loose as the lights went out.

ᐃᑉᖅᐃᑉᖅ

Shannon was nearly at the door.

The person doing most of the talking had to be Olivia.

Roy was moving forward now, hidden in the darkness past the edge of the light coming from the room. He tilted his head a bit more to the side, then pulled back.

In sign language, he pointed to his eyes then flashed the number six, followed by a shrug.

Six people in the room, maybe more. Several of them could be armed. Not the kind of situation to inspire confidence.

A few moments later, she breathed a sigh of relief when she heard Jackie's voice, although her words came out as if she had the world's worst sore throat.

When Olivia said something about shooting people, Shannon knew she couldn't wait any longer. She covered the remaining ground in about two seconds. She could see a light switch on the wall just inside the room, but it was on the opposite side of the door. Still, she felt she could make it since all eyes would be on Olivia.

She didn't have a chance to move before it was too late.

Jackie's voice shrieked, "Olivia!" as two shots were fired.

Cursing, Shannon leapt for the light switch and plunged everyone into darkness.

She was about to enter the room when Roy's hand on her shoulder yanked her back.

"Both sides of the door. Now!"

Shannon took the left side, Roy the right, both using the jamb as partial protection. Someone stumbled towards them and felt along the wall.

The lights went back on.

"*Everybody freeze!*" Roy bellowed and moved forward.

The volume of the sound in the confined space made everyone in the room hesitate for just that extra moment.

Shannon had her eyes fixed on a big man over near one of the room's windows. He had a gun in his hand, but it was down. Next to him was a shorter man whose face reminded her of a rat.

"Drop it!" Shannon yelled. He looked at her with astonished eyes, but the gun did rattle to the floor.

"Two on the right!" Jackie croaked.

Knowing she might regret it, Shannon dove into the room, trusting that Roy would cover her. Landing on her side, she had her pistol trained on two large men. One was Maxine's butler, and the other was the man who'd knocked her down on the street in New York. Both froze with their hands halfway into their jackets.

Roy stepped into the room behind her, gun targeting the men at the far end of the room.

Shannon's gun was swinging back and forth between Maxine's two heavies. "Now, gentlemen, use two fingers on your other hand to pull your lapel back very slowly. I don't like how fast you move, and you're gone. I don't miss at this range." She carefully rose to her feet, keeping her gun trained on her two targets as they disarmed themselves. "Kick them over to me."

Smith had crouched over Maxine St. James, who was on the floor, moaning. "She's hurt."

"Too bad," Roy said. "Get your sorry butt up and get those needles out of my girl, then put your lab coat over her. She's going to catch a cold."

"Next to me," Jackie croaked as Smith did what he was told. "Olivia's been hit."

Shannon picked up the two guns and stuck them in the waistband of her jeans, then slid around to the other side of the table.

Olivia lay there, crumpled on her side, eyes closed. Her face was drained of colour and her breathing rapid and shallow. A finger of scarlet was snaking out from under her back.

"Christ, Roy," Shannon said, "this is bad. Can you handle the crowd without me?"

"Sure thing, babe. Do what you gotta do."

The girl had a light jacket on. When Shannon pushed it to the side, a small ring of blood around a neat hole in her white T-shirt was the only evidence of the bullet that had ripped through the centre of Olivia's chest. Experience and the trail of blood soaking the knee of her jeans told Shannon that the worst of the damage would be in the back.

Slipping her hand underneath, she found the exit wound with her fingers. Sliding her hand further under, she pressed up hard with her palm, hoping the pressure would slow the leaking blood.

Shannon touched her other palm to the side of Olivia's face. "Olivia," she said softly. "Andy Curran sent me. Hold on. Help will be here soon. Just hold on. You'll be all right."

Olivia's eyes fluttered open, and she tried to take a deeper breath. It bubbled ominously, and she winced from the pain, but oddly, she smiled at the woman kneeling over her. Then her eyes slowly shut again.

"Roy, we're losing her!"

"Shit!"

Jackie snarled. "Smith, you're a doctor. Do something!"

Smith stood above Shannon, looking stricken. "I'm a psychologist. I really don't know about these things."

Shannon bent down further, her mouth next to Olivia's ear. "Olivia, don't give up! Stay with me. We're going to pull you through."

The girl's eyes barely opened again, and her mouth moved. A trickle of blood came out of the corner, held for a moment, then flowed down her cheek. Shannon wiped it away with her sleeve.

Olivia's mouth moved again, and Shannon put her ear directly above it, knowing she wanted to speak but couldn't because of the blood filling her lungs.

The words came out in a pain-filled whisper. "I did...what I had to."

She shuddered once more, and the last breath of Olivia St. James's short life left her body as a long sigh.

Filled with anger, regret but mostly deep sorrow, Shannon's slumped as she bowed her head over the dead singer.

Down below, running feet could be heard, then, "Police! We've got the building surrounded."

The cavalry had finally arrived.

Marvell, obviously not in good shape from the crack on his head, was sent off to the hospital, but Jackie flatly refused to go. Since she wasn't outwardly marked, they didn't overrule her. So Shannon, Jackie and Roy were put in a downstairs conference room to cool their heels as the official wheels ground slowly forward. Roy paced the room ceaselessly, muttering to himself. Jackie had been given a blanket, but she was still shivering and looking ill.

Shannon, surprisingly, felt calm and focussed for the first time in several days. Procedures were being followed. Each of the three had been interviewed in a separate room, and she knew the same was being done with Maxine and her crew. As a former cop, she desperately wanted to hear what sort of spin they were trying to put on the situation.

About every ten minutes, Roy complained that things were taking too long, and one or the other of the two underlings watching them would answer wearily, "The sheriff will deal with you when he's good and ready."

Close to three in the morning, the door opened and a new person entered. An older man with a grey buzz-cut and sharply pressed uniform, he sat down wearily on the chair at the end of the conference table, then slid Shannon's and Roy's wallets down to them. No sign of their guns.

"I'm Sheriff Newmark," he said.

"What's going on?" they all asked at once.

He pursed his lips and stared at them for a long moment. "Well, as you know, Ms Olivia St. James is dead. The ME has told me that the bullet tore her up real good inside. There was nothing anyone could have done for her."

Shannon sagged, then asked, "And her stepmother?"

"Maxine St. James was hit in the shoulder. She lost a lot of blood, but she'll be all right."

Jackie smashed her fist down on the table. "Goddammit!" she croaked, "Why is it *always* the wrong way around?"

Once the three had been given the thumbs up by Newmark, the sheriff's men became a lot friendlier. A female deputy accompanied Jackie back to her room so she could get some clothes. Still, it was nearly five o'clock before they were allowed to leave.

Seen in daylight, the damage to Roy's Hummer was even worse than expected. He didn't seem to notice.

It was a subdued group that dragged themselves back to the motel in Portola.

"I'm going over to the hospital and see how Marvell's doing," Roy said with a sigh. "He looked pretty rough. I don't know how I'm going to explain to his momma what's happened."

Shannon gave him a big hug. "Thanks for everything, Roy. You've been a rock throughout this."

He looked at her sadly. "I just wish it had turned out better."

"We all do."

After the door closed behind the big man, Jackie looked at Shannon. "How are we going to tell Andy?"

Her boss sat down on the bed and put her head in her hands. "I don't know, Jackie. I just don't know."

Even though she was falling-on-her-face tired, Shannon called Toronto after gathering her thoughts for a few minutes. The last thing she wanted was for Curran to hear something about Olivia's death through the media.

"Shannon!" he said. "Thank God. It's almost three, and I've been going crazy with worry. What's happening?"

"It's all over, Andy, and...well...I really don't know how to tell you—"

"Is Olivia okay? That's all that matters."

"No, Andy, she's not. Everything went horribly wrong. She had confronted her stepmother by the time we got there. She had a gun and there was...there were some shots fired. Olivia was hit in the chest." The PI squeezed her eyes shut, trying to find the inner strength. "She's dead, Andy. I wish I could tell you anything else. I am so sorry." The phone was silent for quite a long time, until Shannon finally asked, "Andy, are you still there?"

"Yeah. How did it happen?"

In a calm, unemotional voice, Shannon told him everything that had taken place the previous evening. She felt certain Olivia's actions had saved Jackie's and Marvell's lives, and she told him that.

"And that bitch of a stepmother?"

Shannon sighed deeply. "I really don't know what's going to happen to her. I'm not a lawyer, but you can count on me not resting until she's brought up on any charges we can make stick."

"And what charges would those be?"

"I wish I could tell you. She's in the hospital. She's certainly an accessory to what happened last night, but past that, I just can't tell you at this point. I'm sorry I couldn't call with better news."

"So am I." Curran sighed heavily. "So what happens now?"

"We've been told by the sheriff to stick around. You'll hear from me the minute I find out anything. You have my word."

"Thanks," he said and hung up before Shannon could say anything else.

Jackie lay in bed all that first day, face to the wall.

Shannon knew she was wrung out by her ordeal, but this response was more than that. The girl would never admit it, but she was a wreck.

What they'd done to her had been unimaginable.

About five, Shannon went out and picked up some Chinese food at a place down the road from the motel. She also bought a bottle of whiskey. But when she got back to the room, the first thing Jackie said was, "I'm not hungry."

Shannon put the food on the dresser and sat on Jackie's bed. Giving the younger woman's shoulder a squeeze, she said, "I know how you're feeling right now. I feel the same, but what happened is part of this game. It sucks, but things don't always turn out the way we'd like."

Jackie flinched under her hand. "If I hadn't screwed up, we wouldn't have failed, and Olivia wouldn't be dead."

"You didn't screw up. If you hadn't held out as long as you did, Marvell, you *and* Olivia would probably all be dead. And Olivia being in that room wasn't just about saving you. She finally had a chance to confront her stepmother. That's why she was there. That's what you have to remember. You have to keep that fact in the front of your mind. You. Did. Not. Fail."

Jackie made no response.

"Do you still want to work for me, Goode?"

Finally, Jackie turned over. "Yes."

Shannon nodded and got off the bed. "Then the first order of business is to get something in our stomachs. I've also bought a bottle of Jack Daniels. Tonight we're going to tie one on. Forget all about the bullshit world we live in. Tell stories about ourselves. Maybe even laugh."

Looking out of red-rimmed eyes, Jackie asked her boss. "And what about tomorrow?"

The older woman's eyes blazed. "Tomorrow we go after Maxine St. James with everything we've got. She is not going to walk away from what she's done."

But for all her brave words to rouse the troops, Shannon knew she had lied.

They had indeed failed.

EPILOGUE

I faced Shannon O'Brien for what would likely be the last time.

The original plan had been for me to go to her office in Unionville, but packing up the rest of the house had been taking more time than I'd expected. Since the movers were coming the next morning, she'd said she would drop by in the evening.

It seemed a fitting way to bring that chapter of my life to a close.

Shannon had been arrested on her return to Canada, and she'd admitted later that only some fancy footwork by her friend Roy had saved her from the same fate in Portola. Even though Palmer had spoken at length to the sheriff in California, he was still angry enough at her that he was determined to get his pound of flesh. It had taken two days to get her sprung from jail.

I'd had a devil of a time making Kate understand what was going on when she saw a news report about Shannon's arrest on TV. She was so incensed about it she'd written a blistering letter to Toronto's chief of police, which I actually encouraged because it distracted her for awhile from the loss of Olivia. It was my child's first experience with death and something I would have shielded her from if I could have.

Typically, Shannon had shrugged off her arrest, not wanting the cops to look any worse than they already did. If Palmer had even an ounce of sense, he would have fallen on his knees and kissed her feet for the information she'd provided.

We'd been in touch sporadically over the past three months but hadn't talked face to face. Palmer and his men, along with cops from Florida and New York, had trooped through Olivia's room at my house, taking photos and asking pretty much the same questions each time.

When all of them were satisfied, I painted over everything. I couldn't bear to look at it.

As I listened to what Shannon was saying, I just wanted with every fibre of my being for it all to be over with.

"Smith provided most of the information," Shannon was saying, "once the DA made a deal with him."

"So when are Haggerty and Colville being brought back to Canada for trial?"

"Palmer is pushing hard to get them, but the U.S. always does things in its own way and in its own sweet time. Believe me, if they thought they could make a murder charge stick against Dave Haggerty for Olivia's death, they'd never give him up. He isn't fighting extradition. California has the death penalty."

"And Palmer? What's he got on Haggerty?"

Shannon's face had an unreadable expression. "With my information, Palmer's men got hold of the rental car they had in Toronto and unbelievably found a couple of Maggie's hairs still in the trunk. They probably had her body wrapped in a plastic sheet, but that's seldom foolproof. The pathologist also found a tiny bit of Haggerty's skin under one of Maggie's nails. So Dave will go down, along with that little rat Colville as an accessory."

"What's the latest on Maxine St. James?"

"Seems she personally owned Sunnyvale and had installed Dr. Smith as its head. That makes her an accessory to what he was doing to Olivia, as well as for his torture of Jackie," Shannon said disgustedly, "and, of course, for Olivia's shooting. Maxine let Smith do whatever was needed to keep her stepdaughter anxious, lost and totally unable to deal with anything. It isn't hard when you use the right psychological techniques on someone as vulnerable as her. The drugs were the worst, though, a combination of heroin and cocaine."

"Speedballs?"

"Kind of a cute name for something so horrible, isn't it? Maggie figured out pretty quick what was going on, and after they got away, she probably had to get Olivia over the worst of the addiction by herself. Once free of Sunnyvale and the drugs, Olivia actually began to heal a bit. I don't know if she ever would have been completely right, but she certainly was doing better, as you know."

"But why didn't Maxine just arrange for her stepdaughter to have an accident?"

Shannon finally smiled. "When they got a look at Bernard St. James's will and the date it was drawn up, it became pretty clear. Somewhere in the back of his mind, he must have suspected his wife might have had something to do with his son's death. Part of it was that he couldn't believe his darling daughter would ever have done anything like that, nor did he believe the police version that the murder was possibly committed by a bunch of partying kids. The retired butler, Jim Davis, admitted that much to me a few weeks ago."

"So the father changed his will?"

"Yes. He had a new one drawn up two months before he died but didn't tell Maxine. In it, his widow would be the trustee for the estate and have full control of it until Olivia either married or died. Once either of those things happened, Maxine would get a cash settlement of twenty-five million dollars, and the rest of the estate would either go entirely to Olivia or to various charities and St. James relatives. The solution was obvious: all Maxine had to do was keep Olivia at Sunnyvale the rest of her life, and she was home free."

"She must have freaked out when Olivia got away."

"You bet. One of the servants in the New York mansion remembers the day well. Maxine was throwing things and screaming at Smith, who'd flown in to talk to her. She was completely out of control."

"But why go to all this trouble? Surely twenty-five million dollars would have been enough for her."

"Maxine's whole life revolved around playing with her late husband's estate. That's the best way to put it. She's got the value of the damn thing up to one-and-a-half *billion* dollars. *That's* how she gets her ya-yas."

"I've been thinking a lot about the last thing Olivia said to you—"

"We all have. I believe she knew *exactly* what she was doing. She knew about the provisions of her father's will."

"So she was willing to die to beat her stepmother? I find that hard to swallow."

"How can we say what was going through that poor girl's head? I only know what she said...at the end. You can believe what you want."

At that point, I just couldn't sit there, so I made an excuse about getting a glass of water from the kitchen. I brought one back for

Shannon too. We drank, neither of us willing to look at the other. Eventually, the silence became too much.

"Do you think Maxine killed Olivia's brother, or were those sketches upstairs something out of her imagination?"

Shannon pursed her lips. "How's this for a scenario? The son finds out about his stepmother's indiscretion with Taggart and threatens her with it. He loves his father and does not want to hurt him in any way, especially since he's dying, so he tells Maxine he won't tell his father what he knows. Could she take that risk? No. He's going to take over the business. There was the very real possibility young Bernard would boot her out as soon as his father died.

"When I spoke to his fiancée, she told me Bernard III had been edgy all that last week, but wouldn't tell her why. He did say something about how he had to protect his father. She also heard Bernard arguing loudly on the phone with Maxine two days before the family left for Florida."

I nodded. "That all sounds logical."

"We'll never prove it unless Maxine develops a conscience. Hell, she's going full tilt with a slate of high-powered lawyers to prove she's innocent of all charges." Shannon smiled again. "But there are some things she's not going to wiggle out of. She'll do time, but most devastating to her is that the estate is now out of her control forever. *That's* Olivia's revenge."

"And this Taggart guy, what happened to him?"

"Unless someone squeals, we'll never know. I doubt he's alive, though. He was screwing Maxine. It's my belief he asked for a big pay-off to keep his mouth shut about it, and she couldn't count on him to do that. Maybe Maxine was involved with the drugs he was supplying to Olivia. Our only hope there is that either Haggerty or Colville knows something and lets it drop.

"Maxine had known Richard Colville for a number of years. He used to be a PI, and I'll bet he did her dirty work. He has a bad reputation in the business. He might have been the one who took care of Jack Taggart. The only thing we've got going for us is that Dave Haggerty is not too bright. The DA in California has them separated, hoping that will shake something loose. Without the brains of the outfit around, Haggerty might say something interesting."

"That sounds like a long shot."

"I don't think so. There are too many people around who know too much. Sooner or later, somebody is going to slip up or cut a deal for a lighter sentence, and Maxine St. James is going to go down for something really big. The trouble with people like her is that they believe no one can touch them. Jackie and I, not to mention my friend Roy, are committed to seeing justice done. We won't let this one go."

"By the way, thanks for sending over the series of articles that reporter wrote. She really gave it to everyone involved with Sunnyvale. I'm surprised she hasn't been sued. Or has she?"

Shannon laughed. "Not the last I'd heard, but the articles have garnered a lot of notice in the New York press, and it's taken some of the wind out of old Max's sails." She closed her notebooks and looked at me closely. "There's one thing I haven't told you yet."

"What's that?"

"The reason Haggerty and Colville got sent to Toronto is that somebody ratted Olivia out."

"Who would have—" I stopped. I knew who it was.

Ronald.

I guess I'd known it all along. Always on the computer when he wasn't playing piano, jealous of the notice Olivia was receiving, the way he'd acted that last night at the Sal. It all made too much sense. He would have had no more trouble than Jackie in finding out who Olivia was. I didn't know if it was worth the energy to confront him about what he'd done, but I probably should. If he hadn't opened his mouth, Olivia might still be alive.

Shannon let me mull that over, then said, "Andy, how are *you* doing?"

Looking down at the floor, I answered, "I have my ups and downs. Kate has been a great help. We bought a condo down near the waterfront. Lots of windows looking out over the lake. She's fallen in love with it."

Even with the fact that a body had been dumped on my porch, the house had sold very quickly – and for an absolutely astronomical sum.

I'd paid cash for the condo, bought a new car and still had enough money left to invest and to pay Shannon's bill – which I felt sure had not reflected the actual amount.

When it was announced that a revival of *The Lion King* was being mounted in Toronto, I'd auditioned for the drum chair and had gotten it with no trouble. I was actually looking forward to doing something so different.

"And you?" I asked Shannon.

"After this, I'm thinking of packing it in. Actually, I discovered I've been thinking that way for awhile, but was too busy to notice."

"What are you going to do?"

She shook her head. "I honestly don't know. But first I have to sell the business if I can."

"To whom?"

"Jackie's been making noises about buying it. I don't know if she's ready, though. As good as she is, she's pretty green. She's also still beating herself up about what happened to Olivia, no matter what I tell her."

"I still can't believe she's gone. It was such a tragic, useless ending."

"Yes...it was. Olivia was a truly exceptional talent, and I'm incredibly sorry we couldn't manage to save her. The way life treated her is just completely unfair." She looked up at me. "I just want you to know, Andy, that you did the very best you could for her. It was everyone else who failed Olivia."

Again trying to control my emotions, I could only nod. "By the way, there's something I want to show you," I finally said, getting to my feet. "It's in a box out on the porch. Wait here."

The chalk outline of Maggie was long gone, but you wouldn't have been able to see it anyway because of all the boxes piled up for the movers in the morning. Opening one box, I removed a new frame with a beautiful mounting of Olivia's drawing of Kate reading on my sofa. I took it back into the house.

"Kate and I have promised that this is going to be the first thing unpacked at our new place."

Shannon looked at it for a long time, then said, "The other night when I got to his apartment, Michael was playing the CD you gave me of Olivia singing. I walked in just as 'A Case of You' came on."

I looked away. "I don't think I'll ever be able to listen to that song again. It tears me up inside worse than ever."

The detective was silent for a moment, then said, "She wrapped that song around your soul, didn't she?"

A nod was all I could manage.

She leaned forward and gave me a clumsy hug. "I'm sorry you're hurting so badly. If it's any consolation, it will get better over time." Shannon snuffled and dabbed her eyes with a tissue she'd dug out of her pocket. "Sorry I brought up that song."

"You didn't know."

"Her performance is just so stunning. It's a shame no recordings will ever be available to a wider audience."

"Maybe it should be," I said, voicing something I'd been thinking about for a few weeks.

"Michael said he'd be glad to help if you decided to do that."

I looked out the front windows again. Sunset was beginning to colour the clouds in brilliant oranges and purples.

"Why don't we just let it ride for the moment?" I answered as I switched on a lamp.

It was getting dark in the old house, dark in my old life, and I found I was yearning more and more for the light.

ACKNOWLEDGEMENTS

This novel, while wholly a work of fiction, owes a great deal to a number of very real, very generous people.

First, my wife, Vicki, is always the person I rely on most. Having known each other as long as we have, and especially since we're both musicians, she can always be counted on for candid and cogent appraisals of what I've written. For that, I am grateful beyond measure.

Andre Leduc has again provided all the photographs used, and I think they're some of his best so far. Visit his website if you'd care to see more of his work: www.andreleduc.com.

Preliminary editorial evaluation by the insightful Cheryl Freedman. Agental assistance by Patrica Moosbrugger. Promotional assistance by Jesson Artmont Communications. Vocal stylings at the book's launch by Nina Richmond of the Advocats Big Band. Gracious hospitality by Pat and Gill Maloney of Vineyard Alpacas (www.vineyardalpacas.com). Their Beamsville home provided the refuge where I wrote a good portion of this novel.

The following kind people provided assistance for the book's cover: Sasha Maslow, Paul Delong and Pat Morrison, Pam and Jeff Fong, Johnson Attong, my son Karel, and John at the Black Swan Pub. I'd be very remiss if I did not also mention Frank Basile, who gave me the shock of my life.

Travel companionship provided by Raymond J. MacDonald. Research help in Portola from Dee Dafa of Dee's Station Café (when in Portola, CA, you must eat there!), Ida Larrieu and Linda Knudson. Many thanks for your information and personal insight.

Howard Heller provided no help whatsoever, but wanted his name mentioned, so I made him a criminal lawyer. He's actually a musician.

If I've missed anyone, please forgive me!

And last but *definitely* not least, at RendezVous Crime, my publisher, Sylvia McConnell, and my editor, Allister Thompson, need to be especially singled out for their insight, advice, dedication and support in making this book a reality.

Any errors in the novel are entirely the author's own – and have been made despite the very best intentions.

The fact that Rick Blechta has been a musician all his life is clearly apparent in his writing. His five previous novels, *Knock on Wood* (1992), *The Lark Ascending* (1993), *Shooting Straight in the Dark* (2002), *Cemetery of the Nameless* (2005) and *When Hell Freezes Over* (2006) have all been critically praised for their insider's knowledge of the music world. *Cemetery of the Nameless* was a finalist for the Arthur Ellis "Best Crime Novel" in 2006.

Rick, who began his professional music career at the age of fourteen, is accomplished on several instruments. After receiving a B. Mus. from McGill University, he formed a progressive rock band, Devotion. He taught instrumental music for twenty-three years, and for sixteen years he was a member of the faculty at the Royal Conservatory of Music. He currently plays with the Advocats Big Band.

For the past sixteen years, Rick has been a member of Crime Writers of Canada and was recognized with their Derrick Murdoch Award in 2000 in recognition of his contributions to the organization.

He lives with his wife, prominent flutist and educator Vicki Blechta, in Toronto, and they have two sons.

For more information on Rick's writing and music, visit his website:

www.rickblechta.com

More musical mysteries by Rick Blechta and
RendezVous Crime

Michael Quinn, former rock star, turned his back on a band on the verge of superstardom twenty-four years ago. He's spent his life since hiding from everything he'd been. When a woman chased by thugs jumps into his car, he tries to help. But this sets in motion a chain of events which turns his life upside down.

Now he must confront what he was, what he is now and what he might have been.

ISBN 978-1894917-41-4
$16.95 CDN, $15.95 U.S.

"If this is the future of crime writing in Canada, it's a bright one indeed."
-Calgary Herald

Victoria Morgan, violin virtuoso, is on yet another European tour, currently stopping in Vienna. While playing to a full house, she leaves the stage and disappears in the middle of the concert, leaving behind a puzzled audience. Why would a seasoned professional do something so damaging?

Rumours of her disappearance involve the accusation that she has committed a brutal murder. While the press hounds everyone who knows her, it appears she is running from them, the police and her long-suffering husband. Or is she?

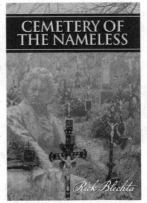

ISBN 978-1894917-17-9
$16.95 CDN, $14.95 U.S

"This new novel by Rick Blechta is excellent. Whether it's the terrific plot or the spectacular location, or just plain good writing, the book is hard to put down."
-The Globe and Mail